"It doesn't happen every often, but once in a while you come across a new voice that does everything right. Virginia Lanier is one of those lights in the darkness that makes up so much of what's offered to booksellers and readers today. In a story that is funny, well-developed, and satisfying in all respects, *Death in Bloodhound Red* gets our vote as a shoo-in for an Edgar nomination this year. . . . Lanier has an ear for dialect and mannerism that rings true in her depiction of the Good Ol' Boy inhabitants of the Deep South. In Jo Beth she has created a character with biting wit, backbone, and enough faults to keep her likable. The bloodhound lore woven into the story is fascinating, as is Lanier's obvious familiarity with the region she has set her story in. There's danger, duplicity, humor, and yes, murder in this first offering—enough to satisfy the most discerning mystery buff."

—*Southern Book Trade*

"Literate, well-modulated prose, satisfyingly detailed descriptions, elements of Southern decadence, and a leisurely pace punctuated by thrilling moments of action all characterize a very appealing first novel."

—*Library Journal*

"This first novel has more mysteries than fleas on a dog's back, and every one is neatly resolved. . . . Run, don't walk for your own copy of *Death in Bloodhound Red*."

—*Meritorious Mysteries*

Books by Virginia Lanier

Death in Bloodhound Red
The House on Bloodhound Lane
A Brace of Bloodhounds
Blind Bloodhound Justice

Published by HarperCollins*Publishers*

THE HOUSE ON BLOODHOUND LANE

Virginia Lanier

HarperPaperbacks
A Division of HarperCollinsPublishers

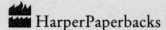 HarperPaperbacks

A Division of HarperCollins*Publishers*

10 East 53rd Street, New York, N.Y. 10022-5299

This is a work of fiction. The characters, incidents, and
dialogues are products of the author's imagination and are not to
be construed as real. Any resemblance to actual events or
persons, living or dead, is entirely coincidental.

ISBN 0-06-101086-3

HarperCollins®, 🏰 ®, and HarperPaperbacks™
are trademarks of HarperCollins*Publishers*, Inc.

The hardcover edition of this book was published in 1996
by HarperCollins*Publishers*

Cover design © Designed to Print
Cover illustration © Peggy Leonard

First mass market printing: July 1997

Printed in the United States of America

Visit HarperPaperbacks on the World Wide Web at
http://www.harpercollins.com/paperbacks

❖ 10 9 8 7 6 5 4 3

To my sons
In loving memory of Robert W. Lanier, Jr. (1950–1970),
to Mike, Les, Quinn, and Rex, who gave me gray hair
and a world of joy and happiness.

ACKNOWLEDGMENTS

I wish to thank the following people for giving me advice and information and for sharing their expertise on bloodhounds:

Mary Michener, editor of *American Bloodhound Club Bulletin,* Ellensburg, Washington.

Jan Tweedie, chief of corrections, Kittitas County Sheriff's Department, Ellensburg, Washington.

Marlene Zahner, veterinarian, a former resident of Raleigh, North Carolina, now living in Switzerland.

Bill and Martha Butler, owners of the Jennings House, off Interstate 75, Exit 87, Jennings, Florida.

A heartfelt special thanks to Mary Nix, owner of Mr. Employer, Inc., Valdosta, Georgia, who had the infinite patience to instruct and guide me while I grappled with my new computer and who advised, corrected, cajoled, and sustained me during the hard times.

To the wonderful bloodhound owners and owners of other breeds who send me photographs, sharing the joys and sorrows of their beloved companions—you have brightened my life forever.

All the above-mentioned people gave me the correct information. Any mistakes are mine and mine alone.

All the small rural counties in southeast Georgia in this book came from my mind, not a map. All people, incidents, and law-enforcement personnel are fictional and are not patterned after real people or situations.

THE HOUSE ON
BLOODHOUND LANE

Prologue

The trauma of turning thirty years old two weeks ago made me sit up and smell the flowers and decide to review my bad habits. I recently read where the American philosopher William James espoused the theory that, by the age of thirty, one's character is set like plaster and will never soften again. I hoped I was still living within the window of opportunity. I vowed to eat the right foods, quit smoking, get more exercise, treat my fellow humans more kindly, and love my animals more. So far I've managed to keep two vows, and I'm failing miserably with the other three. So much for good intentions.

Last April, after receiving a modest inheritance from my father, I embarked on a risky venture that entailed hiring six new dog trainers, two part-time domestic employees, and a videographer. My newly hired group, plus Wayne and Rosie Frazier, Jasmine Jones, and yours truly, have trained, fed, treated, and nursed fifty-seven adult bloodhounds of different ages through a difficult and vigorous six-month period. Six bloodhounds are ready to go to their new law-enforcement masters next week. All six qualify as mantrailers. Four specialize as drug sniffers, and two excel in search-and-rescue efforts. Not only have I quadrupled the payroll, I have squeezed the cash flow to a trickle by hanging on to all the qualified dogs for training. Next week I'll find out if I made a wise decision or stuffed the greater part of seventy thousand dollars down a rathole.

My name is Jo Beth Sidden. I'm five feet seven inches tall with naturally curly, short brown hair. My skin is pale even though I spend most of my time outdoors. I live in Balsa City, a small town in southeast Georgia, and earn my living working in three counties that border the Okefenokee Swamp. I do search-and-rescue and drug raids and track prison escapees, using bloodhounds I breed and train in my kennel. I'm a staunch feminist and a loyal Georgia peach, and I love southeast Georgia and all its critters with the exception of snakes, spiders, and gators— not necessarily in that order.

If I had been given an inkling of the mystery—the weird, dangerous, and chaotic events of the next few weeks—I would have promptly packed a bag and fled to a more peaceful clime, possibly the Everglades in south Florida. It would have saved me a lot of grief, debilitating night sweats, and harrowing nightmares of being buried alive. However, it's hard to travel with eighty-seven bloodhounds and one large tomcat, and I cannot bear to leave them.

The events that follow are what happened in November.

1

Confusion Reigns
Somewhere, Sometime, in the Dark

The man awoke and stirred in the inky darkness. His head was throbbing with each heartbeat, and the pain blended into a continuous roll of agony. This was the most horrendous hangover of all time. He squeezed his eyes tightly closed and opened them again, hoping he would be able to penetrate the black void. Nothing. His actions seemed to increase his pain and didn't improve his vision.

What happened to the lights? He was confused but not yet wary. He tried to swallow, but the inside of his mouth was as dry as ashes, and his lips felt crusty and swollen. He moved his tongue slowly over their rough surface and felt a stab of pain deep in his throat. Don't try that again.

He took a cautious breath and tried to reason. The night-light bulb had burned out, or maybe the electricity was off due to a sudden storm. Struggling to raise a hand to his head, he felt soft resistance. He experienced a flare of panic and hastily tried to work his hands upward, keeping them close to his body. It had been years since he had drunk enough to get a hangover like this. Panic bubbled like air in his throat. His fumbling hands felt a zipper. What was a zipper doing among his sheets and blanket?

Sudden nausea overwhelmed him. He fumbled with the zipper and managed to lower it enough to move sideways in a crablike motion about half of his body length before he started retching. Great dry heaves, nothing coming up. His body was racked with more spasms.

He lowered his head weakly to the carpet—but it wasn't carpet. The surface felt hard and alien against his cheek. For the first time he felt the cold surrounding him. A tremor started in his spine and radiated throughout his body. He was shivering. He worked backward feebly until he was in the same position as when he awoke and then managed to pull up the zipper before he surrendered to unconsciousness.

2

Give Me One Good Reason Not to Cry
November 12, Friday, 6 A.M.

The clock radio blared out the national news, but, being slow to wake, I missed the lead story. Surely nothing had happened overnight on the world level that would have any impact on my tiny empire. I semi-snoozed through several commercials while waiting for the local news and weather report. I became aware of Rudy, my large tomcat, softly kneading my right hip with his paws as he purred his wake-up song of contentment. I reached down and idly scratched his ears. But I was awake and alert in a heartbeat when I heard the announcer report, in the appropriate solemn tones, that an officer had been killed in the line of duty in Collins. I listened with dread for the name. None were close friends of mine, but I had worked with several on search-and-rescues and prison escapes.

It was Mavis Johns. She had stopped for coffee at a convenience store and walked into a robbery in progress involving two black males. Both suspects had fired multiple rounds, killing Mavis instantly.

I turned off the radio and went to the bathroom. Mavis

was an acquaintance, but we hadn't gotten along too well. Tears blurred my vision. I wished she had been able to draw that damn gun she was so proud of and blown those suckers away. Wherever she was now, I knew she was fuming at the lost chance of nailing them. From what wasn't announced in the broadcast, I knew either the clerk had recognized the robbers or there was a witness. Also, the investigators knew how the suspects left the store. No descriptions were given out, and I hadn't been called in with my trackers to search. It's routine to call for the dogs when suspects leave on foot or when their mode of transportation is unknown.

I stepped into the shower. As the hot water pounded my neck and shoulders, I played the mental memory tape of my last encounter with Mavis Johns. It hadn't been exactly pleasant. Now she was dead and I'd never be able to retaliate as I'd planned. She was a novice in the blackmail department, and, since I'm a seasoned pro and it's my favorite weapon, I use it often. I said good-bye to Mavis, as tears mingled with the cascade of steamy water, and felt both clean of skin and cleansed of uncharitable thoughts.

After dressing, I went to the kitchen and carefully measured a half serving of dry cat food and placed it in Rudy's dish, taking the same care with a special mixed portion of nutritious goop for Bobby Lee. They'd return soon from their morning constitutional. All three of us were overweight, and if I had to diet my roommates had to diet.

Rudy weighs twenty-three pounds, and our vet insists that he drop at least three. Bobby Lee, a pedigreed bloodhound puppy, at eight months weighs in at ninety-three pounds. With his bone structure, he should weigh about eighty-five, so he has to lose at least four pounds for starters. I weigh one twenty-eight and want to go down to one twenty—to look willowy. I've never looked willowy in my life, and in bleak moments I admit I probably never will.

Having stalled as long as possible, I distractedly poured my first cup of coffee, sat down at the kitchen table, and commenced suffering. This was my fifteenth morning without a cigarette, and it wasn't any easier now than on the first day. With glum resignation, I pondered how long this vicious longing for nicotine would last. I'd smoked since I was fifteen and wouldn't be surprised if it took another fifteen years to get over the craving.

I heard the squeak of the cat door as Rudy and Bobby Lee returned from their morning run. I still call it the cat door even though it was enlarged threefold so Bobby Lee could come and go too. They went directly to their bowls for their skimpy breakfast.

After two dainty bites, Rudy emitted a quarrelsome sound between a growl and a hum to inform me that he hadn't forgotten what a normal breakfast dish should hold. "Don't fuss. It's for your own good," I told him.

Bobby Lee's head didn't emerge from his dish until he had scarfed down the last morsel and moved the raised dish in its holder in a semicircle, checking to see if he had missed a crumb.

I watched as Bobby Lee walked unerringly across to me, skirting the right side of the table to sit precisely one inch from my right foot. He leaned his upper body against my leg, so I dropped my right hand to his head and fondled his ears. Rudy would take his place on the left side in another few minutes. He ate slowly, savoring every morsel, and sometimes catnapped between bites.

Bobby Lee is twenty-six inches to the shoulders and still growing. He is a perfect specimen of a pedigreed bloodhound champion—with only one defect. His coloring, size, wrinkles, and bone configuration are excellent. Even his large hazel-colored eyes are naturally formed and look expressive, but Bobby Lee was born totally blind. He's one of twelve from Gloria Steinem's last litter.

Gloria was an excellent mother and performed her duties correctly, but with each litter she grew more dejected, put upon, and depressed. She hated her fat little charges pulling on her teats and crawling all over her. She became red-eyed with fatigue and lack of sleep. Her expression telegraphed her feelings so expressively I took pity on her and switched her to scent training. She was so grateful, she repaid me by becoming one of our best drug trackers.

In early May, when we discovered Bobby Lee was blind, I moved him in as my houseguest. In July, he blossomed into a miracle. The present head count in the kennel is eighty-six. Six are going to various law-enforcement agencies and their new masters at the end of next week after the completion of our first seminar. Bobby Lee is the crème de la crème, the very best.

I sat at my desk and dialed Hank's number. When he answered I leaned back in my chair and cradled the receiver on my shoulder.

"Hi, Hank, it's Jo Beth. I just heard about Mavis on the radio. They called you in early?"

"They woke me up a little after two. I've been setting up roadblocks and hunting suspects ever since. Damn their hides, I hope we get them soon. Sheriff Scroggins is really stressed out on this one. I'm worried about his high blood pressure."

"So am I; he should have retired last year. At least he has you to work with now, instead of asshole Carlson."

Hank Cribbs is our new sheriff, just 10 days into his first elected four-year term. He is also my former lover, for some three months earlier in the year, and is still a close friend. Our love, infatuation, or whatever couldn't survive intimacy, but our friendship prevailed.

"I'm not helping much. We have the clerk, an eyeball witness, giving vague descriptions, and she thinks she's seen one of the guys before. She's looking through mug shots and trying to place him. Nothing, so far."

"Who are you looking for, generally?"

"Two black males. Young. I'd guess their ages at under twenty-five. No beards, goatees, or extraordinary hair growth."

"That's half the black males in this county."

"Tell me about it." He sighed. "Listen, Jo Beth, changing the subject, I need to ask for a favor. I have a deputy I've heard some rumors about: John Stringer. He lives over in Mercer. Know him?"

"Probably, if I could see him. What's he done?"

"A snitch says he's growing marijuana for distribution and smokes it himself. I require a gifted nose. Not yours, one of your dogs. I can't bill your services through the county because he may be innocent. If he is, I don't want anyone to know I was investigating him. You know how suspicion sticks. I can't afford your exorbitant rates on my salary. Will you check him out for me for free?"

"Sure," I said, "as long as it's crack, heroin, LSD, gunrunning, or cigarettes smuggled from North Carolina. All other substances need not apply; it's a resounding *no.*"

"I understand he has his own pot patch. He's supposed to have a good-sized operation going."

"Whoa, hoss," I said with firmness. "Back up. You know my policy on local pot growers and moonshiners. I don't snitch on them—ever. They know I never see pot patches or stills when I'm working in the flatwoods and swamps. We have an understanding, an unwritten code. I honor it. If I turn in a pot patch or still, I might as well hang up my rescue suit and retire to Florida. I'd be dead meat in the woods. They know I work the towns, business, schools, and roadblocks. That's acceptable. Their own pea patch is another matter. They don't get mad, they get even. You know this. How could you even ask?"

"Jo Beth, hear my lips." He sounded grim. "He's a D-E-P-U-T-Y. He's sworn to uphold the laws of this state. His private life has to be above reproach. I will not have a dirty officer on my force. His patch is supposed to be within walking distance of his house. I've been sitting on him for seven mornings, and he hasn't taken a stroll in the woods. He works swing shift, three to eleven. I can't be there Tuesday morning. I have to testify at a civil service hearing. I can take care of it through Monday. If he goes in Tuesday, wait until he comes out. Verify he's growing, and I'll take over from there. I have no one else I can trust with this. Will you do it?"

I sighed. Decisions, decisions. I knew Hank was right, but I was also right. I make only a small portion of my income from search-and-rescue in the woods and swamps. The reason it's so important is not the search fee but the reputation I've built and the publicity I receive from successful rescues. The publicity has sold trained dogs to law-enforcement agencies and spread my reputation to several states. If I make the Associated Press or a major television network, one rescue is worth thousands of dollars in sales, opening up new markets for my animals. Was I stupid enough to take the risk of losing this? I sighed again and decided I was.

"I'll sit on him Tuesday, but only Tuesday. My seminar will have started, and I'll need to be available here. I'm just praying I don't get called out for a search next week."

"Thanks, Jo Beth, I owe you. Something else has come up. This is for your ears only. Do you know Frank the Second of Cannon Trucking?"

"He's the father of three sons who work there, right? I haven't met him, but the youngest son hired me to do random drug sweeps."

"Yep, Frank's the dad. He runs the place, or did. He's been missing now for eight days. We're working it as a kidnapping."

"Why wasn't I called in?"

"Because the sons kept it under wraps for five days. They didn't even tell their grandfather; they lied to everyone. On the fifth day, Gramps came down and got me to go with him to Frank's house. When Frank's sons saw both of us on the doorstep, they invited us in and came clean about the abduction. The trail was five days old, so I knew you wouldn't want to tackle it."

"Amen," I agreed.

"Also, the initials are now in charge. I'm just the simpleton who runs the county force and furnishes them with warm bodies from time to time, upon request."

"Which one's fucking up?"

"Both of them: the powerful FBI and the mighty GBI. We call them FIB and GIB when they aren't present."

I chuckled. "That's strange. I didn't think they liked working together. They turn over a new leaf?"

"Nah." He sounded disgusted. "One son called the FBI while another was dialing the GBI. Now we have a lot more chiefs than Indians. It's like a cat-and-dog fight around here: screeching and hollering and wrangling over territory."

"I'm glad I'm not involved," I said happily.

"I wish I'd called you in three days ago. Now it's eight, and we still have nothing. After all this time, we both know he's somewhere out in the swamp. Sooner or later, someone will walk up on what's left of him. Until then, keep your eyes and ears open. You're out among the merkle bushes more than most. Maybe your hounds will walk him up."

"Bloodhounds, please. When you refer to my dogs as hounds, it sounds like you're talking about a pack of blueticks."

"Picky, picky," he said with a chuckle. "Bloodhounds. See you around, kiddo."

"Take care."

"You too."

For a while after Bobby Lee moved into the house, Rudy was jealous, claimed priority, and used his claws and body to physically shoulder Bobby Lee aside to keep him from getting near me. He thought Bobby Lee was his dog, not mine. Bobby Lee quickly memorized the location of each object in the house. As soon as he gained confidence in his surroundings, he gently but firmly let Rudy know they were equals, not master and slave. He still allows Rudy to boss him around occasionally, inside. But outside he is my dog and devoted worker from his gifted nose to the tip of his tail. Rudy, after all these months, still sits on the back porch and grumbles and whines when I hook Bobby Lee to his lead; he is one stubborn cat.

I decided to visit Jasmine and call the weather line from her place. I looked at my watch; it was half-past seven. I walked through the courtyard, past the second gate, and up the stairs to her apartment. Built above a double garage, it's very small, thirty feet by thirty feet. One half is living room, dining room, and kitchen combined; the other half is her bedroom, large closet, and bath. It would give me a touch of claustrophobia, but Jasmine designed it, the Jensen brothers built it, and we all were happy with the results.

Jasmine Jones and I formed a firm bond of friendship when Hank Cribbs, then a lieutenant in the Dunston County Sheriff's Department, sent me to her. Hank was trying to keep me out of the sheriff's clutches—and the county jail.

In turn, I offered her a job as a tracker, and she had lived with me for the two months it took to build her apartment in the compound.

I gave one perfunctory knock on her door and went in. It was the method we all used. When she called for me to enter, I was already halfway through her living room. She was standing in the kitchen area pouring herself a cup of coffee.

Jasmine is truly lovely. She's twenty-five and one inch shorter than I. She's African American and her skin is one shade lighter than milk chocolate. She weighs in at one-thirty, and every pound is in the right place.

"Want a cup?" She knew I never turn down an offer of coffee. She commented on my suffering countenance as she poured. "Still bad?"

I nodded—she was asking about my fanatical craving for a coffin nail—as she knelt to say good morning to my escorts.

Jasmine tapped Bobby Lee on the left shoulder. When he presented his left paw, she shook it and leaned closer to whisper sweet nothings in his ear. She turned to Rudy, rubbed her knuckles over his chest fur, and purred endearments. So far, he had refused to present either paw for shaking, but I knew he understood my request when I spent some time with him trying to get him to cooperate. I finally quit trying to teach him. He shakes when he feels the urge or on alternate Tuesdays that fall on the twelfth of the month, whichever comes first.

Jasmine sat down at the breakfast table, indicating I should join her. As I sipped the delicious coffee, I spoke with glum resignation. "Tell me again why I quit smoking."

"You want to live to be old and gray?"

"Sure, but there has to be more. That's not enough."

"To prove you have the backbone and willpower to lay them down when you want to?"

"Nope, I know I've got backbone and I know I've been short-shirted in willpower; there has to be more."

"You don't want an oxygen tank strapped to your back when you turn forty, do you?"

"Stop! Christ, that will do for now."

"You're doing great. It will be easier soon."

"I need to call the weather line."

She handed me the phone and cleared the cups. I glanced at the open textbook on the table. Jasmine earned her GED last month and was now attending junior college three nights a week. She's striving to catch up on her education; with her heavy schedule here, I was beginning to wonder when she had time to sleep.

"How's school?" I asked as I punched in the number.

"Great. I have tons of homework assignments. I'm learning a lot, fast."

"Need more time to study?"

"Nope. I'm organized as all get out. No need."

I made a mental note to suggest to my manager, Wayne, that he juggle the schedule and cut her sweeps down.

I listened to the recorded weather message. The weather was fine at least for another two days. Highs in the upper 70s, lows in the middle 50s, southeast winds ten miles per hour, and—the best news—lowest relative humidity near 55 percent today and around 65 tomorrow. High humidity and light winds are excellent tracking conditions. Low humidity and strong winds can play havoc with a rescue attempt. Today and tomorrow would be good. I'd have to wait for Sunday's forecast. My guess on the weather is right about half the time, and so is the forecaster's. Only two types of people try to predict the weather—damn fools and Georgia Crackers.

I told Jasmine I would see her later.

3

Once More into the Breach
November 12, Friday, 7:30 A.M.

With the feline on my left and the canine on my right, I crossed the courtyard and climbed Wayne and Rosie's staircase. Giving another perfunctory knock, I entered and held the screen door open for my entourage. Wayne hurried into the living room, because I had also activated the pulsing light over the inside sill of the living room doorway. He couldn't hear my knock. He is hearing impaired to the politically correct, deaf and dumb to the local rednecks, and deaf to the rest of the population, who are too embarrassed to use the old term *dumb*. Most local uneducated rednecks think that being politically correct is being a Democrat or knowing someone who claims to be a member of the Ku Klux Klan.

Wayne Frazier is twenty years old, with six feet of muscle, brown hair, brown eyes, and a large open face. He's worked with me for almost two years. I've congratulated myself many times for being smart enough to see his potential and lucky enough also to snag his mother, Rosie— she goes where Wayne goes; she raised her only chick by herself. She turned forty last month, but it didn't bother her one bit.

Rosie has our local fire chief, Simon Clemments, wrapped around her little finger, and they are tying the knot December fifth. She's one of my best trainers, and I dread to think about losing her, even though she swears nothing much around here will change after the marriage. She says she'll be here as much as she'll be at her new house, but I know better. Clemments is in his fifties, and he'll want his new spouse at home, waiting on him hand and foot. Wayne and I plan to wean her gradually from trying to take care of both of us. When she goes to her new husband, we want her to be happy and content.

Wayne grinned and said good morning in sign language as he lay on his back on the carpet and roughhoused with Rudy and Bobby Lee—another morning ritual. I stepped around them and went to the kitchen to greet Rosie. She was peering into the open door of the oven and using a fork to probe a pot roast that could easily sate a dozen hungers. I groaned inwardly. She still hasn't forgiven me for hiring a cook. She protested that she could handle the cooking for the seminar along with her regular duties as trainer, which is impossible. She hates the idea that Wayne and I are now being fed by a stranger down in the common room. The seminar doesn't start until Monday, but the cook, Jansee Tatum, started this morning.

I thought it would be a good idea for Miz Jansee to have a couple of days to learn her duties, and it would give me a chance to have all the trainers together today and tomorrow to go over the schedule for next week. We were all supposed to be downstairs at eight for a working breakfast. I watched Rosie take out a large pan of biscuits from the oven and realized that, even though I was on a diet, I would have to eat two breakfasts this morning: one here to placate

Rosie and the other to give a vote of confidence to Miz Jansee Tatum.

Rosie loves to wear bright colors. She's barely five feet tall and plump. I have to guess her weight; she tells no one—not even Wayne. I would say in the neighborhood of one seventy-five. This morning her ensemble consisted of bright red slacks and an orange-colored tentlike top with large bold lemon-colored stripes. The way the colors clashed made your teeth ache and your eyes run water at the same time. Her hair is jet black, which I suspect is an expensive dye job, and is always elaborately coiffed. She must get up at four in the morning to achieve such a masterpiece of curled harmony.

"The biscuits smell delicious. Buttermilk?"

"Clabber biscuits, smoked country ham, red-eye gravy, grits, and scrambled eggs," she said, as she deftly slid the huge biscuits onto a platter. In my pre-thirty and pre-diet days I would eat three.

"Did you forget I'm on a diet?" I asked with sweet restraint. She caught the implied irony.

"There're others around here who eat besides you," she retorted. "Eat just a dab and quit. Use your willpower."

"You know I don't have any willpower. You're shameless."

She grinned. I helped her put the food on the table. Bobby Lee sat quietly next to my right foot, but Rudy started his beggar-stalker routine. I told Rosie and Wayne to ignore him; it was imperative that some of us remain on our diets. I stared pointedly at Rosie.

Wayne put his fork down and started signing: "Doc and Carol have promised to help this morning, if no patients arrive. I have three part-timers coming in. With six trainers and the four of us, we should be able to finish bathing the dogs by noon."

"Including the puppies?" I signed with a frown. We had

twenty-one puppies old enough to be bathed. With the fifty-seven grown dogs, it would be quite a feat to finish by noon even if everything went smoothly.

"I'll save the puppies to wash last; it will be warmer then. If we can't finish, I can bathe them tomorrow."

"You can't count on Jasmine or me. I have grocery shopping this morning. You won't believe the list I have, it's a mile long. I'll need Jasmine to help, but we should be back by noon."

Wayne shrugged. "We'll make out."

"Is the conveyor belt working properly?"

Any machinery I own sooner or later becomes infected with gremlins. The latest victim was the conveyor belt we use to move the animals for bathing or grooming.

"I tried it this morning when I unlocked the gates. It's working fine." He knocked on wood—the dining table—when he finished signing.

When I started to help with the dishes, Rosie shooed me out of the kitchen, so the animals and I went downstairs. I watched Bobby Lee as he walked beside me. He has a special sense that warns him if he's approaching an obstacle in his path or if there's a void beneath his next step.

Bloodhounds are started on basic obedience training at six months. They are eighteen months old before they're ever started on scent tracking and trailing. They have to be mature to learn to use their talents. It takes a grueling six months to teach a bright dog to scent trail and be a successful tracker. When I found out Bobby Lee was blind, I moved him into the house as a pet.

In three weeks he was getting around so effortlessly, I began to take him with me almost everywhere. He loves the sound of traffic, people moving about, and the wind blowing his ears while we're moving. When I get out of the van he always goes with me, except when I enter a store. I attach his leash to my belt and forget about him. He's so sensitive he never gets in the way and I never step on him. He senses the way I'm going to move or turn before I do it.

In the office I picked up a clipboard and returned to the back porch. I reached for Bobby Lee's lead and attached it to his harness.

"Rudy, you can't go. It's a no-no. Bobby Lee's working."

I didn't want Rudy circling the breakfast table begging for handouts. He sat and wound his tail around himself and stared off into the distance—as if he couldn't care less—but I knew he was hurting. I attached a clip to a belt loop on the right side of my jeans and fastened Bobby Lee's lead to it. I gave him a quick caress behind his right ear, gave him the command to heel, and we departed. I was going to have that second breakfast.

The common room was built to house, feed, hold meetings with, and entertain participants of my seminars, which include trainers, trainees, and my employees. It is roomy: forty feet by forty feet. A compact kitchen is in the far left corner. There is a steam table, small salad bar, and a six-foot counter for desserts, serving utensils, and dishes.

In the far right of the room is a six-foot wet bar holding nine different types of booze. I don't try to stock everything a regular bar holds. These were law-enforcement guys, and since the booze was free they could drink what was offered or abstain. I had been foolish when I purchased the jukebox, but I wanted a replica of the 1955 Wurlitzer; I thought they were fabulous. It cost over five grand, but since I'll have to work the rest of my life to pay for all this other stuff, I should at least treat myself to something I want and admire.

The door on the right of the room opens into the kennel area, and the door on the left opens into Wayne's office. Even with large windows, there's still a lot of wall space to fill, so I hired a college student majoring in art to paint seven large oils of my favorite subjects: bloodhounds. The ceiling has three huge skylights, giving enough light even on dark, dismal days.

Placed against the walls are two leather couches, seven comfortable loungers, and four small potted trees.

Placed in the middle of the room are four eight-foot picnic tables made out of soft white-pine slabs. The carpenter brothers built them, and a painter finished them with about a dozen coats of clear polyurethane so the lovely grain and knotholes are visible.

My maternal grandfather left me a large two-story farmhouse built out of the best seasoned lumber. Every structure in the compound is built out of lumber from that old house.

The two carpenter brothers, who had been unhappy in their retirement, worked ridiculously cheaply. Many of my friends commented that I had a horseshoe up my ass to accomplish all this with so little cash. I didn't bother to explain the humongous mortgage hanging over my head like a sword, which still gives me night sweats on occasion.

Wayne and Rosie walked through the door behind me, and the three of us headed to the tables, where Jasmine, five of the six trainers, and Donnie Ray Carver, videographer, were already seated. Also present was Lena Mae, my newly acquired maid. I saw Miz Jansee behind the steam table, and when she looked my way I gave her a smile. I slid into my chair, and Bobby Lee settled at my right foot.

I noticed the message light on the wall phone was lit. Our ten o'clock scholar, W. A. Beckham, a college student, hadn't arrived. He runs a little late most mornings, but I try to be understanding. I decided to check the phone messages and give W. A. a few more minutes before starting. I told everyone to fix their plates and start eating. I dialed the message code and heard the voice of Hank Cribbs leaving a message for me to call him immediately; it was important. My gut tightened. This did not sound like good news. He would have mentioned the fact if it was a rescue call-out.

I dialed Hank's private number at the courthouse and whispered my calming mantra: *I will not get upset. It could be nothing. I will not get upset. Amen.* Hank answered after the first ring.

"This is Jo Beth," I said quickly.

"Have you heard anything from the parole board lately?"

"No," I said, through suddenly numb lips.

"Those assholes up there are still as inefficient as ever. You should have been given a call at least thirty-six hours ago—it's the freaking law! I'm sorry, Jo Beth, they released Bubba at twelve-oh-one this morning. I checked, and your restraining order is current and on the computer. They're a bunch of screwups."

I was stunned into silence.

"Are you all right? Jo Beth, answer me!"

4

Bothered and Bewildered
Somewhere, Sometime, in the Dark

The second time the man opened his eyes he wasn't so confused by the dark and his inability to see. His subconscious had prepared him while he slept. His head was throbbing, but the pain was now endurable, and he could think and reason more clearly. He still had a dry mouth and a raging thirst. He forced his mind to concentrate. How long had he been here and how long had he slept? He remembered the zipper and raised one arm slowly, lowering it to his waist. He wasn't going to make any sudden moves yet, not wanting the gut-wrenching nausea to return. Fingering the material, he knew he was in a sleeping bag and lying on a hard surface. He raised one hand to his face and felt the stubble. Being a creature of habit, he had shaved every day of his adult life, even on camping trips with his father and when he had been laid low by colds or flu. Feeling the stubble, he thought it was probably three days. He couldn't be sure his estimate was correct; he had never tried to grow a beard.

The boys. He remembered he had three sons and a wife

and what he did for a living. He ran his free hand into the sleeping bag and felt for his wallet. Bringing it to his chest, he could tell by its feel there was a healthy stack of bills inside—he had always carried plenty of money. It hadn't been robbery. He laid the wallet beside the sleeping bag and slowly raised one leg at a time until he had achieved the maximum height the zippered bag allowed. He squeezed toes, flexed calf muscles, and felt no injury or soreness. Weakness in his legs caused him to lower them quickly. The weakness reminded him of when he had been bedridden with flu for seven days. Lord, he couldn't have lain here for a week, could he? His thirst distracted him from logical thought.

He had to find water or he would continue to weaken and possibly die, he reasoned to himself. The sobering thought of dying, lying flat in a sleeping bag, gave him a jolt of adrenaline and enough energy to run the zipper as far down as possible without rising. He turned on his left side and propped his head on his left elbow. He was dizzy and felt the nausea building in the back of his throat. He closed his eyes and remained motionless. After his stomach settled, he opened his eyes and was elated to find that his eyes could penetrate a few feet of the darkness. The few inches of height he'd achieved in propping his head up had made a difference.

Using only his eyes, he scanned the room slowly, trying to find any trace of light in the inky darkness. There seemed to be light far away. He blinked to focus his eyes and stared. It was a tiny hole in the ceiling. What was a hole doing in his bedroom ceiling? Cut it out, his mind cautioned, you're jumping the gun. You already know you are on a hard surface in a sleeping bag and not in your room.

Placing both hands palm down on the hard surface, he raised his body to a sitting position. Dizziness struck quickly, and he drew his knees up and rested his head wearily on folded arms supported by his knees. Right, he thought, conserve your strength. Just don't sit here too long. You need water. When the dizziness passed, he focused on the lighter area and by straining his eyes he could make out three blobs at floor level. They had to be white for him to make out the shapes. He turned his head and shoulders slowly to the right and then to the left. There was nothing—just darkness. He was afraid to stand, so he placed himself in a crawling position and slowly traveled in a straight line toward the objects so he could find the sleeping bag again. He felt the cold seeping into his bones. He was dressed in a soft wool shirt and gabardine pants, socks but no shoes. He couldn't pass out now, away from the bag; he had to have its warmth. He counted every time he placed his right hand in front of him while moving forward. This way, he would know how far he had traveled and could return to the bag.

After approximately twenty feet he could see the three objects were white plastic five-gallon containers, each with a sturdy handle and screw-top lid. Beekeepers used them for transporting sugared water to their winter storeyard. Moonshiners used them to transport white lightnin'. He kept one in his pickup in case the radiator overheated and he was stranded in the middle of nowhere. Nearing the jugs, he reached out a shaking hand, pushed against one, and met solid resistance. His heart soared and started chugging like a locomotive traveling up a steep hill.

"Please, God, don't let them be filled with industrial cleaners or used motor oil," he prayed in a ragged whisper. Still kneeling, he straightened and gripped the screw top but couldn't turn it. It had been tightened firmly, and he was so goddamned weak. He whimpered in frustration and strained until he saw brilliant stars floating in his area of vision. Just then the cap started to move under his grip. He quickly removed the lid and placed it on the floor. He gripped the handle and slowly tilted the jug until some of the liquid splashed into his cupped hand.

He smelled it and forced his dry tongue into the liquid and quickly drank the balance that hadn't trickled through his fingers. It was cold fresh water, nectar of the gods, a chance of survival. He continued to tip, pour, and drink. He refused to speculate on the fifteen gallons set here for him: either as to who had put them here or who had placed him here among them. He just kept drinking the life-giving elixir, his mind a blank slate, no visible writing on its surface.

5

The House on Bloodhound Lane
November 12, Friday, 8:15 A.M.

"Don't yell in my ear, Hank. I have an Excedrin headache the size of a basketball," I said. "Christ! I don't believe this. I've actually felt safe these past few months, thinking I'd be notified well in advance of his release. They really taught him a lesson this time, didn't they? Seven months served on a two-year sentence! My insurance company filed a civil suit against Bubba to recover what they paid in April for his last rampage. They haven't even been given a court date. It seems to me they should have a chance to collect what he owes them before he gets out and starts running up another bill."

"I know, I know, justice sucks," he said, sounding upset. "After I hang up, I'm going to call the superintendent at Patton and chew his ass. What if I'd been out today? No one else would've bothered to call to see if you'd been notified of his release."

"Don't call the prison. I'll handle it from this end. When they finally get around to notifying me, I'll pass on the time lapse to Carolyn Braithwaite. She won her old seat back as state representative from this district, in case you didn't know."

"Are you serious?" He sounded wounded. "I ran for sheriff of this county. Of course I keep up with statewide elections!"

"Who won the judgeship in superior court for the Fifth District?"

"Up yours," he said, chuckling. "Are you okay?"

"I'm fine. Thanks, friend. I owe you one."

"No, you don't. Take care, buddy."

On hearing Hank call me buddy, I felt hollow. We couldn't be lovers without hacking at each other, but I wasn't ready to be called a buddy so soon. It seemed inadequate for my feelings. But I knew I had to concentrate on Bubba.

I returned to the table, noting that W. A. had arrived. There were thirteen for breakfast, and the fact that thirteen is an unlucky number was not lost. Ramon Fontaine, our in-house vet, and Carol, his wife, were no-shows. They must have had an early morning emergency. I took a sip of coffee to ease my constricted throat and felt such a sharp pang of desire for a cigarette, my stomach cramped in shock. I managed to push back my chair and stand.

"Enjoy your breakfast, everyone. Wayne?" I looked at him so he could read my lips. "I need to see you in your office for a minute. Please excuse us." I forced myself to make a dignified exit and waited for him. He was only seconds behind me.

I closed the door and signed to him. "The phone call was from Hank. They released Bubba last night after midnight. The prison has yet to inform me. I need a cigarette. I need lots of cigarettes. No lecture on how well I was doing. My nerves are shot. Will you please go get me some?"

I tried not to whimper. I was his employer and felt I

should always appear calm and in control. He glanced once at my expression, moved to the filing cabinet, and pulled out the bottom drawer. He turned and placed a carton of Dorals and a new Bic lighter in my willing hands.

I stared at him. "O ye of little faith." As soon as I had released the words into the air, I wished them back. He loved to tease and I had just handed him enough material to feast on for weeks. He patted me on the shoulder, and, as he left the room, he softly closed the door behind him.

I tore into the carton and got a cigarette going without dropping anything, then flopped into his chair and propped my feet on the desk. I knew the first cigarette would taste funny and make me dizzy, but who cared? I felt deep pleasure with each drag. My lungs would have to survive— in spite of me.

I reached into the desk drawer, took out a stack of photographs of Bubba, and returned to the breakfast meeting. Bobby Lee settled next to me.

"Before we go over the schedule for the seminar, I have an announcement to make. When each of you was hired, I explained why the compound is so elaborately secured. However, our precautions have become a little slack in the past few months because the object of concern was safely behind bars. This isn't the case any longer.

"My ex-husband, Bubba Sidden, was released at midnight from Patton Correctional in Sebring, Georgia. You all know about his last rampage here.

"I was married to him for three years. In 'eighty-five, he criminally assaulted a woman in a neighboring town. The woman still has physical and mental scars. I doubt she'll every fully recover.

"I divorced him while he was in prison. In 'eighty-seven, after he was released on a conditional parole, he came after me. I spent six months in the hospital and had to have three corrective surgeries before I was well enough to return to work. He was sent back to prison until last March. He was out less than thirty days when he breached the security gates here because of inadequate locks. The alarms woke me and I was able to stay out of his reach, but he did slightly more than seventeen thousand dollars in damages on the property—using a lead-filled baseball bat.

"Pictures of Bubba will be posted in all areas of the compound. I'll leave some on the table by the door. Take one home with you. Study the photograph and memorize his face. This man is dangerous. He may come today, next week, or next year, but he will try to get at me. It may be in the daytime when the gates are open. Every time the gate alarms sound, be very cautious until you are positive it's not him. If you do recognize him, alert others. Stay out of his way. Try to leave the compound. There is a possibility he might try to get to me by using one of you as a hostage. You're not paid enough to take that risk. Anyone who wishes to quit may do so right now. I'll understand. I'd appreciate knowing right away so I can make plans for Monday."

I listened in the silence and wondered what they were thinking. Had I convinced them of the danger, or did they think I was exaggerating? Did a hint of violence add spice to their bland existence or was it a sad commentary on America's progress, that a job paying a dollar more than minimum wage was worth the risk of personal injury? I hesitated and waited a bit. When no one yelled they were quitting or bolted for the door, I decided to proceed.

"If you change your mind, please let me know. Just be careful at all times.

"Each trainer has an information sheet about the officers who will be here next week. Take it home and study it. Remember, they'll be taking the dogs you've been training for the past six months home with them. Give them all the knowledge you have about your animal. If the dogs have any special quirks, like circling in place two or three times before starting a sweep, pass it on. If they like their tummy rubbed or their chin scratched a certain way, tell them. If your dog doesn't like jerky treats, tell them."

This made everyone laugh. All bloodhounds are born hungry. I grinned at them.

"Just kidding, but you get the point. If you have questions, ask. That's all from me. Wayne has a message for you."

Wayne stood and slowly gave the bathing schedule in sign language. He picked up his pad and marker to reinforce his message: "We wash seventy-eight dogs this morning."

There were several good-humored groans. The trainers all understood slow signing and were getting better each day, some faster than others. Wayne tried to make each message clear so he wouldn't be misunderstood. His patience was boundless.

The meeting broke up, and I turned to Jasmine. "I need you to help with the grocery shopping this morning. Before we go, I want to speak to Miz Jansee and Lena Mae, but I'll be ready in five minutes."

"Have I got time to change?"

"Why? You look sexy in those pants. If by any chance we should run into Eddie Murphy and Tom Cruise in the Piggly Wiggly, they'll have to understand we're working girls. Let me rephrase that last remark: We're women and we work."

Jasmine smiled. "They're both married, I believe."

"Really? You mean I've been having sexual fantasies about a married man? Remind me to pick up a tabloid at the checkout lane. I'll have to replace him."

"When will you have time to read?"

"Good point."

I walked over to Lena Mae. "Are all six units ready for our guests?"

"Yes, ma'am."

"Good. You can help Miz Jansee until we get back with the groceries. I'll have some more things to be placed in the rooms."

"Yes, ma'am. Miz Jo Beth, I need to tell you something."

I had told her several times to call me Jo Beth, but she couldn't overcome her southern upbringing.

"What is it, Lena Mae?"

"I have to help my family on the day before Thanksgiving. It's the day we make the syrup."

"Sure. No problem. Is that the twenty-fourth?" I was looking at a large calendar on the wall. When I'd first interviewed Lena Mae, I'd been told by the state employment agency that she had quit school in the sixth grade. At nineteen, she didn't seem interested in fashion, men, or any other subject I'd tried to discuss with her. She was the second child of eleven in her family, and the money she brought home was very important. I'd been tutoring her for her GED for the last six months, but her heart simply wasn't into studying even though she wasn't simpleminded.

I thought of Jarel Owens, and a pain echoed in my heart. He'd been fourteen when I started tutoring him four years ago. He had been eager and learned fast. I'd also given him a huge dose of pride in his race by introducing him to books about famous African Americans. He learned too fast and too well. He'd graduated from high school this past June, an honor student and a fire-eating racist who preached—to anyone willing to listen—the violent overthrow of our "corrupt" government. It made me wonder what Lena might become.

"What's your job on syrup day?"

"I feed the grinder and skim kettles some, when somebody wants to rest."

"Sounds interesting. I'll tell Wayne so he can change your schedule."

"Yes, ma'am."

I knew the family would send over three or four quarts of homemade cane syrup, a delight to most Southerners, but I can't stand the stuff. Openly admitting my preference for maple syrup would be like saying I wasn't patriotic or belonged to a witches' coven.

I went to speak to Miz Jansee. She was washing dishes. She is a small woman with wispy brown hair coiled neatly into a bun. Her thin legs are roped with broken veins and her hands and arms are covered with liver spots. She is only forty-five years old.

"How did the first meal go, Miz Jansee? I got the bad news about Bubba and lost my appetite."

"You weren't the only one who didn't eat. The food was hardly touched." She sounded tired. She had six children and a husband who deigned to work only when game wasn't in season and the fish weren't biting.

I'd spent some thought on how I would phrase my next topic. Poor but proud egos are fragile.

"Miz Jansee, the Bible tells us 'Waste not, want not.' There're a lot of Styrofoam containers in the pantry. Any food left over, I'd appreciate your taking home. What you can't use, you can take to the Salvation Army's kitchen. Do you mind doing this for me?"

"Thank you, ma'am. I'm obliged." She sounded too humble. I had a sudden urge to kick her husband's lazy ass around the courthouse square.

"I'm looking forward to dinnertime," I told her with a smile. "I'll just get my purse," I told Jasmine.

In the bedroom, I opened the top drawer of the nightstand, picked up my .32 snub-nosed revolver, and inserted six rounds. I then gathered up six more rounds from the drawer and placed them in my bag along with the gun.

Jasmine was waiting in the van. I unhooked Bobby Lee's leash, and he hopped nimbly in and sat on his cushion in the walkway between the seats. I fastened his safety harness to the chassis. When we were alone he rode in the passenger seat, which also had connections for his harness, so I didn't have to worry about his being thrown through the windshield in case of an accident.

Reaching the end of the drive, I saw a Balsa City work truck parked on the verge directly in front of the mailbox. Two men were watching a third man digging a hole, using posthole diggers. He was digging six feet from the curb. I pulled up even with them and hopped out. I recognized the man who was digging. He took a couple of steps toward me, and all three of them made the motion of touching their cap brims in greeting.

"Hi, guys. What's up, Ron?"

"Howdy, Jo Beth. Nice day, ain't it? We're here to put up your new street sign." He gave a sly grin. "We heard how you were just tickled pink to be in-cor-por-ated into the city and all." Now all three were grinning. They were getting their jollies waiting for me to explode.

I bared my teeth in a poor imitation of a smile.

"What's the name of my street?" I was trying to be polite. I was remembering my birthday pledge to be nicer to my fellow human beings, but sometimes it's downright hard.

"Well, the city commissioners sure must not hold a grudge against you, Jo Beth, what with you fighting against taking this three-mile section into the city limits and making them hold a special election for the residents out here to vote on it. They gave your street a right purty name: Bloodhound Lane. Has a nice ring to it, don't it?"

I had to admit it didn't sound bad. I glanced back at the eight-foot fence, the first gate, and the hardtop driveway that made a broad curve back about fifteen hundred feet to the second gate and inside fence of the courtyard. It wasn't a lane, really, just a driveway, but it did have a nice ring to it. Our city engineer, who named our new streets, sometimes got too cute. I was expecting something like Hummingbird Throat or Red Cardinal Flight.

I tried it out loud. "The house on Bloodhound Lane. I like it," I told Ron.

In July, after forcing the commissioners to let us vote on the city's proposal, I'd visited the property owners to discuss exactly what was happening. We would receive nothing we didn't already have and would have to pay city taxes based on their assessment. We already had fire and police protection. We would not get garbage collection, city water, or a sewage system for years—if ever. We were admitted into the city by a ten-vote margin. I was patiently waiting until we received the first tax bill, and when the neighbors started complaining I would blister their hides with my tongue.

"Uh, Jo Beth, the sign has some numbers on it. I think it's one hundred. I think you'll have to use the numbers."

Ron walked over to his truck and slid the sign out for my inspection. He was right. It had ONE HUNDRED E printed after the name.

"Screw the numbers," I said sweetly. "I'll use my idea."

That drew snickers from the three of them. Ron tried again.

"You ought to be ashamed, cussing out our bosses like you did, just because they're trying to make more revenue for the city. It wasn't ladylike."

"You're mistaken," I said calmly. "I didn't *cuss* them out. All I said was, 'They don't have the good sense to pour piss out of a boot with the directions printed on the heel.' That's not even close to cussing." I wiggled my fingers in farewell and went back to the van.

Jasmine was silent as we drove away. When we were

out of sight and earshot, I pounded the steering wheel in frustration.

"Damn! Why do I always have to retaliate and let them pull my chain? I let them goad me into it every blasted time!"

"Do you think it's because you're a redneck feminist who likes to dish out more than she gets?" She sounded serious as she voiced the question. I burst into laughter and she joined me.

"You hit the nail on the head," I told her, with satisfaction.

6

Happy Trails, Worthless
November 12, Friday, 11:30 A.M.

We didn't get back to the common room until eleven-thirty.
Jasmine and I started unloading the van, and Lena Mae ran
to help. After the first trip, I opened the grooming room door
and glanced inside. Wayne and his helpers were bathing
puppies, so he was right on schedule. All were wearing
heavy rubber aprons and elbow-length gloves. The room
was hot and steamy and the floor awash with suds. The
washer and dryer were rotating and agitating, and a hamper
on wheels was piled high with wet towels. The radio was
blaring country music, faces were red and sweaty, and most
of the puppies were howling their outrage and dismay.
Everything was normal.

In the kitchen I noticed we were having peach cobbler
and pecan pie. My God, how could a woman with lousy
willpower lose weight around here?

We freeze, can, and store fresh food in bulk all year. You
will eat very well in south Georgia if you are ready and able
to sweat, pick, prepare, and pack the land's bounty. This also
entails stooping, bending, squatting, tying up, weeding,

hoeing, fertilizing, spraying, and praying for rain. Nothing comes easy in south Georgia, either.

At ten after twelve, we had all the supplies and food put away. I had time for a cigarette before the dog scrubbers came in, so I released Bobby Lee from his leash and told him to go play. He scampered out, toenails clicking on the varnished floor. I went to fill a plate.

After lunch, I was in the office paying bills and keying information into the computer. It wasn't my idea of an afternoon of fun. Bobby Lee was asleep on my right, an innocent sprawl of limbs. He was emitting tiny sounds of a dream chase along with an occasional spastic twitch. Rudy was curled into an artistic ball on my left, dead to the world. All this somnolence was contagious, making me toy with the idea of going to the bedroom and grabbing a snooze. The windows were open and the wind was making soft soughs from the southeast. Muted bird sounds and the occasional drone of bees drifted inside on the 75-degree air currents. Perfect.

My reverie was disturbed by one rap on the door as Donnie Ray Carver charged across the carpet with unbridled enthusiasm.

Donnie Ray is my videographer. He's nineteen, small in stature (only five feet five inches), and weighs one hundred and thirty-five pounds. He has wispy blond hair and green eyes. He's feisty and loves to make snappy comebacks.

"I told you I'd finish Rosie's videotape on time!"

I raised my head, frowned, and clucked my tongue at him.

"Sorry. *Miz* Rosie. I don't forget when I'm talking *to* her. Honest. It's just when I'm talking *about* her."

"Noted. Go ahead," I told him.

"She's not poetry in motion, but the message comes

across loud and clear. I despair of ever making an actress out of her. She just can't stand constructive criticism."

He gave a theatrical sigh and flopped into a chair, but he was too happy with the film to maintain his disapproving air. He jumped up and began to give me a frame-by-frame critique. He paced back and forth in front of the desk, using his hands as much as his voice. . . .

I tuned out his hype and remembered last June when I'd needed someone who could make training tapes of search-and-rescue methods and shape them into a commercial product. I knew I couldn't afford an expert, so I'd decided to search for an amateur who wouldn't cost a bundle.

After talking with the faculty adviser for the camera club at the Dunston County High School, I'd decided on Donnie Ray. I was assured that Donnie Ray had raw talent but was very difficult to work with. I'm a sucker for difficult people.

I'd checked on him and found he was raised by a lazy slut of a mother and had an absentee father before he was three. His small stature made him an easy target for school bullies. He'd survived by wading into each fray with an unquenchable belief that he could win the battle. He never did, but they finally left him alone because it took too much effort to win a fight.

Handing him a videocam, I'd told him to spend some time in the library studying angles, lighting, and editing. During the first month, you couldn't turn around without bumping into him or his camera. When he brought me his first effort, I was brutally honest and told him it sucked.

"Listen, Donnie Ray, Spielberg you're not. I don't need slanted angles or cutesy puppies or glamour photos of Jasmine. I want clean, clear shots and a walk-through of our training procedures, something you can view without turning your head sideways to see what's happening. *Comprende?* Go forth and film again."

He left with a bruised ego, smarting from the criticism. But, wonder of wonders, he had a determined look on his face and he wasn't pouting.

Three weeks later, he filmed the search for Mary Ann Miles, and after viewing the tape I knew it was a winner. It was raw and had lighting problems and the picture wobbled in several places, but he had caught the essentials in clear and horrifying detail. I gave him the highest praise of all. I told him he was going to make one hell of a videographer. . . .

". . . and she's ready to roll. You want me to load her up?"

I tuned back in time to hear his last remark.

"Why don't you check with Wayne, Rosie, and Jasmine? See if they want to watch with us."

"Rosie is baking tarts and doesn't want to be disturbed." He grimaced. "I really don't think she has any desire to see it. Wayne is showing puppies to a prospective buyer, and Jasmine left for a locker check at Elliston Elementary over an hour ago. It's just us chickens, unless you want to wait till later."

He tried to sound offhand, but I could hear disappointment in his inability to draw a crowd for his just-finished effort.

I really didn't need a soothing nap. I summoned up some enthusiasm. "How long does the tape run?"

"An hour and twelve minutes."

"Start her up," I said, sounding eager. "I'll watch it again when you show the others."

He gave me a huge grin and ran to fetch the cassette. He had been so certain I would wait for the others that he hadn't brought it with him. His pleasure made me glad I hadn't put him off.

*   *   *

At a quarter till six, Jasmine stuck her head in the door and yelled hello. I answered her from the kitchen, where I was filling water dishes and serving up a measured meal for Rudy and Bobby Lee. We met in the hallway.

"This dress would look fabulous on you if it isn't too short," she said, indicating a gold-colored wool sheath draped over her arm.

"It won't be too short, it'll be too tight in the bust. I'm top-heavy."

"Nonsense," she said, laughing. "You're too hard on yourself. You fill a thirty-six C bra beautifully."

"Oh, yeah?" I retorted. "Then how come I look like a nursing mother when I stand next to your thirty-four C?"

"Cut it out," she said impatiently. "Try it on. Right now." In the bedroom, I wiggled out of my jeans and yanked my T-shirt off. She had unzipped the back of the dress and was holding it forward. I slipped it on, walked to the full-length mirror, eyed my image critically, and turned for the rear view.

"My butt sticks out," I remarked.

"It suits you to a T. I knew it would look good on you," she crowed.

"How much did you pay for it?"

"Seventy-nine dollars. I wore it three times. I'll settle for sixty."

"Jasmine, you're jeopardizing your chance of attaining the rapture and entering the pearly gates. 'Thou shalt not fib,' remember?"

"I paid one-twenty-five, and one hundred is my final offer."

"I'm over budget this month and my overhead has soared."

"I'll trust you."

I looked at her. She raised her hands. "I remember. I remember. I have it memorized: 'We will not let business, money, or playtime affect our friendship. Amen.' I'd do this for any of my friends," she protested.

"Maybe."

"All right already," she said. "I'm stealing Wayne's thunder by telling you this. You have to promise to act surprised and delighted when he tells you. Promise?"

"Promise," I said.

"Wayne sold Worthless for full price this afternoon to a seventy-two-year-old man who wanted, quote, A good companion in my old age, unquote. They can eat and take naps together."

"My prime procrastinator? My perpetual panhandler? The biggest failure in the history of the kennel? Worthless?"

She was nodding yes, rapidly. I turned to the mirror.

"I want the dress! I want the dress!"

I felt like dancing. Worthless was registered as Sidden's Prince of Promise but failed miserably to live up to his name. Even as a puppy, he didn't like getting his feet wet in the morning dew. He thought searches were silly games and refused to participate. He couldn't tell marijuana from cocaine and declined all opportunities to learn. Even Wayne had finally given up on him. He was a three-and-a-half-year-old failure. His only successes were sniffing out food in visitors' pockets and mooching treats from the handlers. His working (ha-ha) handle was Prince, but when Rosie tried to teach him arson procedures and pronounced him worthless, the name had stuck. He had mastered basic obedience and then retired from learning anything new.

I groaned aloud. Jasmine looked surprised. "What?"

"Bloodhounds don't have the life expectancy of other breeds. Their average life span is eight to ten years. He's three and a half now. What if—"

"Never fear." Jasmine read my mind. "I saw the nice old

man, and I know Worthless. I predict Worthless will grieve for his lost master and return to us in a few years."

Jasmine was referring to a promise I incorporated in my sales contract. Simply stated; any animal that grew too old, or was injured and could not function, or needed a home could retire and live out its life here at the kennel. Sinclair Adams, my CPA, said I might regret this guarantee farther down the road, but it was too soon to tell. I had only been in business a little over four years.

"Let's eat," I told Jasmine. We took off for the dining room.

Miz Jansee had outdone herself: pot roast, veggies, salad, home-baked bread, and, for dessert, peach tarts and currant pudding. I ate sparingly, keeping the image of the form-fitting wool dress in mind. Wayne had told me about selling Worthless. I had hugged his neck and waltzed him around the common room. He and Donnie Ray were missing from Miz Jansee's feast. They had received an invitation from Rosie. I guessed I was temporarily off her A list—she hadn't invited me.

I was lounging on the sofa in the office when Susan Comstock arrived at eight. Susan was one of my oldest and dearest friends, going back to first grade at Elliston Elementary School. Jasmine would be over shortly. Her apartment was connected to the gate's security system, so she knew Susan was here.

Susan dropped her large handbag on the sofa, crossed to me, and gave me the obligatory hug and kiss on the cheek that all southern sisters, friends, and relatives bestow on each other, whether it's four hours or four years since the last meeting.

Susan is divorced. Her marriage lasted only seventeen months, at which time her husband ran off with a high school senior. Mine had lasted three miserable years, only because I had stubbornly tried to make it work. She was more fortunate than I. She never saw or heard from him again.

Susan is a natural redhead with green eyes. She is tall with a well-developed body kept that way by working out on a regular basis at the local gym. She also rides horses on weekends at her parents' farm.

Susan, Jasmine, and I usually wear jogging suits for our Friday night get-togethers. Susan's is pale green, Jasmine's pink, and mine is a faded yellow. I had commented that we looked like pastel Easter bunnies who couldn't find a male bunny on a bet. We eat popcorn, drink beer, watch old movies, and tell outrageous jokes. Compensation for our dateless existence.

"Sidden, how many times have we watched this movie?" Susan said in her rich, deep voice with its melodious Georgia twang.

"*Casablanca* is not just a movie, it's a happening. A classic. Would you rather watch something else?"

"No. Not really. But I find myself reciting most of the dialogue with the actors. Another thirty or so viewings and I'll have it completely memorized."

"That's half the fun, knowing what they're going to say next."

Susan said, "I agree. I still get chills when they play the French national anthem."

"Me too," I said, as I went to get the beer.

Jasmine arrived, carrying a big bowl of popcorn. I asked her what she had found on her search this afternoon.

"Four rocks of crack, sixteen tabs of LSD, nine home-grown hand-rolled joints, three poor-boy baggies, and a twenty-two target pistol—unloaded, thank God."

"Where?" Susan was startled. "High school?"

"Elliston Elementary," I said with disgust. "You'd think

the little shits would learn, as often as we go there. But no. We could reappear tomorrow and find almost the same thing."

Susan pointed her finger at me. "I sometimes think it's retribution. School officials finally getting paid back for the way they treated us." She turned to Jasmine. "I apprenticed under a master. After years of following her in all her escapades, now that I'm grown and more knowledgeable, she doesn't use my experience or talents. I must have failed the course."

Ah, so. She felt left out because I don't include her in my wheelings and dealings. The main reason is to keep her out of trouble. I can take an occasional chance of getting clobbered—and arrested—but I don't want to drag her into danger. Also, to be honest, Susan loves to gossip and sometimes has difficulty in sorting out what is tellable and what is not. Live and learn. I needed to make amends somehow.

"Hey," I said, being glib. "Speaking of using your experience and talents, maybe you can help me figure out a way to thwart Bubba and get him tucked back into the clink."

"He's out?" she glared at me. "When?"

Oh, boy, now I had torn it. From the frying pan into the fire.

"Last night at midnight," I said. "Hank called me this morning. The prison officials haven't gotten around to notifying me—yet."

"You didn't call me," she said, her voice rising. "I'm supposed to be your best friend!" She hesitated, realizing she was about to yell. "Is that why you started smoking again? I was being tactful by not mentioning the fact that you were puffing away as usual. I was not going to say, 'I told you so, you don't have the willpower to lay them down.' My, my."

"Sorry. I knew I'd see you tonight. That's why I didn't call."

Jasmine was dividing an apprehensive look between us. "Uh, ladies, are we going to watch a movie or fight?"

Susan and I both erupted into laughter, breaking the tension.

"We never fight," she explained. "We just nag, nag, nag."

"Nag, nag, nag," I echoed.

We ate popcorn, watched the movie, and guzzled beer. Just after eleven, I rode with Susan to the first gate.

When I got out of her car and walked around to the driver's side she said, "Do you have your gun with you?" She was going to worry, I could tell.

I patted the pocket of my jogging suit, stepped back one step, and, with my arms akimbo, I said, "I am woman. See me fly. Watch me leap tall buildings with a single bound."

"You're a nut. I'll be at the farm for the weekend. Call me if you need me. Take care."

"Will do. Don't fall off any horses."

"Have I ever? See you Sunday morning." She gunned the motor of her Lumina minivan the few feet to the highway, stopped abruptly for a second, turned right, and sped off into the night. I watched her taillights disappear before turning to lock the gate. While walking back up the drive, I looked up at the stars. The clouds had dissipated, and with the moonless night they looked bright and twinkly. I caught the tiny blur of a falling star. My wish was automatic: *Make Bubba disappear from my life.*

7

Random Thoughts

Somewhere, Sometime, in the Dark

He lay on his side, his left shoulder pushed under the skimpy pad sewn into the sleeping bag. A couple of years ago he'd casually mentioned to Milt Phillips, his doctor of twenty-three years, that he'd taken to sleeping on two pillows. Seemed more comfortable. Milt had blasted him with a caustic harangue on his two-packs-a-day smoking habit, along with a dire diagnosis of encroaching emphysema. He manfully endured Milt's tirade, promising to seriously think about quitting. Instead, he went back to sleeping with just one pillow, positioning one corner between his shoulder and neck to give it added height.

What in God's name had made him remember a mundane conversation between himself and Milt that had taken place two years ago? Maybe the need for nicotine was returning. He'd felt no desire for a cigarette since he'd opened his eyes here—wherever here was. He felt no pressing need now for nicotine; hot coffee sounded better. A nice steaming-hot cup of coffee, heavily laced with Coffee-mate. He hadn't drunk a cup of coffee without lighting up for over thirty years.

Why yearn for caffeine without its constant companion, nicotine?

His mind was playing tricks, but he hadn't been so stupid as to pinch himself to see if he was dreaming. He had to admit, however, that fleeting thoughts, both ridiculous and beyond reality, had fluttered across his reasoning process. He could've caught a rare virus: tiny infectious agents harming his vision and causing nightmares too powerful to comprehend. He could see himself waking up under bright lights with a tired but elated Milt grinning beside his hospital bed. Nope, that scenario wouldn't fly. Milt retired last year. If he was standing over something, it would be a fishing rod or golf putter. He could've found some humor in his nonsensical musings if he just didn't feel so rotten. His stomach was distended from the volume of water he'd drunk. He reached down and undid the top button of his pants.

Since he couldn't remember throwing up any of his stomach contents, whatever drug he'd been given could've been reactivated with all the liquid he'd consumed.

He turned carefully onto his right side, bunching the head pad over his shoulder, and opened his eyes in the darkness. Into the empty space surrounding him and in a firm voice that didn't tremble, he spoke aloud. "I am a fifty-six-year-old male in peril and feeling damned uncomfortable. I've been having random thoughts. I'm going to rest now and preserve my strength." He felt better after the effort. Presently, he slept.

8

Button, Button, Who's Got the Button?
November 13, Saturday, 7 A.M.

While sitting at my desk, working on my third cup of coffee, smoking a cigarette, and enjoying the nicotine as it coursed throughout my system, I checked the voice mail for messages and was pleased there were none. I then dialed the weather line and listened to the recording as it informed me that the weather conditions were optimal, if I were called out on a search, even with the wind. So far, the morning was perking right along.

In the past, when Bubba had been released from prison, his modus operandi was a few days of silence, followed by phone calls where he just hung up after the voice mail recording or my answer. I had no reason to believe he would change his plans; Bubba wasn't great at improvising. My guard was up, but I felt I still had a few days of grace.

Looking out the window, I noted the grass was still green this late into fall. It was going to be a mild winter. The woolly bear caterpillar said so.

The phone rang just as I was leaving for the breakfast

meeting in the common room. I ran back and caught it on the second ring. "Hello," I said.

"This is Patton Correctional's parole office in Sebring, Georgia. I wish to speak to Ms. Jo Beth Sidden," said an officious-sounding female voice.

"Oooh," I moaned, speaking with a southern mush-mouth accent. "Oooh, dat po' chile, dat po' lamb. Done been cut off 'fore her time! Lordy! Lordy! Dat bad man! He done come and got her. He got her on her own porch, bless her sweet soul. May he burn in fire and brimstone! Oooh, my po' sweet missus!"

I was treated to a long silence but kept panting heavily and sniffling into the receiver.

"Is . . . she dead?" The voice was almost a whisper.

"My chile be with Jesus! She be in the hands of her Maker! Praise the Lord! Allelujah! Blessed be the Lord!"

I was hamming it up, thoroughly enjoying myself. I continued the heavy breathing and could hear a continuous litany only partly muffled by a hand over the receiver.

"OhGodohGodohGodohGod!" The line was disconnected.

I smiled with evil relish. Let them sweat while they passed the bad news up the chain of command. When it reached the people responsible for damage control, they would check and find the story false.

Still smiling and stepping lightly, I entered the common room and approached Jasmine, who was standing by the bulletin board.

"Mornin', Jasmine."

"Mornin' to you too," she said with a smile. "Feeling chipper are we?"

When I related the phone conversation word for word, she clapped her hands together, her eyes dancing with mischief.

"I would've paid good money to have seen her face

when she listened to you. Just think what's being said right this minute up there."

"I know, I know," I said with satisfaction.

Everyone was present for breakfast except Ramon and Carol, who were missing again today. I'd have to stop at the animal clinic on the way to town this morning. I had several items to discuss with him about the speech he was to give next week to the new dog owners. Will wonders never cease? Rosie was here—and eating. Could it be she was accepting the fact that Miz Jansee was the cook of choice? Nah, probably not.

"How's the breakfast, Rosie?"

"The red-eye gravy is a mite salty, and there're some lumps in the grits. Her biscuits didn't rise enough, and the ham is a trifle overdone. I'll speak to her after we finish." She smiled sweetly.

I swallowed. "Uh, Rosie," I said, as I leaned closer and lowered my voice, "did you notice how tired Miz Jansee looks this morning? Maybe you should wait until Monday. She may have had a sleepless night. What do you say?"

"Well, if you say so. It makes me no never mind."

I drew a breath and went to fill a plate. A temporary reprieve to the coming showdown.

As I was leaving for town, Jasmine followed me to the door. "Are you taking Bobby Lee?"

"Nope. It's too hot today for him in the van."

"Do you mind if I use his talents this morning? I'm reviewing sniff commands with W. A.'s dog, Hemingway."

"He'll love it. But why?"

"I've noticed that Hemingway is slow to respond to some of the commands. He probably won't like having a younger male besting him in every exercise. Hemingway is slow but competitive. He'll pick up speed fast when he sees Bobby Lee in action."

"Good idea," I agreed. "Come on over." We walked to the porch. "Bobby Lee," I called.

Both he and Rudy were quickly in front of me with expectant looks, awaiting instructions.

"Rudy, my love, you can't go. It's a no-no."

He stretched and stalked into the house. I could tell he was furious.

"Bobby Lee, fetch your leash and go with Jasmine." I'm sure he only understood three of the words: *leash, go,* and *Jasmine.* He took two hops and reared up on his hind legs precisely in front of the post where the large nail held his leash. He positioned his mouth directly under the large loop handle and carefully lifted the leash up and over the nail. He scooted to Jasmine with his tail working overtime and shook his head as he presented it to her, spraying drool over her shoes and ten feet of floor. Jasmine laughed as she pulled on her gloves.

"The only flaw of a bloodhound: drool, drool, drool."

Like a proud parent whose first grader has remembered his lines in a school play, I stood by and watched them cross the compound with Bobby Lee's stride matching perfectly with hers.

I braked at the end of the driveway, checked for traffic and turned right on the highway, drove five hundred yards, and pulled into the hard-packed dirt parking area in front of the veterinary clinic. I was proud of this creation. It had everything a small-animal clinic needs: waiting room, treatment rooms, operating room, small lab, and storage room. Out back were kennels for twenty patients and ten long fenced-in runs with covered and uncovered areas.

Ramon Fontaine is of Spanish, Italian, and Irish descent. He has dark hair and an olive complexion and has grown a pencil-thin mustache during the past year. He had just graduated from a veterinarian college when I found him and his young bride, Carol. She is a slim blonde who blushes when anyone speaks to her. Ramon has been here three years, repaid the government loan for his education, and is now saving money to open his own clinic. He's fiercely independent, and I know I'll lose him in three or four years. In my opinion, he has a damn good thing going here, but some people yearn to be their own boss. I can't fault him for that, and he has built a respectable practice.

I reached into the back of the van and picked up my purse. It held only the essentials: lipstick, comb, tissues, cigarettes, billfold—and gun. The purse bulges unfashionably, but with Bubba free, the gun goes where I go. This gun is my search-and-rescue weapon, along with a .22-caliber rifle. My serious protection gun is the .357 magnum in the nightstand by my bed. The gun I carry today I once used to shoot and kill an escaped convict during a search. So far, I haven't been traumatized by the event or had any bad dreams.

Petula, the young black receptionist, didn't hear me enter. She was standing behind the waist-high partition with her head turned toward the hallway, listening so intently to the conversation taking place in one of the treatment rooms, it startled her when I spoke.

"Hi, Petula, how are you?" I said loudly. Since no cars were in the parking lot, I assumed the voices were Ramon's and Carol's.

She jumped with nervous surprise and returned my greeting in an even louder voice than I had used.

"I'm just fine, Miz Jo Beth! My, don't you look nice! Got a date, I'll bet!"

Both our heads swiveled in unison toward the hallway, and neither of us tried to pretend that nothing was going on. We heard a brisk smack, then total silence. Our eyes met in consternation. Unless I missed my guess, someone had just gotten the hell slapped out of them.

Carol came barreling down the hallway and burst into the waiting room. Her face had a rosy glow. She lost a step when she saw me but quickly recovered and stomped her way out the front door. Ramon was right behind her and stopped dead in the doorway when he saw me.

"You need me?" His voice was harsh. I tried not to stare at the red handprint that glowed on his right cheek.

"No," I said lamely. "Just wanted to say hello."

"Good," he said brusquely, as he turned on his heel and disappeared down the hallway. I heard a door slam somewhere in the rear of the building.

I looked at Petula. "I'm not asking as the owner of this establishment—and their employer—I'm asking as a friend. Is there trouble in paradise?"

"You bet," she answered promptly. "Started about six weeks ago and it's gotten much worse here lately." I saw tears form and spill over her lashes. "'Scuse me," she said, as she took off to the ladies' room.

Talk about emptying a room. Shit. I wondered what Ramon and Carol were fighting about. I had had no idea they were having problems. It would be better to let them cool off and pump them individually tomorrow. I picked up my purse and got out of there.

Downtown, I pulled into the alley and parked behind Alice's Flower Pot. When I entered, Alice was sitting on a high stool by her workbench twirling a streamer of blue ribbon.

"Hi, Jo Beth." She came forward to hug my neck. "Where you been hiding yourself? I've missed you."

"Tending to business. You're looking good. Mason must be taking good care of you. How's Toby?"

"Likes school but dislikes his third-grade teacher. Ain't seen you in a coon's age," she complained.

"I've been busy, but I hope you aren't too busy to make some floral arrangements and deliver them to the compound this afternoon."

"Busy? You're pulling my leg. A little spurt at Thanksgiving, pretty good at Christmas, and then nothing till Saint Valentine's day. What do you need?"

Alice always sings the blues about business. She doesn't think she's making money unless she's running way behind on the orders, which hardly ever happens. She has lots of time to devote to the business since her husband, Mason, who drives a semi for Cannon Trucking, is on the road five days out of seven.

"I need six arrangements that will appeal to men and a larger one for the common room. They have to stay fresh until next Friday—and not cost a fortune. I've spent so much lately, I'm one step away from the poorhouse."

"You start running a hotel I haven't heard about?"

I explained the motel-like units and the week-long seminars.

"God, girl, think of the available poontang. Here I've been feeling sorry for you lately, thinking you weren't getting any."

"Bite your tongue. I should be so lucky. Don't spread it around: Bubba's out."

"Again? What they got up there, revolving doors?"

"Seems like," I agreed.

"Gal, why don't you just blow him away, like you did that escaped prisoner—when, last April? Solve your problem and get on with your life. Quit messing around."

"Why do I have to be the one? It's the law's place to protect me. They should handle it, not me," I said in anger.

"Yeah. But they ain't gonna, you know that. Besides, what's the difference between Bubba and the escapee man you shot and killed? You still got feelings for that piece of garbage?"

"Nah. I wouldn't piss on him if he was on fire, but one of my dogs was killed during a search, and I lost it. The bastard deserved to die."

She shook her head and grinned. "You're something else, Jo Beth. Here's Bubba, a no-good animal who's tried to kill you more than once, and you can't pull the trigger. Remind me to never kick one of your dogs."

"It's a capital offense," I said with a weak smile.

Glancing back at the cooler where the cut flowers are stored, she said, "How often you gonna hold them seminars?"

"Once a month or until the trained dogs run out. We're trying to time their training to match that schedule."

"Silk arrangements cost more, but I could fix them up with fall colors and they'd last for three months. Then you could go with spring colors. Save you money in the long run."

"Wouldn't they look tacky?"

"I don't do tacky!" she retorted. "I went to school to learn *not* to make tacky. I get colored illustrations from the florist people monthly, showing me how to do the latest arrangements."

"Sorry," I said. "I stand corrected. Here's my MasterCard. I'll let the cost be a surprise. I know you'll take it easy on me."

"After tacky, don't be too sure," she muttered.

9

Illegal Speculations
November 13, Saturday, 11:45 A.M.

I pulled up at Chester's Restaurant at a quarter till twelve, knowing they wouldn't be crowded. They serve twice the food at twice the price, and it is simply delicious. Also, we would have time and space to talk without being seen. I didn't lock the van; car theft is practically unheard of in Balsa City, and so far carjacking hasn't appeared on our streets.

I stood in the foyer waiting for a waiter. When he appeared, I pressed a ten-dollar bill into his hand and said, "My name is Sidden and I'm expecting a guest: Ms. Dawson. I need a secluded table, fast service, and time for a lengthy conversation. If everything jells, that bill has a twin."

"Right this way, ma'am." He led me to a high-backed booth with an ornate flange running the height of each seat.

"Would you care for a drink?"

"Imported beer," I said. The beer here is delicious and, heathen that I am, I drink it straight from the bottle. I had finished about half the brew when I saw the waiter walking ahead of Sheri. She was wearing yellow, her favorite color. I have only really known her for seven months, but I've never seen her in any other color. I pictured her closet holding thirty or so yellow outfits with maybe a basic black looking lost at one end.

Reaching around the flange, she hugged me awkwardly and slid in opposite.

"Would you like a drink?" I asked.

"A glass of white wine," she said. I tipped my bottle of beer at the waiter and he took off.

Sheri giggled. "You must have tipped him already. I had to trot to keep up with him."

I smiled and did some appraising. She was two years my senior and looked eighteen, at the most. Five feet four inches, a hundred pounds dripping wet, shoulder-length ash-blond hair, blue eyes, and gorgeous. At eighteen, she had won all the local beauty contests and was third runner-up in the Miss Georgia Pageant.

We had alternated in treating each other to lunch for the past six months. I wanted to pick and probe to see if she was worthy of Wade Bennett, my friend and attorney and her intended. Also, I had to know what made her tick. Could she be trusted with a big, big secret that would bind us as co-conspirators and co-criminals for the rest of our lives? I wasn't sure if there was a statute of limitations on the particular crime I was about to suggest to her. Unfortunately, I couldn't ask Wade or any other attorney in this small town. Only time would tell if I was doing the right thing or stepping into a pile of doo-doo.

"How was your week?" I asked. She had dark circles under her eyes from worrying too much and for too long.

She didn't answer because the waiter was deftly serving the wine and beer and asking if we were ready to order.

"I'll have the seafood salad with the house dressing and rolls," I told him.

"Fried prawns, coleslaw, and rolls," she said.

The waiter disappeared in a puff of smoke.

"Sheri," I began, "I have a long story to tell you."

She laid both hands over mine and spoke quickly. "Can I go first? My first date with Wade, when you saw us at Attenburg's Steak House. You were with George Harris. Do you remember?" I nodded. "You scared me to death, Jo Beth. I sensed your hostility. I had already fallen for Wade. He was so damn tentative about asking me out, and then he was so embarrassed when he saw you sitting there in the restaurant. I thought you were staking a claim on him. I've never mentioned this before, I was afraid to ask, but I really have to know. Did you ever want him?"

Giving her an open grin, I said, "I thought about it off and on for about three days. But we turned each other off every time we opened our mouths. We found out very quickly we weren't compatible. After two weeks of some hectic and trying times, we managed to become friends and that's really all we ever wanted."

"I'm so glad," she said, beaming with relief.

"And Sheri, if I seemed hostile that night, I apologize."

Tears welled up in her eyes and she removed a tissue from her purse and blotted them. "Jo Beth, I'm weepy all the time now. My nerves are shot to hell. Talk nice to me and I'll start bawling."

"You and Wade can't figure out a solution?"

"We've tried. Oh, how we've tried! We've discussed mortgaging the house for this year's taxes, but what about next year? He could sell some of the land, but a few years' taxes will gobble that up, and we'll still lose the house. Wade never knew how much he loved Tara until he found out he is about to lose it. It breaks my heart. I want that pile of wood so much I can taste it, but his practice will never be big enough to support that house—and a family. On top of everything else, he wants me to quit work and us start a family right after we get married next month!"

I let her sip her wine before asking the next question.

"How much did Wade's father leave when the probate finally cleared?"

This question was way out of line. Asking pointed questions about someone's finances is not socially acceptable southern etiquette, but Sheri didn't seem to notice.

"Less than five grand. I could kill the old fart, if he wasn't already dead. All those holding companies and offshore accounts. It took them almost two months to unravel those tangled webs he wove, and then he got cold feet—"

Sheri broke off the conversation as the waiter arrived and began serving our food. I looked at him. With one eyebrow raised, he asked if everything was jelling.

"I trust you removed the calories."

"Ran the food through the decalorizer—personally," he returned.

I smiled and nodded approval and he bounded off like a gazelle.

I was intrigued with the sentence Sheri had broken off when the waiter arrived. She couldn't possibly know about the money—I didn't think—but it sure sounded like she knew *something*.

We both ate with good appetites and finished the meal with plenty left over. I wiggled a hand out in space; the waiter's eyes were glued to our booth.

"Want another drink, Sheri?"

"Just coffee."

The waiter cleared the table quickly and took my MasterCard and the order for two coffees. When he returned, I placed the promised ten-dollar bill on his tray.

"Sheri, before the waiter interrupted, you were saying

something about Carl Bennett: 'and then he got cold feet.' What was that all about?"

She pulled on her left earlobe and took a deep breath. "The old crook made some illegal money in the last years of his life. I firmly believe that. I got my hopes way up when the probate took so long. I thought there would be enough so Wade could pay those god-awful taxes each year and we could survive. I thought he had set up all those convoluted real estate transactions to fool the IRS. It was us he fooled. He closed them all out and didn't put his money in them, just shuffled them around and left almost nothing. I guess he realized it wouldn't be safe."

"What makes you think he made illegal money?"

"Come on, Jo Beth, give me a little credit for brains. I didn't just pop out from under a cabbage leaf. I know you and Wade fought because you thought his father was a crook and Wade thought he was honest. He told me."

"Okay, Sheri—God help us both—I'm going to tell you a story. Willing to listen?"

"I'm sitting on dead ready. Have been for six months."

"Before I start, I want to stress one vital point: This is all supposition. When Wade came down from Boston to bury his father, he went through the old man's files. As a result, he came out to the compound to talk to me about *my* father's will, and we spent that first day together discussing our daddies. I showed him around the kennel, and he was still there when I got a call-out to search for Ancel Tew. Do you remember the details?"

"I read about it, and Wade told me a little. Hearing it from you sounds very interesting. I'm all ears."

"Being a silly female, I wanted to show off to impress him. I asked Wade if he wanted to tag along and see what I did for a living. He did, and you know about him getting injured during the search. Ancel Tew's son-in-law threw him halfway down a flight of stairs, which resulted in three broken ribs and a mild concussion. He had to spend the night in the hospital. Wade was living alone at Tara, so I invited him to stay in my guest room."

"Did you?" Her eyes were bright. "He conveniently forgot to mention being your houseguest, and I know why. I would have given him the third degree about the sleeping arrangements." She said this good-naturedly.

"Sheri," I said, "there are a lot of things you're not capable of with three broken ribs, and screwing is right at the top of the list. He only stayed one night. And he was in a great deal of pain."

"I know," she said softly. "I was only kidding. I know you're just friends." She grinned impishly and added, "I still would have grilled him, even with the broken ribs. You can see why he decided not to tell me."

"During our conversations," I continued, "I gathered enough clues to grow suspicious of Wade's father, clues that Wade didn't realize the importance of. When I told him about my suspicions, he hit the ceiling. He didn't believe any point I tried to prove. I wouldn't have brought up the question of Carl doing anything illegal so soon, but it was three weeks after Carl's death. I was afraid the IRS and the DEA would swoop down as soon as the will was probated, and Wade would lose everything. You know how they love to grab houses, cars, bank accounts, and anything else of value lying around."

"DEA? Drugs?" She was shocked, her eyes wide open and round as saucers. "Wade's father dealt in drugs?"

I sighed, and Sheri noticed my expression.

"Sorry. Tell the story. I promise I won't interrupt."

"Wade didn't want to believe his father was a crook. He buried his head in the sand, got angry with me, and wouldn't discuss it further."

Sheri was listening closely, her lips pressed together, and she was scowling.

"You haven't heard any of this?"

"No. But this explains why Wade is so defensive of his father. I've learned the hard way to quit taking potshots at Carl. What made you so sure he was a crook?"

"I'll give you the clues I gathered and let you decide. You've seen the mansion. Do you think Carl kept it up on about twenty thousand a year—after taxes?"

"No way," she said, grim-faced. "I've done a lot of figuring since Wade and I started discussing marriage. Money has been spent lavishly on that house. It gleams. It's burnished. It's in tiptop shape."

"The same conclusion I reached. Eight to ten years ago, Carl suddenly gave up hunting. Was 'just plum tired of killing those purty little creatures.' And guess what? He stopped all his old buddies from hunting on the six hundred or so heavily wooded acres at the same time. Add the fact that Hector, Carl's gardener, was willing to work 'for free' until the probate cleared when he heard Wade was short of money. He even offered to loan Wade money until he received his inheritance."

"I never knew anything about Hector," she commented.

"Hector was into pot. When I made the mistake of telling Wade about it, he said he was going to the DEA and ask them to check into it. I knew they would laugh themselves silly, think Wade was a fool, and confiscate everything he owned down to his socks, if they found any pot growing on Carl's land."

"I would have been as positive as you. Anyone around here is thought to be growing pot if they own a hundred acres and buy a new truck every year." Sheri was almost breathless with excitement.

"Fifty acres," I said with a smile. "The rule of thumb is, if they have fifty acres they are suspect."

"What happened next?"

"I want you to understand, Sheri. I have a compulsion to

help my friends neaten up their lives and solve their problems. My life is such a mess and since I can only force myself to play defense—not offense—against Bubba, there's really no solution to *my* problem. Maybe that's the reason I meddle in other people's lives. I don't want you to think it's because I want Wade, the house, or the money. I helped him because he's a buddy."

"I'm glad you told me. I was afraid we'd never be close."

"After I finish telling you this story, we'll probably become even closer. Now, about how I helped Wade. I gathered a team of four men and one woman. These are people I trust completely, and some of them owed me big-time. We found pot growing on Wade's land. It took us all day, but we managed to destroy the plants and any evidence of their existence. That was the same day Wade visited the local DEA's branch office, told them about the rumor, and said he wanted them to check it out. Thank God, it takes time for them to gather a task force and helicopter for a search. We cleaned out the property on Monday. The DEA began their search on Thursday with the chopper, spent Friday with a ground search team of twenty or more, and didn't find a blessed thing."

"That's amazing. If you hadn't helped Wade, he would have lost everything. He hasn't told me one word of this! How in the world can he still believe his father was innocent of any wrongdoing? After the will was probated and there was no money, I tried to tell him his dad had to be into something illegal. Carl spent money like water."

"Sheri, Wade didn't tell you anything because he doesn't know anything. I never told him. He wants to believe in Carl's innocence, so I hope you'll keep this a secret. Why spoil his memories of his father?"

"I'm not believing what I'm hearing," she said. "You risked everything to save Wade's butt, his house, his reputation, and everything else, and never even told him?"

"Right. If I'd told him, it would have proved his father was a crook."

Sheri stared at me as her eyes filled with tears. "Thank you from the bottom of my heart for all you did for Wade. He can't thank you because he doesn't know, but I thank you for him. It kept him whole for me."

"Thanks aren't needed. That wasn't why I told you."

I waited. She wiped her eyes and took a sip of cold coffee. The waiter was giving us our time and space. Glancing through the small opening, I could see the diners were thinning out. Appetites had been sated; the hum of activity was muted. It was half-past one.

"Sheri, I'm curious," I said slowly, as if thinking out loud. "A hypothetical 'what if.' What if the money was available and you knew it was from drugs, would your conscience let you keep it? Could you spend it?"

I smiled and watched as her eyes lit up.

"So fast it would make your head swim," she said with a big grin. "I solved that dilemma of ethics back when I thought some would show up. At first, when I knew Carl had overspent and lived way beyond his means, I made some promises to myself. If he had been embezzling from little ol' ladies, the money would be returned promptly—if there was anything left. But drug money? The buyers can't be reimbursed, and I surely wouldn't give it to the government. Yes! Yes, I would spend it. Would you?"

"In a New York minute," I agreed. "What if you had to make this decision alone, with Wade not aware of the money? Could you keep it from him? Feed it slowly into your budget? Live with the secret and all it would entail? It would take vigilance, and you would be under constant pressure for years to come."

She rubbed her nose and sat there thinking it over, then

said, "Every woman keeps secrets from her mate. Some are good, some are bad. This would be a good secret."

Leaning back in the booth, I relaxed and lit a cigarette. Sheri had come up with all the right answers.

"Jo Beth?" I saw a small frown of consternation on her face as she formed the coming question. "You didn't tell the story about clearing out the pot for praise, and it happened seven months ago. Why are you telling me now?"

"I just wanted to be sure you could handle the secret and had the guts to stick it out for the long haul. I think I know where the money is hidden."

10

Criminal Shenanigans
November 13, Saturday, 1:30 P.M.

Sheri didn't scream, jump for joy, faint, keep a stiff upper lip, or remain calm. She pushed aside her coffee cup, placed her head on her folded arms on the table's surface, and commenced crying as if her heart were broken. Her shoulders shook in rhythmic accompaniment.

People in this town are the most avid gossips on earth, male and female. The males swear they don't gossip, they "cuss and discuss the issues." Bull. They gossip. Sheri's position as head librarian made her as recognizable as the mayor—only prettier. Rumors would fly with the speed of a sonic boom and would be as diverse as chalk and cheese. They would have her dumped by Wade, pregnant, or dying of an incurable illness (possibly AIDS; you just can't trust ex-beauty queens).

"Sheri," I said acerbically and softly, "put a lid on it! Thirty seconds into your future life of crime, you're giving people reason to speculate. This is definitely a no-no. Are you listening?"

"Sorry, I lost it there for a minute. God, I'm a wreck. Excuse me while I go fix my face." She started to rise.

"Keep your buns on the cushion, my friend," I said evenly. "Do your repairing right here. The rest room is not necessarily empty."

She patted her face and outlined and lipsticked in silence. When she finished, I gave her a tight smile.

"I must be slipping. I could have sworn I added a disclaimer right in front of the last sentence. Didn't I say *I think?*"

"You did, and I overreacted. I'm sorry," she said in a humble voice. "But I've been under such a strain worrying where the money would come from to pay the taxes on Tara. I confess, I've caught myself lately mentally casing two banks and the check-cashing store on Flatland Road. I've made you angry with me."

"I'm not angry. Just suddenly apprehensive. The minute you and I entered into a conversation about this money, we became co-conspirators to defraud the United States Government out of a whole heap of money, along with other charges such as spending profits from the manufacture and distribution of illegal drugs, withholding the evidence of a crime, guilty knowledge, and God knows what else. We can't even consult an attorney to find out just how many laws we'd be breaking."

"You can count on me, Jo Beth."

"Where's Wade today, playing golf?" I asked.

"No, he had to go to Waycross. He's taking depositions from three locals there who were involved in a car accident at Three Forks last week. He told me he wouldn't be back until eight or nine tonight."

"What did you have planned for this afternoon?"

"I'm getting my hair done at three. Wade says we're going to church tomorrow morning."

"Why don't you cancel your hair appointment. You'll have plenty of time to do it yourself before Wade returns. Let's go and see if I'm as smart as I think I am or have a swelled head and don't know diddly-squat."

"Now?" She looked strained.

"No time like the present."

"God, Jo Beth, my hands are shaking."

"You have the shakes after twenty minutes of speculation. I've had seven months of 'Am I right or am I wrong?'—and it's not even my money."

"You'll get some, I promise," she said.

"No way. Don't start. It was left for Wade and his heirs. I don't qualify."

"Finder's fee, maybe?" she persisted.

"Read my lips." I said the words slowly. "Nada. No more discussion of this topic, it's finished, over. Let's go home, change clothes, and meet at Wade's. See if you can find a round-point shovel in his garage. We'll also need a plastic trash container. I'll bring another shovel and a heavy tarp."

"Do you know where to dig?"

"I've seen the treasure map," I said, with a smug expression.

Sheri's yellow Camaro was parked in front of Wade's mansion when I arrived at three. Low smudged clouds hung in the southeast, slowly moving toward the northwest. A sufficient breeze kept the insects grounded. It was a pleasant 85-degree afternoon, but even with the breeze we were going to sweat.

For a moment I sat in the car and admired the house. When Wade's grandfather built it sometime in the early 1900s, he copied the antebellum look of the plantation mansions. At the time, Margaret Mitchell was just learning to read and write. But after *Gone With the Wind* premiered in Atlanta in 1939, the locals had promptly dubbed this house Tara, and Tara it would remain until the great chimneys crumbled to ruin and moldered to dust away, to use a description borrowed from Longfellow.

The fifty acres surrounding the house include a long curving drive lined with magnolia trees and artistically arranged flower beds and shrubs. The five hundred and fifty acres behind the house are in their natural state and were where I had tromped with my dogs and my friends to eradicate the last crop of marijuana to be grown on this land—maybe.

The house has fourteen rooms and a modest ballroom. It's furnished with genuine antiques purchased almost a hundred years ago. It's a pity its present owner has his head in the clouds about his modern-day pirate of a father, and his bride-to-be and friend are forced to grub for tainted money to maintain the property in the style to which it has become accustomed.

Sheri appeared from the south side of the house, dragging a shovel in her left hand and awkwardly balancing a large sturdy plastic tub on her right hip. She dropped the tub at my feet and leaned the shovel against the van.

"It's the only thing I could find. Will it do?"

"The two wide handles will enable us to carry it easier than a trash can."

I opened the door at the rear of the van and unloaded the items I was going to contribute to the search: another round-point shovel and a straight-edged shovel, a heavy-duty plastic tarp twelve feet square, two pairs of dog-handling gloves, and a fitted vanity case that matches my set of luggage.

Sheri eyed the case. "What's that for?"

"To transport the money," I said. "I forgot to tell you to bring yours. You can return mine when you've found a safe hiding place for the loot."

"I'm heartened by your optimism," she said with a wide grin.

I'd forgotten to unload a roll of black plastic bed-liner

and garden shears. I removed them from the van and tucked everything under my left arm except the shovels. I carried them under my right arm, balancing their weight and steadying them with my right hand.

"Load up and follow me," I told her.

I headed for the north side of the house, traveled the graveled path about fifty feet, turned right, and entered the rose garden. In this section of the yard grew all the roses, so the lady of the manor could cut blooms for floral arrangements without having to wander too far from the house. The bushes were in small groupings, and all were outlined with carefully tended gravel paths that wove in and around the beds.

When I arrived at a white concrete bench firmly embedded in concrete footings, I turned to Sheri. "Unload and let's rest awhile."

The finely graveled path widened at this point and edged up to run along the front of the concrete bench, and then gently curved back to its original width. Straight across from the bench it widened the same amount to form an open area for the huge oak tree that shaded most of the rose beds from the scorching sun during the hot summers. I used a glove to wipe two areas of dried bird droppings from the bench.

"Sit," I said, patting a spot beside me. Moving my feet back and forth across the surface of the ground, I could feel the white pea-sized gravel roll smoothly beneath my shoes.

Sheri sat down and gazed around with pleasure. "It's beautiful here, especially with that big oak in front of us. I've cut some lovely roses out here in the past six months. I hope I'm still cutting them next year," she said pensively.

I lit up a cigarette and settled back. "Before we start digging and sweating, I'm going to explain how I discovered where to dig. When I unloaded my suspicions about Carl on Wade, I also told him I suspected a letter from his father would show up, either when the will was filed for probate, in Carl's safety deposit box, or hidden in the house. Of course, Wade didn't believe me, but during the three days he had to wait for the DEA, he did search the house from top to bottom for a letter or some sign of his father's guilt. He found nothing.

"What he failed to realize was that the letter had simply been delayed. His father's ex-law partner, Andrew J. Carpenter, had retired five years before Carl's death, and he and his wife were literally on a slow boat to China.

"When the partner returned home, he found out about Carl's death. Carpenter was holding a letter from Carl to Wade. I asked Wade if he would let me read it. He was glad to oblige, he was so relieved to find out his letter was not a confession from his father about his criminal past. He also wanted to rub it in a little, that I was mistaken. Has he shown it to you?"

"Yes. Carl must have really missed his son when his wife divorced him and moved to Boston, taking Wade with her. He wrote page after page about Wade's childhood exploits. A very tender letter of love for his son."

"Tender? Maybe. Just maybe. The truth is that the old thief was skewered on the horns of a dilemma. If he told Wade about the money, he would lose his son's admiration. If he didn't tell him, Wade might lose the estate. He straddled the fence and couldn't decide which way to jump—even after his death—so he hid the money and left clues. Carl must have reasoned this way: If Wade ever got a hint about his illegal activities and questioned how he could afford his grand lifestyle after seeing the bottom-line profits in his law practice, Wade could find the money. If Wade didn't find the money, Carl knew Carpenter, who had no children, had named Wade as his heir. Carl also knew Wade's mother had money. He was hoping that even if

Wade didn't find the money, some future recipient of his genes would."

"Wade could have found the money if he had known there was money hidden," she said loyally.

"Absolutely," I agreed. "And I know to look because I knew damn well Carl was dirty."

"So how do we find it?" She was trying to be patient.

She was right, I had stalled long enough. A feeling of trepidation ran through me. I'd really look like an ass if there was nothing to find.

"Do you recall the first incident Carl referred to in his letter about Wade's boyhood?"

She stared off into space in concentration, then shook her head.

"I can't remember the first one. I know he mentioned several."

"Well, I may not quote it verbatim, but he wrote, *I remember the sack swing hanging from the oak tree in the rose garden where you fell and broke your arm when you were nine years old. After your mother took you away, I sat there many times on the concrete bench across from that oak and knew that beneath my feet was the dirt upon which you played as a child.*"

"So?"

"The letter was a treasure map, Sheri. Here's where he placed the first *X* to mark the spot. *Dig here,* he said." I rolled the pebbles beneath my feet.

Sheri watched the movement of my feet and then stared at the big oak directly opposite us across the path.

"By Jove, Holmes, I think you're brilliant!" She was high with excitement, and her eyes were dancing with delight.

"Elementary, my dear Watson," I said smoothly. "Shall we begin?"

"You bet!" She jumped up and grabbed a shovel.

"Hold your horses," I said with good humor. "We have to be very careful not to make a mess. It has to look exactly like it does now when we finish. Who did Wade hire when Hector quit last May?"

"The Henderson twins. I still don't know who's who."

"Do they ever work or come by on Saturday?"

"Never. They both work somewhere else on Saturday."

"Great. Now I'm going to scoop up the gravel very carefully with this shovel and put it in the tub. We'll try a three-foot square first so as not to disturb the ground anymore than necessary."

"Anything I can do?"

"Yes, you can look around and locate the nearest water faucet. It'll probably be low to the ground. Look in the middle of the flower beds. I forgot that we would need water to pack the dirt back into the hole. The ground is very dry."

While Sheri searched for a water spigot, I cleaned a three-by-three-foot area and brushed it clear of rock residue. Using garden shears, I cut a slit in the plastic and cut out the square.

After figuring out where the money was hidden, I'd speculated on what Carl had buried it in. In the old days people used glass fruit jars to thwart robbers and revenuers. But modern technology produced metal detectors, and jars all had metal lids or glass lids with metal fasteners. Technology also gave us plastic. That would have been my choice: a plastic wide-mouth thermos jug, the gallon size so you could toss in lots of those little packets that absorb dampness. Put rolls of hundred-dollar bills with those moisture-proof packets, add some waterproof glue, and screw down the plastic lid. Guaranteed to last a lifetime. Protected from water, fire, insects, and all government agencies.

I stuck the shovel into the middle of the small plot. With

the help of my foot for added weight, it sank with ease into the dry powdery dirt. Picking up the first load with the shovel, I dumped it onto the twelve-foot tarp I had spread out on the right side of the hole.

"There's one here!" Sheri yelled.

"See if you can find a fifty-foot water hose and a spray-nozzle attachment!" I yelled back.

The hole must have been about a foot deep when I saw the bluish damp streak. Just my luck. I tried two more shovels, half full, and actually heard a sucking sound on the second try; the damn clay didn't want to come out of the ground. I was getting nowhere fast. A glance at my watch told me it was ten minutes to four. At this rate we would be here, digging away, when darkness overtook us.

Laying the shovel down, I returned to the bench and lit a cigarette while watching Sheri roll a small hose cart to the spigot and attach it. The hose was about fourteen feet short.

"That's a twenty-five footer," I remarked. "Somebody goofed."

"Well, it sure as hell wasn't me!" she said with asperity, as she turned the cart where well-defined numbers in white read 50 FEET.

"Sheri," I said, ignoring the hose and her remark, "do you know what posthole diggers look like?"

"If," she said with crisp diction, "they are those thingamajiggers that look like two paddles scooped out on one end and joined in the middle with long handles, then I do indeed know what they look like. Why do you ask? Do you possibly want me to fetch them?"

"Come sit," I said with a chuckle. She walked over to the bench and plopped down in silence.

"We're getting a little tense here. I'll explain. This is my operation, Watson, so I'm the foreman. The next position is gofer. You know, go fer this and go fer that. I take it you don't like this job and would like to advance to a new position?"

"Change is nice," she said in a half-joking way.

"Good, because we have a small problem," I said casually. "We've struck clay."

"Clay is a problem? What do we do?"

"I'll tell you what we *should* do, partner-in-crime, we should repair the mess we've made, put up the tools, have a few beers, and wait for Wade to go out of town for a week."

"I couldn't," she said. "The gospel truth is I couldn't stand the suspense. It might be weeks before he leaves again, and the taxes are due in thirty-seven days. Can I have my old job back?" She scooted off to find a longer water hose and posthole diggers. I sat and contemplated the hole. The jackass should have found a different spot. Maybe he couldn't recall another childhood incident, or he could have been stubborn, or—hell, the ground might never have been dug up at all. I could be dead wrong about something being down there.

11

The Pig and the Rainbow
November 13, Saturday, 4:30 P.M.

Returning to the task at hand, I grabbed the shovel and started widening the hole. Sheri came back with another hose cart, a picnic jug, and posthole diggers, trying to balance the diggers so they wouldn't drag on the ground and leave a mark. She just might have the right stuff to last out the years ahead.

"If there's liquid in that jug," I told her, "you can have my job."

"Lemonade, and I have a job, thank you very much. I'm the best damn gofer south of the Mason-Dixon."

"Hear, hear," I said as she poured me a cup of the cold drink. It eased my throat and cooled my insides. I drank a second cup and refused to check the time.

Eyeing the posthole diggers, I said, "I have serious reservations about either of us having the strength to be effective with these suckers, but we won't know until we try." Planting my feet on each side of the hole, I raised the diggers above my head as far as possible and put everything I had into the downward plunge. The rounded edges penetrated about four inches. I moved them back and forth to open the gash and then brought them down a second time, missing the first cut completely. Balancing the diggers upright, I panted, trying to catch the breath that cigarettes had stealthily taken from me during the past fifteen years.

"Sheri, by any chance do you work out with weights, throw barbells around, anything like that?"

"I run laps three times a week on the track at the high school. I doubt that gives me much upper-body strength, but I'm willing to try."

My arms and shoulders had almost daily workouts from the large dogs straining against their leads. If I couldn't do it, she couldn't do it. Maybe Sheri and I could each hold a handle and together raise the digger as high as our arms could reach and plunge downward at the same time. We finally worked out a routine that furnished pitiful results, but it was our only chance of hacking through the clay. We raised, plunged, and pulled the handles, and when we had a jaw full of clay we deposited it onto the tarp. Our clothes were ruined. You can't completely remove blue clay from suede, fabric, and shoes.

We had an eighteen-inch-square hole approximately two feet deep when the diggers produced a dull-sounding thud on a downward plunge. We stared at each other in awe.

"Have we reached China?" Sheri sounded too weary to care.

"We've reached something," I said, breathless with exhaustion. I went down on my knees and started scooping out wet clumps of clay with my hands. Almost standing on my head, I could feel a rounded surface that felt smooth through my wet glove.

"Sheri, I need a garden trowel." She didn't answer, but when I came up with another handful of clay, she was gone. I knee-walked across the plastic to the cigarettes on the bench, shook one out without touching it, slipped off a glove, and lit it.

Sheri returned with the trowel and knelt in front of the hole. "Let me try awhile. You finish your cigarette."

"Be my guest." I stood slowly and eased my left glove off enough to check the time. It was ten minutes after five. The sun was over the yardarm and I needed a drink. I poured a cup of lemonade and sipped it while I smoked.

"See if you can clear an outline of the object to see if we have to increase the dimensions of the hole, God forbid."

A grunt was her only reply. I couldn't sit on the white bench with my butt covered with clay, so I eased back down onto the tarp.

Sheri, looking excited, raised her head and unloaded a trowel full of clay. "I've dug past the top and it appears to be about eight by ten inches around. I don't know how deep it goes, but I don't think we'll have to enlarge the hole. It has a knob on each side. Maybe we can work it back and forth."

"What does it look like?" I was slowly working up some enthusiasm.

"It's pretty dark down there. My first thought was a crude statue. Maybe a pig. It feels like wood even with all the clay stuck on it." Her upper body disappeared into the hole.

"Swell," I said thoughtfully. "We've either hit pay dirt and found Carl's piggy bank or a long-lost pirate's treasure worth millions. We can't lose either way."

Sheri came up giggling. "Wanna look?"

I peered into the hole and could see the object. Pulling one of the knobs toward me, I could feel it move a little. Sheri tried the same move but she was too short to be effective. I pushed back and forth, dug a little more around the edges, and finally the object broke the suction of the wet clay and, with a small *plop,* came free. I rested it briefly on the bottom of the hole. My arms seemed permanently damaged, and my shoulder sockets felt like I had been stretched on a torture rack. I finally brought the thing up with willpower alone. I had no strength left. While I rubbed my shoulders, Sheri rubbed the surface of the container. It was indeed a pig.

I sighed. "Sheri, let's put our motors in high gear. We have tons to do, and the clock is ticking fast."

Now we had to get the statue out of the garden without leaving clay marks anywhere and fill up the hole without leaving any evidence of the ground's having been disturbed. While Sheri lugged the pig to the garage, I started filling up the hole by layering the clay and spraying water on top of it. It was slow going: a layer of clay, then water, and *chop, chop, chop* to pack it firmly so as not to leave a sunken tattletale square. Sheri came back for a load of tools to be cleaned, oiled, and dried and returned to my van or Wade's garage.

"How's the pig?" I asked.

"Soaking in bleach and soapy water in the laundry tub in the garage. It must weigh forty pounds. I thought I would never get it into the sink."

She looked at the hole and then at the clay on the tarp. "What if you don't have enough clay to fill the hole?"

"There will be clay left over. Obviously, your moon science is spotty. Dig a hole on the waxing of the moon and you'll have dirt left over. Dig on the waning and you'll never have enough. Works every time."

"You don't really believe that crap, do you?" she said, dripping scorn.

"Trust me," I replied with ease.

"If you say so. If you don't need the shears and that roll of plastic, I thought I would cut a big square and put it by the kitchen door. When we finish, we can stand on it and undress and not get clay on the floor."

"Good thinking. When you return, bring a large plastic bag and a twist tie."

I finally filled the hole, covered it with plastic, and very carefully replaced the gravel, spreading it evenly.

Sheri arrived with the plastic bag, and we crammed the bulky tarp inside it. We looked around carefully to see if there were any telltale signs of what we had been up to for the past few hours. We saw none. On the way to the garage I let myself check the time. It was six. We weren't out of the woods yet. I didn't like the possibility of Wade's interrogation under oath being canceled and him arriving early—all hell would break loose.

Sheri had the pig washed, dried, and sitting on a wide workbench. The stubby statue had looked better with the clay covering. It was an ugly piece of work, a crude pot-bellied creation supposedly standing upright, its eyes, snout, and hooves daubed with ocher-colored pigment. The rest of the surface was a dark brown. I could see no discernible seam, but it made no difference where it had been joined; we were going to be forced to break it open to get to its contents. From its weight I couldn't even guess what it was made of. I know absolutely nothing about this kind of work.

"Sheri, what if we're destroying a genuine piece of art?" I don't believe in that much of a coincidence, but strange things do happen.

"I happen to know it isn't art and certainly not valuable. I'll prove it later. *Trust me*." She repeated my recent words.

We lined the floor of the garage with plastic, covering approximately a ten-by-twelve-foot area.

"Help me with the pig," I told her. We each grabbed an end and, by taking short sliding steps sideways, stood finally at the edge of the plastic.

"We're gonna swing this sucker and try to hit the middle on the count of three. Ready?"

"Count! I'm a nervous wreck," she yelled.

"One . . . two . . . three!" I cried.

The statue landed near the center and burst into a jillion pieces. Overkill, Sidden, you should have held it just a foot or so above the surface.

The late pig was splattered across the garage floor. Some pieces had traveled as far as twenty feet. The banded packets of money, however, fell mostly onto the plastic. In the dim light, the green of the bills looked too dark to be real; the entire concept was ridiculous, our eyesight questionable. All we could do was stare at the money.

12

Jo Beth's Fickle Finger of Financial Finagling
November 13, Saturday, 6:15 P.M.

I recovered from the currency shock before Sheri; the main reason—it wasn't mine. She had the dazed look of a lottery winner, which in a sense she was. It was found money, not earned or anticipated. She lunged across the space between us and held me in a fierce embrace.

"Thank you. Thank you. Thank you! God! Just look! I've never seen so much money!" She laughed with pure joy while I patted her back and made soothing replies. She ran to the workbench and returned with my vanity case.

"Careful of your knees and hands," I cautioned. She had dropped down beside the packets of money and begun packing them into the case.

Looking around for a broom and dustpan, I made a large detour around the crash site to avoid exposing my bare feet to the shards from the statue. I found them hanging near the doorway and started sweeping in a large circle, pushing the broom in front of me to give my feet a clear path. I remembered the time.

"Is there a phone out here?"

"On the wall over there." She waved in the direction of the workbench. I walked over and dialed the common room. Rosie answered.

"Hi, Rosie. I've been delayed. Any problems?"

"Wayne hasn't mentioned any. Are you gonna get here in time to eat?"

"'Fraid not. That's why I'm calling. Will you act as hostess for me? Poor Miz Jansee gets so upset when she thinks her cooking is going to waste. It would really help me out."

"Sure," she said in a booming voice. "I can understand a body getting upset when her cooking ain't appreciated. I'll smooth her feathers."

I flinched. I hoped Miz Jansee was far back in the kitchen rattling pans and hadn't heard.

"Thanks, Rosie. Tell Wayne I'll be home about eight. See ya."

I returned to sweeping. Sheri walked over with the case of money and the lemonade jug.

"Scoot. I'm almost finished. I'll join you shortly," I told her.

"I'm going to hide the money and wash the thermos. There's clay all over it. Sure you don't need me?"

"Go, go, go."

"Strip at the door. I may be in the shower when you come in. Use the bathroom off the maid's room. First door to the right as you enter the kitchen." She turned and fled.

I finished sweeping up the shards and dumped them into the middle of the plastic. Then, starting on one side, I began rolling and folding the plastic inward until I had a compact package the size of a medium suitcase. I took it to the van and then plodded back to the kitchen door. I was pooped. I stripped at the entrance, added my clothes to Sheri's, and discarded the plastic matting.

Upon entering the laundry room, I tried to think of a

snappy reply if by chance Wade came home early and yelled "Honey, I'm home!" as he strode into view. I was so damn tired I couldn't think of a thing.

After standing under the hot water and scrubbing clay stains, I finished with a long blast of cold water to revive my flagging spirits. Sheri had left me a fluffy lace robe in pale yellow (what else?), and I felt a tight pull across the shoulder seams when I put it on.

She had made coffee and was pouring a cup when I entered the huge kitchen. It looked like something out of *Good Housekeeping*. She led me to a large semicircular booth that filled the front corner of the kitchen where at least eight people could lounge with ease. She had her hair-roller kit on the table and began wrapping wet hair around huge rollers. I'd already toweled my hair dry and I reached over, borrowed her comb, and quickly gave my hair a few licks. That was all I'd need. It would dry and kink into curls without any effort on my part. I really didn't know where she found the strength to lift both arms over her head to manipulate the rollers. Of course, she had a man who was coming home tonight. Bobby Lee and Rudy didn't notice if my hair was perfection or chaos.

"Would you rather have a beer or booze?" she asked.

"Nope. This coffee is great. Accompanied by a cigarette, there's nothing like a hot cup of good coffee."

"What's next, Jo Beth? You've promised to guide me every step of the way, so start guiding."

"God, Sheri, you make me feel like a pimp meeting a sixteen-year-old runaway at the bus station. I sprang this idea on you less than six hours ago. You haven't had time to consider all the issues here. I have to tell you, I don't envy you from this moment on. You'll never be able to confide in Wade, your mother, a best friend—anyone. You'll have to be manipulative, secretive, use guile, and watch everything you say and do. Are you sure you want to support the house that much? Think about it."

"Wade loves this house and wants to keep it so badly, and hell, Jo Beth, I want it too. I feel this is what I would have accomplished if God, when he was passing out height, had made me five-eleven instead of five-three. I had beauty, a perfect body, and enough talent to have made the grade in several professions that pay big money. I married a man who conned me into believing that and spent eight miserable years trying to make it work. I feel God has reconsidered and decided to give me one more shot at my dream: a wonderful husband, a great house, a chance for children, and a productive life. I'm more than willing to live with these conditions."

"I thought you were five-four," I said with a smirk.

"That's what I tell everyone else," she said with a grin. "You get the truth."

"What did you tell Wade?"

"Five-four. I told you even good women lie to their husbands at some point. I'm sure Wade has some secrets. He hasn't told me the one-hundred-percent honest-to-God truth about all things. Little white lies don't count."

"If you can hold on to that perspective, you just might make it. But I'll still retain my guilt, thank you."

"Start guiding," she said in a stern voice.

"The very first step is to clean the money."

"You mean launder it, don't you?" She giggled.

"No, I mean clean with a dry wash. Get a plastic dishpan and fill it with a mix of cornmeal, cornstarch, baking soda, and a half cup of Seven Dust. Scrub each side of the bills with your fingers. Don't forget to wear heavy rubber gloves that reach to the elbows, and don't breathe in fumes from the Seven Dust. That stuff is very toxic. It should remove cocaine residue, fingerprints, and all traces of marijuana."

"Where did you get that recipe?" she quizzed.

"I washed some bills in the washing machine in anticipation of finding the money. They lost color and looked different. The dry wash should be sufficient. I'm no chemist, so I picked ingredients that are easy to obtain and reasonable to have around the house. You know those small mesh bags you use to wash stockings and unmentionables?"

"I have two," she replied.

"Buy three more. I forgot to ask, how much is there? Did you count it?"

"I didn't count a bundle to check for accuracy, but each bundle is banded with folded notebook paper with five thousand written in pencil. It's all hundred-dollar bills. There are twenty packets. One hundred thousand dollars!" Her voice quivered in awe. "What are the mesh bags for?"

"Put one bundle of money in each bag and air-dry it in the dryer. No heat. That should remove the residue and make the money smell normal. We're experimenting. Let me know how it turns out."

"Right," she said, putting confidence and understanding she didn't really feel in her voice. I didn't blame her. Even if the mixture didn't work, it was better than doing nothing. I'd read about the Miami bank that had its inventory of one-hundred-dollar bills tested. All had shown some cocaine residue.

"I did some computer doodling on this problem. You have to save twenty-five thousand dollars a year— legitimately. Until Wade's practice picks up, it's gonna be a bitch. By this time next year you must have twenty-five thousand dollars in savings. That will cover your taxes and insurance on this money-eating pile of wood."

"But the taxes are due soon. How can I explain a payment of almost seventeen thousand that I don't have?"

"I have the first payment all figured out. It will work

only once. I'll explain later. Right now you can start with the basics. These are your golden rules. Never ever deviate, or you'll be a goner. Have a long talk with Wade and tell him you want to handle all the finances. You've had courses in money management and you want to prove how good you are at saving. Get his permission to handle everything. Bank every check, yours and Wade's, without fail. The object is to get every dime of legitimate money into the bank and use Jo Beth's fickle finger of financial finagling to keep every dime you possibly can in the bank without arousing suspicion. Another hard-and-fast rule: write a check for cash every month for two hundred dollars. Give Wade a hundred for walking-around money and pocket expenses. You use the other hundred."

"That seems to be a contradiction of what you just told me. Why do that? That's two hundred that could stay in the bank. I could use the hidden money for miscellaneous expenses."

"If you are ever audited by the IRS, how would you explain your walking-around money? You need to have cash withdrawals. Trust me."

"Gotcha. Lead on."

"These tips on frequent purchases for your household have to be consistent. You can't pretend to practice thrift one week and buy lavishly the next. Buy your groceries at different stores and never let Wade go with you. Sometimes write a check. About half the time, use cash. Keep a household journal so your checks will average about the same each month. Clip coupons and learn where the bargains are. Bore Wade and all your friends with constant talk of what you can't afford.

"Use your charge cards sparingly. Always write checks on provable purchases. If you buy two dresses, charge one and pay cash for the other. Wade loves fine wine. Surprise him every other week or so, telling him you saved up from your household budget, with a couple of bottles of his favorite vintage. The object is to keep anyone from being suspicious, including Wade, about how you can afford something. You're going to learn a whole new system about easing cash into your economy. Never unload your purchases in Wade's or anyone's presence. Go out of town a couple of times a month and, using different banks, change your hundreds into twenties. Around town, never carry more than two hundred dollars in cash. Every other time you fill your gas tank use cash. Borrow Wade's car and fill it up as often as you can get away with. There are a hundred ways to slop cash into your purchases without getting caught. We'll find them all and soon, and they won't be so hard to remember. What do you think?"

"With your help I can handle it. I'm going to have a million questions."

"Over coffee once or twice a week we'll tailor the plan as you spend."

"More coffee?" I nodded. She had finished with her hair, popped a frozen package into the microwave, and refilled my cup.

"Think the wash has finished?"

"I'll check." When she returned, she was laughing. "Boy, you were right about the clay. You can still see stains. I just put your clothes into the dryer. We're gonna have to toss everything. I'm defrosting lamb chops. Want to have supper with Wade and me?"

"Some other time. I'm pooped. As soon as my clothes dry, I'll head on home. It'll be wise if I'm gone when Wade gets home. You'll be able to act more natural. You've had some heavy excitement today. This is the start of a long journey for you, so take it one day at a time."

"I will. I promise. Don't look so sad. I'm happy."

"Tell me you'll be happy two, four, six years down the road, Sheri. When you start to interfere in other people's lives, you feel guilty. I could have screwed up your happiness *and* your future."

"You hush now," she cautioned. "You're just tired. You did the right thing. You've given me a chance at having what I want. That's great, and I thank you for it. You're not responsible if, in the future, something bad happens. I accept the burden of the money. If I screw up, it's not your fault. Rest easy."

"Sure," I said with a smile. "I'm just tired."

"You need a laugh. Follow me." She led me into the large entrance hall, with its fabulous chandelier, and stopped in front of an ugly small idol-looking object, sitting on a large table.

"See what I mean? This is the ugly pig's first cousin. It was a gift from Constance Dalby to Wade's father. You did know they were secret lovers for years, before he died? I hate these ugly pieces. She made them with special river clay; she has her own kiln. They're all over the house. Wade says I can't destroy them because it would hurt her feelings."

"God, it's terrible looking! No wonder you were positive that the pig was not great art."

We chuckled. Sheri walked me outside and waved as I left. I was elated. The chief justice of the Tenth District, Judge Constance Dalby, had fired the monster pig that Sheri and I demolished. This meant she knew about Carl's illegal deeds and had helped him hide the money. Judge Dalby didn't know it yet, but if I ever needed her help I had a great calling card. We were now sisters in crime.

On my way I stopped at a county dumpster and deposited the tarp containing the leftover clay. I arrived home at eight-fifteen wearing dry clay-streaked clothes and still-damp shoes and managed to gain my bedroom without anyone's seeing me. The animals were happy about my arrival and followed me closely.

"Let me change clothes, guys, and I'll feed you." I put

on a wine-colored jumpsuit and lounging socks. In the kitchen I placed their food in their dishes. I spotted a covered plate on the kitchen table and walked over. There were two notes and a plate of food.

Rosie had written that she had saved me a plate and everything was fine except the string beans were overcooked. I grinned. The second note was from Jasmine, saying she had fed the boys at six and not to let them con me. I looked over at the animals and smiled. It was Saturday night and I hadn't increased their portions since last week. Let them enjoy an extra supper.

While the food was heating in the microwave, I checked for phone messages. There were none, which was great. In the living room I selected a book. Next week was going to be a bitch, and I needed a quiet night. I returned to the kitchen and ate supper: sweet-and-sour spareribs, green beans, and potato salad. Rosie hadn't brought any dessert. Good. If I really started craving something sweet, I had two candy bars hidden away.

I was on page ten of the novel and almost finished eating when the front gate alarm sounded. Shit. I stood at the kitchen window and waited for the vehicle to reach the drive where the night-light would illuminate whomever was arriving. Recognizing Ramon's Bronco, I caught a glimpse of blond hair behind the wheel before she disappeared around the curve, heading for the inner gate. I stood on the back porch and waited for Carol to leave the vehicle and start toward me. When I saw she was alone, I peered up at Jasmine's window, saw her profile, and gave her the clenched fist, then the palm opened with fingers spread wide. It was the all-clear signal. She gave a wave and disappeared.

"Hi, Carol. Come on in. Did you lock the gates behind you?"

She stopped walking and glanced up in surprise. "No. Should I go back?"

"It's okay. Come on in." They didn't know. Carol and Ramon hadn't been at the meeting yesterday when I made the announcement about Bubba, and I hadn't had a chance to say anything this morning, they had disappeared so quickly.

On the way to the office I explained about Bubba and asked her to tell Ramon. After she settled on the couch, I served coffee and made sure tissues were on the table.

"I hate to barge in on you. Are you sure you don't have something planned?"

I reassured her and asked sympathetically, "What's the problem, Carol?" I wanted to get right to it and then get to bed early. It was already after nine.

"I'm just so miserable," she said and promptly burst into tears.

Going for the tissues, I tried to console her. Carol has never, even on a bad day, looked a day over sixteen, but when she raised her head and finally dried her eyes, I saw she had aged some since I had last noticed.

"I'm sorry to unload on you, but there's no one else I can talk to. I have no friends or family who cares within five hundred miles of here."

"I'm glad you're confiding in me." When they moved here three years ago, they had made friends with the younger couples around town. For the first year or so, I had invited them to whatever was going on around here, but I sensed Ramon wanted to keep our relationship on a businesslike basis. "Take your time and start at the beginning, Carol. I can't help you if I don't know what's going on."

"I was so bored, I took the car a couple of times and just went for a ride without his permission," she said. "Then suddenly the car wouldn't start. Ramon said it needed repairs, but when he had to run errands it always started for him. One day, I couldn't find my car keys and he wouldn't give me his to get them copied. He began to accuse me of leaving to meet men. He said I was meeting them at motels behind his back. He stares at me all the time and almost never leaves the premises. For the last three weeks he has been talking about this seminar—constantly. He says I'm looking forward to being around all those men, and he won't put up with my actions any longer; he'll find a way to stop me. On Wednesday he knows he has to make an appearance at the seminar. He won't let me stay at the clinic alone—which I would be happy to do—he's going to make me come to the meeting. I don't know what will happen. I've had it.

"Tonight, he went to bed early. A few weeks ago I found where he hides the car keys. I took the car and came here. I can't go back. I need help, Jo Beth. I'm scared."

I sat in stunned silence. How could I have missed something like this, so close, without realizing what was going on? I tried to gather my addled wits about me.

"My God, Carol," I said in shock, "why didn't you tell me sooner?"

She looked exhausted now that she had gotten her story out.

"I didn't want to get him fired. You're his boss. I just couldn't run over and unload when it first started. It would have sounded petty and silly. I kept hoping things would get better. Tonight I made the move because I don't know what will happen on Monday with all those men around. It's sorta like I've gone a little nuts myself. I guess I wasn't thinking clearly."

"Did he . . . did he ever hurt you?" I asked softly. I might as well hear it all. What she had described—Ramon's trying to cut her off from her friends—was a classic case of domination.

"No," she said. "No physical abuse. He's always remote and contained. Never any fire or passion in his actions. It's almost like he isn't emotionally involved. He hasn't made love to me in over a year."

This was surprising. He's part Latino, and I thought they were passionate and had violent tempers. So much for type casting. It looked like no female was getting laid around here, with the possible exception of Rosie. Many times I'd felt a twinge of envy seeing Carol and Ramon together and thinking about them lying close. Goes to show, you never know what goes on behind closed doors.

"Can I stay here with you tonight?" She sounded wistful and beat.

"Of course," I quickly answered. "You're going to take a soothing bath and go to bed. I'm going to move the Bronco into the garage, lock it up, and then lock the gates. Come, I'll show you to the bathroom and get you something to wear. I'll be back in about twenty minutes."

I returned to the office and took the .32-caliber snub-nosed revolver out of the desk drawer and tucked it into the slash pocket of my jumpsuit. After I parked the Bronco in the garage, I went to the first gate, locked it, and then back down the drive and locked the second gate without mishap. Maybe Bubba had gone on a long vacation to Alaska. Fat chance. You couldn't get him to leave this county with a case of dynamite wired to a rocket and inserted up his ass.

Back in the kitchen, I tidied up and set the coffeemaker for morning. Would Carol want to sleep or talk some more? I sat at the table, lit up, and watched Rudy groom himself for sleep. Bobby Lee was sitting at my right side with his head turned toward the doorway when Carol entered. He'd anticipated her approach.

She appeared in my terry robe with a towel wrapped around her head. I went to get the hair dryer.

"Have you made any plans, Carol?" It was mostly business, not nosiness. I needed to know how much she and Ramon might rock the boat. This was a hell of a time for their marriage to go belly up. True, part of my worry was for them, but mostly for me. I needed a vet to talk to the men at the seminar next week.

"If you can help me shake some get-out-of-town money out of Ramon's pocket, and I can take the car, I'm long gone. I'll probably go back to my mother's. She's alone now and has room for me."

"Are you sure?" I asked her.

"Absolutely. I'm gone. I can't take it any longer." She sounded awfully sure.

Oh, God, why me, Lord? I silently recited my calming mantra: *Don't be alarmed. Things will work out. Don't be alarmed. Amen.* I continued to listen to her complaints and future plans. She alternated between the two subjects for over an hour. When I thought I had listened as long as custom required, I packed her off to bed, telling her she needed the sleep.

I solve many of my problems at night while lying in the darkness and listening to the hum of the washing machine and the refrigerator. Night sounds seem to intensify in the stillness. The distant hoot of an owl warning small rodents he's patiently waiting for a rustle of foliage or a mad scamper across the pine needles. The screech of a startled loon, lonely and sad. An occasional croak of a bloated bullfrog from the slough behind the kennel. The monotonous buzz of the bug zapper on the back porch as insects fly toward the purple death light. In these moments, I can see the solution to my many problems with a clarity seldom experienced in the bright light of day.

The washer finished, and I could hear the click of the well pump as it turned off and on to keep the water pressure constant. Rudy moved near my left knee and turned for a more comfortable position. I turned for a more comfortable position for myself and closed my eyes. The last time I looked at the clock, it was after two.

13

Settling In

Somewhere, Sometime

The man had awoken a few minutes earlier and felt almost normal. His strength was back. The water, soup, and the nap he had taken had restored him. He finished his housekeeping by moving the sleeping bag down the length of the room and placing it near the water and moving the boxes of food by sliding them slowly and carefully. He would use the far corner, near where he had previously lain, for his toilet. He was as far away as he could get. The cold was constant, not any warmer during the day and not colder at night. The temperature was about 50 degrees. Moving back and forth, establishing his habitat more comfortably, made him seem more in control. His confidence had risen. The movements also kept him warm enough for a while, but he knew when he stopped he would be too cold out of the bag.

Checking the food boxes, he was elated to find two extra batteries for the flashlight. He now knew with the water and food he could last at least a month if he rationed them. He was too damned fat anyway. Too many sandwiches ordered from the canteen and eaten at his desk. Too many pizzas and take-out fried chicken at the office at nine or ten at night while he still labored with the problems of his business. It was time to take charge of his life and change some of his bad habits. The food here was loaded with salt and fat. He couldn't diet properly, but he could cut down on the amount he ate. There was only one loaf of bread and it was at least three days old. He would eat the bread first, after it was gone there were boxed crackers.

He'd decided on his late supper. He was in the sleeping bag zipped to the waist, sitting with his back to the wall. He had a pull-top can of Vienna sausage and three slices of bread in his lap. There were seven sausages. After pulling the label off the soup can, he'd used it to drink water before each meal while dreaming of a hot cup of coffee, freshly brewed, faint steam rising as he stirred in a teaspoonful of Coffee-mate. He hated black coffee.

He thought of how much he had loved camping trips with his dad. Just the two of them, hunting, fishing, hiking. These were precious memories. The trips had continued even after his marriage to Helen and until his first son was six. He'd planned just a half-day fishing trip because he knew his son was too young to stay interested all day without tiring, but Helen had refused to let the boy go. He'd believed he was master of all he surveyed until that day. He was wrong. He encountered a fierce tigress defending her cubs. He'd never won a skirmish with her, let alone a battle. She was perfectly willing to fight to the death of the marriage in every confrontation, and he wasn't. The marriage wasn't great, but he hung on, hoping for change or at least a mellowing on her part. It never happened. He had tried and failed and had lost his sons. They were hers, body and soul. He had put up his strongest defense when the oldest boy was twelve, going so far as to consult his attorney. This was a period in which fathers rarely gained custody of children under the age of twelve.

His lawyer advised compromise, but Helen didn't compromise. She fought back by moving out and taking the boys with her. She was gone a month before he capitulated and she returned triumphant.

His sons hadn't participated in sports. He'd sat in the school gym a few Friday nights and watched other fathers cheering for their sons, but it grew too painful and he stopped going. He was sad but patient. He'd wait until they were older, then he'd form an adult bond of friendship. It never happened. He'd been outclassed, outfought, and soundly defeated.

He'd thrown his energies into the company his father had started, and his only satisfaction was watching it flourish and grow—for the benefit of three sons who didn't care about him or their grandfather.

His father had been supportive, and their relationship had deepened. His mother having died when he was twenty, his father had been his rock, his constant pillar of strength through all the disappointing years. Six years ago his dad had retired. After a slow progression from a cane to crutches to a walker, arthritis had put him in a wheelchair. God, how he missed his father being just down the hall from his office, their business trips together! It was painful knowing they would never sit around a campfire again. He sighed and finished the meal.

These days his father sat at home making intricate model airplanes, refusing to let painful fingers and joints force him into watching daytime television. He visited his dad most evenings, two men growing old together, discussing business, Civil War battles, the big ones that had evaded their hooks, the bucks they had missed, and the three sons who didn't give a tinker's damn about either one of them.

He brushed a few crumbs from the sleeping bag, picked up the soup can, and drank some water. He was going to get a good night's sleep. Tomorrow he would begin exercising. He was going to defeat the bastards who had done this to him. He planned to inspect this prison and look for a way out. He would check the small round hole in the ceiling when the light reappeared. Maybe, with the aid of the flashlight, he could get a glimpse of something that would give him a clue as to where he was being held.

He turned off the flashlight and placed it by his side inside the bag. He no longer thought anyone was going to come and take it away from him, but just in case they tried he was prepared. He wasn't drugged any longer and was in fair shape because of not overindulging in alcohol; however, these past six years of inactivity had produced extra weight.

He had always controlled the purse strings in the family, but he gained no satisfaction in keeping the boys on a modest budget during college. Helen had used all her personal account and household account, which was more than generous, to supplement their college spending money. He had taken over the household accounts and cut down on her spending money. He forced the boys to work in the business during their summer vacations if they wanted extra money during their college years. He had hoped they would get involved and learn to love the business, but they had been sullen and withdrawn, showing up most of the time for work but taking no interest.

Helen no longer had a weapon to hold over his head. Her threat of leaving him was no longer valid. He would have welcomed her absence in his life. She now pretended they were one happy family, insisting on a weekly Thursday-night family dinner. It was a command performance and he took perverse enjoyment in the whole thing and never missed attending. He sat at the head of the table, ironically pleased with Helen's efforts to make the dinner a happy family occasion. He would watch his wife, three sons, one daughter-in-law, and one three-year-old grandson pretending to enjoy themselves. He did not participate in this farce, and they had learned to leave him out of the forced chatter. He would watch the candles' flickering light play over their faces, and sometimes he was rewarded with a quick guilty glance or an occasional embarrassed silence, which they would try to fill with inane chatter. It was his only retaliation for years of heartache and frustration.

He smiled grimly in the darkness while he stretched out and tried to find a comfortable position for sleep. He went back over the last time they had been together—Thursday night—and the events that had happened after the dinner was over. His mind was free of drugs now, and he remembered each detail of the evening in perfect clarity: the end of the meal, his preparation and departure to visit his dad, and finally the abduction itself.

He didn't know where he was, but he now knew who had abducted him, drugged him, and brought him to this place. He also knew the reason behind the crime.

14

Who Knows Where the Wild Goose Goes?
November 14, Sunday, 3 P.M.

I cornered Jasmine and made my pitch. "I need a giant favor. Feel free to say no if you can't do it. Promise?"

"I'll take Carol off your hands and keep her out of your hair, but it's going to cost you," she said with a smirk.

"How did you know that's what I was going to ask? Have you started reading minds?"

"Sometimes."

"I'm more than willing to pay your price. Carol would drive me up the wall. Name it."

"Before you know what I'm charging?" Her eyes were glittering—with excitement or amusement, I couldn't decide which.

"I know you won't be too hard on me," I said. "Will you?"

"Promise!" she demanded.

"You have my word," I said, with trusting innocence.

"Gotcha!" she cried. "Starting in January, you will enroll in Psychology One, room two-twelve, with a very handsome and charismatic professor. Once a week, eight to ten on

Thursday nights. You have to stick it out, at least to the end of March."

"I'm wounded. I trusted you not to exact too high a price."

"Bull," she said gleefully. "I snagged you fair and square."

"Look," I said, "I'm under a lot of pressure right now. If you're so fired up about me meeting this hunk, I'll agree to a blind date and promise to be on my best behavior. Will that suffice?"

Jasmine placed an imaginary fiddle beneath her chin and sawed away with the pretended bow. "Such a sad story. I can't believe you're trying to welsh on a promise."

"We'll discuss this later," I said.

"Now," she said firmly. "Before I move her upstairs."

I thought about it. January was seven weeks away. Bubba could be snuffed out in a bar brawl, or catch a rare pneumonia bug, or embrace some passive religion. Anything's possible when the sun's shining.

"You win," I said with a theatrical sigh. "Go collect your houseguest."

As I watched her skip across the driveway, I realized she'd picked up one of my bad habits—blackmail.

Inside the office, I checked for messages. One hang-up. *Too soon!* Ol' Bubba hadn't forgotten me. He was out there waiting to pounce.

I turned on the bathtub taps and padded to the kitchen for a beer. I heard the second gate's buzzer and returned to the bathroom, stepped up on the toilet seat, and stretched my upper body out in the three-foot-square atriumlike extension. It holds no plants or knickknacks. It was built to give me a view of the driveway from the bathroom. It was Jasmine in her blue Geo going to the clinic to pick up some clothes for Carol. I climbed down, stepped into the tub, and took a sip of cold beer. There's nothing like a hot soak and a cold brew.

Six men were arriving tonight. Wayne and Donnie Ray were leaving for Jacksonville's airport after five to pick up two of them: a Deputy Sergeant Ralph Vaughn from Zion County Sheriff's Department in Phelton, Georgia, and Corporal Randall Jordan, Georgia state patrolman from Monrose. The other four men were driving and should be arriving between six and eight.

The units were ready for guests, and Miz Jansee would be here at four to start cooking their supper. The temperature should be in the 70s when they arrived, and their rooms would be comfortable with just the ceiling fans, hopefully without the air conditioners. I knew when the bill for next July, the hottest month of the year, arrived—along with Georgia Power's 28-percent rate hike—I'd crumple in a dead faint.

Since some of the men had to drive over two hundred miles and it would be difficult to estimate their arrival, I dressed and fed the animals early. I'd picked out a lightweight cotton sundress, dark blue with tiny white flowers, spaghetti straps, a full skirt, and a matching jacket. I placed the .32 in the large patch pocket of the skirt, padded barefooted into the hall, and turned on the corner-mounted floodlights at the north end. I bent over and put my head at knee level, checking to see if I needed a slip. The mirror on the south wall said my briefs were sufficient. The bright lights and mirrors were for checking my body for ticks after a tromp through brush or swamp. No matter how much you bundle up in protective clothing, ticks can find their way to a warm vein. I hate the bloodsuckers, and they can be deadly. If you happen to pick up a light-brown minuscule tick with tiny white dots on the top, that's the species that carries the Rocky Mountain spotted fever virus. If they attach themselves to you and drink for twenty-four hours, they can end up killing you. I check very carefully after each outing.

I picked up the clipboard with the list of expected arrivals and prepared to depart. My roommates wanted to tag along, but they didn't beg; they had too much class. They were sitting near the door of the office, expectant expressions on their faces, looking like job applicants.

"Sorry, guys, you can't go." Bobby Lee would decorate my slippers with drool and Rudy would forget his manners and beg for handouts.

Crossing the driveway, I heard the first gate's alarm. I went inside and watched from the screen door until I saw it was Jasmine returning. I turned on the lights and started setting three of the four tables, complete with six wine goblets down the center of each. I was placing the silverware when I again heard the alarm. It was Miz Jansee.

"Sorry I'm late. Had to get jumped off. My battery's weak." She said it with a small, weary grimace.

"No problem," I assured her. "We probably won't eat until after eight. You have plenty of time."

I was at the door when the alarm sounded again. I stepped back inside and watched a fairly new car with a male occupant make the turn at the second gate and drive into the courtyard. A Canton County sticker was on the front license plate. Which one was from Canton County? I drew a complete blank. I grabbed the clipboard and scanned the list. Here he was. I was as nervous as an actress on opening night. Sergeant Mitchell Stone, thirty-five years old, six feet two inches, one hundred eighty-five pounds, brown and brown, single, from Eppley Police Department, Eppley, Georgia. Eppley was in the northernmost part of the state, just across the line from Chattanooga, Tennessee. His was the longest journey of the six, and he had arrived first. It was only four-thirty.

I rushed to the door and then made myself slow down and walk like a dignified person. As I approached his car, he opened the door, stood, and straightened up to his full height. I suddenly realized something was wrong with this picture. From about twenty feet, I stopped. The smile vanished from my face as I spread my feet another six inches, placed my right hand in my pocket, wrapped my fingers around the butt of the .32, and thumbed off the safety.

"Sergeant Stone?"

"I'm afraid not," he replied and slammed the car door hard.

Before he could take a step, I'd raised the .32, holding it with both hands, body turned sideways in the correct firing stance. He glanced up and froze in his tracks, surprise wiping all expression from his features as he took in the sight of the gun and the expression on my face.

"Don't make any sudden moves," I said, in an ice-cold voice. "Turn slowly and place your hands palms down on the car's roof. Do it now!"

Without speaking, he moved slowly to do my bidding. I heard Jasmine's screen door slam, and I flicked a brief glance in her direction. She was streaking down the stairs, catching every second or third step, left hand hovering above the railing in case she stumbled. Her right hand was held aloft with her .38 aimed at the sky.

The man placed his hands flat on the top of his car and continued to watch me and didn't attempt to turn his head, even though we both could hear Jasmine's running footsteps. She closed at a right angle so she wouldn't be in my line of fire. She stopped, assumed the firing stance, held her gun with both hands, and nodded to me.

"Who are you?" I strove for a normal tone, but I knew Jasmine heard the strain in my voice.

"Chief Jonathan Webber, Eppley Police Department, Eppley, Georgia. Sergeant Stone broke his right leg yesterday while on a rock-climbing trip. I stopped by to tell you on my way to visit my brother in Tampa. I'm on vacation this week. You must be Ms. Jo Beth Sidden, owner of Bloodhounds, Incorporated, five-feet-seven, one hundred and twenty-eight pounds, medium brown and dark brown. *We* requested a dossier on you from your local officials, just as *you* requested one on Sergeant Stone, and I'm *not* too pleased to make your acquaintance."

His voice was deep and showed hardly any displeasure until he almost finished. He ended up sounding pissed.

"Humor me, Chief Webber. Reach for your wallet with your left hand and place it on the roof of your car. Push it backward, okay?"

He did as I asked. Jasmine tucked her .38 inside the waist of her jeans, reached for the wallet, and stepped back quickly. She read every word of the information on his driver's license aloud.

Jasmine grinned at me, placed the wallet on the trunk of the car, and took off for her staircase. She had no desire to be introduced to the chief right now. Neither did I.

"Chief Webber, I'll apologize shortly, but right now I need a cigarette. I'll just go inside to fetch one. I'll be right back to eat crow." I was so rattled, I'd forgotten they were in the pocket of my dress.

"Have one of mine," he said gruffly. "I feel the need for a little nicotine myself."

I took the cigarette and held it over his lighter. My fingers were trembling, and I couldn't connect the tip to the flame. He reached over and steadied my wrist until I got it going. I inhaled twice before I spoke.

"I have an ex-husband who was released from Patton Correctional two days ago who desires my destruction. He's tried twice in the past and is stalking me as we speak. He wouldn't forego the pleasure of doing me himself, but it is possible that he could send someone to pick me up and deliver me to him. He knows I'm waiting for him, and he believes I'm prepared to blow him away at first sight."

"It was my height and weight that alerted you. Am I right?"

He no longer sounded pissed, just curious. He was taking his unusual reception better than I had expected.

"That and the way you slammed the car door. I thought it was to distract me. Can I buy you a drink?"

"Only if it's poured out of a bottle with BOURBON printed on the label."

"Follow me," I suggested and led him inside to the bar. I poured a shot glass to the brim with bourbon twice, dumping them both into a glass, added ice cubes, and lifted a brow in question.

"Just branch."

I added water to his drink and retrieved a beer from the small refrigerator behind the bar. Making a slight motion with the can, I said, "Cheers."

I took a healthy swallow and sat down, leaving an empty stool between us, and tried to relax. He looked around the room, missing nothing. He wasn't attractive, he just looked solid and dependable.

He smiled at me. "You really need more firepower than that little peashooter. It could get you into trouble. If you're gunning for someone, you need something that will bring him down with one shot. It might be the only one you can get off."

"I have a three-fifty-seven magnum by my bed. The last man—besides you—I pointed this one at, I put three bullets in his chest. He didn't get up." I regretted the words the minute they left my mouth. It sounded as if I were bragging about shooting a man. "I'm sorry," I said in haste, shaking my head. I rubbed my face and drew in some air. "I'm not right yet. I'm pumped with adrenaline and shaky. I apologize for that rotten remark."

"Relax. I know how you feel. It affects people differently. Usually, I have to run to the head over a drawn-gun episode. The fear goes directly to my kidneys."

"Has it happened to you often?" I inquired.

"Three times in a twelve-year career, but nothing fatal."

Well, I'd forgive him for this zinger, I had it coming. I gave him a shaky laugh and stood.

"Please excuse me." I took off for the ladies' room. I splashed water on my face until my normal paleness appeared and then studied my reflection. I hadn't used makeup because of the heat. After the temperature cooled down a little, I'd put on my face. Holding up a hand, I could see it was steady. The shakiness had moved to my gut. I returned.

"Chief Webber, I have to open up the units to air them out. Want to walk with me? You can stretch your legs. You've been sitting for hours."

"Good idea."

I saw Wayne and Donnie Ray walk by the front windows on their way to feed the dogs. Chief Webber drained his glass and we walked outside.

He stopped and turned to me, offering his hand. "I'm Jonathan. May I call you Jo Beth?"

"You may," I said with pleasure, as I shook his hand.

We strolled across the driveway. The units were about thirty yards away and Rosie's rose garden was between my house and the guest quarters. Jonathan took a deep breath, smelling the roses. He was taking in all the landscape.

"How many acres do you have here?"

"The kennel complex is fifteen acres, which are fenced. There're five additional acres up front with the animal clinic and residence, which aren't fenced."

"Is the fence hot?"

"From a foot below ground to the eight-foot height, plus

those three strands of bob wire leaning outwards. I only arm it at night when I lock the gates."

"Both gates have pressure plates?"

I glanced his way. "Anything that weighs over thirty pounds triggers the alarms."

He stopped walking. "You have very good security. How did he get to you—twice?"

I gave him the story on Bubba and his nefarious activities.

"Where were you while he was destroying your property during his last rampage?"

"I was cowering in a hidden place, listening to the destruction till the local police arrived."

"My next question is—"

"Why didn't I blow him away? Solve all my problems, wouldn't it? It's not my damn job, that's why! I have to live in an armed encampment with the measly protection of a restraining order, which you and I and everyone else who has one eye and half a brain know isn't worth diddly-squat. He was sentenced to two years for criminally destroying my property and had his parole revoked from the prior attack. He had three years left to serve, which is a total of five years, right? He's free now after serving less than seven months. In the past nine years, he has received sentences totaling twenty-eight years and he's served less than eight."

"I should be used to hearing stories like this, but this still sounds wrong. Georgia has been stricter than more liberal states like California, for example. What gives?"

"His daddy can pull some mighty strong strings all the way up to the capitol in Atlanta. He's a good ol' boy and pays his dues."

He shook his head, and I gave him a weak smile. "Let's discuss something more pleasant."

He smiled and followed me into the first unit. We opened windows, turned on the fan, and sprayed air freshener. I admired the small floral arrangement of silk flowers. I would have to remember to call Alice tomorrow and thank her. Jonathan complimented me on the unit and we continued down the line.

Outside, I faced him.

"Look, Jonathan, this unit was for your Sergeant Stone. Why don't you stay over tonight? Miz Jansee is cooking a delicious meal, which will be served at eight. I have plenty of bourbon, and five more lawmen will be arriving soon. You'll be able to converse with your peers. How about it? Best of all, it's all free."

"Sounds too good to miss. Sure I won't be in the way of your school?"

"Tonight's social. You'll get to meet some nice people who work with me, and my best friend. Are you single? She's a lovely redhead. You're sure to like her. She has startling green eyes, and she's loads of fun."

"Yep, I'm single. My divorce was final almost six months ago. But if I have the freedom of choice, and she's not committed to anyone, I'd prefer five feet seven inches, one hundred and twenty-eight pounds, medium brown, dark brown, with a small smattering of freckles across her cheeks, if it meets with her approval."

I looked into his dark brown eyes. They seemed to have specks of gold floating near the irises.

"Well . . . sure, if that's what you . . . are you sure?"

My God, I was simpering. I couldn't even finish a sentence! I could feel the flush on my skin rising and climbing into my hairline.

"Very sure," he said, with certainty. "It sounds great."

"Well, that's settled," I said, sounding inane. "Let's walk back so you can move your car, unpack, and freshen up."

On the walk back, I couldn't think of a thing to say— which is rare for me. When we reached his car, he climbed in and looked at me. "See you later."

"Okay, fine, see you later," I said, moving numb lips. All of a sudden I couldn't string six words together to form a sentence. This was ridiculous.

Donnie Ray and Wayne were coming down the stairs from Wayne and Rosie's apartment. Wayne waved and went into his garage to back out the spare van. Donnie Ray loped across the courtyard.

"We're leaving for the airport a little early. Wayne wants to know if you need anything."

"Nope. Don't forget the folding chairs for your passengers. Tell Wayne to drive carefully. He's going in on county roads through Callahan, isn't he?"

"Yes, Ma," he said, teasing. "Drive carefully and use the back roads. Gotcha."

"Show some respect for your elders," I admonished him.

"Yes'm," he called, as he scooted back to the van. Oh, to be nineteen again and know what I know now.

I decided to call Susan to make sure she was coming. Busy me. Trying to keep from thinking about Jonathan's remarks. Today was almost over, and tonight promised to be even busier. I had to keep focused on seminar business. Carol and Ramon's spat was a further distraction, and I didn't need a new complication—namely, Jonathan. I decided I would force myself to relax and go with the flow. I needed some romance in my life, however fleeting. Here today, gone tomorrow. No problem. I gave a carefree skip up the steps to the back porch.

Bobby Lee and Rudy were there, acting weird. Bobby Lee was huddled behind a miniature rubber plant contained in a half-barrel planter. Rudy was stalking back and forth in front of him, stiff-legged with anger, fur standing straight up. He was whining guttural threats. I watched in confusion. They usually napped away warm afternoons in the office and didn't go outside until the cool of the evening.

I stooped and felt Bobby Lee's muzzle. He was trembling. I aimed a pat at Rudy, but he dodged my hand and kept stalking back and forth.

"It must've been some argument," I remarked as I went inside. Their behavior was odd.

I dialed Susan's parents' number and received no answer. They must be outside making the stable rounds. I then dialed Susan's number and listened for the recording. At the beep, I told her to call me. I listened for several seconds to see if she might pick up, then disconnected.

I wandered into the bedroom and dug out some expensive perfume I keep in my save-for-special-occasions drawer and squirted it behind my ears. I seldom wear perfume because of the dogs. It deadens their sense of smell as effectively as chloroform. If I was called out tonight, I'd have to shower first. I decided to take a look at the green strapless I'd planned on wearing tomorrow night. I just might wear it tonight—Jonathan was leaving tomorrow.

I pushed open the double sliding louvered door to the closet. My jaw muscles dropped, my mouth flew open, and my mind froze in shock. I was staring eye to eye, nose to nose, with a skinny black man in a dirty T-shirt. He had wild-looking eyes, and he held a large-bladed knife defensively at chest level in his right hand.

15

Birds of a Feather Stick Together
November 14, Sunday, 5:30 P.M.

Recognition was instantaneous, even in shock. It was Jarel Owens, my former part-time employee. We'd first met when he was fourteen years old. I'd discovered he was illiterate and taught him to read.

I refused for the moment to think about the knife he held and its implications. First things first. My tongue finally came unglued from the roof of my mouth.

"What are you doing in my closet?" My voice was more or less natural, but I was seething inside. His eyes showed more white, and he wiped at his sweaty forehead with his left hand, not moving the hand that held the knife.

"They're after me. You have to help me. I shot at the floor. Johnson is the one that killed her. I have to get out of this jurisdiction immediately. I have a number to call in the underground movement. I've tried it twice since I've been here and haven't got an answer. You have to drive me to Waycross. I have friends there who will help. If they catch me they'll hang me in my cell—the pigs."

The sickening news entered my brain, shifted to my

heart, and landed in my gut. This boy, whom I'd labored to teach, was involved in the cold-blooded murder of Mavis Johns. Deputy Sheriff Mavis Johns was lying in a funeral parlor somewhere in the next county awaiting her killed-in-the-line-of-duty funeral tomorrow at three o'clock.

I reacted without thought or reason. Grabbing his shirt with both hands, forgetting the knife, I pivoted to the left and pushed him with all my strength. The back of his legs struck my stiffened right leg, held rigid with tension, and he toppled backward. Twisting, he managed a couple of steps, trying to gain his balance, before he landed head first on the edge of the dresser. There was a sickening thump as his head struck the wood. I limped forward quickly and stomped down on the hand that held the knife. I watched in fear until his hand relaxed and the knife was free. I snatched it up and backed to the panic button wired to the edge of the nightstand and pushed it with numb fingers.

I slid the knife under my pillow and prayed that Jasmine was still upstairs. My heart pounding, I reached down and felt for a pulse, watching for any movement. I felt the blood pumping through his neck vein and was grateful I hadn't killed him—as yet. I didn't know how badly he was injured; he could be dying for all I knew.

I sat on the bed to keep from falling and also to take the pressure off my right leg. Gingerly, I probed the bruised area. His leg or shoe had caught me in the fat part of my right calf, but with the adrenaline flooding my system, I couldn't feel much damage. I didn't hear a whisper of movement, but suddenly Jasmine was framed in the doorway, her gun held with both hands, her eyes wide with fright.

"We have to stop meeting like this," I croaked.

She pointed the gun at the ceiling, pushed the safety catch, and leaned weakly against the doorframe.

"Who is it?" Her voice was husky. She'd worked with

Jarel, but he was face down and half crumpled with both arms behind him. I slid the knife out from under the pillow and showed it to her.

"Our friend and fellow worker, Jarel. He was waiting in my closet with this when I opened it to look at a dress. He told me in a calm voice that I had to get him out of town. He'd shot at the floor, but Johnson had killed Mavis."

"Oh, my God," she whispered. "I bet he meant the kid who was here with him last week. He didn't look a day over sixteen and he worships Jarel. He lives in Collins." We stared steadily at Jarel. "Is he dead?" she asked.

"Not yet," I replied, feeling weary.

"Shouldn't we be doing something?" she asked softly. "What if he comes to?"

"I need a time-out. To think." I sounded peevish and put-upon. I was trying to plan my action but my mind was not cooperating. At least the mystery of the animals' weird behavior was solved. A bloodhound isn't the least bit aggressive. They'll greet an intruder with the same enthusiasm they show on their master's return. Bobby Lee had probably gone up to Jarel to greet him and been met with a swift kick. Rudy would've bailed out quickly and then shown anger from a safe distance.

"What time is it?" I was rubbing my temples, trying to get my mind in gear. I was wearing a watch, but Jasmine answered with patience.

"Five minutes till six."

"Swell," I said with irony. "Time sure flies when you're having fun."

I picked up the portable phone and dialed the number for the common room. It rang seven times. This gave Jonathan a chance to tell Miz Jansee the phone was ringing and for her to reply that she'd been told it wasn't her responsibility to answer. He'd hesitate for a couple of rings, then take the chance of answering because a ringing phone can almost force you to answer.

"Hello?" Tentative.

"Jonathan?" I was forcing my voice to sound calm.

"Yes." Much more positive.

"Jo Beth," I said unnecessarily. "Do you, by any chance, have a pair of handcuffs with you?"

Silence, then a low amused chuckle. "I feel I should apologize for what I'm thinking. Should I?"

"Yes, you should," I said evenly. "Do you have a pair?"

"Yes."

"Would you please bring them over to the house, posthaste. Don't bother to knock. Turn right in the hall. I'm in the bedroom."

"I'm on my way."

Just making conversation cleared the fog from my brain. I dialed Wade's number. Please, God, let him be home! I heard a groan from the floor. Jasmine stepped back, removed her gun from the waistband of her jeans, and pointed it at Jarel. She risked a glance at me. I nodded. She looked down at the gun and released the safety catch. I was counting the phone rings. A breathless Sheri answered.

"Hello?"

"This is Jo Beth. Is Wade there?"

"Yes. He's barbecuing spare ribs," she said, laughing. "You want to talk to him?"

"No. Listen carefully and don't ask questions. Get him dressed in a suit and tie with briefcase in hand and on the front steps of Tara in fifteen minutes. I'll be in a blue Geo."

"Got it," she acknowledged.

I dialed Hank's private line at the sheriff's office. Jonathan walked in and stood behind Jasmine, surveying the scene in silence, handcuffs dangling from his right hand.

"Get a towel from the bathroom and dampen it in case there's blood," I requested. He turned and left the room.

After five rings I hung up. I then dialed Hank's home number. Jonathan reappeared with a damp towel. I motioned him over, handing him the phone. "If a woman answers, ask to speak to Hank," I said.

"May I speak to Hank?" Damn, he had a good telephone voice, smooth and authoritative. He quickly handed me the phone.

When Hank said hello, I spoke. "Don't mention my name." All Charlene had to hear was my name to go ballistic. "You are receiving a call from an informant who wants a meet. This is important, Hank. You don't recognize the voice, but you're not worried about a setup because you're meeting on the high school grounds. Mention all this to Charlene so she can be your witness. Say you think it's a student who wants to turn in a fellow student for smoking pot. Can you grab P. C. in a hurry? You need a friend for a witness on this one to keep me out of it completely."

"Yes."

"Hank, be careful. This is big, really big! Meet me behind the visitors' dugout on the baseball field, ASAP. If I'm not there, wait on me. If there're any kids hanging around, get rid of them. Got it?"

"Yes."

I tossed the phone on the bed and searched the bureau for a clean T-shirt, listening to Jonathan as I searched.

"You can't move him. Wait for the ambulance."

"Is he still alive?" I asked, kneeling beside Jarel. Jonathan was feeling for a pulse.

"His pulse is strong and his heartbeat sounds normal." He leaned almost to the floor as he looked at Jarel's forehead. "He's got a large goose egg on his head, but I don't think the skin is broken, and I don't see any blood. Probably a concussion. How long has he been out?"

I deferred to Jasmine and she checked her watch. "Twenty minutes," she said.

"What are you doing?" Jonathan's voice was sharp.

"Jonathan, I want you to listen carefully." I rolled Jarel over to try to remove his dirty T-shirt. "You don't know me, but I'm asking you to trust me. I'm handling this the only way it can be handled."

I looked at Jasmine.

"I need your car. After you bring it around to the front door, I want you to go to the common room and act like nothing has happened. When the lawmen arrive, I borrowed your car and you don't know where I went. If I don't make it back, you, Wayne, and Rosie can handle the seminar just fine. Please get the car."

"You're going to get arrested," she wailed. "I'm the reason you can't pick up the phone and call it in, and you know it! Let me go with you," she pleaded. I saw surprise on Jonathan's face.

"Nonsense," I said firmly. "I need you here. There're three lawmen arriving any minute. My clipboard is in the common room. Greet them and settle them into their rooms. Jasmine, get crackin'!" She turned and left.

I finally had the shirt on Jarel, with Jonathan's help. I was cleaning his face with the damp towel.

"You are out of this as soon as you help me get him into the car and put the cuffs on him. Return to the common room and act like the three monkeys."

Jonathan looked into my eyes. "What's next?" he said.

I could have hugged him. I opened my purse and put my wallet in my pocket, along with my cigarettes. I picked up the .32, opened the cylinder, pushed the six loaded rounds so they would drop into the nightstand drawer, and then laid the gun inside and shut the drawer.

"We load him into the back seat of the car and you return to the common room and have a double bourbon and relax. I'll be back shortly."

"Uh-huh," he said with sarcasm. "Jasmine thinks you might be arrested, and she knows the situation better than I do."

"Only if I get caught," I replied with a grin.

He gave me a shocked look. "You're enjoying this!"

"Just a little," I admitted. "Let's load him up."

Jonathan waved me away, braced one bent leg, placed his arms under Jarel's legs and shoulders, and came up with the dead weight in one smooth motion.

"Wow!" I said in admiration. He had risked a hernia or slipped disk just to impress me with his strength. He followed me down the hall, through the living room to the front door. I pushed it open and held the screen for him. Jasmine had pulled the car level with the steps to the small porch. She opened both back car doors and squatted at the far door to help slide Jarel across the back seat. They loaded him.

"Put the cuffs on him and fasten them in front, please."

Jonathan reached in and cuffed him. I held out my hand for the key. He ignored it, climbed into the front seat, and slammed the door.

"Get in," he told me. "It won't do any good to argue. The cuffs have my initials stamped on them and I have the key. The only way you can keep me out of this is to get in and quit wasting time. Let's get it done, whatever we're doing."

I entered on the driver's side, made a circle on the grass, and waved at Jasmine as I took off.

It was dusk, when car lights are needed but don't do too much good, just a yellow smear in the failing light. I quickly took the car up to fifty miles per hour but watched that I didn't exceed the speed limit. It was six miles across a blacktop county road to Wade's mansion. I explained to Jonathan exactly what had taken place since we'd parted earlier.

"Jesus H. Christ," he said, when I explained Jarel's identity and quoted his confession. He didn't speak again until I pulled into Wade's driveway. Jonathan gave a long, low whistle at the opulence of the house and grounds.

"We locals call it Tara," I said with a laugh.

"I can understand why," he said with feeling.

Wade and Sheri were standing on the front steps. He looked fabulous in a light-gray summer suit. With briefcase in hand, he quickly came down the steps and I called out to him.

"Get in front." I waved to Sheri and she waved back. Wade veered to go around the front of the car, glancing in the back seat as he climbed in. Jonathan had slid over close to me, but it was still a tight fit. Thank goodness, Jasmine didn't like bucket seats or Jonathan would've had Wade in his lap. I pulled away as Wade closed the door.

"Wade, I would like to introduce Police Chief Jonathan Webber from Eppley, Georgia. Jonathan, this is my attorney and friend, Wade Bennett, who has a practice in Balsa City." The men awkwardly shook hands in the confined space. I dug out my wallet and handed it to Jonathan.

"Hand me a bill," I requested. Jonathan reached in and pulled out a dollar bill and passed it to me. I leaned across him and handed it to Wade. "I'd like you to accept this retainer and to represent me in the event of charges being filed against me for my actions this afternoon."

"I am your attorney of record," he answered calmly. He'd learned in the seven months since we first met not to be too surprised at anything I said—or did. He was born here and had lived his first fifteen years here and then spent the next twenty in Boston. When he came back here he was a prude and somewhat inhibited. I'd started loosening him up, and after he met Sheri she'd completed the process. He is six feet of easy grace with brown hair and brown eyes.

He is attractive, and he and Sheri make a very handsome couple.

"Jonathan, hand Wade a bill and say the words," I said.

Jonathan freed his wallet and held out a twenty to Wade.

"Will you be my attorney?"

"I am your attorney," Wade answered him.

"The object in the back seat," I informed Wade, "is Jarel Owens. He's almost nineteen years old. This past June he graduated from Dunston County High School with honors. I met him when he was fourteen and taught him to read. Got him interested in famous black men so he could be proud of his heritage—much to my sorrow. He became a dedicated terrorist who espouses the violent overthrow of our government.

"I opened my bedroom closet this afternoon around six and he was twelve inches from my nose, wearing a dirty T-shirt and holding a knife in his hand. The blade is approximately five inches long. It's at the house now."

I heard Jonathan's sharp intake of breath. This was the first he had heard of the knife.

"He calmly told me that I had to drive him to Waycross, he had friends in the movement there, and he—and I am quoting his exact words—'shot at the floor. Johnson is the one that killed her.'"

"Hot damn," Wade said with relish. He realized the implications immediately. This case would make every paper in Georgia and could well be picked up nationally: BLACK TEENAGE ACTIVIST SHOOTS WHITE LADY COP DURING ARMED ROBBERY TO FURTHER HIS CAUSE. It had high-profile written all over it. Wade was struggling with a practice his father had left him, which was almost nonexistent, and he needed exposure. This case could make or break him.

"I also want you to know that if the court won't appoint you as his lawyer and give you sufficient funds for his defense, I will pick up the tab."

"It could be very expensive, Sidden," he cautioned.

"Not to worry," I said with confidence. "Easy street is just around the corner. You tell me what you need to do a good job, and I'll dig it up."

Sheri would get a kick out of "dig it up." This would be a good way to get a hefty advance into Wade's bank account so he could meet the taxes next month. Sheri, Susan, and I could form a committee to collect money for Jarel's defense. Sheri and I could slip in some heavy money from the buried treasure and no one would be the wiser. If anyone contributed, they'd most likely want to keep it a secret. This way, we wouldn't have to give receipts and could get away with cooking the books.

We were getting close to the meet. "Here's your story, Wade: You received a phone call from an unidentified source who assured you that he or she was guardian of Jarel Owens's affairs and you would find him—injured and unconscious—lying in the visitor's dugout at the baseball field at Dunston County High School. Your caller assured you that Jarel was injured by friends trying to keep him from hurting himself over his remorse about being present when the fine officer was shot. He was afraid to turn himself in because he feared being killed by officers who worked with Deputy Johns. This source assured you that he was not injured by any law officers. Hank will arrive with Sergeant P. C. Sirmans and humanely rush him to the nearest hospital. You'll be able to testify that he was injured before the officers arrested him. If any accusations are leveled against Hank and P. C. and your word isn't sufficient, I'll come forward and attest to the fact that I was the one who injured him."

"You can't, Sidden," Wade shot back. "You know you have too many enemies. Between ex-Sheriff Carlson and Buford Sidden Senior, who both have clout in the courthouse, you'll be crucified."

"I won't let Hank and P. C. be accused. They're doing me a favor. Accusations are hard to erase. In a lot of cases, people remember the wrong information."

Jonathan spoke. "If needed, I'll testify that the officers received the prisoner after he was injured."

"No way," I said bluntly. "Wade, disregard his remark." I glared at Jonathan and almost missed the turn. "You're not stepping into this shit, Jonathan, and that's final."

"After giving it some thought," Wade remarked, "I don't think we have much to worry about. Charlene Stevens would have to prepare the charges, and she wouldn't indict Hank on a bet."

"Bull," I said, still upset. "You don't know the barracuda like I do. She'd prosecute her own mother if it would further her career. She wants to be DA instead of assistant DA."

"She doesn't stand a chance," Wade said, scoffing.

"Don't count on it," I told him sharply. "Tread softly around her. She has the support of the good ol' boys. She wins all her cases, except where the fix is set in concrete; then she looks the other way. They all had grown tired of Bobby Don Robbins screwing up long before Charlene arrived."

"I'll tread *softly,* Sidden," he said, with evident amusement. I let him get away with it because I understood his reaction. He wanted Jonathan to know I wasn't leading him by his nose. Men. When would I learn to soft-pedal instructions to keep from wounding fragile male egos? Never, never, never, amen.

We entered the school grounds by the south gate, which is left unlocked at all times for emergency vehicles on weekends. I know this, and everybody else in town knows this, so I think it's ridiculous to lock the other three gates, but that's the school board for you.

"Battle stations," I said quietly as we stopped in back of the dugout. "The law will be here quickly. Wade, insist on sticking to him like glue. I'm counting on you to keep him alive."

"I think I can handle it from here on out, Sidden," Wade answered in a take-charge voice. Then he looked over at me and said "Thanks," in a nice way.

"Get back here on the double so we can flee the scene," I whispered to Jonathan. He patted my thigh and got out. Wade and Jonathan unloaded Jarel and half walked and half dragged him to the bench in front of the dugout. I scanned the parking lot and finally spotted Hank's car nosed in close to the school building, partially hidden by a large hibiscus hedge.

With Jonathan back in the car, I gave it a tad too much gas and slung gravel from the parking lot. "Let's not mention this rough start to Jasmine. She really cares for this little car. It's the first one she's ever owned."

"Mum's the word," he agreed.

I hung a fast right and sped down Collins Avenue.

"We're looking for a phone booth. You check the right side. When we find one, I'll dial the newspaper and you do the talking. Fred would recognize my voice. Tell him, if he gets his photographer to the hospital's emergency entrance real fast, he can get a picture of one of the men suspected of shooting Deputy Johns. Make it clear that the deputies didn't cause his injuries. Tell him the payment for this tip is a good clear picture of both the lawyer, Wade Bennett, and Sheriff Hank Cribbs on the front page tomorrow. At least three columns wide. Say you have to remain anonymous. But, so he knows he's printing the truth, tell him the tip came from a relative of Smiling Jack."

"Who's Smiling Jack?" he asked, still looking for a phone booth.

"A relation of mine, currently under indictment for the attempted murder of my ex."

"You do lead a colorful life," he said with a chuckle.

"Well," I said defensively, "Fred is a stickler for the truth. He has to lock up the front page by ten o'clock at night. I have to let him know the tip is kosher or he won't defend the officers."

"My, my, aren't you the devious minx. Now I know why Wade was all gussied up. I was wondering if he was planning on attending court or about to get his picture taken," he said.

"Wade and Hank can both use the—"

"Hold it," he said sharply. "Slow down, on the right there in front of the Amoco station." I slowed and whipped in beside the phone booth.

"Do you have a quarter?" I had forgotten to bring change.

He dumped his pocket change into my hand, and I dialed the *Dunston County Daily Times*. After hearing the first ring, I gave the receiver to Jonathan, turned sideways, and eased out of the booth.

16

A Fly in the Ointment
November 14, Sunday, 7:30 P.M.

I drove into the courtyard and backed into Jasmine's garage. Overhead fluorescent tubes illuminated the neat interior, revealing the workbench, equipment, and rescue van occupying the other half of the space.

As Jonathan opened the door he asked, "How's the leg?"

"Stiff," I complained as I tested my full weight on it. I reached down and prodded the bruised calf with a finger.

"Pity. I noticed the jukebox earlier. I was hoping to dance with you."

"Sorry."

"Whoever customized this van really did you proud," he remarked.

"Thanks."

Jonathan ran his hand down the side of an aluminum cage. The van is light green with bright yellow lettering. The name BLOODHOUNDS, INC. and the address are outlined with a thin black line of a bloodhound's silhouette. The county seal of the Dunston County Sheriff's Department is underneath. About halfway down the door is SEARCH AND RESCUE NO. 2.

My van is number one, and the backup van is number three. Wayne has a pickup with the same colors and lettering. All the vehicles have flashers on the roof, sirens, and police-band radios. All gadgetry is furnished and installed by the county, per my contract. I'd paid for six aluminum dog cages, three to a side, and I was proud of them.

"I didn't want the damn flashers and sirens, but the county insisted. I get even by not using them."

"You should," he said. "They'll sure clear traffic ahead when you're in a hurry."

"Most county boys here drive with their eyes glued to the side and rearview mirrors. Some of them are doing things that're not legal, so when they see the top lights in their mirrors they suddenly become solid citizens, slow down, pull over, and get out of my way. My biggest problems are the very young or very old females. You have no idea where they're going. The only direction you're sure they won't go is straight up."

"Tell me about it. I break out in a cold sweat when I come up behind *any* female."

"I refuse to discuss female drivers. I'd betray my sisters. 'Nuff said."

He sighed. "You're a feminist."

"I lean in that direction. Is this a problem?"

"God, I hope not," he said sincerely.

It was my turn to sigh. "Don't tell me you're an MCP."

"The *M* I'll readily admit. A male and proud of it. I have a problem with the tag of chauvinist pig. Generally, I'm not, but I have to admit to a few gray areas."

"Such as?"

"Jo Beth, darlin', I want you to like me. I want to impress, not distress. Can we sorta feel our way here as we go?"

"Agreed, with one provision. Tonight when you go to

your room, will you please make a list of things you don't agree on? Then I can see how far apart we are."

"Are you ser— yes, you're serious. I can tell by your frown. If you're absolutely one-hundred-percent sure the list is vital to our budding friendship, I have no other choice but to agree."

"Fine," I replied. "Let's go eat and mingle with your cohorts."

Just inside the common room, Nola Faye was standing near the bulletin board studying Bubba's likeness. Her eyes flicked over Jonathan and then locked with mine. She is short and pear-shaped, with the constitution of a horse. She is eighteen going on thirty, a good dog trainer, smart and alert. She views the world through Coke-bottle-thick glasses. Last May, when she started working here, she weighed one-sixty-five. She is now at one-fifty and holding. I introduced her to Jonathan.

"Pleased to meet you. Are you taking Sergeant Mitchell Stone's place this week?"

Jonathan glanced my way and I smiled. "She has the trainees' list memorized, is my guess," I told him.

"No." He answered her pleasantly. "I only stopped to explain his broken leg. It's so nice here, I just might stay awhile to watch and learn."

Nola Faye divided a glance between us, adjusted her glasses, and simpered. "I'm sure Miz Jo Beth can teach you a lot."

"You're not too old to spank, you know," I said, delivering the line with a straight face and level tone. Her face flushed. She nibbled on her lip and was smart enough to disappear quickly.

"What was that all about?" Jonathan asked, looking perplexed.

"One glance when we entered the door and she had us pegged as lovers," I said, annoyed. "She was trying her hand with a double entendre."

Jonathan winked. "Bless her. May all her pegging come true."

"Idiot," I said lightly as I mentally counted the house. Looked like everyone was present except the airport group.

Wendell Grantham, another trainer, walked up to us with a guest in tow who fit the description of the man he was paired with to train this week: six feet, blond, and blue-eyed. Handsome enough, I guessed, in a brutish sort of way.

"My dear," Wendell proclaimed in a formal tone, back held ramrod straight, "I'd like to introduce Deputy Sergeant Adam Gainey, my partner in training, and the future handler of Gloria Steinem. Deputy Sergeant Gainey, I'd like to present Ms. Jo Beth Sidden, owner of Bloodhounds, Incorporated."

Wendell has the look of an ex-colonel in the British army. Sixty-seven years old and a retired druggist, he can't weigh more than one hundred and forty pounds. Wispy white fringes of hair form a semicircle around his tanned head. His arms and legs have ropy muscles, and there's not an ounce of fat around his waistline. I've always envisioned him with a swagger stick tucked under his arm and almost called him colonel several times in the past few months. Although he's never been in service, he carries himself like a four-star general.

I presented my hand to Gainey, but he had other ideas. Capturing my hand with both of his, he gazed into my eyes.

"Since I'm an Adam, I hope to hell you're Eve," he said with passion, insinuation, and God knows what else as he played a tune on my fingers with his.

"Not for all the tea in China," I said with good humor. I noticed a narrowing of his eyes, a fleeting bleak expression before a brilliant smile appeared.

"Ah, a fighter. I love a fighter. It makes the chase more

interesting." His blue eyes seemed to darken as he stared at me.

"Miz Jo Beth," Wendell said as he smoothly eased into the space between us, "could I speak to you privately in Wayne's office? It won't take but a moment."

I turned to Jonathan. "Why don't you get us a drink? Make mine a beer. I'll join you shortly."

I took Wendell's outstretched arm, and we walked across the room. Inside Wayne's office, Wendell's pale eyes were flinty with anger. "That cretin is an abomination to man," he stated angrily. "He's rude and crude, and I'm thankful that I got the unlucky draw instead of one of the ladies. You should send him packing."

I put a hand on his thin, knobby shoulders. I was only two inches taller, but it seemed he'd shrunk a little lately.

"Don't worry, Wendell, I can handle a creep like him. He's one of those men who think they're God's gift to women. He has a giant ego and a fast mouth, but he's harmless."

"He isn't why I wanted to speak to you. He just got under my skin for a moment. I have some rather bad news, I'm afraid. On my way here this evening, I spotted your ex-husband parked on the verge as I made the turn into your driveway."

My heart made a couple of high leaps in my chest before remembering it had to deliver a regular beat. When it was back to normal, I spoke. "What did his vehicle look like?"

"Just before I turned, I spotted him parked on the opposite side of me, so I slowed even more for my turn. I scanned his truck and got a good look at his face. I know you told us the enlarged photograph is nine years old, but I'm sure of my identification. The truck is red and has every accessory you can possibly install: over-cab spotlights, roll bars, extra-wide side mirrors, toolbox, high-tech wheels.

I'm afraid I don't know what they call them, but chrome spokes. There's also enough chrome here and there on the cab and body to keep Detroit running for a week. It had one of those Confederate flag murals on the back window. You know what I mean. One where you can see the design, but not inside the cab from the rear."

"I wouldn't have thought he'd keep the same truck," I mused. "You just described his truck of nine years ago."

"No, no," he said in haste. "The truck is new. I could tell by the design."

"Then it's a gift from his daddy. He hasn't had time to get one customized since his release. His daddy wants to celebrate his release from the slammer—however brief it may be."

"Are you going to call the authorities?"

"It wouldn't do a bit of good, Wendell. The highway is a public road. He was far enough away from the house not to violate the restraining order."

"But he's stalking you!"

"Let's go back to the party. We'll just have to keep a sharp eye out for him."

A little after eight I told Miz Jansee to start serving supper. I'd seen Wayne drive by the front windows; they were back from the airport. Before that, I'd spoken briefly with all the guests. I'd saved Susan for last. She looked stunning tonight in a black silk tube-style dress that complimented her curves. She was wearing flashing silver accessories, large dangling earrings almost reaching her shoulders, and four-inch fuck-me spike-heeled slippers. I saw Adam Gainey with his head solicitously close to Susan's bright tresses. Like a moth drawn to a flame. I invaded their space.

"Hi, Susan." I greeted her with bright gaiety. "Has Adam been telling you about his lovely wife and three daughters? How old are they now, Adam, seven, five, and two? I bet they're adorable." He turned toward me, and if looks could kill I would've been on my way to the morgue. He turned and left Susan's side without speaking.

"You truly have a gift for running off my men," Susan said, giggling. "Did you see the look on his face? If I were you, I wouldn't turn my back on him for a few minutes until he calms down."

"He's a pig. Let's go eat."

As we lingered over dessert, small conversational groups were forming around the room. The jukebox was delivering some nice background music. Jonathan sat to my left and Susan to my right. She was talking to Corporal Randall Jordan, a Georgia state patrolman. He was proudly showing Susan pictures of his two children. They were deep into a conversation on children's books. Susan owns and runs Browse and Bargain Books, and she enjoys talking shop. I glanced over at the second table and saw that Deputy Sergeant Gainey had moved in on Carol. They were doing a lot of talking and very little eating. I would pry her loose after dinner.

Susan and I helped Miz Jansee clear the tables. When the dishes were done, we returned them to the serving table.

"Thanks for the help, Susan. Now, go mingle. You don't have to work for your supper."

"I know that, Sidden. You two looked exhausted. I had a relaxing day, a nice long horseback ride, and a short nap. You and Jonathan seem to be hitting it off. How's it going?"

"Like a house on fire," I said, feeling upbeat. "Wish me luck."

"I'll cross my fingers," she said.

Jonathan and I walked Miz Jansee out to her wreck of a car and stood by as she tried to start it. She finally succeeded. Going back into the common room, I stumbled at the threshold and Jonathan helped me regain my balance.

"Are you all right?"

"I've had one hectic day. My sawdust is leaking out through my stitching," I admitted as I straightened.

I saw Jasmine standing by the jukebox with the only black man at the seminar, Sergeant Curtis French from the Faircomb County Sheriff's Department's drug squad: thirtyish, with a light complexion, a visible contrast to her darkness—and single. They seemed to have naturally gravitated to each other. It appeared Jasmine was enjoying herself. I hated to pull her away from the first friendly male she'd shown any interest in for a long, long time. It wasn't her responsibility to run this place, it was mine. Surely I could remain upright for another hour or so.

Across the room, I spotted Carol and Deputy Sergeant Gainey slow-dancing. I waited impatiently until the dance was over, asked Jonathan to excuse me, and walked over to where they were standing. I gave Carol a brief smile. "Say good night to the deputy, Carol, it's your bedtime."

Her face flamed with color. She ducked her head and left without speaking.

"Leave her alone, Gainey. She's had a fight with her husband and she's vulnerable."

"What are you, the morals monitor around here?" He fumbled out a cigarette and angrily started to light it.

"You bet your ass I am," I said. "Get your act together, friend, or take it on the road. Do I make myself clear?"

He gave me a harsh bark of laughter. "I know all about you and your hangups. I stopped by the courthouse and had a little visit with the county boys before coming out here. They filled me in on you and that black whore over there who's acting like she's never had any. Mess with me and I'll spill the beans to all the nice people around town about what kind of a place you're running. Still want me to take my act on the road?"

I took a quick step closer and lowered my voice. I was crowding him in his personal space—deliberately. With a mean-minded bully, you have to let him know who's running the show.

"I hope they also told you that when I say 'Jump!' Sheriff Cribbs says 'How high?' Another point: Seven months ago, I put three rounds into the chest of a man who killed my dog. I think a lot of Jasmine. *Comprende?* So if you still feel the urge to run your mouth, just be willing to pay the price I've just outlined."

"Don't threaten me, you bitch. You wouldn't dare. You've got too much to lose."

"What's to lose?" I gave him an evil grin. "The boys down at county are setting you up, asshole. They all know I also have the chief justice of the Tenth District in my pocket. I'd walk on all charges."

"You're bluffing," he said, now sounding uncertain.

I gave him a laugh free of guile. "The only way to know for sure is to give it a try. 'Course, you won't be round to find out the outcome."

He tossed down his cigarette, grinding it into the floor with his shoe. "This is a pile of shit. I'm going to bed."

As I watched him walk away, I sensed Jonathan at my side.

"Have a problem?"

"Nah. Deputy Sergeant Gainey's gone to bed. He told me he was sleepy."

"Yes," Jonathan said wryly. "I could see how sleepy he was when he left."

I glanced at him when I heard the irony in his voice, but he was giving me a bland smile.

"Let's tell these folks to wind it up and send them off to bed," I suggested. He agreed, and that's what we did.

A little after eleven, Jasmine, Sergeant French, Jonathan, and I were left. It took the four of us ten minutes to tidy up so everything would be ready for the next day.

Jasmine and the sergeant wandered toward her stairs. Jonathan and I walked to the back porch. At the office door, he turned me by my shoulders and gave me a soft casual kiss on the lips. "Get some sleep. You're beat," he said. "See you at breakfast."

"Want some coffee?" My voice was husky with fatigue.

He laughed. "You couldn't last until it was ready. See you tomorrow."

I mumbled good night and fled. Leaning briefly against the office door, I turned to see if he was still there. He wasn't, but I saw the sergeant stroll by on the way to his room. Then I remembered that Carol was upstairs. Jasmine and I both would remain chaste. I went to bed and didn't dream.

17

Somber Reflections
Somewhere, Sometime

The man lay warm and comfortable in his sleeping bag, dozing and then waking up in the darkness. While awake, he'd catch a glimpse of his past. His mind wasn't selective, simply showing a certain day or year, and he'd remember what had actually happened. He tried to play the "what if" game, but his imagination wouldn't allow him to go down a different path. He'd always lived in the real world, not fantasy. He seldom daydreamed.

Earlier, when the light was brightest, coming straight down from the pipe to the floor, he'd tried to see where it was coming from. He'd stacked all the canned goods in one box and dragged it directly under the pipe. It raised him an additional eighteen inches when he stood on it. He'd removed the paper wrapper from a package of cookies and rolled it into a cylinder so he could look through it. It was long enough to reach the pipe. By closing one eye and squinting the other almost shut, he was able to see a tiny patch of blue sky.

Now, lying in the sleeping bag, he put together all he

knew about his surroundings and shivered—from his discovery, not the temperature.

The view up the pipe told him he wasn't in a building with an automatic temperature control. Looking through the pipe, he tried to estimate the distance to its top. His subconscious had told him soon after the drug had worn off what the container was in which he was imprisoned. He couldn't acknowledge the fact in his conscious mind because it also confirmed who his abductors were. Now he had to face the dismal knowledge that he was buried in the ground and, from the estimated length of the pipe, at least six feet deep. He shivered again and tried to ignore the thought of tons of solid earth above his head. He longed for sleep that wouldn't come. He clung to the fact that the coconut macaroons included in his survival packages were his favorite nighttime snacks, usually eaten, along with a glass of milk, before bedtime. Another concession for his comfort. He still couldn't make himself count the people who were aware of his choice of cookies. He knew the list—when he totaled it—would be quite short.

18

Seeing Is Believing
November 15, Monday, 6 A.M.

After the alarm finally woke me, I drew up my leg and gently touched the bruised area on my calf. It wasn't as bad as I'd feared. I stood and decided the limp would go away as soon as the muscle warmed up. Rudy stayed close while I loaded the dryer. When I was seated on the john, Bobby Lee appeared and sat in front of me. "What good ears you have, Bobby Lee," I said softly, as I crumpled the generous folds of his skin. Then I stroked Rudy's chest and shoulder area.

In the kitchen as I started the coffee, I mimicked my blatant invitation of last night: "Want some coffee?" God, how stupid! I'd sounded like a sex-starved female who hadn't had a man in months. I was, but that was beside the point. I dressed and didn't bother with makeup because you can't handle dogs and look elegant at the same time. Jasmine could. Maybe it was just me.

I stepped out the door to get my paper. Wayne brought it into the compound every morning when he unlocked the gates. I'd ordered extras this week for the trainees. The early morning air was wonderful. Heavy dew dripped from the trees. Little wisps of ground fog were faintly visible in the night-lights. By ten o'clock it would be hot and dry with warm winds, but now it was perfect.

While having coffee I stripped the rubber band from the paper and spread its thin contents, mostly advertising, across the kitchen table. I sipped, smoked, and stared at the picture on the first page, which covered four columns. Fred had come through in spades: a sharply defined Hank to the right, Wade on the left, both pushing a gurney with Jarel on board through the double doors of the emergency room. Wade was holding Jarel's hand; the black and white clasped fingers showed compassion. Nice touch, Wade. Hank looked grim and efficient in his tailored uniform. The picture couldn't have turned out better if I'd staged it myself. I grinned with pleasure. Sometimes my scheming plans work out.

When I entered the common room at five after seven, the wonderful smells of a Georgia-style breakfast filled the air—enough cholesterol to permanently clog your arteries, so many calories you'd lose count, and a divine taste that makes it worthwhile to live so dangerously. I counted heads: Rosie, Wayne, Donnie Ray, Jasmine, Carol (surprise, surprise), and Lena Mae, along with four trainers and three trainees. The missing trainers were Clifton Holcombe and W. A. Beckham. W. A. was always late. The missing trainees, Gainey and Vaughn, worried me. Gainey might be cooking up some funny business and possibly have an ally in Vaughn. Both would bear watching.

Nola Faye was at the steam table. She saw me and walked over. "Sorry about last night, Miz Jo Beth," she mumbled, trying to sound contrite.

"No problem, kiddo," I acknowledged graciously. "Remember, when trying to pull one, you have to be subtle. Make it go over their head, *then* you can laugh.

Also, when you apologize, strive to make it sound humble. Take it from a pro, you're good. Just practice. It'll come."

"Thanks, I think," she said, moving away, slightly puzzled. She was trying to discern if I'd given her a compliment, some constructive criticism, or just a put-down. She's a sharp little cookie. Actually, I'd tagged all three bases lightly to keep her on her toes.

Jonathan entered and walked to my side.

"Good morning," I said with a smile. Just seeing his rugged and dependable-looking face light up when he spotted me made my day.

"Good morning. Who's your companion?" He returned my smile, knelt, and balanced gracefully in a squatting position.

"Jonathan, I'd like to introduce you to Master Robert E. Lee. Shake hands, Bobby Lee." I leaned over and lightly touched his left shoulder and he promptly stuck out his left paw and laid it unerringly in Jonathan's right hand.

"What a nice dog," Jonathan said as he rubbed Bobby Lee's ears. "Is he your favorite?"

"Absolutely."

"Is he for sale?" His eyes were twinkling.

"No way."

Jonathan grinned. "I gathered from your look that he's the apple of your eye. He's a very handsome dog."

"He is," I agreed. "Let's eat."

We filled our plates and sat at the middle table. I'd put extra bacon on mine to share with Bobby Lee. We had white tablecloths this morning. Miz Jansee is a traditionalist.

Gainey and Vaughn entered the room. Gainey headed to the coffee urn and Vaughn went to the steam table. They didn't sit together, so maybe it was a coincidence that they came in together. I fed Bobby Lee a bite of bacon. Jonathan caught me eyeing his plate.

"I refuse to eat sensibly on my vacation. It's un-American," he said.

"I went on a diet two weeks ago when I turned thirty."

"How are you doing?" He glanced at my plate.

"I'd have to be locked in the toolshed for a week to shed a pound around here. I have no willpower."

He laughed. "You're perfect just the way you are. Don't lose an ounce."

"You're flattering me because you want some of my bacon, but it's earmarked for Bobby Lee." I fed my handsome dog a half strip and watched it disappear.

"I see who rates number one around here."

"Well, if it's any consolation, your second-place finish was a very close decision."

As I stood to begin the seminar, I spotted the message light blinking on the wall phone and went over to check it. It was from Hank. I dialed his number.

"Hi," he said softly when he recognized my voice. "Just wanted to thank you for the gift last night. P. C. is on the way out to your place to return the cuffs. I told him to put them in the mailbox."

"Did my name come up during questioning?"

"Not so far," he replied. "Our boy is awake. Wade sat up with me last night in the hospital room. I have a feeling that he won't let Jarel open his mouth until after he has a conference with him. This means I'll get zilch after Wade cautions him."

"Great picture in the paper." I was testing the waters.

"Yep," he said, chuckling softly. "Your timing was perfect. Neil popped out from behind the door and caught us totally unprepared. It's a God's wonder I didn't have my mouth open in surprise. The flash came out of nowhere. By the way, who is J.C.W.?"

"A friend from out of town. You don't know him," I said casually.

"Wouldn't be Chief Jonathan C. Webber, Eppley Police Department, Eppley, Georgia, by any chance, would it?"

"Quit showing off, Hank," I said, stung. "How did you know?"

"Babe, when requests for your record started trickling in from different law enforcement offices around the state recently, I decided to keep a list of the people who were asking. You never know when some information could be valuable. Lo and behold, I found the same initials on the cuffs that were on the list. See how smart I am?"

"You're a nosy bugger!"

"Thanks again," he said, and laughed as he hung up.

Back at the table, I tapped on a water glass with a spoon. The room became silent.

"I want to welcome our guest trainees to the first seminar held by Bloodhounds, Incorporated, for the purpose of training officers to handle the dogs your departments have purchased. This morning you'll meet the dog that goes home with you on Friday. This dog will be your responsibility: its care, feeding, grooming, and future health. All of us here hope you'll grow to love and admire the bloodhound as much as we do.

"In your indoctrination sheet, sent to you before your visit, we suggested you bring a full-dress uniform for the purpose of taking a picture of you with your dog upon graduation. This picture will be sent to your local paper with the appropriate copy for a press release.

"I'm sorry to say we have a sad duty to perform this afternoon that also requires you to wear your uniform. A fellow officer, Deputy Mavis Johns, was killed in the line of duty during a robbery in Gilsford County. Her funeral procession will start at three this afternoon in Collins, thirty-five miles from here.

"Will the trainers please watch the time and break off promptly at noon. We'll have lunch, get dressed, and leave here at one-thirty. We have four official vehicles in which to transport everyone. Supper will be served here at six-thirty. After the meal, an eighty-minute rescue tape will be shown. Then your time is your own. See you back here at noon."

Just after I'd finished my speech, W. A. and Clifton arrived and both approached me at the table.

"Sorry, Jo Beth," W. A. apologized, "my clunker wouldn't start this morning and I had to call Clifton."

"No problem," I said with a smile. "Go find Deputy Sergeant Vaughn and introduce him to Hemingway."

"Sure. See you later."

I turned to Clifton. "As you know, Clifton, Sergeant Stone isn't with us. You can exercise Rhett Butler and work with the next seminar dogs."

"Thanks, Miz Jo Beth." He went away happy.

Everyone was clearing out. I saw Carol walk over to speak to Gainey. She saw me watching, cut the conversation short, and left. Lena Mae went to clean the rooms. Jasmine had an early sweep. Wayne had gone to help the trainers, and Donnie Ray was wandering around with his camera recording our first seminar.

"Rhett Butler?" Jonathan said with amusement. He'd just returned with our coffee cups replenished.

"We have lots of fun naming the dogs. Drug dogs are named after famous writers. Search-and-rescue dogs are southern symbols and famous and infamous people. Rhett Butler is your department's dog."

Jonathan motioned toward the phone's blinking light. "I think you have another message."

"I'll be right back and give you a tour of the kennel," I said.

I dialed in the code and listened. "This is Tim Fergerson in security at Cannon Trucking Company. I'm calling from a pay phone and leaving the number. It's eight-twenty now. I'll wait here ten minutes for a callback. If we don't connect in the next ten minutes, don't call me at work or at home. I'll try and get in touch later. This is important, Jo Beth. Thanks."

Glancing at my watch, I saw I had four minutes to return his call. What in the world did Tim want? We weren't close friends, just business acquaintances who'd done each other favors in the past. I quickly dialed the number for the pay phone.

"Tim, it's Jo Beth."

"Thanks for returning my call. I need your help. Can we meet this morning?"

"Today?" I exclaimed with dismay. Christ, weeks and weeks of the daily grind, and suddenly I'm busier than a bee in a tar bucket.

"Sorry, but I'm in deep shit. Are you free?"

"Sure. When and where?" He'd come through last April when I needed him. How could I do less now?

"Great," he said, relief clearly evident in his voice. "It'll be tricky. I'm being tailed by a combined task force of GBI, FBI, and off-duty men from the sheriff's department. I don't know who has the duty this morning. I just left my house for work and stopped to call. Do you have a car, other than the vans?"

"I can borrow one," I said.

"Help me think of a place I can go in through the front door and then meet you in the alley. I don't want them to know about you. You're my secret weapon." He was trying for humor, but I could hear the strain in his voice.

"Do you know Browse and Bargain Books?"

"Yes. I've bought books there," he said.

"What have you read recently?"

"Ah . . . *Bootlegger's Daughter* by Margaret Maron."

"I'm gonna put you on hold," I told him. "Hang on."

I quickly dialed Susan's number. She surprised me by being there early.

"Jo Beth here. I'm involving you in some skullduggery,

and I need information fast. How much is *Bootlegger's Daughter*?"

"Let's see. . . . Sixteen ninety-one," she answered.

"I'm putting you on hold; don't go away."

"Tim?"

"I'm here."

"Write a check to Browse and Bargain for sixteen ninety-one." I glanced at my watch. "At eight-forty, enter the store, drop the check on the counter, and pick up the book. Continue straight back to the rear, go through the door marked PRIVATE, turn right, and go out the door marked EXIT. I'll be in a late-model black car in the alley. Got it?"

"Gotcha. Just be there."

"Susan?"

"Sittin' on dead ready!" She was enjoying this.

"At eight-forty this morning, Tim Fergerson will enter your store, give you a check, pick up the book you'll have in a bag lying on the counter, with receipt, and go out your back door. Lock it behind him. If you don't know him personally, take a good look and memorize his features. He'll be followed by someone. The object here, Susan, is to stall, stall, stall. Ask for identification. Don't be alarmed if he's GBI, FBI, or whoever. Make him prove it. Do you think you can handle this?" I tried to sound doubtful. I wanted her on her toes.

"Piece of cake," she asserted.

"Good girl," I said with warmth. "I'll call back later for details."

I scanned the room. Miz Jansee was close and I explained to her that I'd return soon and to pass this message along to Wayne. Jonathan was waiting patiently for me, and I gave him the news.

"We have to leave quickly, and we need to take your car. Meet me at the back door, ASAP."

In the bedroom, I put my wallet, keys, cigarettes, and

gun in a brown shoulder-strap bag. I told Bobby Lee and Rudy they couldn't go with me and hit the door. Jonathan was behind the wheel with the motor running.

"Move over," I said, opening his door. "I forgot to tell you, I have to drive."

He slid over quickly. I waited until we were on the highway before I spoke.

"What's your opinion of the GBI?" I was busy adjusting the rearview mirror and the left outside mirror and moving the seat up a notch closer. I quickly took the car up to sixty-five.

"The Georgia Bureau of Investigation is a worthwhile organization." He lectured me as if he were holding class for a bunch of raw recruits. "They are sorely needed by the small counties, which can't afford an investigative unit, lab, or pathologist to perform autopsies. This means about ninety-five percent of rural Georgia qualifies for their services. They respond when we request help and treat us like we just fell off a turnip truck. They pretend they want us to work as a team but really treat us like gofers and look down their noses at us. Shall I continue?"

"Nope. How about the FBI?" I was scanning the rearview mirror, all side streets, and oncoming traffic, trying to spot the law before they caught me speeding.

"You concentrate on driving," he remarked pleasantly, "I'll ride shotgun. The FBI is in a league of its own. They are total assholes. No pretended cooperation, nor do they show any compassion for our fragile egos. They treat us like dirt. Need any more?"

"No, sir, I get the picture, thank you very much. I have a working acquaintance with Tim Fergerson, second banana in security at Cannon Trucking. We do random drug sweeps for them. He's ex-police because he lost control of his car chasing a drunk and slid into a semi. He can walk all day but can't run fast enough to catch the bad guys, so he's on partial disability. I owe him and his cousin John, who also works there, a very big one. This morning he called in my marker."

I was trying to guess which streets would have fewer cars, traffic lights, and stop signs. I slowed, turned on Lily Pad Lane, and picked up speed again.

"Tim told me he was in deep shit. He said he was being followed by a, quote, task force of GBI, FBI, and off-duty county deputies, unquote."

"So we're galloping to his rescue?" Jonathan quizzed. I glanced in his direction and saw him smile. "I too would have my shorts twisted if that combination were following me," he added.

"We're heading for a meet as we speak. I need some input from you, Jonathan. You know more about combined task forces than I do. Could it be drugs?"

"No way. The big boys don't like to share press conferences. It would be GBI or FBI but not both."

"Damn. I don't have a clue. What's your best guess?" I was fibbing. After Hank's phone call Friday, I was positive this was about Cannon's kidnapping.

"Beats me. The only thing that comes to mind is the hijacking of some government shipment during interstate hauling or possibly a kidnapping. Even then, for both to be involved, both would have to be notified before either one could put a lid on it and seal it tight—I would think."

I grunted. I was weaving on and off short stretches of streets. There were three traffic lights I couldn't avoid in reaching the alley behind Susan's store. I made the first one just fine but had to slow for the second one with several cars in front of me. Two cars near the front of the line had their left blinkers on. No left turn signal. I was in the inside lane and had to turn.

I checked my watch again. It was gonna be close. Three cars cleared the light going straight. The first signaler was trying to ease forward, but turned chicken and sat just over the white line, letting a string of cars go by; they had the right-of-way. I fumed. The light finally turned green and the chickenshit driver in the first car played the waiting game again. When the driver finally took the plunge and turned—in a space large enough to accommodate a seven-forty-seven jet—the light turned from amber to red for the second time. Finally, the woman just ahead of me and I were slowly easing forward, waiting for a break.

"I hope you appreciate the fact that I'm not going to mention that the driver of the car who caused the bottleneck was a woman," Jonathan said.

"Suck a lemon," I retorted. "So's this one."

"I want you to notice that it was not me who mentioned that fact," he said with good humor.

"Some of us know how to get through an intersection," I informed him smugly. I rode the woman's back bumper as if there were a tow bar connecting us. Oncoming traffic had to stop because we both inched out, totally ignoring them, and made the turn.

I cut into the alley behind the Southern Union Commercial Bank and whipped out of its parking lot, almost clipping a slow-moving car to my right. My watch was dead on eight-forty, and I was a block away from the right alley. I gunned across the intersection without slowing down and noticed a short intake of Jonathan's breath and the squeal of brakes. I didn't hear glass breaking or feel a bump so I knew we were clear. I floored it to the next alley, which was the right one.

I said, "Open the back door as soon as I stop."

I felt Jonathan shift position so he could reach the door handle behind him. I coasted to a stop and he popped open the door. I glanced at Susan's rear shop door and saw it open. Tim closed it and made a dive into the back seat.

"Go!" he yelled, and I gunned the car down the alley.

The momentum of the forward surge slammed the door closed. I flinched when the tires squealed as I turned left. I hadn't slowed enough. After several blocks, Tim raised his head and spotted Jonathan. I'd been checking the rearview mirror.

"Good morning, Tim," I said, using my right hand to indicate Jonathan. "I'd like you to meet a friend, Police Chief Jonathan Webber from Eppley, Georgia. Jonathan, my friend Tim Fergerson."

"Great," Tim said. "Did you also call the editor of the paper?"

"Shake his hand, Tim," I said, in my best no-nonsense voice. "He's a friend and you're in need. I trust him as much as I trust you. It sounds like you may need both of us."

"And many, many more," said Tim with feeling. "Sorry," he said to Jonathan as he extended his hand. "First time I've ever dodged the law. It's made me a little edgy."

"Glad to meet you," replied Jonathan amicably. "I can empathize."

"Tim," I explained, "I'm heading for Jefferson Park. It's close and usually deserted this time of the morning. We can talk there."

"I watched as we pulled out of the alley," Jonathan said. "I didn't see anyone come out the back door."

"Good," said Tim, relaxing in the seat.

We three didn't speak again until I'd pulled into the small park and driven down a twisting drive. The car was easily shielded from the road by thick shrubbery and trees. We got out of the car and sat at a nearby picnic table, Tim on one side, Jonathan and I on the other. We lit up.

"Thanks for coming," Tim said. He took a deep drag on his cigarette before he began.

"Eleven days ago, a Thursday night, at approximately nine o'clock, the owner and CEO of Cannon Trucking Company was kidnapped from his car about halfway between his own house and that of his father. The car was abandoned on the side of the road. No sign of a struggle. The road is paved, so no car tracks. The owner's name is David Franklin Cannon. Since there are three men with that name, I'll explain what they're called so you'll know which one I'm talking about. The patriarch is Frank Senior. He retired from the company six years ago, when arthritis put him in a wheelchair. He's seventy-six years old. His son is called Frank Junior. He runs the company, and he's fifty-six. Frank Junior's son is the third but he's always been called David, which makes it easier to tell them apart. I'll use Frank Senior for the old man, Frank for the boss, and David for the third." We both nodded in understanding.

When Frank didn't arrive at Frank Senior's place by ten-fifteen, the old man called Frank's house and spoke to David. David, knowing his father had had time to reach his destination, left to follow his usual route to see if he'd broken down or had a flat tire or something. He found the car abandoned, unlocked, keys still in the ignition, and no sign of his father.

"What happened at Frank's the night he disappeared?" I asked.

"The whole family was there for dinner. Seems like it's a Thursday-night ritual. There're three sons: David is thirty, Philip is twenty-seven, and Donald is twenty-five. David's son, David Franklin the fourth, is three years old. David's wife was there also; the other two sons are single. And of course Frank's wife, Helen, the boys' mother, was present."

"Go on with your story. What happened next?" I didn't know how long the tale would take, but I was conscious of the clock ticking away the minutes, and I wanted to get Tim back before they got more suspicious of him than they were now.

Tim seemed to sense my urgency and quickened his

speaking pace. "The sons conned their grandfather—called him and told him their dad was ill. They kept up the pretense for five days. Finally the old man contacted Sheriff Cribbs, and they finally got the truth of the kidnapping. When I heard about it, I went to Frank Senior's house."

"Why would you go there?" I was curious. "Was he a friend of yours?"

"Not really. We'd talked a few times when he came into the plant. I went there to tell him my theory about the kidnapping and to try to enlist his help. He heard me out and agreed with me completely. We both think we know who kidnapped his son."

"Who do you suspect?" I asked, breathless with suspense.

"Frank's no-good, lazy, and ineffectual sons. All three of them. Possibly their mother also; I'm not sure about her. But you can take it to the bank, those three boys arranged the kidnapping of their own father."

19

Questions Beg for Answers
November 15, Monday, 9 A.M.

Jonathan and I sat quietly and digested this denouncement of Frank Junior's three sons and possibly his wife. Frank sure didn't sound as if he had much of a family life.

"What's the basis for your theory? Any proof?" Jonathan beat me to the essential question. I lit another cigarette and listened closely.

Tim held up four fingers of his left hand. "One," he said, bending a finger down, "they hate the company, all three of them. They take no interest and don't try to learn anything about handling it for the future.

"Two, they try to hide it, but all three show their contempt of their father in their actions and attitudes. It isn't just me. Several others at the plant have noticed and commented on how they treat their father.

"Three, Frank seems to know how they feel about him. He'd have to be an idiot not to, and he's a very smart man. For almost a year he's been working on a merger with another trucking company out of Atlanta. The sons are dead set against it. They don't give a fig for the company or their father, but they know that when they're no longer the owner's sons they won't last thirty days in their jobs.

"Four"—Tim continued to press down fingers—"he hasn't answered their questions about what he'll do with the big chunk of money he'll receive with the merger. They know he wouldn't work under anyone in a business he was raised in. They're afraid he might invest it unwisely, give most of it to charity, or sit back and use up the principal. They want to be sure he doesn't spend it. They think it's their rightful inheritance, and it might not be there a few years from now."

"Is that all you have to go on?" I asked. I thought it was plenty, but I wanted to find out if he had any proof.

"No," he said slowly, and hesitated.

"Give," I said bluntly. "If we're to help, we have to know."

"What I gave you are all facts that can be checked out. What's left is purely speculation on my part."

"We need your thoughts," Jonathan remarked. "You've been observing them closely or you wouldn't have jumped so quickly to enlist the aid of Frank Senior and air your suspicions about his grandsons."

"You're right," he admitted. "It's only a gut feeling. As I told you, the merger has been hashed and rehashed for close to a year now. The boys screamed their heads off the first six months. They tried reasoning and cajoling and finally escalated to open defiance. About six months ago I noticed a change. They stopped ranting and raving about the merger and started being polite to their father. They didn't fool me. They hate him and they want out of the company—with lots of money—so they can live their dream life of not having to work. I've seen the way they look at him, glances passing among them when they think no one's looking. I knew back then they were planning something. I worried about them doing something really stupid like hiring a hit man or doing him in themselves. I actually thought about going to Frank with my suspicions but chickened out 'cause I didn't have one ounce of proof. Don't you see? The kidnapping is brilliant. They'll end up with a big chunk of money, will still own the company, and can either sell it or run it themselves. All they have to do is work the money into their finances—slowly. They were smart enough to plan the snatch; they'll be smart enough to ease into the money."

"How big a chunk are you talking about?" I asked. "What was the ransom demand?"

"Three million is what they claim a caller demanded," Tim said.

I whistled. "Is the company good for it?"

"They don't have that much in the safe," Tim said with dry humor, "but they can dig it up—the company, not the family. I understand everyone's willing. They're already at work getting loans and arranging financing."

"If they want to inherit quickly, they'll have to have a dead body," Jonathan said softly. "I don't imagine they'd want to wait five years until he could be declared legally dead."

"I know," said Tim quickly as he looked into my eyes. "That's why I called you, Jo Beth. I think they're keeping him alive until they can get the ransom money. I want you to find him before they get the money and kill him."

I said with surprise, "Me personally, or Bloodhounds, Incorporated?"

"Either, both, whatever it takes," he answered. "I've spoken to Frank Senior twice. Told him I wanted to hire you and needed some expense money. He agreed." He reached for his wallet, pulled out a slim sheaf of bills, and laid them in front of me on the table. "Here's a thousand dollars in advance for expenses. If you need any more, just holler.

"We have to assume Frank Senior's phone is bugged as well as mine. I've been instructed to tell you, if you try to find Frank and fail, you'll receive a fee of five thousand and what's left of the expense money. If you find him— dead or alive—the fee is fifty thousand."

"You've got to be kidding," I said with feeling. "You don't understand about dogs and a cold scent trail—" I stopped. I was remembering back to the long, long day we'd worked side by side. I'd filled his head with a lot of facts on how the dogs worked because he'd been interested, and I always love to brag on my animals. I began to smell a rat. "Just what did you tell him about me?" I asked, staring into his eyes.

"I told you were smart—brilliant, in fact. Operated with guile. Were devious and not afraid to get your hands dirty and to bend the law, if necessary," he said, returning my gaze with a steady look.

"Did you give him any specific examples?" I asked in an ominous voice.

"Two," he admitted, his voice steady. "The only two I'd personally witnessed and could vouch for. I disguised the innocent and protected the locals. I had to do it, Jo Beth. I had to convince Frank Senior that you are more than 'a slip of a girl leading some dogs around,' his original estimate of you. I need his wealth and contacts behind you in case you get into trouble. Will you forgive me and will you do it?"

"I'm not sure," I said doubtfully. "I'm swamped with work at the kennel, and, truthfully, I wouldn't know where to begin. What makes you think I'd even consider such a hopeless task?"

"Because you can't resist a challenge? Because you thrive on excitement and trying the impossible? Am I right?"

Seeing the wide grin appear on Tim's face, I glanced at

Jonathan and saw the same grin spreading across his features.

"Shit," I said and stood up abruptly. Then I walked off a few feet, furiously dragged on my cigarette, and stared at the morning. The sun was getting warmer with every passing minute. The dew was almost dry, even in the shade. I was trying to think. I hadn't been honest when I'd told Tim I wouldn't know where to begin. Purely as a mental exercise, I'd been flitting along thinking of all the places to check into and look over even as Tim was telling his story. He was absolutely correct; I couldn't resist. I was just pissed off that he could read me so easily—we weren't bosom buddies. And Jonathan must agree with Tim, judging from the shit-eating grin on his face.

I sighed, threw the cigarette butt down, ground it into pieces with my shoe, and walked back and sat down.

"Okay," I said, with a casualness I didn't feel. "I'll give it a whirl, but don't expect too much. I've got a question, Tim. Did you mention me to Frank Senior the first night? If not, why not, and when did you get around to it?"

"I didn't mention you the first time because frankly, Jo Beth, I didn't think of you then. I was going to do the investigating on my own and find him myself, which, from your questions, you've already figured out. I didn't tell him about you until late last night.

"You see, yesterday afternoon at four o'clock a GBI and an FBI agent served a search warrant on my house. When I got home from work, according to my wife, they'd been searching for something small enough to hide in a book. She said they'd picked up every book in the house, even my daughter's schoolbooks.

"They were still searching when I arrived at five-thirty. I blew my stack and they questioned me, not giving me any reason. I knew then my hands were tied, because from what they said I knew my phone was bugged. I'm guessing

Frank Senior's phone is bugged too. By now, they've listened to the tapes from Frank Senior's house and they are really suspicious, I bet.

"Late last night I sneaked out the back of the house, used cousin John's car, which was parked four streets away, and went to see Frank Senior. I knew I was being followed everywhere I went. I convinced him to let me roll him out by the pool, only I continued past the pool and stopped by a noisy fountain. I didn't want them to know about you. It wouldn't surprise me for them to pick me up for questioning, when I get back. It's up to you, Jo Beth."

"If they had two cars on you, how come they didn't cover the alley behind Susan's store?" I asked. A logical move, I would think.

"You don't know these guys, Jo Beth," said Jonathan. "Even using two cars, one is bound to screw up. Stop for cigarettes or go to the john or something."

"They would fuck up a wet dream," Tim agreed.

"We've got to get you back to town. You've been gone too long," I said.

On the way back, I said, "Tim, take your book and turn down page twenty. You supposedly told Susan you wanted to go to McDonald's for breakfast, the reason you went out the back door. When you got outside you changed your mind. You were still upset about the search warrant and the grilling. You decided to take a walk. Later, you retraced your route and went to Dunkin' Donuts instead. Buy something and sit and pretend to read. If they pick you up at any time after you leave this car, your story will sound okay. What do you think?"

Tim was in the front seat. I'd seen Jonathan wave him to it because he knew I'd want to talk to him on the way back. Tim turned to Jonathan and laughed. "Now do you understand why I call her devious?"

Jonathan laughed with him until he caught a glimpse of my glare in the rearview mirror.

"Call me between twelve and one each day. Use a different phone booth each time. What I want to know tomorrow is anything, no matter how silly or trivial, anyone can remember happening at the terminal six months or so ago. If they get curious, tell them you bet a fellow employee that if you remembered something unusual or trivial happening around that time, you could find someone else who could too. Your friend is betting you can't."

"What do you think happened?" Tim asked.

"I have no idea. I'm just trying to cover all bases, and that's one I can't handle and you can."

"Sure," he said with disbelief in his voice.

"Honest Injun," I said truthfully. "And Tim, don't get discouraged. I'll fill you in on what we've found out every time you call, even if it's nothing."

"Thanks," he answered, sounding happier.

"Out you go," I said, pulling to the curb.

"Good luck," he said as he crawled out and quickly put distance between us. I eased back into traffic as Jonathan rubbernecked out the back window.

"Didn't see anyone resembling fuzz," he said, as he slid forward on the back seat. His warm breath was tickling my right ear.

"Where've you been? Fuzz is old-fashioned," I said.

"*I'm* old-fashioned," he commented. "Showing my age."

"By the way, now you can give me that list I requested last night," I told him.

"What list?" His innocent brown eyes met mine in the rearview mirror.

"No, no. It won't work. I asked and you promised. Give."

"I truly forgot," he said with a winsome smile.

"You charmer, you," I said sweetly. "If the list isn't in hand in sixty seconds, you're a dead man." I put my hand, palm up, near my right ear. He caught my fingers with his and kissed the palm of my hand, lingering over the caress, brushing his lips across the surface. I felt my blood rise to meet the sensation following the movement of his lips. I cupped his chin with my hand, trailed my fingers across his face, and tweaked his nose.

"Ouch!"

"That was much too erotic for a person to deal with while operating a car at forty miles per hour. I trust you have sufficient insurance?"

"I guess we're back on the subject of the list," he said gruffly.

"What list?" I wouldn't meet his eyes in the rearview mirror. He chuckled manfully into my right ear.

I detoured three streets and pulled up under the canopy at the first drive-in window of my bank and glanced to see who was working it.

"Hi, Cathy, how ya doing?" I asked in greeting. I put a deposit slip and the thousand dollars from Tim in her drawer. Jonathan moved from the back seat to sit beside me.

"Just fine, Jo Beth. Is your passenger one of them lawmen that's staying at your place this week for your see-men-ar?" Her southern accent was dripping with peach juice.

"Sho 'nuff is," I drawled in return. Regardless of how busy you are, you can't rush these conversational exchanges. It's part of our inherent politeness.

"Cathy, this is Chief of Police Jonathan C. Webber. Chief, this is Ms. Cathy Porter, a good friend of mine."

"Pleased to meet you, Chief. Where y'all from?"

"Pleased to meet you too, Miz Porter. I hail from Eppley, up near the Tennessee border."

"Isn't that just amazin'?" Cathy exclaimed. "I have a

first cousin lives near there, in Franklin. Pearson Porter? Maybe you know him?"

"I know several Porters in Franklin, but right this moment I can't recall a Pearson Porter."

"His daddy's Simon Porter. Raises hunting hounds." Cathy was determined to find a connection, regardless of how tenuous. This could take awhile. Two cars were patiently waiting behind us. Cathy was aware of them so it was her place to move them along, not mine.

Jonathan was leaning forward at an angle so he could talk. "Well, I'll be!" he said happily. "Well, sure, went over to look at some hounds with a friend of mine not too long ago. Isn't that something. It's a small world, isn't it?"

Cathy beamed and peeked at the waiting cars. "It sure is," she said as she sent the drawer out with the receipt. "You both have a nice day and I hope you enjoy your visit, Chief. Y'all come back, you hear?"

"Thanks, nice meeting you," answered Jonathan. I gunned the motor and got us out of there.

"Sorry 'bout that. I feel sorry for her. The louse she was engaged to found out she had to quit work so she could take care of her mother who'd had a stroke. He was looking for a meal ticket so he switched to her second cousin, married her, and now they live just four houses down from Cathy. Her mother died less than six months later. Not only does she see him often because he's part of the family, but she has to smile and smile at every family get-together to keep proving she's not heartbroken. She should go after his gonads with a broken bottle."

"Ouch," he said with a grimace. "Remind me never to leave *you* standing at the altar. I must confess, Franklin isn't *near,* it's about sixty miles from Eppley, and I've never gone looking for a hunting hound in my life. She furnished the clue so I pounced on it."

"Well, since we're being honest here, her daddy is one

of the three county commissioners who signs my search-and-rescue checks. I was also doing a little political toadying."

"Tell me about it," he replied. "I do it every day, on and off the job."

"Does it ever make you feel two-faced and repulsed?" I questioned.

"When it builds up in me, I take it out on my horse by punishing him."

"How?" I asked sharply.

"He's lazy and officially retired. I saddle him and we go for a two- or three-mile stroll. He hates exercise and pouts for days."

I laughed and relaxed. I had thought he meant something like kicking the dog in anger.

20

The Devil Dances When a Fool Advances
November 15, Monday, 10 A.M.

When we arrived back in the courtyard, I sent Jonathan to the common room, telling him I'd be along in about ten minutes. I spoke to the animals, checked their water, and gathered my working tools: portable phone, my little black book of telephone numbers, two spiral notebooks, and three black pens. It would be easier to hold the brain trust here in the office. I chuckled. I was fairly sure if Jonathan and I worked here alone and got comfortable, lounging on the sofa, it wouldn't be my brain or any other body part I'd trust. Jonathan spotted me crossing the courtyard and hurried to open the door and relieve me of my bundled items.

"It's not heavy, just awkward to carry. I should've gotten a book bag."

"You should've gotten me. I don't know if I've told you, but men are put on this earth to carry objects for women." His head was cocked to one side, and a small superior smile played upon his lips.

I mumbled sadly, "Just when everything was going so well."

"I beg your pardon? I didn't hear what you said." He took a step closer.

"Jonathan," I began with a crisp flourish, "your smug, superior male attitude, while blathering male platitudes, can be an irritant to a dedicated feminist such as myself. It's like waving a red flag at a bull. Well, you now have my atten—"

I stopped and stared at Jonathan. He looked as if he had been poleaxed. I couldn't utter a word. You've done it now, Sidden, I thought with bitterness. The first decent man who's even looked at you in all these months and you . . . ah, hell. . . .

Jonathan recovered first. He rubbed a hand across his face and tried an uncertain smile. "I bet it was something I said. Am I right?"

The sound that burst forth from my throat couldn't be called laughter. It spewed forth in solid waves of noise. I had to stop to catch my breath. That's when I discovered Jonathan, bent at the waist and lost in the same hysterical mirth as I. I wiped my eyes with my fingers, but the sounds he was making set me off again.

We finally staggered to a chair and collapsed. He brushed his hands across his eyes. They were tearing like mine. He wouldn't stop making those horse-whinnying noises.

"Shut up," I said weakly. "Please hush."

He clamped both hands over his mouth, turned his back, and staggered toward the rest rooms. His shoulders were jumping in an uncoordinated rhythm as he passed through the door.

I walked over where Miz Jansee was stirring a pot. I nodded and smiled, not trusting myself to speak. At the sink I rolled off a paper towel, dampened it, pressed it to my face, and slowly walked back to the table.

Where was my mind when I needed it? Usually my

body parts were quick to point out my stupidity, but not now. Jonathan lives way up there, somewhere close to the Tennessee border. He has a farm, a life, and a city to police. I live way down here in southeast Georgia, run a kennel housing eighty-seven dogs—with no freedom at all.

Jonathan returned. "Sorry. My mouth does this to me all the time. I apologize for the sexist remark."

"No apology needed," I said swiftly. "My temper gets me into hot water too often lately. Please sit. We have less than two hours before lunch. Let's start making lists. I always tackle a problem by making a list. How do you operate?"

"Spur-of-the-moment random thoughts, seat-of-the-pants approach, coupled with standard police procedure. I have to admit, though, it doesn't always work. Are we still friends?"

"Friends, and fast becoming buddies," I said with a wide smile.

He frowned and studied my features. "I heard something in your voice, something new and scary. It wasn't there thirty minutes ago. What happened?"

"You're imagining things," I said succinctly and pleasantly. "Let's get started, okay?"

"Sure," he said. "You start on the list. I think better on my feet. Is it okay if I just wander around your land? Any vicious dogs? Resident skunks? Agitated alligators?"

"None of the above. Feel free to roam. Lunch is at twelve."

"Wouldn't miss it," he said with a wink. He turned and strode out.

I stared at the area he'd just occupied. The room felt empty and cold, same as my heart. I was quick to hope, to fantasize romance. I was also fast with the chop when I came to my senses.

I dialed Susan's number. "How'd it go?" I asked when she answered.

"Slick as owl shit," she replied, laughing. "I wish you could've seen my performance. Not two minutes after your Tim left—and I didn't recognize him, by the way—a dude walked in the front door. He purely reeked of a stereotype fed. Sports jacket, white shirt and tie, and those little round sunshades their imitation counterparts wore on *Simon and Simon*. You remember the TV series a few years back?"

"I remember. Go on."

"Are we on a timetable here? Should I condense?" She sounded disappointed because she wanted to give me the blow-by-blow details. Knowing how she could drag it out, I could honestly tell her I didn't have much time.

"Sorry, babe, but I have to have it fast."

"Right," she said crisply. "It took him two minutes to enter, two minutes to check the stacks, another two minutes to check the balcony stacks. I stopped him from entering the back storage area. Stalled and stalled. It was a total of ten minutes before I slowly unlocked the back door. He was FBI. I made him prove it."

"You did great, partner. Don't forget a word or look. I want to hear what happened in its entirety when we have time. See you at supper."

"You got it," she said cheerfully, as we hung up.

On the first blank page of the new notebook, I wrote: *Computer: all real estate holdings of the David Franklin Cannons, I through IV.* I felt silly adding the kid's name, but I'd heard somewhere that property in Georgia could be placed in a minor child's name with the parent named as guardian, and it would be listed as such in the courthouse records. I also added the other two Cannon sons and the two wives, along with everyone's age, if known. These were all the people Tim had mentioned. I didn't know if there was a living wife for the grandpa, but I doubted it.

Before going any further, there was one inquiry I could get off the ground at once. I wanted to call Little Bemis at work, but first I'd have to decipher the code *du jour* or he wouldn't talk to me or even acknowledge that he knew me. I sighed. I felt foolish going through the charade he demanded for working with me, but not so foolish as to refuse, because, even though the locals think he's a few bricks shy of a full load, he's a topnotch computer whiz.

Little Bemis works for Apex-Semex, Inc., which has its home office in Dunston County. They located here because the county offered them free land, no taxes in perpetuity, free water, and free garbage disposal and still calls them every Monday morning asking if there's anything else they can give them. Just ask—please.

In turn, the company brought in about ninety of its own personnel and hired about forty locals, of which Little Bemis is one. The newcomers meant more homes and the county could charge them taxes and water and garbage fees up the ying yang. They also bred a new country club and several specialty stores. All in all, the county made a sweet deal.

Now, back to the code. After a few minutes of juggling convoluted data, I came up with the code word *contribution*. Well, this one was easy; not long ago he came up with *quodlibetic*. Try working that tongue-twister into a normal conversation. I dialed his number.

"Computers."

"Mr. Bemis, this is Lila of Fennoy Farms. We haven't received your contribution for this month."

"Let me check. Hold, please," he said in a very pleasant voice. Lila's my code name, but I couldn't resist adding different names of imaginary business enterprises. I must have a touch of whatever's afflicting Little Bemis.

"Lila, I'm ready for input."

I explained that I needed to know all the real estate owned by the following people and read him my list.

"What's the time-frame need?"

"Immediate. This man's been kidnapped."

Little Bemis didn't turn a hair. He was used to all sorts of fantasy allegations. Your reason for needing the information he could provide had to have a fairy-tale ring to it: saving the queen, rescuing the princess, putting down an insurrection, et cetera.

"Name of operation?"

"The Case of the Kidnapped Caliph." I didn't roll my eyes over the absurdity this time, because the imaginary title was my truest to date.

"Your printout will be at drop five by five-fifteen. Wait one hour before pickup." He hung up. I set the phone down with relief. Once again, Little Bemis had saved my legs and fingers from doing the walking.

Gazing into space, I thought, What next? I knew I had to see the old man, Frank Senior, and it would have to be late tonight. Might as well call. I looked up the number in the phone book.

"Cannon residence."

"I'd like to speak to Mr. Cannon, please. My name is Jo Beth Sidden."

"Please hold," said the male voice I supposed was his servant or nurse.

"Frank Cannon." The voice sounded angry.

"Mr. Cannon," I said with a bright chirp, "this is Jo Beth Sidden from Bloodhounds, Incorporated. You remember the puppy we discussed two weeks ago? Well, he's ready to leave his mother, and I think you'll be very pleased with him. I'd like to show him to you tonight, but I'm afraid it will be nine or later before I can bring him over. Is that too late? I apologize for the late hour, but I have a list of prospective buyers that has more names than I have puppies. I'll bring all seven so you can literally have the pick of the litter." I tee-heed vacuously and continued.

"Will it be too much of an inconvenience to view the puppies from your driveway? It's best not to handle them too much at this age. Will that be satisfactory?"

"I can manage," he said, sounding somewhat mollified. "Sound your horn and I'll come out to look at them."

"Thank you so much and I'll see you at nine or so," I trilled and hung up.

What the hell? Did the old fart really think I was dumb enough to call him on a phone we all suspected of being bugged and start blabbing about his son's kidnapping?

I saw Wendell Grantham's reflection in the large mirror on the wall in front of me as he entered the hall leading to the bathrooms. My watch said it was ten minutes till noon. I wanted to snag him before dinner and see how Gainey acted this morning with Gloria Steinem. She's Bobby Lee's mother and a good friend. Gainey is such an asshole, I wanted assurances that he was going to treat Gloria right.

I gathered my materials and decided to make two trips this time. As I returned from my first trip, Donnie Ray and Wayne were present. I asked Donnie Ray if he'd carry my second load to the office. I filled his arms and spotted Wendell emerging from the bathroom area. I motioned for him to join me and made my way to Wayne's office.

Wendell stood ramrod straight, I could almost hear his heels click. I asked him how it went this morning.

"Fair, is my assessment," he said after a slight hesitation. "He handles Gloria with confidence and retains all the commands, but he worries me."

"In what way?" I valued Wendell's opinion because he seemed to be a good judge of character.

"I don't mean his filthy speech or his habit of sneering at each of my sentences or explanations. I believe he lacks kindness. Have you ever met a man who wasn't kind?"

"One or two," I said with a sigh. A person can be cruel,

egotistical, and selfish and still have a fondness for animals. I was hoping Gainey was one of them.

"We have a problem, Wendell. You don't think he'll be good to Gloria?"

"It's a feeling. He doesn't jerk her chain or show displeasure when he speaks to her. It seems he knows he's being watched and evaluated and makes all the right moves. I could be letting my dislike for the man color my judgment, but I'm worried."

"So am I," I said truthfully. "Watch him like a hawk. I'd have to have some proof of cruelty toward her to refuse to let him take her Friday. I can't tell his department head we had a feeling he'd abuse Gloria in the future. As far as they're concerned, the purchase is final. We're just spending a week training the new handler as part of the purchase price. It's something I overlooked when my lawyer and my CPA were helping me write the purchase agreement. It *will* be corrected before any additional contracts are signed, you can bet on that."

"I'll watch him," Wendell promised.

I went to the house to freshen up for dinner. When I returned to the common room, I found Jonathan sitting between Jasmine and Carol. The three of them were chatting away like old friends. I sat at the head of the table with Wayne at my left and Cora Simmons at my right.

Cora is fifty-five years old and retired from the postal service. She retired early because of her varicose veins. She's short and squat and weighs about a hundred and sixty pounds. She has tightly curled blue-tinted hair. I'd been reluctant to hire her as a trainer because of her medical condition, but she asked for a month's trial. She turned out to be a natural teacher and she loves the animals.

After she knew me well enough, she confided that her veins weren't a problem. She said if she had stood one more day in the same spot, hearing the inane and repetitive remarks the customers made, she knew she'd do something drastic. She said she'd had dreams of yanking off all her clothes, running through the post office lobby buck naked, and squirting the customers with a water pistol. When her dream changed, and she was holding a real gun, she decided she needed to seek new employment. She never married and is full of mischief and fun.

"How's Sergeant French getting along with Margaret Mitchell?"

"It was love at first sight." She beamed. "I'm really jealous. She hardly notices I'm around anymore. He's a nice man and quite taken with our Jasmine. He's been pumping me all morning about her love life and such."

"What have you been telling him?" I was eating a delicious pork chop, candied yams, green beans, and only one buttery sourdough roll. I'd seen the lemon meringue pies as I filled my plate.

"I told him Jasmine had only three men she really paid any attention to: a college professor, a local disk jockey, and a pro football player who commuted from Atlanta."

"You should've made the football player a wrestler. They have more muscles."

"Well, I didn't want him to feel defeated before he even got started." She and I leaned closer to each other as she whispered. "You can actually see the steam rising from their bodies when they're in close conversation."

I laughed and went to get a piece of pie. Wayne put down his slice of chocolate cake and signed to me. "Did you see the two envelopes I put on your desk? They were in the mailbox when I picked up the mail."

"Where're they from?" I signed.

"They didn't come through the mail. Just have your name on the front."

I remembered. Hank had said P. C. would drop off the

handcuffs. Before I ate my pie, I went over to investigate. The large envelope held the handcuffs and key. The small envelope held several small black bands for the officers to slide over their shields at the funeral. It was nice of Hank to remember them.

After informing everyone that the bands were by the door on the table, I sat down to eat my pie. Jasmine and Carol had left to dress for the funeral. I was cynical enough to wonder if Carol would've attended the services if Gainey hadn't been paying court to her. It seemed her marriage had less of a chance of success than my original estimate. None of the trainers were attending the funeral and I'd given them the afternoon off.

"How's it going?" Jonathan said, as he gave me a big smile and slid into the chair next to mine. "I had chocolate cake."

"I love chocolate cake, but I haven't tasted homemade lemon pie in ages. Did you come up with anything I could start checking or any suggestions?"

"Tim is a nice guy, but I think he's making a mistake in narrowing down his suspects so early. If the sons are guilty, everything will work out, but if they aren't, valuable time's been lost barking up the wrong tree. I think he should check out present and past employees, say, at least five years back. Some guys carry a grudge a mighty long time."

"I'd guess the FBI and GBI would be checking them out," I said.

"Oh, yes, they will. It's routine. I just think Tim shouldn't dismiss them so easily from his investigation."

I finished the pie. While we were talking the common room had emptied. The trainers had gone home and everyone else was dressing for the funeral, I supposed.

"I have to get dressed," I told Jonathan.

"So do I," he said as we started outside. "See you in a few minutes."

21

A Hero Laid to Rest
November 15, Monday, 1 P.M.

After a quick shower, I moved to the bedroom and placed my navy-blue voile two-piece suit on the bed. I tried on the three-inch heels and flexed my calf muscle as I walked back and forth. The bruised area was sore when I poked it, but I didn't think the heels would cripple me for the few hours I'd have to wear them. I donned underwear and the handkerchief-linen white blouse I usually wore with the suit. It would be in the high 80s while we were standing in the hot sun at graveside, and I'd swelter in silk or rayon. When I finished dressing, I combed my hair and applied minimal makeup and a couple of dabs of perfume. I put the essentials into a crushed leather navy blue shoulder-strap bag. I checked my gun, then tossed it and six extra shells into the bag and laid a navy and white silk scarf on top. The tiny scrap of navy-colored velvet ribbon with a froth of navy net veiling shaped to the top of my head was called a hat. Tiny pearl earrings and a pearl necklace completed the ensemble.

I picked up my cloth flats and purse and went out to

the courtyard. Wayne and Donnie Ray had lined up the three vans and had Wayne's truck at the rear. Wayne kept the vehicles washed and polished at all times, but he and Donnie Ray had spent part of the morning putting an extra gleam on their surfaces.

Jonathan would ride with me, along with Jordan and Vaughn. Jasmine would drive her van with Curtis French riding shotgun and Carol and Adam Gainey in folding chairs in the aisle. I hoped Ramon wasn't lurking around the corner spying on the arrangement.

Jasmine was a vision in a simple dark-green dress with light-green piping on the neck and sleeves, but she'd look good in a croaker sack. Even Rosie looked subdued in a black and white check. Carol looked very nice in a powder blue dress with a full skirt and sandals, but it certainly wasn't funeral attire. Everyone was standing in the shade talking, so I told Jonathan, Jordan, and Vaughn to load up. I knew they'd start moving when I cranked the van.

I pulled out at one-thirty on the dot. On Highway 301, our caravan kept a steady speed of forty miles an hour. We had plenty of time, and it seemed inappropriate to speed to a funeral.

"You look sensational," Jonathan said to me.

"So do you," I told him. He hadn't packed his dress uniform to vacation with his brother, but he had brought a lightweight navy suit, white shirt, and gray and blue tie so he could attend church.

"Were you close friends with the slain officer?" he asked.

"Nope. I keep thinking about the last things we said several months ago, and how I planned to get even with her." I told Jonathan about our last meeting.

He gave a sad chuckle. "At least you didn't lose a close friend."

"I feel so damn lousy because I really didn't like her at all," I admitted.

"Hey," he said softly. "Getting killed doesn't make a person a saint."

I grimaced. "Around here it does, especially the way she was killed. I couldn't admit to a local that we didn't get along. The only way she'll be remembered now is with loving kindness, and that's fine with me. I'll agree with them, as a penitence, for thinking badly of her these last seven months."

Jonathan suppressed a smile and shook his head. "You're something else."

We rode in silence for several minutes. Then Jonathan leaned closer to me. "Would you please explain why I received the freeze in the common room earlier today?" He waited for my answer.

I glanced in the rearview mirror and saw that Jordan and Vaughn were deep in conversation, so I guessed they couldn't hear me.

"Jonathan, you live way up there and I live way down here. What if we clicked? It's a sobering thought. I really don't have any time to spare now or in the near future for a romance, even a long-distance one. There're too many problems attached."

"Whoa, hoss, whoa," Jonathan said in haste. "You're talking commitment? Long-range commitment? My thoughts were leaning toward . . . ah . . . "

"A one-night stand?" I supplied with a chuckle. "A little slap-and-tickle? Wham, bam, thank ya, ma'am?"

"Not funny," he said, with pressed lips. "Why don't we just wait and see what happens? Haven't you heard about going with the flow?"

"Let me explain my position. Say we like each other and we get it on several times in the next few days. We screw like minks and have a hell of a good time. You then ride off into the sunset to Eppley with a smile on your face. I'm left here with fading pangs of the ol' libido. This puts another thin coating of hardness on my personality and the way I feel about men. I want to believe that someday love will come knocking, and I don't want to be so hardened and cynical I miss the soft rapping on my heart."

"With your approach, a lover won't get past your gate, much less your door," he said with irony.

"Maybe," I admitted, "but that's the way the ball bounces on my side of the court."

"It stinks," he stated.

I looked to the left and saw the turn coming up to take Fenmore Street all the way to the courthouse. The funeral procession would drive down Main Street so the townspeople could view the many official cars that had traveled from all parts of the state to show respect and solidarity for one of their own. At the end of the line, I pulled in behind a City of Valdosta cruiser. Today people would see an estimated two hundred law-enforcement vehicles making the slow journey to the cemetery. The revolving lights were on and each car was highly polished. All were driven by solemn uniformed men and women thinking about their own mortality. The next time all these vehicles lined up—it could be for them.

Since no church in Collins was big enough to hold all the mourners, we went straight to the cemetery. After the ceremony, I searched the throng for Sheriff Philip Scroggins, who'd been my father's friend and was now mine. I had to get in line. Officers were lined up to pay their respects and shake his hand. When it was finally my turn, we hugged instead of shaking hands.

"Thanks for coming, honey," he said, with the booming voice that always shocked your senses. His eyes were red-rimmed and spoke of sleepless nights.

"Get some sleep," I said with compassion. "He's

behind bars. Please take care of yourself." I moved on to let others express their thoughts.

Later, as I turned onto Bloodhound Lane, I said to Jonathan, "As soon as we unload, I have to make a fast trip to pick up something. Want to come?"

"Sure."

We left the driveway at six twenty-five. I hoped to hell Little Bemis hadn't pounced on the site at one minute past six-fifteen, found the material unclaimed, and taken it with him. Anything's possible with him. I'd never been late at a drop before. Thank God, we were only about eight minutes away.

I turned on Baker's Mill Road and sped down the dirt surface like crazy, kicking up dust behind me so thick my entire rearview was blocked. Jonathan, sitting silently beside me, hadn't asked a single question. I slowed to a crawl when the odometer read just under two miles.

"We're looking for an X made of white adhesive tape on a pine tree at eye level. It's only two inches long. You'll have to look closely."

"Hold it. There it is," said Jonathan, pointing toward a sapling. "I almost missed it."

I reached under the seat and pulled out the pair of jeans I'd placed there earlier. The voile skirt I was wearing would snag if I even passed close to a briar bush.

"Turn your head," I ordered. "I'm not going to risk this skirt in the bushes."

He obediently stared out his window while I stepped out of the skirt and wiggled into the jeans. I'd been wearing my driving flats so it was easier than I'd anticipated.

"All clear," I stated. "Would you mind getting the tape? The path looks clear from here."

"Be glad to."

I loped across the sandy road and jumped across a dry narrow ditch. I stood in front of the first pine tree and turned to make sure it was lined up with the one that had the tape. It looked right. I walked straight back to the third tree and found the black plastic-wrapped package propped against the trunk. Son of a bitch. Little Bemis had come through! My heart danced a couple of extra beats and my gut eased a little. My pessimistic mind kept its thoughts to itself. I made it back to the van unscathed by briar or thorn. After changing back to my skirt, I reversed the van and tossed the package into Jonathan's lap.

"Open it, and we'll see if it's treasure or trash."

"Ve-ry mysterious," he said with amusement. "I hope we don't need my decoder ring. I left it at home along with my spyglass. When I was twelve years old, I had to eat five boxes of cereal in order to get them and then wait six weeks for delivery."

I bit back an angry retort. Little Bemis is unpredictable, so I didn't know if I had anything yet. It was too early to stick my neck out.

Jonathan used a small pocket knife to open the package. He pulled out several pages of a computer printout.

"Let's see." He scanned the top page, snorting as he read the heading.

"Data for the Case of the Kidnapped Caliph? My God, Jo Beth, I'm not believing this!" he roared.

"Has anyone ever told you that you sound exactly like a constipated horse when you make that whinnying sound?" I was striving for composure.

"Sorry," he mumbled as he pulled out his handkerchief and wiped his watery eyes. "I got carried away. Let's see now, there are five pages of land descriptions and real estate, and . . . oh-oh."

I didn't like the sound of that oh-oh. "What?" I said

impatiently. I was now driving through the dust storm I'd created a few minutes earlier. Dust is slow to settle without wind, and I couldn't see a damn thing. I had to slow my speed. "What?" I repeated.

"The last three pages are printouts from NCIC."

"I'll translate for you," I volunteered in a sweet voice. "I'm sure your one-horse town doesn't have anything but antiquated equipment for your police department. It stands for National Crime Information Computer."

"I know what it means, and I use it almost daily," he said, sounding a bit testy. "Your tame lawman is risking his career *and* criminal charges for using the service to help a civilian. This can easily be traced to the source who requested it. You've put your man in the hot seat because of your curiosity. You should be ashamed."

"My source, snitch, informant, or rose by any other name is neither lawman nor government official and is in no danger of getting caught. Trust me."

"I don't believe you," he retorted.

We were within a block of my driveway. As I eased up on the accelerator, I gave him a quick glance. "See, I told you we'd never work out. Look how quickly I was proven correct. You weren't listening closely," I said with anger. "I said *trust me* and you ignored it. Case closed."

We didn't speak again, and upon arriving we parted and went our separate ways to change clothes.

We were a little late for Miz Jansee's supper. The mood at the tables was light because it seemed everyone was trying to put aside the trappings of mourning. Sometimes people try to hide their sorrow with nervous laughter.

I passed on dessert and, while everyone turned their chairs and grouped them around the large television, I went to the house and told Bobby Lee and Rudy they could come over and watch the videotape. I hooked Bobby Lee to the belt of the gold lightweight wool dress I was wearing that had caused Jonathan's eyes to widen when he first saw me in it. It was worth the hundred bucks I'd paid for it. In my profession, I don't get many of those kinds of looks.

With Rudy at my left and Bobby Lee at my right, I returned to the common room to view the videotape of the search for Mary Ann Miles.

22

The Search for Mary Ann Miles
July 13, Tuesday, 10 A.M.

We had been in the midst of a heat wave, the July temperature soaring to 100 degrees every afternoon. About every other day we experienced violent short or prolonged thunderstorms, and the rain turned to steam when it hit the pavement. After the storms the air felt thick enough to slice, and there wasn't a whisper of wind.

I'd just come into the office from a two-hour workout with five puppies. I was sopping wet with sweat and well covered with puppy drool. I'd tossed my clothes into the washer and was standing under a cold shower when I thought I heard the phone. The water felt so damn good I ignored it. The answering machine would handle it. After drying and putting on a terrycloth robe, I walked barefoot into the office and played the message. Hank wanted me to return his call ASAP.

I sighed. Please God, don't let it be a swamp search. My rescue suit seals off the air and I sweat gallons when I wear it. I dialed his number.

"Sheriff Cribbs."

"Please don't say swamp. Anything but swamp. It's just too damn hot," I begged.

"You think it's hot?" he said wearily. "This fan on my desk is absolutely worthless. I'm sticking to my chair, my shirt is sticking to me, and I'm sick of working in pools of sweat. We all should walk out and let the hoodlums take over this town until the voters give us enough money to air-condition the courthouse. This is ridiculous."

"Yes. I saw where the county commissioners were sad that there isn't enough money again this year."

"I just might move my desk over to the annex and share their space," he muttered, sounding in a black mood. "Listen, you read about Mary Ann Miles, the kidnapping?"

"Yeah. Any news? Any clues?" I asked.

"Plenty of news. No clues. None," he said. "We have the creep who kidnapped her. Picked him up less than two hours after he threw her into his truck in broad daylight in front of two witnesses and took off. Deputy Tom Selph was coming in from a call on Turkey Creek Road when he came up behind him, coasting along about ten miles an hour in his truck, acting cool as a cucumber. Tom called in the license plate number to make sure and pulled him over without backup. I scorched his ass about that. Anyway, the fucker is Preston Little, forty-two, works in logging. He'd been stalking her for almost a year now. She finally applied for a restraining order about four months ago. You know from personal experience how much good that does. He's been sitting in the interrogation room off and on since yesterday morning, smiling a creepy smile and not opening his rotten mouth.

"His lawyer made us quit last night at midnight. It gave him six hours of sleep, but we started in again at six this morning. He still hasn't said one cotton-picking word."

"Well," I said for comfort, "you've got him cold. The DA ought to offer the bastard a deal. Life instead of the electric chair, so you can find her and the family will be able to bury her."

"This is where it gets sticky," he said with intense disgust. "One witness is a ten-year-old kid, Billy Jennings, who may have an equal somewhere who can lie as well as he can, but I doubt it. He already has a reputation for telling more whoppers than a United States senator. The other witness, Miz Mabel Deloach, age sixty-nine, doesn't like to wear her glasses in public and didn't have them on when the truck was thirty feet away and she had a ringside seat. It might as well have been three hundred yards, because she couldn't see well enough to make a positive identification. I'm ready to pull my hair out."

"Bobby Don, our esteemed DA, won't make a deal?"

"Absolutely not. He has visions of being on the cover of *True Detectives* next month. A deal would put closure to the crime, and he doesn't want closure. He wants exposure."

"I don't know if the county can take four more years of his boo-boos," I remarked.

Hank chuckled. "Let me tell you why I called. I want to prepare you. I apologize in advance for sending him to you, but he was driving me bananas, and I know you can calm him down."

"Who?" I was suddenly suspicious. I should've caught on when Hank had been so open in discussing the case. He's usually tight as a clam when a case is in progress.

"The fiancé, Fenton Hamilton, age twenty-three. He's been here at the station ever since he heard she was taken. I hope you can convince him to go home and get some sleep. This bastard Little's gonna cave in eventually, they all do. What we find isn't gonna be pretty. This Fenton Hamilton is a nice guy. Convince him there's nothing you can do to help him."

"You son of sea cook," I said, without heat. "You

shouldn't have done that to me. You know how softhearted I am."

"It needs the feminine touch," he replied.

"Get stuffed. When will he be here?" I asked.

"Any minute now. He left the station over twenty minutes ago."

"Hank!" I yelled, but he'd already hung up. Damn him anyway. I went to the bedroom and dressed. I was combing my unruly hair when I heard the harsh *bing-bong* of the first gate's alarm. Jasmine had just moved into her new apartment, but she was out on a drug search with Wayne. I started outside with Rudy and Bobby Lee walking beside me.

When I reached the back door, Donnie Ray was standing outside Wayne's office waiting to see who was driving in. He was a good kid, caught on quick. I was hoping he'd be able to get some good video footage of training under his belt soon. He needed one success to get his jaunty attitude back.

The young man who climbed out of the compact car was about five feet nine inches tall and appeared to be about fifteen pounds overweight. He had dark hair and dark eyes and looked haggard. His hair needed combing, and he could use a bath and fresh clothing. Sitting at the sheriff's office all night must have been nerve-racking.

"Miz Sidden?" he said.

"Call me Jo Beth. Hank called. You're Hamilton?"

"Yes, ma'am. Did Sheriff Cribbs tell you why I've come to see you?"

"He did, and I'm sorry you wasted a trip. You need to be home in bed."

"I can't give up, Miz Sidden. If I give up and go to bed, Mary Ann will die. I need her so much in my life, Miz Sidden. Please, you have to help me. She's still alive, I know it. I'd know if she'd died, Miz Sidden. We have a strong bond of love between us. I'd sense it if the bond was broken. She's alive, Miz Sidden. Please help me."

Tears began to roll down his cheeks, but he didn't seem to notice. Looking at his dirty tearstained face and his earnest manner, my heart spoke first: *You have to help him, he knows she's still alive.* My mind scoffed at such nonsense: *Send him home, you can't do anything. There's nowhere to start.*

When I didn't answer right away, Fenton began talking again.

"Whatever you charge, Miz Sidden, I'll double it. My dad owns Hamilton Hardware. I know he'll lend me the money. I have almost three thousand in the bank. That's yours as soon as I can draw it out. I'll sign a note for the rest and pay you every cent. I promise. Plea—"

"Shut up!" I yelled. After I had his attention, I spoke more softly. "I'll help you, with the following conditions. One—"

"I agree," he butted in. "I'll agree to anything."

"Are you listening to me?" I spoke in a barely audible voice.

"Yes, ma'am, I hear you."

"Don't say another word until you hear me out. Don't mention money again. If I can help, I'll get my fee from the county. If I can't help, it's on the house. I want you to be completely truthful with me. If you lie for any reason, you could get us both in a lot of trouble. Do you understand me? Please answer."

"Yes, ma'am. I'll tell you the truth. I promise."

"Do you have any medical problems? Heart? Diabetes? Breathing problems? Anything at all?"

"No, ma'am. Mary Ann and I are both a few pounds overweight from working long hours in the store. We started walking two weeks ago, five miles a day. We walk at night. Yesterday, Mary Ann decided to walk to work. It's less than two miles, and she's anxious to lose weight fast. We plan on getting married in September. That's when he picked her up. We hadn't seen him for weeks, and it was eight in the morning. We thought it was all right. I'm just overweight. Honest."

"Are you allergic to any medications?"

"Not that I know about," he said.

"Wait here," I told him. I went inside, pulled a desk drawer out, reached all the way to the back to a wadded-up handkerchief. There were four bennies tied up in one corner. Untying the knot, I took out one, retied the knot, stuck the handkerchief in my pocket, and returned to the back porch.

"Have you ever taken a bennie before? It's a form of speed."

"No, ma'am."

"Take this." I pointed to the outside spigot. He stooped, cupped water with his hand, and swallowed.

"It'll kick in in about ten minutes. It's powerful. Do you and Mary Ann live together?"

"She stays over at my place occasionally. She did last night, but she still officially lives at home with her mother. Her father's dead."

"Does she sleep in a nightgown? T-shirt? What?"

"Usually a shorty nightgown," he answered.

"I want you to drive home under the speed limit and not jump any lights. You're now under the influence of an illegal substance, and if you're tested it'll show up in your blood. Understand? When you get home, take a bath and change clothes. Dress in heavy jeans or chinos, heavy walking shoes, and a long-sleeved shirt. Bring a denim jacket. Wear heavy socks, and bring an extra pair. Put the nightgown Mary Ann slept in last night in a gallon-sized Ziploc bag to retain her scent. Have you eaten since yesterday?"

"No, ma'am."

"When you're cleaned up and on the way to meet me, stop somewhere and eat a full breakfast. If you're gonna be any help to me, you have to have food in your stomach. Do you understand?"

"Yes, ma'am."

"Will you please call me Jo Beth?"

"Yes m—yes, Jo Beth."

"Thank you. When you finish everything I've outlined, I'll meet you at the gate of the county's impound lot, three blocks from the courthouse on Gorton Street. Do you know where that is?"

"Yes, I do."

"Don't tell anyone where you're going, and don't say anything at all to any reporters. Okay?"

"Yes, Jo Beth."

"Get going, and no speeding!"

"Thanks, Jo Beth." He forced himself to walk to the car, knowing I was watching. God help us if he tore through town, high on the speed I'd supplied. It was stupid to let him go with me, but he was so broken up, it would be hell for him to just sit and wait. At least this way he felt he was doing something to help. I have a soft spot for lovers. The world needs more of them. I went inside to call Hank. They had to get him out of the interrogation room. When he came on the line, I told him I was going to try to help Fenton.

"Do you think there's any chance?" he asked.

"Right now, I'd say slim to none, but I've got to try. You knew that when you sent him over here."

"Guilty as charged," he said, sounding more cheerful.

"Keep the GBI off my back, if you have to call them."

"Will do. Call if you need me. I didn't mention to them that I sent Fenton to see you."

"Let's keep it that way. What was Little's appearance like when he was picked up?"

"Freshly showered and shaved. Clean clothes. Not a

trace of Mary Ann on him. Two deep scratches about two inches long on the left side of his face. Had flesh-tone Band-Aids over them, and an antiseptic had been applied."

"When you checked where he lives, was the shower or tub wet?"

"Nope. Bone dry. Wherever he went, it wasn't back to his apartment."

"Does anybody know where he's currently employed?"

"Next-door neighbor said he was hauling for Champion International. The nearest branch office is in Fargo."

"See if he's currently employed, and if he's been hauling anywhere near where he was picked up."

"I'm way ahead of you. Called them over an hour ago. We should be hearing any minute."

"Were any dirty clothes found in his apartment?"

"A whole pile of them. It was a pigsty."

"Get someone to pick out the smelliest object they can find—socks, pants, T-shirt, whatever—and bag it. Is his truck in impound?"

"Yep. But there isn't a thing in it. It's been cleaned, and recently. Butch tells me the mud on it is from the past twenty-four hours. He must've washed and vacuumed the inside before the crime."

"Great. At least we don't have a lot of trips to weaken the scent. Hank, can you have the ripe article of Little's and Deputy Tom Selph at the impound when I get there? I have to load the van."

"They'll be there," he promised.

"Hank, I'm getting a slight tingling behind my ears. In case our esteemed DA changes his mind, don't let him offer Little a deal for the next few hours. Okay?"

"I gotcha covered. Good luck."

"See you."

I called Wayne's office and Donnie Ray answered.

"Have you ever loaded the van by yourself for a search?"

"Once, when we went after the cat," he said with disgust.

I smiled in remembrance. "This is the real McCoy. Load up for a search. I need Caesar and Mark Anthony. Fill up six canteens and the five-gallon water jug for the dogs. Don't forget their water dishes. I need the full pack: rescue suit, rifle, shoe guards, and skate key. Anything else?"

"You didn't mention deer jerky," he said with pride.

"Good man. Load your camera gear. Have I forgotten anything?"

"I don't think so," he said after a moment.

I pulled out the map of Dunston County that was plotted in five-mile grids for search purposes. I grabbed a drawing compass and went to the bedroom. I checked the .32, picked up six extra bullets, and took two pairs of thick socks. I yelled for Bobby Lee. I hunted for my denim jacket in case I was caught in the woods overnight. He appeared from the kitchen area, bumping into the bedroom doorjamb in his haste.

"You want to go?" I asked him. His whole body went into motion as he wagged his tail vigorously.

"Go get your long and your short leash," I told him. He took off for the back porch like he'd been shot.

I met Rudy in the doorway to the hall, scratched his ears, and went to check the water dish. I left a note for Jasmine and Wayne. Bobby Lee was on the back porch proudly clutching both leashes, with drool dripping from his jaws. I wrapped the long leash around my waist, hooked him up to the short one, and attached it to my belt.

"Heel, sweetheart, we're going for a ride," I told him

with a smile. He was a wonderful puppy, so full of life, and had never glimpsed the world he lived in.

Donnie Ray had the rescue van on the tarmac in the courtyard. The water hose was running into the five-gallon jug. I checked, and everything seemed to be loaded, even my gloves, which I'd forgotten to mention.

"I'll watch the hose. Grab a chair for yourself. We're picking up a passenger in a few minutes."

I loaded Bobby Lee, strapped him into his safety harness between the front seats, and fed him a piece of deer jerky. Donnie Ray climbed into the back, and we were ready to roll.

I stopped at Hardee's about a mile from town. "Get six big roast beefs and lots of packets of horseradish sauce while I go to the bathroom," I told Donnie Ray, and gave him a twenty. When I returned, he'd put the sandwiches inside my pack.

When I drove past the gate at the impound yard, Deputy Tom Selph was leaning against his car talking to Cuthford Jethro Layton, the county farm agent, known to some as Butch and to the ladies as Lothario. Deputy Tom Selph looked like an anemic shoe salesman standing alongside his tanned good looks. Tom is short, thin, and wiry, with sunburned skin and thick glasses. He certainly wasn't what you'd expect to see arriving at a store robbery or burglary call. He's a far cry from the typical good ol' boy deputy of south Georgia.

I pulled the van into an open space, and Donnie Ray and I walked over to join them.

"Hi, Tom, Butch," I said in greeting.

Tom tipped his hat and Butch winked, grinned, and started to close the gap between us.

"Stop right there, you octopus. Don't come an inch closer," I said crossly. "I haven't got time to wrestle with you this morning."

He pretended to feel hurt. "You wound me, Jo Beth."

"I'll hand you your goodies in a paper sack if you mess with me," I said. He loved it. He folded his arms and leaned on Tom's vehicle, giving me another lavish grin and salacious leer.

"Tom, can you find out the exact time you called in for a license plate check on Little's truck?"

"The dispatcher'll have it; I'll check," he said, and went to his radio.

I looked at Butch. "Which one's Little's truck?" I was glancing around the lot.

"The green one behind you," Butch said, pointing.

I turned and walked toward the beat-up dark-green truck, nosed into a parking space next to the equipment shed. Donnie had gone for his camera and was back to taping as he walked toward me.

Butch had joined us and was eyeing the camera. "Is he shooting a video?" He looked surprised.

"Yes," I answered, "and stay out of his way." I was looking at the tires on the truck. They looked new. The grooves between the threads were deep and held packed mud level with the surface. I went back to the van and hooked up Bobby Lee so he could get some air. It was already too hot in the van for comfort. I opened my pack and took out a pint-size Ziploc bag and my small penknife.

At the rear of Little's truck, I crunched the bag open and scraped dried mud from the crevices into it, using the knife.

As usual Bobby Lee was staying close to my right leg. Squatting there behind the truck put me level with Bobby Lee's head so it seemed we were both interested in the tires. He was sniffing as if he was enjoying the earthy aroma in front of his nose. On an impulse, I thrust the bag under his nose and said, "Seek!" He stiffened his whole body and started eagerly sniffing the tire down to the ground. He reversed his position, tugging on the leash, and started on the path of tire prints the truck had cut into the damp earth, softened by yesterday's rain. I turned and let him have slack on the leash. His nose was three inches off the ground, following the precise path of the indented ruts he couldn't see. He tugged urgently. I went forward with him, increasing my speed.

At the gate, he followed the gentle arc of the ruts to the asphalt of the paved street, turned left, and continued to travel on the hardtop. I was so engrossed in his amazing performance, I forgot that cars have the right-of-way out here on the street. A car stopped within a few feet and the driver sat patiently waiting to see what the idiot leading the dog would do. I came out of my trance and hauled up on the leash before we walked into the car's grille. I threw the driver a wave and a quick smile of apology and tugged Bobby Lee over to the safety of the grassy verge. The driver stared curiously at us as he drove slowly by.

I knelt and hugged my puppy and told him how marvelous and gifted he was, unashamed of the tears brimming over my eyes and making tracks down my cheeks. I was stunned with his ability to track, my nineteen-week-old miracle. I rose and said "Heel" and started back to the van.

Donnie Ray had been behind us with the camera. I'd learned to ignore the fact that he was filming me. When he'd started a few weeks ago, I'd found myself glancing toward the camera and not facing the person I was speaking to. When I'd seen the results on the TV screen— after laughing until I cried—I vowed never, but never, to look at the camera again. I was getting better at pretending it wasn't there.

I closed the bag containing the mud scrapings and tossed it into the van. I grabbed the grid map and compass and walked over to Tom, standing at the rear of his car watching us.

"Did that pup just do what I think he did?" Tom asked casually as he propped his foot on the back bumper.

"He did indeed," I said softly in wonder, as I spread the map on top of his trunk. I was studying it, my mind reeling, trying to figure out my next move.

I heard Tom say, "Isn't that right?"

I raised my head. "Sorry," I said absentmindedly. "I was thinking. What did you say?"

"He wasn't scent-tracking, he was following the tracks visually, right?" Tom raised deer and bear dogs, with Rhodesian Ridgebacks mixed with bluetick hounds and God knows what other choices. He knew a lot about scent trailing. I'd heard many of his tales of bear hunts and the prowess of his animals.

"He's blind," I told him.

"You're shittin' me," he said.

"Nope." I went back to the map. In my peripheral vision, I saw Tom move and glanced up just as he made a fake jab a foot from Bobby Lee's face. Bobby Lee didn't flinch, of course. He just sat quietly thinking whatever he thought about when he was sitting quietly.

Tom gave me a sheepish look for doubting my word. "He really *is* blind. He was scent-trailing, not tracking visually. How old is he?"

"Nineteen weeks."

"I'll be goddamned. You've got a good one."

"I do indeed," I agreed with pride.

I'd had no idea he had any ability at all. For the past month, I'd fastened him to my side because he seemed to love it. I'd done it out of sympathy for his blindness. I didn't know he'd absorbed the verbal commands I'd used to train the grown dogs. He had obviously listened and soaked up everything he heard. My God, he was brilliant! I cursed the tiny defect in his optic nerves that caused his blindness. Then I realized that fact just might be the cause of his brilliance. It still hadn't fully registered in my brain just how accomplished he was. It would take me awhile to find out. I knew one thing: I was going to give him his chance before I ever tried to put Caesar and Mark Anthony on the search pattern. He deserved it.

23

Young Pup Gets His First Break
July 13, Tuesday, Noon

I stared at the map. "Did you get the time you requested the license plate run yesterday?"

"Nine-fifty A.M.," Tom answered.

"Can you get Hank on your radio for me?"

"I can try."

I saw Fenton pull his compact onto the graveled space outside the fenced compound where the posted signs directed visitors to park. He locked his car and came toward the gate, carrying a small bundle under his arm. His jacket, extra socks, and Mary Ann's nightie, I presumed. His walk was brisk, and, when he was near enough, I could see he was bright-eyed and bushy-tailed. The speed had kicked in. He was alert and in control.

"Did you eat?" I asked.

"Yes."

"Good. If you'll wait over by my van, I'll be there shortly."

He didn't hesitate. So far, so good. He was doing what I

told him. The real test would come later. Then I'd know if I'd been foolish to include him in the search.

"I have the sheriff on the line," Tom yelled.

I walked around the car and accepted the outstretched mike.

"Hank, what time did the call come in to the station about the kidnapping?"

"Ten minutes after eight," he replied promptly.

"How much time did it take for them to call it in?"

"We estimate fifteen minutes. Miz Deloach walked back to her place, had to find her key, et cetera. She walks real slow. Has a bad hip. She had the boy with her."

"Did either one of them notice how Little drove after getting Mary Ann in the truck?"

"She's no help. All she saw was a blur. Billy mentioned handcuffs and a machine gun. Said the man had a long beard and took off like a rocket," Hank replied wryly. "Take a guess. Neither one's worth a damn as a credible witness."

"Thanks, Hank. That's all for now. Talk to you later."

I got Tom's attention.

"I'd like you to drive to the exact location where Mary Ann was abducted. When we start timing the trip, I want you to drive like you think Little would've driven. Fast start, maybe, for a few blocks, then watching the speed to keep from being obvious. Drive to the spot where you picked him up. Use the same roads you think he took. Time your trip and I'll be doing the same. Got it?"

"Gotcha," he said lazily, with a small tight smile.

"Fine." I turned on my heel and walked to my van. He resented taking the simplest orders from me. I absolutely refuse to sugarcoat them and phrase all my requests as suggestions and simper daintily to relax their damn egos. If a fellow male had said the same thing, it wouldn't have bothered him at all.

Tom pulled around me and turned left at the gate. I backed up, went forward through the gate, turned left, and stopped after several feet. I was getting the hang of what shots Donnie Ray wanted to have for continuity in his video. He ran up, jumped in the back, and yelled, "Go!"

I followed Tom for a few blocks before Fenton spoke.

"You're making a videotape of this?" His voice was strained.

"We'll be training classes of law enforcement officers in a few months," I explained. "They'll handle the search dogs we've raised and trained. We need these videos to help teach them. Regardless of the outcome of this search, I'll let you—and Mary Ann too, I hope—decide if you want the film shown as a training tape. If this was a sanctioned search by the sheriff's department, your permission wouldn't be needed. As this is on spec, I'm not sure if I need your permission. I didn't stop to check with my lawyer. In any case, you have my word that you can make a yea-or-nay decision. Okay?"

"Thank you." He sounded grateful.

"You're welcome. Donnie Ray, look in my pack and find the stopwatch. It's in a small green zippered bag."

I glanced at Fenton. "There's a pad and pencil on the dash. Get it, and let's do some figuring."

When he was ready, I said, "Mary Ann was taken at seven-fifty-five. Deputy Selph pulled Little over on Turkey Creek Road at nine-fifty. What's the total time in minutes?"

"One hundred and fifteen minutes."

"Now comes the hard part. I'm trying to establish the perimeter of the search by using time and mileage."

"I understand that," he said.

"We're going to do some estimating on the time that Little took to do certain things. I speak a lot of times before I think. I'm probably gonna cause you pain with my suppositions. I'm taking you with me in spite of my better judgment. If you think you won't be able to handle it, say so; I'll stop and let you out. You can catch a cab back to your car."

"I can handle anything to get her back alive. She's still alive. I know it!"

I sighed. I decided to give him the easier scenario first. The second one would be a killer-diller.

"I want you to visualize a scene and walk through it with me. What we need is the total time consumed. Are you ready?"

I saw his nod.

"Visualize yourself hurrying, half running up some steps, unlocking a door, going inside and stripping off all your clothes. You put them in a bundle so you can throw them away later. You shave and shower. You clean two deep scratches on your face, treat them with an antiseptic, and put on three Band-Aids. You dress in clean clothes. You look around, making sure you have the wrapping for the Band-Aids and all your dirty clothes. You go out the door, lock it, and hurry to your truck. What's your guess on the time consumed?"

I'd heard his short intake of breath when I mentioned the scratches, but he didn't speak, and I continued with the scenario without pausing. I waited in silence. We were now passing through the suburbs of Balsa City. Small farms, tiny shacks stacked together on small bits of land, large estates with fences, lots of lawns, and imposing houses. They were mingled as if some giant hand had set them down in the wrong sequence.

Fenton surprised me by taking his time and giving the question some thought. "I'd say, if he were quick and well-coordinated, he could do everything you mentioned in ten to twelve minutes. I've only seen Little three times in the past year, once up close and twice from a distance. I got the impression from his actions that he's clumsy. I could be wrong, but I think he'd take longer, as much as fifteen or twenty minutes."

"Donnie Ray?" I looked at him in the rearview mirror. I knew he'd been following the conversation and making his own guess.

"Not under fifteen minutes. No way. Fifteen is the absolute minimum." He sounded positive.

"Well, I don't shave," I told them, "so I'll have to go with fifteen. I thought it would take longer, but majority rules. Subtract fifteen minutes from our one hundred fifteen, and we have one hundred minutes."

Tom slowed and pulled to the side of the road. I pulled in behind him and stopped. He walked back to my window.

"Right here," he said. "I'll start timing as soon as I scratch off. Can you keep up?"

I swallowed a barbed retort and gave him a winsome smile. "I'll try. Don't slow down because you think you're losing me. I'll manage."

As he walked back to his car, I hissed at Donnie Ray, "Wedge yourself between my seat and the wall of the van. Turn sideways."

"I'm okay," he replied.

"Just do it, dammit!" I yelled.

"Okay, okay," he said as he scrambled behind the seat. I cranked the van and floored it. Tom was fifty yards ahead of me and widening the gap every second. I lost another twenty yards on the first turn, but after that it was no contest. After several blocks, Tom slowed to the posted forty-miles-per-hour speed limit, and I stayed a few yards behind him.

"I trust you activated the stopwatch when we took off."

"I forgot," Donnie Ray replied in a small voice.

"Shit!" I was disgusted. I knew Tom was clocking the time, and I didn't want him to know the three of us couldn't manage to push the button on a stopwatch.

"I have a stopwatch feature on my watch," Fenton

said. "I decided to time our trip also. We have the correct starting time."

"Good man," I said. I looked in the mirror and caught Donnie Ray's eye. "You better be glad Fenton was on the ball and saved your bacon, and I don't have to admit to that egotistical macho deputy that we didn't have the time clocked."

"Thanks, Fenton," Donnie Ray said. "Jo Beth would've skint me alive. I owe you, man."

Fenton nodded and said, "You're welcome."

I dreaded what came next. It wasn't going to get easier. I might as well get it over with.

"We now have to decide how long it took Little to move Mary Ann out of the truck, place her where he held her, and return to the truck."

It was the best I could do to spare Fenton. I knew the three of us were imagining the horrors she'd faced. There was no way we could estimate the time frame accurately. We had no clues, either to his intentions or to the depth of his depravity.

Again, Fenton surprised me. He spoke calmly and seemed to ponder each statement to see if he'd phrased the words correctly.

"I know both of you are picturing sexual acts: rape and debasement. Only about half of all stalkers have rape and degradation as their ultimate goals. These are the ones usually known by their victims: ex-husbands and ex-boyfriends, for example. Mary Ann and I did some reading on this subject, trying to get a handle on what makes this type of creep do what he does. We came to the conclusion that this guy falls into the other category. Little is the type who will end up saying that God told him to punish her, or a purple ghost appeared at the foot of his bed and said she had to die for unspecified sins. Does any of this make sense to either of you?"

"What specific actions of his made you come to this conclusion?" I phrased my question carefully. He was doing fine, and I didn't want to derail him.

"I never heard him speak, but on two different occasions Mary Ann remembered a phrase he used. He told her she had to be punished, among other things. Mostly, the times he got close to her—before we realized how dangerous he was—she said he didn't make sense. His sentences weren't structured. He was just babbling."

"So you think he's a nut." I wondered if this made Little more or less a creature of nightmares.

"No. We think he's a religious nut. That seems to be the most dangerous kind, if we read our facts correctly."

I could hear the desolate chill in his voice and knew he was visualizing things too horrible to imagine.

"I don't know if they apprised you of this fact, but it's my understanding that, as of an hour ago, Little hadn't opened his mouth during his interrogation. This tells me he still has some control over his actions. Another thing: He cleaned up and returned quickly. He knew he'd been seen, but he had no way of knowing the witnesses would turn out to be unreliable. He knew he'd be the only suspect. Still, he must've planned carefully for his return. I don't know about you, but this says to me that he isn't completely over the hill. Of course, he has to be insane to even attempt something like this."

"What do you mean the witnesses are unreliable?" Fenton's voice rose during his question.

Oh, boy, they hadn't told him. Me and my big mouth.

"It seems neither one is totally positive of their identification."

"They were there! They saw him take her!" He was beginning to panic.

"Calm down," I cautioned. "I merely meant they're not

ideal witnesses. The elderly lady wasn't wearing her glasses, and the boy has a reputation for telling tall tales." I was crawfishing away from telling him the brutal truth: that neither testimony was worth a plugged nickel in a court of law.

"I see," he answered. I glanced his way. He was staring out the window. We were now on a heavily traveled dirt-packed road called Turkey Creek, a main county connection running from the outskirts of Balsa City to the Gilsford County line. It was used by farmers, hunters, and the local timber industries, and also by the very few who lived out here in the flatwoods surrounded by planted slash pines. There were many sets of ruts, some cut deeply by heavy logging trucks. The ground was still soft from yesterday's rain. Good scent trailing conditions, but too much time had passed. Yesterday's rains, which came after Little used this road, could easily have scattered the scent or blown it into the next county. I had only a faint hope the dogs could find a trail.

On a long straight stretch, Tom pulled over and stopped. I parked behind him. As we left the van, I pocketed a couple of Kleenex and stepped off into the heavy cover of the thick brush for a pit stop. When I returned to the trio, they were standing in a loose semicircle, not having much to say. I hooked up Bobby Lee and joined them, carrying the grid map, compass, pencil, and pad. I spread the map on Tom's trunk. Tom and Fenton moved closer, while Donnie Ray went back for his camera.

"I didn't collect any prizes in school for math," I told them, "so follow along and correct me if I stray. We've already established that Little was missing for one hundred and fifteen minutes." I said it mostly for Tom's benefit. "We've deducted fifteen minutes for Little's bath, changing clothes, et cetera. We'll also deduct twenty minutes for the time he spent in getting Mary Ann out of the truck and confining her." We hadn't decided on a time earlier, but when Fenton didn't speak up I decided to proceed.

"This leaves eighty minutes that Little was missing. Tom, what was the amount of time you clocked getting out here?"

"Thirty-nine minutes," he replied.

"Fenton?"

"About forty seconds more."

"Let's use forty minutes. We know we can't be exact. So, subtracting forty minutes for travel, we still have forty minutes unaccounted for from where we are now. We'll divide by two, because he had to go and come back in that time frame. If we're close on our estimates, we have Mary Ann twenty minutes away from us. That's within ten miles, driving thirty miles an hour."

I waited for comments, searching their faces for any dissent.

"He was driving about ten miles an hour when I came up behind him here yesterday," Tom reminded me.

"This is a long stretch of straight road," I reasoned. "He could've spotted you and simply taken his foot off the gas. By the time you came up behind him, he could've been creeping along at ten miles per hour. It's possible, isn't it?"

He shrugged his scrawny shoulders. "Anything's possible," he said skeptically. He didn't want to commit to any plan, was my guess. That way he could act superior and find fault later if we failed. His attitude burnt my butt.

"Well," I replied with studied ease, "since this is my little red wagon, and I'm pulling it without being sanctioned by my contractor, I'll just go with these figures, if it's all right with you, Fenton. Seems like no one else is busting their rump looking for Mary Ann. What do you say?"

"I say we go with your figures and to hell with the county," Fenton said, glaring at Tom.

Tom bit back a comment. He glanced at the ground, and I could almost see the wheels turning. Hank had sent him along to help, so his ass was covered. "Hey," Tom replied, cutting his flinty eyes toward me. "I'm just along for the ride. It's your decision."

"Good man," I said, mocking him. I folded the map, picked up my compass, pad, and pen, and walked to the van with Fenton beside me. He opened the door.

"I'm going to be working with Bobby Lee. Donnie Ray will be filming. If Bobby Lee picks up a scent and we start forward, follow us in the van. Stay back far enough that if he has to backtrack, you won't be in his path. Okay?"

"I understand. Does he have a chance?" He wanted hope.

"Only God knows, Fenton," I said, giving him an enigmatic smile.

I switched leads, putting on the long lead so Bobby Lee would have freedom of movement. I gave Bobby Lee a strip of deer jerky, then opened the bag of mud scrapings from Little's tires. Sweat dripped into my eyes and stung them. I wiped my forehead with the back of my hand. We were gonna roast out here in the sun. It must've been 85 degrees already. I opened the rear door looking for a cap. Only one hung on the peg, a present from Wayne. He enjoys giving me caps with obvious sexist statements printed on the front, just to tease me. This one read, *I traded my wife for this hat. Boy, I made a great deal!* I put it on and knelt in front of Bobby Lee.

I added a few drops of water from my canteen to the dried mud, closed the bag, and shook it. I handed the water canteen to Fenton.

"Keep it handy. It's heating up."

I stood and walked back to the van, took another canteen out, and hooked it over my shoulder. I tipped the five-gallon jug of water, filled Bobby Lee's water dish, and placed it in front of him. He greedily lapped it dry. I walked by Tom's vehicle, ignoring him. If he didn't have the foresight to carry water in his trunk, he could just dehydrate.

Bobby Lee walked by my side, a foot from my right shoe. His radar was working fine. He padded through the soft clay and dirt mixture, happy as a clam. I knelt, opened the bag, pushed the mud from the bottom closer to the opening, and thrust it under his nose. I placed another piece of jerky on my glove. He took one chomp and swallowed. I presented the mixture again.

"Seek, Bobby Lee, seek."

I stepped back, closed the bag, and slipped it in my pocket. Bobby Lee began the classic search pattern: nose to the ground, moving his head back and forth, ears flapping, drool dripping, walking in figure-eight loops to cover the ground.

I mentally recited a brief mantra: *Let him find the truck's spoor. Let him succeed. Amen.* It's miraculous when a bloodhound can find one particular scent among hundreds—possibly thousands—identify it, and follow its path. Bobby Lee was widening his circled loops. I had him on the right side of the road, where I hoped Little had driven on his trip out to wherever he'd taken Mary Ann. He had been arrested coming back on this road on the left side. If Bobby Lee didn't discover a scent here, we weren't completely dead in the water. He still might find it across the road where we could backtrack. If he succeeded on this side, it would reinforce our theory that this was the path Little had traveled.

With Bobby Lee ranging sideways as much as forward, I had no difficulty keeping up with him. For me, it was hardly more than a stroll. I was about to pull out the bag to reinforce the scent memory when he went rigid for a second. Then he began to pull on the long lead, hurrying forward in a straight motion, straining against the harness.

Damn! It just occurred to me. I'd failed to tell Fenton to take a mileage reading before we started forward. We couldn't use time any longer for measurement. We'd now be using the distance we traveled. I hated to call Bobby Lee off his search just when he seemed to have locked onto a trail. I gave Bobby Lee the command to rest. I still was marveling over the fact that he responded to all the commands. I hadn't been aware that he even knew them. He did what I call the "excited jiggles." He was dancing in a small place, doing some turns, and quivering with excitement. Then he reluctantly plopped his butt on the ground exactly like a seasoned pro when called off a promising scent.

I looked back and motioned for Fenton to advance closer. Donnie Ray stopped filming and started back toward us. I told Bobby Lee to heel, and we went back to meet Fenton.

"I forgot to tell you to check the mileage before we started," I said in disgust. "How far do you think we've come?"

"Not quite two-tenths of a mile," he said, glancing at the pad in his hand. "We'll be using miles, not minutes, from now on."

"Well, that answers two of my questions," I said. I wanted to praise him for his alertness. "One, the distance traveled, and two, you don't need another speed pill just yet. Thanks."

"I have a heavily vested interest in the outcome of this search. I'll do all I possibly can to help." His words held a world of meaning. My heart went out to him.

"Yes, you do," I agreed. "I'm going to try a shortcut."

Donnie Ray had walked back to the van, opened the

back, and was drinking from a canteen. When he heard me say "shortcut," he unlatched the van's back door and sat, dangling his legs outside and resting the camera on the floor of the van.

"It's called leapfrogging," I explained to Fenton. "We'll load and ride to the next road with you driving. Past the road, we'll try to pick up the scent track again. If we can, great, we've saved time. If we can't, we go back where we started and try to pick it up there."

"Sounds good," he said.

"Donnie Ray!" He came around the van. "Go back and explain to our shadow what we're gonna try. Tell him to look closely for a road, path, anywhere a truck could leave the road. If he spots anything we miss, tell him to hit the siren to get our attention. Be nice, but be sure he understands and acknowledges his understanding."

"Gotcha," he said, loping off to pass on the message.

I told Bobby Lee to load up and slid after him. I sat quietly, drank from the canteen, and tried not to think about losing the scent, or what we'd find if we didn't. It was almost one o'clock. Our destination could be just around the corner or ten miles away. It was up to Bobby Lee now.

24

Redemption Depends on Faith
July 13, Tuesday, 1 P.M.

I turned, knelt in the seat, opened my pack, and pulled out two roast beef sandwiches. I groped until I had a handful of horseradish and barbecue sauce packets.

"How about a sandwich?" I asked Fenton.

"No, thanks."

"You sure? There's plenty. We bought six. It may be a long afternoon."

"I ate breakfast a little over an hour ago, I told you," he replied, sounding defensive.

"I didn't question your statement then." I unwrapped a sandwich, squeezed horseradish sauce on the bun, and reached for my knife in the glove compartment. "But I think we should discuss it now. It's natural that you wouldn't have much of an appetite, being up all night and worried. But when I told you it was important not to lie, I wasn't just whistling Dixie. Let's just suppose you were fibbing about breakfast. Now you feel locked into the lie and couldn't possibly be hungry an hour later."

I started dressing the other side of the bun.

"If you really didn't eat breakfast, your stomach has to be totally empty. Twenty-four hours without food. I can tell by your complexion you don't have even a nodding acquaintance with the sun. It's July out there, Fenton. If we have to follow a bloodhound into these woods, and possibly the swamp, you'll never make it in this heat. The sun will flatten you in less than an hour. Determination will take you only so far; then you need energy. If you collapsed, we'd have to stop and administer first aid. In stopping, there's the possibility we could lose Mary Ann. It's up to you."

Fenton sat in the driver's seat beside me, sweating. His extra weight was a liability in the heat. He silently held out his hand for a sandwich. "Sorry," he said. "Just the thought of food makes me nauseous."

"Need any horseradish or barbecue sauce?"

He gave a slight shudder. "No, thanks, I'll eat it plain."

Donnie Ray scooted into the van from the rear and reached for a sandwich.

"Hand me another one," I told Donnie Ray, "and don't you dare squeal on me to Wayne. *Comprende?*"

"Mum's the word," he said with amusement.

I cut the sandwich into quarters and held one portion under Bobby Lee's nose. He took it daintily from my hand and swallowed it in one gulp. For a puppy, he'd shown marvelous restraint when he smelled the food. He sat with dignity and only sniffed and quivered in moderation. I couldn't enjoy my food with him only inches away. We feed each dog an expertly balanced diet that could easily bankrupt a millionaire. Fresh ground beef, the best puppy chow, boiled eggs, cottage cheese, cod liver oil, and vitamin supplements, and on Wednesdays we mix in tomato juice. Wayne would chew me out for feeding Bobby Lee junk food.

"Feel like running one back for our escort, Donnie Ray?"

"Not really."

"Neither do I." I took another bite while I fed Bobby Lee. "Let's roll," I said to Fenton. "You and Donnie Ray check the left. I'll take the right. Drive slowly. It doesn't have to be a road. Look for truck ruts, bent bushes, any places where a vehicle could navigate. With four-wheel drive, you'd be surprised what you can push through."

"You think Little's wreck has four-wheel drive?" Donnie Ray mumbled around a mouthful of food.

I remembered the battered truck. "Good point," I said.

Donnie Ray opened the metal cabinet between the seats and the animal cages and slid out a small ice chest. It held six cold cans of Diet Coke.

"Coke, anyone?" He passed one to me over Bobbie Lee's head.

I passed the first one to Fenton and snapped my fingers impatiently for mine.

"You had them hidden," I accused him.

"You would've drunk both of yours on the trip out here," he explained. "Then you wouldn't have had one for lunch. See how thoughtful I am?"

"I'll forgive you this time," I said with feeling, "because it's cold and delicious, and I forgot to tell you to bring any, but I won't forget your insubordination."

"Uh-oh."

"Just kidding," I said, laughing. "Thanks, partner."

"Sure."

We were traveling about twenty miles an hour. We had our eyes glued to the edges of the road and the ditch, watching for any opening. I'd taken the last bite of sandwich in my mouth when I spotted a small culvert with an overgrown three-path road to the right. I punched Fenton on the arm and pointed. He pulled over and stopped.

I glanced to the opposite side and saw that the road

didn't continue. It wasn't a timber company's grid road, which usually covers a five-mile-square area. The three-path had tall grass between the ruts, slightly bent. Someone had been on the road in the past couple of days. I wasn't an expert. The grass could've been bent yesterday, two days ago, or a couple of hours ago. I couldn't tell.

I pulled on my gloves, picked up the Coke, and climbed out of the van, telling Bobby Lee to unload. I hooked him to my belt and walked to the front of the van. Pulling open the bag of mud, I stopped suddenly and stared at the ground.

"Donnie Ray, front and center!" I could hear him scrambling out the back. He appeared at my side.

"Take a sandwich back to Tom. Ask him to call Hank and find out when we're gonna see that article of clothing from Little's apartment, and hurry."

He took off, and I walked back to Fenton's window.

"Do me a favor. Check Caesar and Mark Anthony's water. If they need any, there's a five-gallon jug in the back."

"Sure."

I inspected the tracks in the soft dirt in front of the van. A vehicle had pulled into this small turnoff and had also backed out. There were two distinct sets of tracks, and both looked like the same tire tread. If it had been Little, why had he backed up? I looked down the small road and saw it made a turn to the left within a few yards. I walked to the middle of the road, Bobby Lee was heeling a foot from my right shoe and he was unconcerned. It was time for a decision. I wanted to give Bobby Lee his chance, but I couldn't expect him to be so advanced that I could switch scents on him. If I went with Little's clothes or Mary Ann's nightgown, I stood a chance of confusing him. If, however, I put him back on the mud scraping scent, I was reinforcing the original scent track.

Donnie Ray arrived back breathless and sweating. "Sheriff Cribbs says there was a bad head-on collision out on Highway Three-oh-one. He hasn't had a spare man to send for the clothing. He's sorry. It'll be another hour or so."

"Shit," I mumbled with emphasis. Fenton had joined us.

"What's going on?" Anxiety made his voice crack. Donnie Ray moved away for his camera.

"Wait till Donnie Ray gets back," I said. I lit a cigarette; we were in the open. A soft breeze was making the foliage rustle. The two of us stood in silence until Donnie Ray came around the van, his head behind the camera, taping as he approached.

"Shut off the camera. We have to talk. Let's see if I can give you a capsule version. So far, Bobby Lee's been tracking Little's truck from the mud I scraped off the tires and doing an excellent job. I have a hunch, a gut feeling, that this is going to be the road Little turned on. It could ramble through the woods for miles, or it could peter out very soon. I think it stops a few hundred feet after entering. I also think this is where Little went in, but he had to back out because there's nowhere to turn the truck. It's the only logical conclusion from viewing these tracks."

I walked them out to the middle of the road, so they could see where he backed and then went forward.

"If my assumptions are correct, it means that Little walked to his destination carrying or supporting Mary Ann, and we're fairly close. He probably carried her. Intimidation and showing how powerful he is, and her helplessness, could've made him make the effort. Here's the problem: If he carried her, her scent trail is in the air, not on the ground. We had some rain yesterday. Light rain and little wind are good tracking conditions. Heavy brief rain and strong winds could blow her scent trail over several acres.

"The two dogs in the van are good, but they aren't capable of air-tracking—not after almost thirty hours. I have no idea what this puppy's ability is, but he's been sensational so far. It makes me want to take the chance. We can give Bobby Lee a try right now or wait a couple of hours for the deputy to deliver Little's article of clothing. Fenton?"

He stared at the tracks in the mud, shifted to the small three-path, and turned his eyes to meet mine.

"Go for it. Use Bobby Lee," Fenton said.

I gave him a smile. "Where's my messenger?" I said, in a loud voice.

"Right here with aching feet," Donnie Ray retorted.

"Tell Massa Tom we're going to check out this road. Will he please wait on the verge, within sight, so when Little's clothing items arrive he can get same and wait right here for further orders."

"I'm gone," he muttered.

I finished my cigarette. Fenton and I walked back to the van. Bobby Lee jumped nimbly onto the front seat with confidence and moved to his cushion in the middle. He was having a good day, if no one else was. Happiness oozed from every pore. He was doing what he'd been bred to do, using the knowledge passed down in his genes, a pure strain, not weakened but strengthened by time. . . .

"I'm back," announced Donnie Ray. "He's notified and happy to wait quietly, doing nothing."

"Let's try the road, Fenton."

Fenton turned the van onto and over the small culvert, moving slowly down the three-path road. I've always wondered why they're called three-path; two-path would make more sense. You can only see two worn ruts, weeds in the center crowding the ruts on each side. But these roads were called three-path in antiquity, so three-path remains the name today.

We rocked along quietly, dipping gently from side to side. We made another sharp curve and were suddenly facing an impenetrable barrier blocking any further forward progress. It was a volunteer stand of young pines and thick brush. The road had continued in the past, but with disuse and time the small trees had grown, along with fast-growing merkle bushes, wild bay-tree sprouts, titi, and an assortment of just plain weeds. For now, we were at the end of our motorized passage.

I turned sideways in the seat. "It's lecture time," I told them. "Sound acts freaky out here. Sometimes it's muffled, and other times it can travel an inordinate distance. Keep your voices down and try to move through the brush as quietly as possible. I've had less than two years' experience out here. I've heard people say you don't see snakes in the daytime in July. It's too hot. Well, maybe you don't see them in town, but this is their territory, and you're invading their habitat. The largest snake I've ever seen, I almost stepped on last July. Watch the ground and where you place your feet.

"I mentioned holding down the noise. We're not sure Little's acting alone. He may have a relative or friend watching Mary Ann. Don't blunder out into the open without looking first. Fenton, Donnie Ray has his hands full with the camera and backpack. If you can carry two canteens, it'll help. Donnie Ray, suit up."

"Ah, jeez, Jo Beth," he protested, "it's July! We'll melt out there!"

"Full gear, Donnie Ray. My suit's just as airtight as yours, and my equipment weighs thirty-two pounds. If I can do it, you can do it."

I put on my bright-colored deep-yellow suit with SEARCH AND RESCUE in bold white letters emblazoned front and back. It has lots of zippered pockets and a built-in belt, upon which I hung quart water bottles. I knelt and fastened the snake protectors and tightened them over my Pro-Wings with a skate key. I can't walk in steel-toed shoes or heavy boots, so the covers prevent snake fangs and blackthorn vines from attacking my feet. My suit is made of a lightweight version of Kevlar, the material used in bulletproof vests. It's airtight and hotter than a sauna. I decided to go with the cap with the cutesy saying instead of the one I usually wore, because it felt cooler.

I slipped my holster strap over my shoulder and fastened it under my breast. I broke open the cylinder of the snub-nosed .32-caliber pistol and checked the load. I fed six extra rounds into the small loops. Fenton held my pack while I slipped the straps over my shoulders and fastened them at my waistline. I took the .22-caliber rifle from the scabbard and pumped out a twenty-two long, checked it, and reinserted the cartridge.

I asked Fenton to back up the van a few feet. I wanted to give Bobby Lee plenty of room. We'd know in the next five to ten minutes if we were on the money or if we'd have to fold our tent in defeat. I pulled on my gloves and attached Bobby Lee's short lead. I'd need to keep him close. He couldn't spot sharp vines and animal traps or, God forbid, a snake. On this trek I needed to be able to pull him back instantly in case of danger.

Fenton returned from backing the van, holding the bag that contained Mary Ann's nightgown. Not a whisper of a breeze penetrated the thick brush and closely planted trees. Hordes of swarming insects were out in force. We couldn't use insect sprays, it would deaden the dog's ability to smell the scent.

I placed two jerky treats on my glove and positioned them. Bobby Lee inhaled them without even a token chomp. I pulled out Mary Ann's nightgown, and he buried his face in the lightweight cotton material. I waited until he lifted his head before I stood. Bobby Lee put his nose near the ground and began his looping eights, trying to pick up the scent.

I patiently allowed him to make two completely fruitless sweeps of the small open area before I pulled out the gown again. This time I held the material, folded in the middle, about three inches above his nose. I raised it higher to make him lift his nose and keep it pointed upward. He sniffed audibly several times. I kept waving it just over his head and took two backward steps to about where I thought Little would've stopped his truck. I walked over where I thought the passenger-side door would've opened. I raised the gown straight up and, after several seconds, wadded it and sealed it inside the bag.

25

God One, Devil Zip

July 13, Tuesday, 3 P.M.

Bobby Lee's head was in the air for three steps; then he lowered it to ground level. I felt despair. Then, as quickly as he'd lowered his head, he raised it again. Using his beautiful nose, he strained upward, casting from side to side. He was covering a narrow invisible corridor that only he could sense, heading in a straight line for the edge of the clearing. My euphoric heart soared, keeping in rhythm with my lungs, singing *I knew he could, I knew he could!* I lifted my left arm above my head and with a clenched fist gave a double pump, the international signal to advance.

Air scents float on fragile air currents and are easily lost. A heavy wind gust, and your mantrailer just might move over twenty feet or more. If the scent trail moves, the dog moves with it. That's the difference between trackers and scent trailers. I didn't want to stop Bobby Lee—he seemed locked onto a scent, maybe Mary Ann's—but it was pure conjecture at this point.

I checked up on the leash, shortening it again, until Bobby Lee and I were side by side. I didn't want him injured. He can sense trees, they're solid, but bushes and vines aren't, and he runs right into them. The path he'd chosen was an old firebreak with at least a two-year growth since a disk plow had leveled its surface. I was constantly hauling him backward, trying to help him negotiate the overgrown path. With his head and nose lifted high, he was particularly vulnerable to hanging vines that dangled thorny tentacles of growth. I had to keep slowing his passage. His muzzle was bleeding, and he had open razorlike slashes on his throat. He was totally engrossed in the elusive wisp of scent he was miraculously pulling out of the ozone. Not once did he hesitate or act afraid to go forward.

We were traveling at an angle from the road in a southeasterly direction. I glanced behind me at regular intervals to see Donnie Ray, several feet behind me, taping our journey. He was trusting his small viewing window to warn him of vines and drooping branches. I spotted a large smear of red on Donnie Ray's brightly colored suit. He'd been unlucky with at least one vine. I also caught a glimpse of Fenton struggling with the tangled flora about six feet behind Donnie Ray.

I was making a rough guess that we had advanced about two hundred yards when I first spotted the tree-line opening in front of us. From the size of the blue space shining up above, it was several missing trees or an intersecting firebreak. I estimated that it was twenty yards ahead. Bobby Lee's head was already held high. All he had to do was open his large jaws to let his wondrous mournful cry pour forth from his throat into the humid air. It's the bloodhound's celebrative bay of success, the triumphant Gabriel's-horn call of victory.

My heart started cartwheeling, with my mind mumbling in total astonishment. The next few yards seemed to take forever. Bobby Lee was straining forward against his lead. He wanted to touch his target, to feel a breathing body, and I was pounding along beside him having the same thoughts.

We broke into the clearing, where I quickly scanned the area and stood motionless for one heartbreaking moment. Then I forced myself into action. I whipped Bobby Lee's lead over a small sapling, praying it would hold him. I yelled "Retreat!" only once; it was all the time I could take. I whirled back to the path, blocking Donnie Ray and his camera.

"Get rid of the camera and help me hold Fenton." My words were terse and guttural. Disappointment had risen like bile in my throat. Stepping around him, I went forward to meet and halt a surprised Fenton. His eyes were on the path, and he hadn't seen me approach.

Placing my hands on his shoulders, I yelled at him. "Fenton! Sit down, right now!" I was counting on surprise and confusion to get him off his feet. I figured that Donnie Ray and I could handle him easier if he were on the ground. Shock and the downward pressure of my hands sent him to his knees.

"Wha . . . " His gaze was blank, his eyes unfocused.

Where in the hell was Donnie Ray? I was going to need his added strength in the next few seconds. I stared into Fenton's eyes, locking his vision onto mine.

"Do you trust me, Fenton?" I was gonna stall until I could get my backpack off and Donnie Ray appeared. I couldn't risk glancing up the trail and breaking eye contact with Fenton.

"Yes, of course." His tone begged for enlightenment.

"Fenton, please trust my judgment," I was speaking slowly and separating each word. "Mary Ann is ahead in the clearing. You don't want to see her like this. There's nothing you can do for her now. Please, take my word and wait here. Will you do that?"

"Mary Ann?" His voice was pitiful. "She's alive, isn't she? I know she's alive!" His strong belief returned. "I have to go to her!" He began to rise. I exerted pressure on both shoulders. I'd managed to drop my backpack behind me. Where the fuck was Donnie Ray?

"No, Fenton!" I yelled, trying to hold him. He rose suddenly, brushing me aside, knocking me off balance onto my back like I was a worrisome fly. I lunged for his feet but missed. He was gone. I rubbed my shoulder. One of the canteens that Fenton had been carrying had caught me as he swung around. I grabbed my backpack and ran after him. I knew I'd be too late to keep him from seeing her, but I had to be near. I had no idea how he'd react. When I reached the clearing, I halted and took in the scene.

Donnie Ray, the little shit, had ignored my order and had proceeded into the clearing to tape Mary Ann. He'd found a burnt stump near enough and level enough on which to place his camera so he could keep taping. He was at the edge of the clearing in the weeds, violently sick to his stomach. He could have no idea just how pissed I was with him. He'd learn the hard way, when I had time to deal with him.

Fenton was on his knees, six feet from Mary Ann, leaning forward and pounding his hands on the ground. He was wearing a borrowed pair of gloves. Maybe they'd help protect his hands from the furious treatment they were receiving. His voice, strained with horror and sorrow, was yelling the same refrain over and over.

"You were supposed to stay alive, you were supposed to stay alive!"

I looked at Mary Ann. Each section of land out here belongs to timber companies or individuals. On the borderline, where ownership of the land changes, taller trees are left and marked with the owner's color. They had scraped off a wide circle of bark and painted a wide band around the tree. The tree must have been forty years old; its trunk was thicker than a fat man's girth. The band was a flat bright pale blue. It originally designated St. Regis Paper Company, but several years ago Champion International had taken over.

Mary Ann was upright and wired to the tree in three places: just under her arms, at waist level, and just below her knees. It was difficult to see her nudity, because the dried blood from many shallow cuts covered her body in a dark wine-and-blackish-colored sheath. A multitude of insects were feeding on her skin. Her head was slumped to the left, with a long spill of blond hair covering her face. The beautiful golden hair contained no blood and was gently lifted by the occasional breeze that eased through the clearing. My eyes were drawn to the foreign object protruding from the deep vee of her pubic hairs. The screwdriver handle looked obscene in the bright hot sunlight.

I was still holding my backpack. I placed it on the ground, put my hand on Fenton's shoulder, and gave him a firm squeeze of sympathy. Donnie Ray's hacking and coughing noise had ended. I knew I had to try for a beat before I took Fenton back to the van. Tom would come and stand guard until the proper authorities arrived.

I slowly walked to her and placed two fingers against her throat. She was warm to the touch and breathing! I quickly put my ear to her chest and heard a steady regulated beat. I was elated but couldn't waste time in wonder. I pawed in my pack and tossed out the inflatable rescue sled and my small tool kit. I rolled out the thin rubberized sled and removed the small plastic squares that became inflated pillows as soon as I pulled the cord. I unzipped the bag and glanced up to see Donnie Ray's approach. Looking sheepish, he rolled his eyes.

I hissed at him. "Get your ass over here!"

He knelt beside me, and I grabbed his chin.

"She's alive, you little shit. Go tell the deputy to get an ambulance rolling and both of you return—on the double! Tell him to bring his collapsible stretcher, which I hope to God he has in his trunk. You got it?"

"I'm sorry I—"

I grabbed his chin again to get his attention.

"Do it now! I'll deal with you later. Go!"

He turned and began to run toward the path. I walked to stand in front of Fenton. I pulled on my right glove and leaned over.

"Fenton!" I yelled in his face. "She's alive. You have to help me. She's alive! Do you understand?"

My news didn't slow the pounding or the repetitive refrain.

I grabbed a handful of his hair and pulled his face up and gave him a good belt on the chops. The blow would smart like the dickens. My gloves were brushed suede and stitched with rawhide.

He froze. His eyes focused on me, his mouth agape.

"Did you hear me? She's alive! Get your ass in gear. I need your help!"

He lunged to his feet. "What can I do?" He was back on track.

"Come hold her. I'm going to cut her loose."

At the tree, he gently put his hands on her shoulders. Little had used electrical fence wire. It was soft, pliable, and had a small diameter. He had wound it over a dozen times in each of the places he'd used to secure her. I cut through three or four strands with each bite of the cutters. Soon, I was pulling it out of the indentations in her skin. Fenton held her under her arms and placed her head on his shoulder.

The wire around her waist was deeply imbedded. The flesh was soft, and the tissue had swollen from lost circulation and the intrusive cuts. After severing the strands, I gritted my teeth and pulled them free. Her ankles were easier to release; that wire hadn't been wound as tightly as the others.

"We have to be careful and hold her legs together," I told Fenton. "If we dislodge the screwdriver, she may start hemorrhaging." I bit my lip. This would be a very bad time for him to lose it, but I had to mention the danger. He didn't lose it.

As soon as I cut the wire, I grabbed her ankles. He lifted her tenderly, as if she were weightless. I eased along beside him, trying to keep her immobile as he lowered her onto the rescue sled. He held her steady while I stuffed the inflatable pillows around her. I eased up the zipper when I felt she was packed in tightly. We worked upward and finally arrived at her neck. I fanned away the insects as I pulled up the tab and locked the zipper. He talked a monologue to her while we worked. He reached over and lifted her hair from her face. Now that we could see her better, she had a cut on each cheek, a bad sunburn, and blistered lips.

"Can't we at least wash her face?" he asked, as he fanned the insects away from her cuts.

"No, we can't. We might cause the cuts to start bleeding again, and we don't know how much blood she's lost. We don't want her to lose any more until she's under medical supervision."

"You're right." He gave me a wide terrific smile. "I told you she was alive!"

"Yes, you surely did," I agreed. I picked up my canteen, poured water into my hands, and washed them. I poured more in my cupped hand, and let it trickle onto her lips. Fenton reached over and pushed gently downward on her chin. I tried a few drops again. I was careful. I didn't want to choke her if she was unable to swallow. I saw her throat move. I tried a few more drops, then screwed on the lid.

"Aren't you going to give her more?"

"She'll be going into surgery, Fenton. I know when I was scheduled for surgery, they took away my water the night before. I gave her a few drops to moisten her throat. Do you think we should let her drink?"

"You're probably right," he admitted. "Let's wait."

We could hear Donnie Ray and Tom long before they arrived. They were crashing through the dry undergrowth and arrived breathless from their efforts and the high concentration of humidity in the air. Tom gave the scene a quick glance. Then he flipped the board over, unfolded it, and slid all the small steel bolts into place to make it rigid. He turned it upright. With Donnie Ray and me standing on the handles, he and Fenton slipped Mary Ann onto the stretcher. Tom pulled out the retractable straps at shoulder and thigh levels and fastened them. I pulled up the hood on the rescue suit and zipped it, to protect Mary Ann's face from further injury on the way out.

Donnie Ray had retrieved his camera from the stump and was taping the action. I didn't learn until later that he'd made sure the stump was the right height and that the camera was taping before he ran into the weeds to throw up. He was a conceited little shit, but you had to admire his grit. He wanted a film of the entire rescue, and he got it. I made him pay dearly for ignoring my orders. I don't think he'll try anything like that again, but I'm not one hundred percent sure. He's a cameraman first, and everyone knows they're nuts.

With Fenton at the front of the stretcher and Tom at the rear, they started back to meet the ambulance. Donnie Ray followed with the camera.

I pulled Bobby Lee's lead free of the sapling. I told him just how much I loved him, and that he was a wonderful mantrailer. He had sat quietly, not knowing what was going on. He trusted me to come back to him. I gave him several hugs. I pulled a plastic bag and a small trenching tool from my pack. I dug a hole, lined it with the plastic, and emptied one of the canteens of water into the basin. Bobby Lee drank it all. Picking up the second canteen, I refilled the basin for him.

I moved over to a shady spot, drank water, and lit a cigarette. Bobby Lee stretched out for a nap. I waited for Donnie Ray to return. I knew he wanted to tape Mary Ann being loaded into the ambulance. It was closure for his story.

I finally heard him approach, after forty minutes. I was on my third cigarette and almost had the normal amount of nicotine circulating through my endangered arteries and veins.

He hesitated when he saw me, then approached very slowly.

"How far can you shinny up a pine tree?" I didn't look at him when I asked the question.

"Well, it would depend on insurance coverage," he said, sounding short of breath from his trip. "There's the possibility of injury. I'd have to be employed to be covered on the company's policy. Am I still employed?"

"Listen, smart-ass, don't push it. I'll decide later. At this minute," I said carefully, "you're still employed. Now, how high can you shinny up a goddamn pine tree?"

"As high as you need me," he vowed.

"Take the binoculars and see if you can spot a hunting cabin anywhere around here and the road leading to it. Look for the sun's flash from a roll of fence wire somewhere out in the weeds. It's doubtful you'll be successful in spotting the wire, so don't spend too much time searching. I expect a structure and a road. Find them."

"Any tree?"

"Any tree except the one where Mary Ann was wired."

He took the binoculars and left without saying anything more, which was smart. His stock was very low with me.

My theory was that Little had discovered the cabin while hauling timber out of here. There should be a lane leading back to Turkey Creek Road. He had avoided it, not wanting to leave tracks leading in and out after the rain. The lane would have a locked cable across it and be a part of one of the hunting clubs. Most of the hunters out here who lease the hunting rights act as if the land is owned and not leased and has been in their family for generations. Their possessiveness borders on paranoia. They spend most of their hunting time traveling their border roads searching for almost nonexistent poachers and examining tire tracks. Little would've wanted to avoid leaving signs leading to the cabin. He probably discovered the short track leading to this clearing. He'd hiked in, carrying Mary Ann, used the cabin to clean up, and hiked out.

By the time Donnie Ray returned, I had cleaned the crime scene of my litter. I'd picked up the plastic bag, filled the water hole, and gathered my cigarette butts.

"I found the cabin." He explained the direction and said the road wound to the southeast, which probably doubled back into Turkey Creek Road. I asked about the wire.

"It's about thirty feet due north from the tree where he used it." I gave him a cool thank-you, strapped on my backpack, hung the empty canteens on my belt, and the three of us left the clearing.

Little was tried and found guilty of all charges against him and is now serving a twenty-year sentence. Mary Ann recovered fairly quickly. The doctors are not certain if her repaired uterus will allow her to bear children. Her numerous cuts were superficial. She'd lost a lot of blood, and she was in surgery for four hours. Donnie Ray supplied this information with a voice-over, as the silent ambulance sped away.

Back in the common room, the screen went black, and Donnie Ray turned off the VCR and turned on the lights. I walked to the front with Bobby Lee by my side.

I smiled. "Quite a tape, huh?" The audience responded with clapping and whistles.

"This tape isn't over. I want to show you a better ending than the one you just saw." I stepped to the side, and Donnie Ray restarted the VCR.

The opening scene was a wide-angled shot of All Saints Baptist Church on Bracton Road. The camera moved to the closed double front door. In the silence of a beautiful sunny October afternoon, just three weeks ago, the triumphant chords of Mendelssohn's wedding recessional filled the air. The double doors were thrown open. A lovely blond bride and a handsome groom stepped out onto the wide steps. Donnie Ray used his zoom lens to capture a close-up of the radiant faces of Mr. and Mrs. Hamilton: Mary Ann and Fenton. The couple ran down the broad steps with their attendants and friends spilling out of the church doors behind them. Ragged clapping turned into solid applause, stomping feet, and whistles of satisfaction as the scene faded.

I'd cautioned all the trainers not to mention Bobby Lee's blindness. I wanted to see if any of the trainees would spot it. Apparently they hadn't, as no one mentioned it, including Jonathan.

I waited until the room quieted and I had their attention.

"I would like to introduce you to the star of the tape, Master Robert Edward Lee. He's named after the commander in chief of the Confederate Army. He's known affectionately to us all as Bobby Lee.

"Would you like to take a bow, Bobby Lee?" I gently tugged his right ear. He placed his right paw a foot ahead of him, lowering his large head until his ears were crumpled and his nose was almost touching the floor. He posed for a moment and then straightened proudly as his tail wagged in harmony with the prolonged applause.

"The most amazing thing about Bobby Lee's part in the rescue is that he found Mary Ann when he was four months old," I said with pride. "He's now eight months old." I hesitated for a couple of heartbeats. "Oh, gosh," I said, snapping my fingers. "I almost forgot. Bobby Lee's been totally blind since birth."

26

Blackbirds Sitting on a Power Line
November 15, Monday, 8:20 P.M.

The rescue film ended a little after eight o'clock. Jasmine, Rosie, Susan, and I were sitting at a table with drinks before us. It was my first beer of the day and it was going down my gullet as smooth as silk. I was staring moodily at Deputy Sergeant Adam Gainey. He was moving Carol around the dancing area in a slow motion that had absolutely no rhythmic relationship to the upbeat country song Tanya Tucker was belting out on the jukebox.

"He's moving a lot more body parts than his feet," I observed.

Susan and Jasmine were drinking margaritas, using the explanation that with two drinking them it was easier to mix a whole blender full. They were helping lower the contents of the pitcher by taking turns topping off each other's goblet. Rosie was sipping on a glass of white wine.

Susan glanced at the undulating couple.

"Remember what we called that kind of dancing in high school, Sidden?"

"Refresh my memory. You've come a long way, Virginia, since high school," I remarked.

"Dry fuckin'," Susan said with a grin.

"A very apt description," I agreed.

"Susan!" admonished Rosie. "You shouldn't use that word in mixed company!" She'd chuckled upon hearing it; she just wanted to set the record straight that she disapproved, generally, of all crude explicit language.

"If you'll carefully note our immediate surroundings," Jasmine said with a casualness that belied her true feelings, "you'll see we're not mixed company—at present."

We all turned our eyes toward the far corner of the common room. Four official trainees and Jonathan were standing in an impromptu bull session near the rest rooms. The loose conversational circle had formed while they were coming and going to the can after the video had ended. Loud laughter erupted and we quickly switched our eyes away, lest we were caught ogling.

Wayne and Donnie Ray had escaped to Wayne's office. Donnie Ray was listening to music and Wayne was catching up on his catalog reading and computer entries. Most everyone had gathered around Bobby Lee, amazed that they hadn't spotted his blindness. Everyone but Gainey had oohed and aahed with enthusiasm and piled on the compliments. Jonathan had been vocal in his appreciation of Bobbie Lee's talents, speaking generally, but he hadn't directed one sentence my way since the video had ended. I was pretending indifference, but my actions were for naught, because the fool hadn't noticed I was pretending indifference. I was beginning to feel frustrated. I sighed and drained my brew.

"Susan, did I tell you how absolutely gorgeous you look tonight?" Her sexy outfit rated the praise.

"Thank you, Jo Beth, for the compliment. However, it

does little to ease the pain," Susan commented matter-of-factly.

"Pain?" I questioned.

"Two hundred plus tax for the dress, thirty for the tricky hairdo, and eighty for the shoes. They had to special-order them."

"The earrings are lovely, dear," Rosie added tentatively. "I was wondering—"

"Don't ask." Susan was shaking her head from side to side. "You would gasp and say I was out of my mind. Then I'd feel worse."

"How much?" I demanded.

Susan mouthed the price, silently.

"*Seven hundred dollars?*" I croaked. "Are you out of—"

"Plus tax," Susan added before I could finish. They were all laughing at my expression.

"Jesus," I said with feeling. "No wonder men think of us as the weaker sex. Susan, with what you have on your back, feet, and hanging from your ears, you could've bought a certificate of deposit, and in five years—"

"I've found"—Susan overrode my speech again—"those certificates of deposits to be scratchy and uncomfortable on a cool November night when I try to curl up and cuddle with them. I've invested in bait to snag a warm male body to romp with me on silk sheets. Just because my props haven't produced so far doesn't mean it's wasted money or a lousy idea."

"True, true," I agreed. I wanted to keep her smiling. I stood. "Ladies, the conversation has been pleasant, but I have a date with a seventy-six-year-old gentleman and seven puppies. I have to go and change clothes. Will you please hold down the fort until I return? I shouldn't be gone long. Jasmine, I hate to ask, I know you're tired of bimbo-sitting, but try to keep Carol vertical and clothed until I return. And ladies, fight the good fight against all the fierce sexual advances those sex-crazed lawmen over in the corner are plotting."

I left them grinning at my nonsense. The night air was redolent with a hint of rose attar, almost masked by honeysuckle and jasmine. The frogs and cicadas had a ragged concert in progress. Only an occasional love call sent by a whippoorwill echoed on the faint breeze. It was too late in the year for him to be courting. The continued heat must have confused him. I opened the van door and told Bobby Lee to load up.

"I'll be back in a second, sport. We're going for a ride."

I checked the first dog box on my side of the van, running my hand over the closely grouped mounds of warm fur. They stirred briefly and snuggled closer to each other. I glanced into the second cage to make sure Wayne hadn't forgotten the puppy carton. It was there. I went inside, stripped off the gold sheath, and donned jeans and a long-sleeved shirt. Rudy was in the middle of the bed. He gave me a sleepy glance, curled into a more comfortable position, and went back to sleep.

Driving to Button Lake Estates, I pondered the question of how the town's forefathers had arrived at the name. The lake is several thousand acres of deep water and perfectly round, but you can't always count on the obvious when names are bestowed on local landmarks. Goose Neck Pond is square. Big Creek is only a rivulet and goes bone dry each fall. Little Creek is thirty feet wide and stays at least five feet deep year round. Who knows?

I was familiar with the lake and its twelve surrounding landowners, thanks to Fred, my friend and editor of the *Dunston County Daily Times*. Once a year Fred will write a scathing editorial trying to excite the local populace to march on city hall, experience outrage, demonstrate, or at least boycott the miscreant owners' businesses to make them pay for their selfishness in not allowing public access to what Fred describes as "a natural resource that should be available to every citizen of the county." It's my personal belief that Fred would achieve more satisfaction if he ventured outside on the correct nights of the month and bayed at the full moon. The lake owners' ancestors had left the fortunate dozen their deeds and unassailable titles, even rights to air above the property, as far as we knew; also solid businesses, investments, and enough cash to hold on to all of the above. They weren't about to give permission for public access where the local riffraff could launch bass boats, fish their water, and invade their privacy.

I followed the curving drive that circled the lake, searching the ornamental gates for Number 4 Button Lake Estates Drive and the residence of David Franklin Cannon, Senior, my now part-time employer and father of Frank Junior, the kidnap victim I was proposing to find. I could laugh at the absurdity of the odds if it wasn't for the spark of challenge and impossibility that never failed to intrigue and ensnare me. I shook my head to clear it. It was too early to feel depressed. I'd barely started.

I pulled into a driveway that was guarded with closed black wrought-iron gates at least eight feet tall. Matching in height was the stone wall that curved and faded into the darkness on both sides of the gate. I left the van's lights on and walked to the illuminated button, read the instructions, and pushed. I glanced around. No cars were parked on the street within my vision. The street was well lit with ornamental light stanchions that looked far too expensive to have been placed there by the Balsa City fathers. The FBI, GBI, or whoever was probably perched on the walled fence, out of sight and using binoculars to keep an eye on Frank Senior. Crows sitting on a power line crossed my mind.

I heard a click and a drone as a small motor kicked on. The gates slowly parted. I drove up the curved driveway for several hundred feet and stopped in front of the house. I was surprised at its modest size. I knew Frank Senior had only one son, but I'd been prepared for opulence on the scale of Wade's Tara. I saw a nicely proportioned two-story brick house with only six double-cased windows facing the drive. A portico to the right covered a paved driveway leading to the back. I stopped and turned off my lights. The grounds were easy to scan. I could read a newspaper standing here in the drive. The idea was to be out of listening range but where the watchers could see what was going on to relieve their suspicions.

I stood there as a wheelchair appeared from the covered driveway, pushed by a man who looked to be in his thirties: sandy hair, wearing light-colored chinos and a white T-shirt. He gave me a friendly smile of greeting as he approached. The occupant of the wheelchair didn't. Even sitting, he had a commanding presence: ramrod straight, jutting jaw, stern countenance, giving me a look that said, I can buy and sell you. This always gets my dander up. I reminded myself that I'd hold on to my temper, that southern manners demand respect for the elderly and infirm. I estimated his height at six feet, broad shoulders, and a body that didn't show much deterioration or muscle atrophy. Snow-white healthy-looking hair, a little thin on top. Tanned face with deeply carved creases around the mouth and eyes.

"Mr. Cannon, I'm Jo Beth Sidden. I'm very pleased to meet you." I held out my hand. He gave me a brisk but bruising handshake. His voice was husky.

"What are you doing to find my son?" His tone was both accusatory and belligerent.

"Mr. Cannon, I don't anticipate giving you a detailed

summary of my actions in trying to locate your son. However, since we've just met and I understand your concern, I'll say I'm actively engaged and will give you my best effort. Will that suffice?"

"And if it doesn't?" he snapped.

"You can go pound sand," I answered calmly.

He flashed a wintry smile. "Tim warned me about you. I should've listened more closely. Why are you here?"

"Do you have any items of clothing here that belong to your son that he has worn at least once without being washed?"

He seemed to be deep in thought. I stepped to the van and opened the cage, picked up a puppy, and handed it to him. He accepted the warm bundle awkwardly.

"Is this necessary?" His distaste was evident.

"It's for the agents with binoculars who are perched on your boundary wall," I said, trying to keep the humor out of my voice and expression.

"They wouldn't dare!" he thundered, lifting not only his voice but his vision toward the nearest stone wall.

"Mr. Cannon, their uncontrolled actions are only exceeded by their arrogance. Who's to stop them?"

"I will, by God!" He pounded his fist on the wheelchair armrest.

"If you frighten the puppy, he may wet on you," I remarked. "Let's get back to business. Can you think of anything that has your son's scent?"

"He keeps swim trunks, a bathrobe, and shower clogs here for the Jacuzzi. We sometimes share it as we enjoy our after-dinner drinks." He shot a questioning look at his employee. "Henry?"

"Laundered after each use, sir," Henry replied, sounding apologetic.

Cannon grunted.

"There're the mohair cardigan and leather slippers Mr.

Frank wears at times. He keeps them in the hall closet. Would they be appropriate?"

I answered Henry's question. "You haven't washed, cleaned, or aired them?"

"No, ma'am."

"When's the last time you remember Mr. Cannon wearing them?"

Henry seemed uncertain. "I believe it was one or two nights before he . . . vanished."

"He didn't vanish. He was kidnapped," Cannon corrected him testily. "He was kidnapped!" He slumped back in his chair and suddenly looked older.

"Can you remember when he last wore them?" I asked gently.

"I can't recall," he said with a helpless shrug of his shoulders.

I picked up the puppy and stepped to the van.

"Come here," I said to Henry. "Stand close and block the view." I took the puppy box out of the cage and, using it to shield my actions, placed the puppy in the van with its litter mates. I passed the carton to Henry.

"Hold the box away from your body. Walk slowly into the house as if you're trying to keep from shaking the puppy. Put the sweater and slippers inside the box. When you return, hold the box by one handle, casually. You can even swing it a little as you walk."

"I understand," he said, giving me a conspiratorial wink.

He performed perfectly, even balancing the box carefully on one knee, to open the screen door.

I turned to Cannon.

"You are now the owner of an invisible puppy. You and Henry mention him a few times each day. Something like, 'Isn't he cute? Catch him before he piddles on the rug. Anything that comes to mind.'" I was being devilish. I wouldn't sell him a puppy for all the gold in Fort Knox. He was tweakable, and I was tweaking.

He snorted.

"If you want to see me urgently or need to tell me something important, call and say the puppy looks sick, won't eat, or something concerning his welfare. Okay?"

I received another grunt.

"Mr. Cannon, this simple ruse is necessary, whether you think so or not. If it's too much for your sensibilities, just say so, and I'll load the invisible puppy when Henry returns and depart—permanently. It's your call."

"Don't be so quick to jump on your high horse, young lady." He stared toward the boundary wall and didn't turn his head when he spoke. "What do you think your chances are of finding Frank . . . alive?"

I took a deep breath. "Slim and none. If you're right that he was taken on the Thursday night he was coming to your house for dinner, he's been out there for eleven days now. We have no leads, no clues, and no further contact since the authorities took over. Maybe they've argued over the original plan. All we have are dire suspicions about your three grandsons and their questionable actions. I want you to prepare yourself. I think something went wrong with their plans. He's been missing too long. That's the bad news. The good news: I'm an eternal optimist and I have a gifted puppy. I'm willing to give it a shot."

"Puppy?" He almost choked with disbelief. "Puppy?"

"Bite your tongue," I cautioned. "I'm very proud of Bobby Lee and will not tolerate any disparaging remarks about him. You don't know beans about bloodhounds, so don't put your foot in your mouth."

While he was off balance I continued.

"I want keys to all your properties that are currently in both your and Frank Junior's names. All the warehouses, storage facilities, and timber acreage. If the timberland is leased to hunting clubs, make sure the name of the club is attached to each key. I also want a written authorization giving me permission to enter and search. When can you have them?"

"Tomorrow by noon." He answered quickly, sounding businesslike. "But I thought you didn't want anyone to know you were searching for my son. Anyway, I don't think you should search Frank's house and grounds. You'll only put them on guard."

"Mr. Cannon, there are several valid reasons for me to be on your property searching. No one is supposed to know about the kidnapping, remember? If I'm challenged, I'll produce a convincing story. Also, I will not be searching Frank's house and grounds. Your grandsons wouldn't stash him there. Don't include keys for property that is fifty miles or more from your house. Common horse sense dictates keeping him near at hand where their presence would be as inconspicuous as possible. I don't think," I added wryly, "they're as incompetent and as wet behind the ears as you think they are."

Cannon was still glaring at me when Henry returned holding the dog carton in one hand and swinging it in a carefree manner. I took it from him and tucked it inside an empty dog cage.

"Thanks, Henry. Do you know Browse and Bargain Books on Main Street?"

"Yes, miss."

"Jo Beth," I corrected.

"Jo Beth," he agreed.

"Susan Comstock, a tall lovely redhead, runs the business. When Mr. Cannon gives you a package to deliver tomorrow, give it to her and tell her it's for me."

"I will, Jo Beth." He seemed happy being part of this event.

I turned to Cannon. "Are we still in business?"

"For the time being," he said, in a civil tone. "Let me know when you have anything to report." He was back in control. I guess he saw bullying wouldn't work with me. He might be seething inside, but he was showing his executive persona in his ability to cope with the unexpected. I told them both good-bye and got out of there.

Entering the common room, I saw the action had picked up. The males and the females were evenly disbursed around the room in conversation and seemed to be enjoying themselves. Susan and Jonathan were dancing. Jasmine and Sergeant French were deep in conversation and oblivious to all that surrounded them. I didn't see Wayne and Donnie Ray. They must still be hiding out in Wayne's office or upstairs in Wayne and Rosie's apartment, or they had gone to bed. No, not bed, or the gates would've been locked.

Rosie was sitting at the far table chatting with Corporal Jordan, Deputy Sergeant Vaughn, and Sergeant Julian Tyre. Rosie was moving her arms energetically and seemed to be holding court. I groaned inwardly. She was telling a joke. Even from where I stood, it was obvious she was animated. Joke-telling is not Rosie's strong suit. She always manages to flub or scramble the punch line. I started in their direction, then stopped. Carol was missing. I scanned the room. Just as I feared, Deputy Sergeant Gainey was also missing.

I changed course and walked toward Jasmine and Sergeant French. The music stopped and Susan and Jonathan arrived at the same time I did.

"How did the date with the old man and the seven puppies go?" Susan asked me.

"Great," I said, not glancing toward Jonathan. "Did Carol call it a night?" I didn't aim the question at anyone, just tossed it out while I took another look around the room.

Jasmine pushed her chair away from the table, standing quickly. Her glance searched the room and returned to mine.

"She was right here a minute ago," she said. "I've been watching her since you left. She must've just cut out!" Her voice rose with each syllable, then faltered. "I'm sorry."

"Not a problem," I said casually. "We're not her keepers. She's over twenty-one."

Jasmine pressed close and lowered her voice. "Deputy Sergeant Gainey has also left."

"I noticed." My tone was droll. "I'm beginning to believe they deserve each other. Go enjoy yourself. I'm going to put the puppies to bed and take a stroll. Be back in a few minutes. Go mingle."

"May I join you?" Jonathan had moved closer just in time to hear my plans.

"Sure."

Outside, Jonathan held the box while I loaded the puppies and carried them around to the nursery. When I had them bedded, we continued around the kennel until we reached the courtyard fence. I leaned my elbows on the top railing, and Jonathan placed his beside mine.

"I'm sorry about this afternoon," he said softly. "I jumped too soon with accusations about someone abusing the system. I'm a stickler for rules."

"Hoo boy. We're in a whole heap of trouble, then," I replied in a bantering tone. "I break the rules more than I observe them."

"Listen, I think I have a solution. You're right in the middle of your seminar. Plus, you've taken on this impossible Case of the Missing Caliph. You don't have any time for us. Why don't I leave early in the morning and spend a few days with my brother in Tampa? Along about

Saturday morning, my sister-in-law and I will be at each other's throats. When I get back here, your seminar will be over, and you'll have a master plan for your search. I'll still have a week left. What do you say?"

"Sounds good." I was being truthful. I didn't have time to start a relationship right now. Also, I'm a world-class procrastinator, especially in dealing with big issues that can dramatically affect my life.

"Then it's settled," he said, sounding pleased. "Want me to help you hunt for Carol?"

"I thought we'd stroll down to unit three, the present abode of Deputy Sergeant Gainey. I bet our search will be over before it begins."

When we reached Gainey's door, the lights were out inside and the drapes were drawn across the double windows. I knocked politely.

Silence. After several seconds I knocked again, this time more vigorously. The door inched open and Gainey's head appeared in the narrow opening.

"What do you want?" He didn't sound happy to see me.

"A blonde who answers to the name of Carol," I replied.

"She's not here. She told me she was going for a walk." He glared at me. "Try the black bitch's place. That's where she's staying, isn't it?"

I raised my voice so Carol could hear me.

"Carol, you have three minutes to get dressed and on your way upstairs, or I call Ramon and give him your room number. There's no back door to this unit, and I'm not going to waste my time standing out here begging you. Three minutes until the fur begins to fly." Gainey slammed the door, and I heard the lock snap. Jonathan and I waited in silence.

Very shortly we heard the lock release. Carol eased through the narrow opening and took off across the courtyard like a startled doe. She didn't speak and neither did we. We walked farther along out of Gainey's vision and hearing range.

"Do you think he'll cause you any trouble?" Jonathan was concerned.

"He's a coward," I said firmly, "or he would've called my bluff. I wasn't about to notify Ramon. I have a feeling that Deputy Sergeant Gainey doesn't have a lily-white reputation back home and doesn't want a showdown on any issue. There's no way he'll ever handle Gloria or any other dog of mine. I'll send him packing in the morning."

"Walk me to my door and kiss me good night?" His broad smile was clearly visible in the glow of the night-lights.

"Sure," I said.

At his door, I cupped both of his ears with my hands and pulled his face to mine. I gave him a thorough, prolonged, and satisfying kiss. At least it was satisfying to me, I can't speak for Jonathan. I slipped out of his arms.

"That ought to hold you till Saturday," I said in farewell and left quickly.

Back in the common room, I told everyone good night and rushed them out. Jasmine and I spent ten minutes tidying up, and I was in bed before eleven.

27

A Destructive Rage Is the Devil's Work
Somewhere, Sometime

Supper tonight was Dinty Moore's beef stew. He supposed it was suppertime. What little light that came from the pipe had slowly faded and darkness had arrived—so it was suppertime. When the light returned, it was daytime and time for breakfast. It was the only division of his time. A little light was day, no light was night. He wanted to scream with boredom. His skin itched and he could smell himself. He snorted in disgust.

What little appetite he'd had vanished as he peered at the cold congealed mass. The flashlight's beam was weaker. This was the second set of batteries he'd exhausted. There was one set left. He'd lost track of the count of light and darkness; his makeshift calendar was useless. He'd tried to reconstruct the lost count, stacking empty cans in the approximate order he thought he'd opened them, then lost interest. What good would it serve if it was ten days or twenty days? It made no difference.

He stared at the congealed fat adhering to the lid and floating on the surface of the can. The food was either reddish brown, red, or brown. It had all begun to taste alike: chili, stew, hash, spaghetti. It looked and tasted the same. He stared again at the contents of the can. He drew back his arm and threw the can into the darkness and was rewarded with a solid *clunk* as it thudded against the far wall. Scrambling from the warmth of his sleeping bag, disregarding the flashlight, he crawled recklessly in the direction of his food supply. He grabbed cans and threw them haphazardly in different directions, hardly pausing to hear the sounds of their impact. He was grunting with each toss. His grunts turned into yells of rage. He threw back his head and howled feral screams.

He searched frantically for more items to throw. A package of saltines, batteries, every item he'd carefully counted and mentally cataloged became missiles for launching. Turning, twisting on his hands and knees in dizzying circles, he exhausted his supply. With nothing left to throw, he crawled aimlessly, changing direction only when he bumped into a wall.

Finally, totally exhausted, he rolled onto his back and slowly drummed his heels on the floor until he could no longer lift them. He was sweating from exertion, but his rage was fading. He felt nothing. He turned slowly on his side and curled into a fetal position before he passed into the oblivion of sleep.

28

What You See Is All You Get

November 16, Tuesday, 6 A.M.

I awoke with the alarm and rushed through my morning routine. Wayne was loading Marjorie for me when I reached the courtyard. Jasmine and I drank coffee while I explained that we were on a mission for a friend and I couldn't give her any details.

"You're not taking Bobby Lee?" She raised one delicate brow.

"Nope, just Marjorie." I drained my cup. We never, ever, go on a search or sweep without backup.

"Your wish is my command, O Great One." She stood and turned a curtsey into a stripper's bump and grind.

I laughed. "As soon as I say good-bye to Jonathan and send Deputy Sergeant Gainey packing, we'll be on our way. You want to eat first?"

She gave me a look of dismay. "What happened with Jonathan?"

"Nothing. He's going to visit his brother in Tampa and return on Saturday, when I'll be able to devote more time to getting to know him."

"Great. I like him. Deputy Sergeant Gainey is out?"

"In spades," I said. "He's not fit to wipe Gloria's paws. I was just waiting for a good excuse to give him the heave-ho. He gave me one last night by having Carol in his room."

"She's of age," Jasmine murmured.

"Carol is a mentally retarded sixteen-year-old when it comes to men. Gainey lost Gloria when Wendell expressed his doubts as to Gainey's ability to be good to her and treat her well. We have no way of proving he would abuse her, so I'm using his actions last night to get rid of him and return the Demeter County Sheriff's Department check."

"Wendell will be pleased. He told me he couldn't bear the thought of Gainey leaving with her. As for food, I'm never hungry this early. Are you?"

"Nope. Why don't you ask Miz Jansee to fix us a sandwich to take with us? This search may take awhile."

I walked outside and met Jonathan crossing the courtyard.

"Coming to kiss me good-bye?"

"In front of God and everybody? No way. Come with me to serve Gainey's eviction notice."

"My pleasure," he said, taking my arm. We walked back to Gainey's room side by side.

As we approached the walk, the door opened and Gainey appeared. He pulled the door closed and grinned at us.

"Coming to apologize for last night?"

"Don't you wish," I said, tightening my speech pattern. I lose my southern drawl when I have an unpleasant chore. "Gainey, your seminar's over, and you failed the course. I want you packed and out of here within the hour. You can tell your people any lie you wish, or the truth—if you have the guts. I'll be returning the department's check with a note saying the chemistry between you and Gloria was wrong and I have no other trained dog available at the present time. I'm letting you off lightly because I don't want a hassle. If you go back and make waves, I'll get signed affidavits from all concerned and demand an official investigation from your department heads, which would also include the local sheriff. Do I make myself clear?"

"You screwing the sheriff too?"

I grabbed Jonathan's arm when I sensed his movement. "Stay out of this, Jonathan! He wants you to take a crack at him. It would give him some justification." I held his arm with both hands until I felt him relax. I glared at Gainey.

"Hit the road, or you'll be meeting the sheriff in about an hour. I mean it!" I tugged on Jonathan's arm until I got him turned around and walking away. I didn't take a deep breath until we were clear.

"Thanks for wanting to defend my honor," I remarked softly, "but it would only have made matters worse. Are you okay?"

"Just peachy," he snapped, shrugging his shoulders to relieve the tension. "Sorry," he said in a more reasonable tone of voice. "I didn't mean to snap at you."

"Point well taken, and noted." We stopped walking and I turned to him. "Are you packed and ready to leave?"

"Yes, ma'am."

"I want you to take off for Tampa this minute!"

"Don't I at least get coffee?" He smiled at me.

"On the road," I said firmly. "I have to leave on a sweep, and I don't trust you two on the same turf."

Jasmine and I stood in the drive and waved as he cleared the inside gate.

I was stretched out on my stomach with the leash in my left hand. My right hand rested firmly on Marjorie's large head.

I didn't trust her to hold the command to remain perfectly still while I took another peek down the trail. We'd been here on our bellies for over an hour, and she was getting restless. When I peeked, she wanted to peek. Nothing. The trail was still empty so I settled back to do some more waiting. Marjorie closed her eyes and nodded off into a light doze. I envied her. Doing nothing for an hour was making me feel sleepy. I was also hungry.

Having removed my pack when we arrived, I stretched and felt inside until my hand closed on the foil-wrapped sandwich. Upon the release of food odors into the humid air, Marjorie was awake, wide-eyed, and expectant. From the slash pocket of my jumpsuit I gave her two pieces of deer jerky. I find it hard to resist her imploring look. Bloodhounds have enormous appetites and seem to need more food than other breeds. She scarfed down the jerky with one chomp and then stared at my sandwich.

"No way." I barely breathed into her ear. "Lie still." She stared fixedly at my hands while I ate and drank some water from the canteen. She saw I was finished and again closed her eyes. I felt sweat pooling in my rescue suit and continued keeping an eye on the trail. I was watching for John Stringer along the route Hank had predicted he'd travel. I'd entered the woods about three-quarters of a mile downwind from his house because I didn't know if he had dogs. His house is isolated and on the immediate edge of the swamp. No close neighbors. He probably has dogs.

By nine o'clock the dew-soaked grass wasn't yet dry. Small insects of every description were flitting around under our noses. They were playing tag in the damp grass and landing on my face in droves. I had to keep blinking and making small limited swipes with my cupped hand to deter them from settling on my eyelids and to keep them out of my nose. Marjorie was dozing and only gave an occasional twitch when they landed around her eyes.

I heard the faint *whomp-whomp* of an approaching helicopter and cursed bitterly as I pawed through the backpack for a twelve-foot square of camouflage plastic. It hadn't been unfolded all summer, and the heat had sealed some of the folds. I wasn't making any noticeable progress in getting it unstuck and was wasting precious seconds. I jumped up and began shaking it and slapping it against my thigh to get it open. I was over three miles from any high-voltage power lines, so I knew it wasn't a Georgia Power reconnaissance chopper. They fly over their high wires periodically checking for fallen trees leaning on their stanchions and for overgrown bushes clogging their rights-of-way. I prayed that the trees and water were distorting the sound. I hoped it was a large cargo chopper from Moody Air Force Base on a flight pattern to Jacksonville NAS, but I knew I was blowing smoke. It wasn't my lucky day. It could only be the damn DEA's pot patrol searching for marijuana patches. From the increasing noise, they'd be appearing in less than a minute—directly over where I was standing.

I risked a quick glance at the trail and saw Stringer frozen by the noise of the chopper and my sudden appearance on his horizon. He was less than thirty feet away, standing with his mouth open in shock.

"Get over here," I yelled loudly. My Day-Glo yellowish-orange rescue suit, along with Marjorie's one hundred and fifteen pounds of reddish-tan fur, made us highly visible. This was fine when you wanted to be seen, but right now, even from the air, they couldn't miss us. We stood out like Christmas tree ornaments. Stringer didn't move.

"Get over here," I screamed again, in desperation. "I'm trying to save your ass!" I knew it was the last chance I had for him to hear me. The noise had risen to a deafening reverberation.

He finally started toward me in a shambling lope. I had about half of the plastic unfurled. He grabbed a loose end and began yanking on it.

"On your belly! To the right of the dog!" I yelled in his ear from less than two feet. I shoved Marjorie downward and dropped my pack on a corner of the plastic to hold it down and flopped down on top of it. I pulled the plastic on top of me and felt it tighten over my body as I squirmed around, making sure all the edges on my side were securely tucked in and under me. I glanced over in the gloomy light and checked out Stringer. I'd seen him around on drug raids and some rescues but hadn't paid much attention to him.

He was within an inch or two of my height and weighed approximately one hundred and sixty pounds. He was wearing jeans and a long-sleeved workshirt. He had dark-blond sun-streaked thinning hair and a receding hairline. He'd lost his cap, but it would pose no problem. I remembered it was camouflaged.

Stringer was eyeing Marjorie and there was about a two-foot space between them. I suppressed a smile. Large dogs with huge heads and big teeth are given consideration and a wide berth.

"Move over," I told him in an almost normal tone of voice. The noise above had abated somewhat. They had turned and hadn't passed directly over us yet. He glanced at Marjorie, who was eyeing him with interest.

"Bloodhounds are not aggressive. She is not trained to catch, hold, or attack. We need to close up the space. If they fly directly over our heads, the wash from the blades could jerk this lightweight plastic loose and blow it away."

He moved over awkwardly, gathering the loose folds of the plastic and tucking the edges tighter. He was now only two feet away, with Marjorie between us. The heat from our exertions and the sun made our little hideaway a sauna. Marjorie started panting. I was holding the plastic in front of my face with both hands. The moisture from our breathing was condensing on our cover and droplets were falling here and there. I rested my left elbow on the pack to relieve the strain.

"I'm Jo Beth Sidden with Bloodhounds, Incorporated," I told him, knowing he knew who I was. "You are Deputy John Stringer of the Dunston County Sheriff's Department, currently growing marijuana on a timber company's land for your own use—also for sale and distribution—and you are in a heap of trouble."

"Sez who?" he shot back defiantly.

"Get real, fellow," I said, sounding bored. "You think I was out here picking wildflowers or birdwatching? I've been sitting on you for eight days waiting for you to go to your patch." I patted my pocket where I carried a camera. "My trusty Minolta here takes very clear pictures. With my snaps of him cropping a few buds, a man has no choice but to plead guilty or look like a foolish asshole. You know, you should wait until the first frost before you cut the first bud. The second frost is even better. It tightens the bud and adds weight and potency. You lose money when you crop early."

I was rambling on, trying to give him time to think. I hoped he was bright enough to see I was leaving a small opening for negotiation. Hank didn't need the embarrassment of arresting one of his deputies for growing pot, especially so soon into his first term in office. With luck, I might be able to scare this dude into going straight. Maybe I could persuade him to destroy his pot patch and convince Hank he wasn't using and dealing.

"Who tipped you?" he said, with a cocky grin. He'd made his decision. The fool was going to try and brazen it out. He thought he could wiggle free. Now I had to get mean.

"Listen, asshole, you're worrying about the past when you should be thinking about your future. Surely, being a deputy yourself, you know what's in store for you: arrest, conviction, and some serious jail time. The judge will be harder on you than on a civilian. You've sworn to uphold the law. After you're released, you'll be an ex-con—with a record. Any kind of job will be scarce as hen's teeth. One thing I forgot to mention. They always promise to separate you from the cons you sent to prison, but with the overcrowding nowadays, well . . . it isn't always possible to keep those promises."

This was the last chance I was going to give this sucker. Either he was going to get smart—fast—or I was going to nail him. I hated the idea of the drug task force now spread over this area catching us out here and making the bust. It would give Hank two black eyes instead of one. Publicly, they'd take credit for the arrest and make it look as if they'd had to root out the bad apple in the new sheriff's bailiwick—the incompetent new sheriff. Privately they might believe Hank and me, but for sure they wouldn't release that information to the public.

There was another small problem. When taking out the one-ounce bag of marijuana from the safe this morning, I hadn't entered a notation in the logbook. The DEA had been very careful in explaining the rules to me when they gave me the drugs I use to train the dogs. They'd given me several ounces of marijuana, crack, heroin, tabs of LSD, and several different types of speed. I'd signed the agreement and couldn't say I hadn't been warned. If I ever removed any of the illegal substances without signing the log, noting time, destination, reason, and amount, I'd be guilty of having controlled substances in my possession without authorization. In other words, I'd be arrested for possession. I was doing a favor for Hank and had known he wouldn't want the information recorded, just in case the guy was innocent.

I'd been following the drone of the chopper. The sound was coming from the south-southeast, about a mile from our position. I knew they'd reappear soon. They always double back, covering the same ground at least twice. This was to catch someone who had successfully hidden the first time, as they were hightailing it out of the woods thinking they were home free. That's why the three of us were still on our bellies and hadn't uncovered.

"You're not concerned about me. You're trying to keep your sweetie from looking like a fool. We all know about you and the sheriff," he said. "Give me the deal—fast. I don't want to hang around here much longer. They'll be back."

"No shit, Sherlock," I said with disgust. "You've figured that out, have you?" I could feel sweat running down my temple and pooling in my left ear. I changed position, bringing my arms down. They were beginning to feel the strain. I cut off the air and most of the light with my movement. Marjorie began to pant again. I couldn't spend a lot more time on getting an agreement.

"Did you go halvesies with anyone? Is there anything at the patch that can be traced to you? If I get you out of this spot, can I trust you not to blab our secret or try to play word games with the sheriff? He's not part of this deal. If you can't control your tongue, you'll be sorry. My ass is hanging out to dry along with yours."

"Shit," he muttered, shooting a quick glance in my direction, which I couldn't read in the gloom.

"What? What?" I was impatient and alarmed. I couldn't deal with this guy in the dark. I pulled at the top section of the plastic to release it and pulled it back for air and light. He began to dig at his corner to help. Marjorie started gulping air and raising her nose to search for a faint breeze. I stared at him.

"I planted alone this year. And I know how to keep my mouth shut," he said, sounding defensive. "I was careful. I needed the money and it don't hurt nobody when I toke up. I never use it on duty. I don't want to get thrown off the force. I've worked hard to get there. I had a partner last year, lives in Mercer. He ripped me off but good. I got less than two grand, and he stepped out with a new truck a month later. He swore the patch was ripped off. It was. He was the one who done it. He had the guts to want to plant together this year. I told him he had to be kidding. He's the source of your tip. I'll swear not to plant again next year. I can't promise to stop smoking it, but I'll be careful and always smoke alone."

He looked at me to see how his story was being received. I remained silent, waiting. He had given me the good news, and I was waiting for the other shoe to drop.

"I'm sure the plants won't be found. I planted in pots in a field of three-year-old trees and only where a tree was missing. I painted the pots the color of pine straw. The plants are about twelve feet high and scattered so widely they won't pick up the colors from the air. But the pots will have my fingerprints, and I'm on file at county, state, and federal."

"Great. Just great," I commented with a dry mouth.

29

I'd Rather Be Lucky Than Rich
November 16, Tuesday, 9:30 A.M.

I didn't have to ask if the plants were located in heavy undergrowth. You can't control-burn with young trees, so the area would be waist-high with merkle, titi, and gallberry bushes, along with dog fennel and twenty other assorted varieties of common weeds.

"Do you have any idea how many actual plants are out there? Or do I search till I drop?" I asked.

He looked insulted. "I run a class-A operation. I started with a hundred plants. I lost nine to rabbits and twelve to root rot when we had all that rain in April. I culled out thirty-seven males. I've got forty-two healthy female plants. Even if the deer find them in the next two weeks and strip their usual amount before harvest, I would've cleared over thirty grand." He gave me a pissed-off look.

"The operative word here is *ran,* not *run,*" I replied with firmness. "The loss of a possible thirty grand compared to serving eight years of a ten-year sentence, being branded a felon, and standing in the unemployment line with your hat in your hand seems like a real bargain to me. But, hey, I'm flexible. Our agreement isn't carved in stone. You wanna change your mind? Be my guest."

"No," he said quickly. "You're right."

"You bet your ass," I said sarcastically. Never leave a guy thinking he has a righteous beef. He could turn ornery and foolish later.

"How's the footing? Wet or dry?"

"Soggy."

It figured. God was busy elsewhere, and this wasn't my lucky day. The vibrations in the southeast remained constant. They must've found a big field over there and were circling so their ground posse could find their way in. Some planters are still using the old method of planting, as in nineteen eighty-four B.C.—Before Choppers. They find an open space, use a garden tiller to cut up the ground, strew dry pot seeds and timed-release fertilizer, cut it into the soil, and then depart. During the dry season, they'll bring in a water pump and enough irrigation pipe to reach the closest creek, slough, or pond, and, after soaking the field, leave the pipe and pump. They're the ones you hear later bemoaning the fact that those dang flying machines found their fields, chopped down their beauties, hauled them out, and burned them in the field behind the courthouse. Surprise, surprise. Those eagle-eyed spotters can find six plants if they're planted together. The brighter and lighter green of the marijuana against the darker green woods and pines sticks out like a sore thumb. Dumb as stumps. They practice the same methods year after year. Maybe one field in twenty goes undiscovered, only because the chopper pilot miscalculated the grid pattern, was running low on fuel, or it was quitting time. The pot growers are too greedy and too lazy to use Stringer's methods. It's too much work. If they wanted to work, they'd punch a time clock, right?

Sitting up and keeping an ear cocked for the chopper, I

used a skate key to remove the plastic guards from my joggers.

"I want you to go home and do some heavy housekeeping," I told Stringer. "Vacuum thoroughly. Empty and wash all your ashtrays, including the one in your pickup. Wash them with soap and bleach. Don't throw your ashes in the trash can. Use a separate bag and don't forget your vacuum bag. I want every smidgen of pot out of your house. I warn you. You better not hold back a stash to smoke later. If you do, and get caught after all this aggravation, time, and sweat you're costing me, I'll shoot one of your kneecaps at the first opportunity and swear it was an accident. Do I make myself clear?"

"Hey, you don't have to threaten me," he said angrily. I had tweaked his macho ego.

I gave him my cool, superior smile. We were now standing eye to eye and less than three feet apart.

"No threat. Just information you can take to the bank."

He thought it over and decided to let it go. He glanced toward the path.

"Don't you want me to show you the way? Locate the plants?" he asked.

When he looked back at me, I gave him a grimace that slid into an open sneer.

"Get serious," I said. "Marjorie can find your plants in the dark of the moon—blindfolded—faster than you can on a Shetland pony in broad daylight. Get crackin'. You're dismissed."

He opened his mouth and closed it, spun on his heel, and took off in a huff for the path and home.

He was in a foul mood and uptight, just the way I wanted him. He'd go to his house and release his anger in scrubbing and vacuuming much more efficiently than if he were feeling cocky and complacent—maybe. I didn't tell him the method Marjorie would use. We'd go straight as a bullet right through the thickest brushes and vines if they happened to be in her path of forward progress. She didn't indulge in the slightest detour in her single-minded attempt to reach her goal. I was in for a rough time.

I let her circle the small clearing in her quest for the perfect spot to pee. She stretched one hind leg in an almost impossible angle, working the kinks out from lying motionless for over an hour. She found the perfect spot and I waited. We walked back where the pack anchored the plastic. I took out the radio, area rescue map, and lightweight waders and placed the radio in my pocket.

I checked the grid squares on the map for my location. Each square represents one mile, which is numbered. It had occurred to me at some point that, when using the radio, I might need to keep my location a secret from hunters, moonshiners, pot growers, law enforcement, and anyone else who shares the same radio frequencies. I'd penciled in different numbers under the official choices.

I opened the bag of marijuana and stuck it under Marjorie's nose. She must love the smell because with most dogs, one sniff, maybe two, they were ready to go. Marjorie just closed her eyes and kept sniffing. On the fourth snort and the fourth command to "seek," I sealed the bag and put it in my pocket.

"That's enough," I told her. "You trying to get high?" She gobbled down the deer jerky I offered. I worked the waders over my shoes, shouldered the backpack, strapped it around my waist, and hooked the two plastic water bottles to my belt again. Unzipping my suit, I stuffed the camouflage sheet inside without folding it—I might need it in a hurry. The sound of the chopper had disappeared and the woods were quiet except for small birds twittering as they chased one another in and out of shrubs. An occasional woodpecker could be heard knocking on a tree, working on lunch.

The almost indistinct path petered out, and Marjorie plunged into the undergrowth. Stringer had played it smart by entering the woods from several different directions. This allowed time for each path to repair itself, so as not to leave a beaten-down trail for a chopper or ground searcher to follow.

Some lowlifes never plant, water, fertilize, cull out males, or spray for bugs—they just harvest. About May or early June, they strap on a backpack loaded with food, a sleeping bag, mosquito netting, and plenty of insect repellent, then sling a couple of water bottles over their shoulders and head for the woods.

They creep very carefully through the brush and swamp looking for faint trails, broken limbs, careless footprints, and car tracks on three-path dirt roads. They locate the plants, draw themselves a map, and go home and rest until November. Then they hit the fields, clipping just the buds. They gather them early, a premature harvest. They couldn't care less about sacrificing weight and potency, having invested no time, money, or sweat. They rip off family, friends, and total strangers without a qualm. If, however, they are caught, they sometimes have difficulty walking and talking for long periods of time. In some rare cases, they cease breathing.

Marjorie pulled me swiftly through the underbrush, entangling me in blackthorn vines, popping back palmetto fronds to slap my legs, and wearing me to a frazzle with her urgency. She has only one speed: high gear. I was kept busy trying to slow her down to a brisk trot and, at the same time, protect my face from sharp thorns and tree limbs. She stopped so suddenly, I almost plowed into her. She turned and looked at me, panting happily, as if to say, We have arrived!

I leaned over, bracing my hands above my knees to catch my breath. From this lower viewpoint, I saw a pot that was almost impossible to detect from six feet away. The terra cotta-colored paint blended perfectly with the surrounding straw. I also saw the sun's reflection from black water less than thirty feet away. Water for Marjorie. Watching where I stepped, I led her to the edge of the cypress pond, not wanting to startle—God forbid!—a water moccasin.

Marjorie waded into the water, easing down until her belly was submerged. She took a couple of casual laps, letting her body temperature cool before she drank her fill. I released my backpack and placed it on a planting mound to sit on it. I drank from my water bottle while deciding if I should call Jasmine now, relieving her of worry, or later, when I was ready for her to pick me up. Now would mean two transmissions on the not-so-private airwaves. Later, I would have the "when" and "where" at hand, so I opted for later.

I gazed up at the tall cypress trees festooned with long streamers of gray Spanish moss. They are mere babies. The lumber companies whack and truck them out to market before they have a chance to reach old age. Just a stone's throw from here, in the federally protected confines of the Okefenokee, are some middle-aged giants about seven hundred years old. In the late nineteenth century the lumber companies logged all the two-thousand-year-old cypress trees. After gazing in awe at the seven-hundred-year-old trees, I would have loved to have seen some of the ancient ones that were seedlings when Christ walked the earth.

Marjorie waded out of the water after drinking, ready to return to work. I strapped on the pack and she led me back to the first find. Placing my foot on top of the pot, I grasped the trunk of the bushy plant and pulled. The whole root structure, matted around the dirt and potting soil, slid out with surprising ease. The tiny white feeder roots resembled vermicelli. I propped the bush sideways between the two trees where it had stood and picked up the lightweight four-gallon-sized pot and carried it to the next plant. When I emptied the second pot, I jammed it inside the first. There was a two-inch flange on top of the pot that was slightly larger than the lower section. I groaned. The flange kept the pot from nesting snugly inside the next one. Damn! I'd seen the type that was sold in sleeves of one hundred, tied with twine and stacked tightly together. Stringer goofed, buying this kind.

On the eleventh pot, I had to stop and bring out the ball of twine from my pack. I read the label and was relieved to see it contained a hundred feet. I had enough string to tie the pots in bundles.

When I'd tied the entire forty-two pots into four bundles, I gave them a gloomy look. They weren't heavy, just bulky. I bet they'd snag on every vine and bough. I tied the four bundles together. Using the remainder of the string, doubled and redoubled, I tied one end to the bundles and the other end to the back of my belt. I was gonna drag the suckers.

I checked the map and compass and decided that Cat Creek Road was the nearest way out. On the way, I thought out key words I could use to convey to Jasmine the name of the road where she could pick me up. Rudy loves to fish in the creek that runs behind the kennel. He sits patiently until a small fish loiters at the edge of the slow-moving dark water. Lightning fast, he scoops a paw into the water. I've yet to see him catch anything or bat one onto the shallow bank. So far, this hasn't deterred him. I feel sure if he ever succeeds, he'll bring it back to the house, flipping and squirming in his jaws, to show off his catch. Maybe Jasmine could interpret Rudy's name and favorite fishing hole as Cat Creek. I knew now I should've renamed the roads at the same time I'd numbered the squares on the map.

It took another thirty minutes to reach the edge of Cat Creek Road. It was now a little after twelve noon. When I'd trekked out with the pots, I'd been wrong about them snagging on every vine and bough. It was every *other* vine and bough. I'll bet I had to stop fifty times or more to untangle, or slice with my knife, the offending limbs. After I'd gotten within sight of the white sandy road, I traveled parallel with it for at least a hundred yards before stopping.

When I loaded Marjorie and the pots into the van, I'd leave footprints. I didn't want any suspicious and enterprising search crews going into the woods in a direct line and finding the pulled-up plants. Given several hours, the weeds I'd flattened on my way out would straighten. Of course, it would be another story if the crews had brought their search dogs from Waycross, but I doubted that had happened. The choppers seldom surprised the locals and caught anyone out in the woods—flatfooted— as they had me.

The pot growers' early warning system rivals the Distant Early Warning line—the DEW line—that protects North America against a surprise missile attack. It's patterned after the local chamber of commerce's scam- artist hot line. Each grower's in a network and has two phone numbers to call in order to warn of anything suspicious. The two they call will call two more, and so on. As soon as the gas truck pulls into the sheriff's department's impound lot or the empty field behind the courthouse, the calls begin, sometimes even before the flyboys arrive in their choppers. Once or twice the DEA has been dumb enough to bring the gas truck in for refueling the night before the flights. This just gives the moonshiners and pot growers more time to let their fingers do the warning.

I'm not aware of how smart the drug agents are about footprints on dirt roads, but the locals are experts. I personally know a planter who has over fifty tire tracks memorized. He can identify the tire prints of close neighbors, the mailman, the bottled-gas-truck drivers, Georgia Power meter readers, and the law. In the early morning, he can stand in his road and recite who passed and didn't return, who made the round trip, and who turned around in his driveway during the night. Locals observe every car and truck and its passengers. If they're unable to place you, they make the calls. They may not trust their neighbors—or even like them—but they unite against the common enemy and make the calls.

After traveling parallel with the road and twenty feet or so back in the brush, I thought I was far enough down from my tracks leading from the pot field. I felt the clock ticking because of the silence in the sky. It was unusual that the chopper hadn't doubled back. I left the awkward bundle of pots, tied Marjorie to a tree, crawled forward to scan the road and almost bumped into Dirty Harry—a deer dummy—standing at the edge of the woods. My adrenaline surged and my heart fluttered until my brain told me it was okay. I snickered and admired the full-sized mounted deer. Mechanical gadgets inside make its head turn, its rump move, and its white tail flick. About five years ago, a state game warden and a taxidermist put it together and named it Dirty Harry after Clint Eastwood's famous character. It's moved weekly to a different spot. Dirty Harry was invented to catch the slob hunters who ride the roads at night and shoot deer frozen in their tracks by the truck's headlights. It's called fire hunting.

Most poachers now drive the dark roads using only a powerful Q-Beam searchlight plugged into their cigarette lighter outlets. The game warden stays hidden near Dirty Harry until the poacher arrives and commits himself; then he announces his presence on his loudspeaker. It's slowed down a lot of night hunters or fire hunting on the lonely dirt roads. If you're caught at night with a light and a loaded gun, your truck, light, and gun are confiscated. If convicted, you face a heavy fine and the loss of your vehicle—possibly forever.

This spot was as good as any. Maybe the track-conscious crews would think someone had stopped with a dog to admire the dummy.

I went back to Marjorie, sat on my pack, and keyed the mike of the radio.

"Hello, good buddy, got your ears on?" I had lowered my voice and was using an exaggerated drawl, hoping to pass for a male. Jasmine had dropped me off at seven-thirty this morning and continued on to the parking lot of a convenience store about a mile down the road where the search-and-rescue van wouldn't be noticed and invite inspection.

"Hey there, Andy," suddenly boomed in my ear. She has a rich contralto voice and sounds a lot like a man over the tinny speakerphone. We just might get away with our impersonations.

"Amos, I can't rightly remember the road ol' Rudy uses to reach his fishing hole. I've tried *four* times. How 'bout you?" I stressed the four, meaning, Search grid four on Cat Creek Road. "Pick me up."

I waited for her answer. It didn't take her long. "Sure 'nuff, Andy," she said gruffly. "Sure took your time."

"Sorry 'bout that. See you soon."

Not knowing what was going on, she'd sweated out the wait after hearing the chopper. This was almost as bad as being pulled through the brush by Marjorie after dumping forty-two pot plants out of their pots and hiking in and out. Almost, but not quite.

It took her twenty minutes. We were just a mile apart, as the crow flies, but she had to reach the intersection of Clemson and Christmas Break Road, turn left, and drive over three miles. She'd made good time and, better yet, still no sign or sound from the eyes in the sky. She'd reduced her speed when she reached grid four and was scanning both sides of the road.

I stepped out of the woods to show my location and quickly went back in for Marjorie and the pots. Jasmine held the rear door of the van open so I could load more easily. I carried the bulky bundles to keep from leaving more tracks on the road. She loaded Marjorie, both of them scrambling over the pots in the aisle of the van, and placed her inside the dog cage. I noticed she'd walked inside the van to the rear door to keep from leaving footprints. Smart girl. I stripped off the waders, backpack, and suit. When I looked up, she'd already separated the bundles of pots and was shoving as many as she could into the remaining five dog cages.

God, the open air felt wonderful on my sweat-drenched skin! Because the suit was water- and fang-proof, it was like wearing a sauna.

I removed a shovel from the van and, stepping carefully, began to scoop sand and spread it over Marjorie's and my footprints. Working backward toward the van's door, I saved the last shovel full, and after stepping into the van, I spread it over the remaining prints. The newly spread sand was damp and darker than the normal sandy road. It would fool no one if they came by in the next few minutes, but in half an hour any evidence that I'd walked out of the woods would be gone.

Neither of us wasted time in conversation. Our four ears were cocked for vehicle sounds and the whomp of chopper blades.

Jasmine started the van and backed carefully about six feet, then drove forward and we were on our way. To my knowledge, she'd never used this procedure in the field, yet she hadn't missed a trick. I was proud of her.

"Perfect," I told her with a grin. From the opened rear door of the van, I'd checked the ground as she pulled forward. The tire tracks were continuous and weren't disturbed by freshly scattered dirt.

She flashed a brilliant smile. "It seemed you were gone at least forty-eight hours. I'm a nervous wreck."

"It wasn't too restful out in the bush either," I replied, as I searched the glove compartment for a comb to tame my ratty, sweat-soaked hair. She looked pristine in her jeans, pink T-shirt, and sneakers. I felt a pang of envy knowing I looked like last year's bird nest. I was wearing jeans and a T-shirt too, but that's where the resemblance ended.

"Did anyone see you on the way here?" I asked.

"No," she answered. "It surprised me. I didn't meet one truck. Isn't that lucky?"

"It wasn't luck. The locals don't move around while a chopper is aloft. They go to ground; specifically they stay off the back roads. They don't want to get caught traveling in a pot area where pot is found. Guilt by association or close proximity."

Jasmine was looking my way, so I saw the cars at the intersection ahead a hair's breadth before she did.

"Maintain your same speed. Look but don't stare. Wave if they do, but don't smile. Stop if they signal. I'll do the talking."

We were moving about thirty miles per hour, a normal speed for this road. I counted six cars and seven men. The cars were their personal vehicles or ones borrowed from the impound lot. No one was in uniform, but they sure as hell didn't look like hunters.

"Steady," I said.

As we approached, I scanned the faces turned toward us and didn't see one that was familiar.

"A casual wave," I ordered suddenly. We both lifted a

hand, and I added a curt nod as we passed. I watched in the van's side mirror as the images of the men grew smaller.

"Why didn't they stop us?" Jasmine's voice was full of wonder.

"Don't run off the road when I tell you my theory," I said, taking my first deep breath since spotting the pot posse. I gave a ragged chuckle. "They thought we were part of the search team."

"You're kidding!"

"Nope. It's the only explanation that fits. You know how they pull the guys in from all over. Anyone who has a day off. County patrolmen, policemen, state troopers. They must've gotten here late or staged in a different area. It's the only logical reason we weren't stopped." Suddenly, my mouth was dry. I needed a cigarette and a cold Diet Coke—in that order. I smoked and drank all the way to a late lunch.

30

Penitence Has a Price
Somewhere, Sometime

The cold woke him. He was freezing. Groggily, he fumbled for the sleeping bag. He was curled up in a ball on the hard floor. He was colder than a well digger's ass in six feet of lime water. Why wasn't he snug and warm in the bag? Where was the damn bag? His mind cleared and he remembered his rage. Minutes ago, or hours? He had no idea how much time had passed. He was shivering and thirsty. First thing to accomplish was to find the damn bag. He was in darkness, unnerved and disoriented.

He started crawling. He crawled until he bumped into something. His knee hit an object and pain lanced up his leg. He brushed the area with his hands until he encountered the object. A can of food. Memories of heaving cans with abandon made him grunt in disgust. How could he behave so irrationally, totally losing control? He was stir-crazy, that's what. He was losing his mind. He gritted his teeth as shivers raced up and down his spine. He kept crawling. Sooner or later he would happen upon the bag. His head bumped into a wall, causing bright dots to dance before his eyes. He slumped against it momentarily, trying to regain his vision. Which wall? The bathroom wall? The water wall? The thought of water started him crawling again, but the pain of rapping his head now made him a little more timid. He stuck out his hand before he brought his knees forward for another foot of space. His hand struck a water jug. At the same time, his eyes detected the white blur. His night vision was returning. Water first, then warmth. His tongue was raspy as sandpaper and the back of his throat ached.

He removed the cap eagerly. Filling the tuna can he used as a water container, he quickly downed its contents. He filled it twice more before he slaked his raging thirst. Knowing the whereabouts of the sleeping bag from the water jug's position, he started crawling toward its warmth. He was surprised to feel comfortably warm before he arrived at the bag. He hadn't been crawling long enough or fast enough to achieve these results so soon.

He crawled into the bag and zipped it up to his chin. He raked his hair from his brow and felt the moisture and heat radiating from his forehead. "Oh, shit," he moaned aloud with dismay. He recognized his symptoms: cold and hot, sweaty, sore throat, and thirst. He either had a cold, flu, or pneumonia. His discomfort had progressed so rapidly, he was willing to bet it was pneumonia. His thoughts flashed to the small plastic bottle that held twelve aspirin tablets he had noticed in his food boxes earlier. "Hoo boy," he whispered in the darkness, "I've stepped in it now."

31

To Move a Mountain, Start Carrying Away Small Stones

November 16, Tuesday, 2 P.M.

Jasmine and I reached the common room too late to eat lunch with the trainers and trainees. Miz Jansee prepared plates for us while Rosie filled us in on the morning's events. Her eyes were sparkling; she enjoyed being the bearer of news. She was telling us about Gainey.

"Then the bum came in and fixed himself a plate, acting innocent as a lamb! Sat alone. Right over there." She pointed at the far table. "He said something to Wendell when he left, but Wendell wouldn't tell me what it was. Something nasty, I bet."

"What did he do?" I asked.

"When Lena Mae came running over to tell me the room had been trashed, the bum was already out of town. I sure would've liked to give him a piece of my mind!"

I threw down my napkin in disgust and started to rise. Rosie reached over and patted my hand.

"Rest easy, honey. There ain't too many items in those rooms that can be tossed. He scattered the flower arrangement, tried to flush a whole box of Kleenex down the toilet, left all the spigots running, and jerked down the curtains. Me and Lena Mae had the room back to rights in no time!"

"Is the carpet ruined?"

"Nah, looks fine," she assured me. "'Course you can't be sure until it completely dries. Donnie Ray used the shop vac to suction up all the water. Wayne unplugged the toilet. Everything'll be all right, I'm sure!"

I forced myself to relax. Worrying before the carpet dried would be unproductive. I was two dogs short of selling my week's goal. Not a very exemplary beginning for the seminar. What else could go wrong?

"Did you get a chance to talk to Jonathan before he left?" Jasmine asked Rosie.

"Sure did," she answered shyly, glancing my way. "Thought Jo Beth had run off another one till he told me he'd be back on Saturday."

I swallowed some iced tea and lit a cigarette.

"Did Wayne say how the trainees were doing?" I had to divert Rosie's inquiring mind from speculating about my romantic nature.

Rosie smiled. "He was bragging on them at lunch. Says they're taking to the dogs like ducks to water. He don't gush much, so I know he's pleased with their progress. 'Course, he feels they need two weeks, not one."

"We can't afford two weeks," I said with conviction, to kill the idea before it escalated into a debate.

"Did Carol appear for breakfast?" Jasmine asked.

Rosie grunted. "Not for breakfast, but she was in time to tell the bum good-bye. I couldn't believe the way she was carrying on! I've got to talk to that little gal as soon as I get a chance!"

"Someone needs to," I agreed. I put out my cigarette

and stood. "I've got to hole up in my office and make a jillion phone calls. I enjoyed the chat, ladies."

"That reminds me," Rosie said. "You got three calls around lunchtime. Sounded like the same man. He wouldn't leave his name."

"It'll happen again in the next few days," I said casually. "If I'm out, he'll call back." I'd missed Tim's calls, but it couldn't be helped.

"Sure," Rosie replied, trying to conceal her curiosity. "Well, I'm off for a sweep at Marcon's. See you later."

"I have one also," Jasmine said. "I'll be here for supper, but I have a class tonight. Sure you don't want me to skip it?"

"Go to your class. I'm sure Sergeant French will be disappointed, but we'll be fine."

I dialed Hank's number and let it ring. He wasn't at his desk; I'd try later. I dialed and reached Wade's temp. He was able to talk and was apologetic.

"Sorry we haven't connected sooner, Sidden." He explained. "I've been busier than an armadillo in heavy traffic. How's it going?" I liked his voice. He sounded confident and pumped. It's amazing how a very big case can fire up a small-town lawyer and get the juices flowing.

"You sound very southernish this afternoon," I said, kidding him. "Sheri is coaching you well."

"Well, you started the process. Sheri's just polishing the finished product. Thanks again for giving me Jarel."

"You're welcome. How are you and Jarel getting along?"

"We're not bosom buddies as yet," he said, sounding cheerful, "but I have reasonable expectations of presenting a vigorous and positive defense in his behalf."

Which didn't tell me a damn thing, but he's a lawyer. That explained it.

"Wade, I have a hypothetical question. Say I'm on a sweep, on land with written authorization from the owner. Also, I have prior knowledge that an official investigation is ongoing. But I'm sorta conducting my own investigation into the same thing. Then there's this higher authority than the local sheriff who's also working on the investigation. What can they do to me if they catch me red-handed?"

"Charge you with obstructing an official investigation. You'd be dead meat." His answer was prompt.

"But the investigation is very hush-hush. I'm not supposed to be aware of it," I countered. "How could I be guilty of anything?"

"But you're caught in the act. It's obvious you *are* aware. Therefore, you're obstructing an official investigation and you're still dead meat."

"Well, it was only hypothetical . . . and confidential," I added.

"Be careful," he warned.

"Sure. Listen, I haven't told Susan or Sheri yet, but they're going to be asked to be co-chairpersons for the Free Jarel Defense Fund. We have to get the community involved in this struggle. I'll be cashing a twenty-five-grand CD in a few days. You're to put it in your personal account and use it any way or anywhere it's needed to make your and Sheri's life run more smoothly. The money the community donates will be in the bank for you to use only for Jarel. I hope you're paying close attention to what I've been saying."

"Gotcha!" he said, with a snap in his voice. "I also hope you heard me tell you, Be careful."

"I did, I did," I declared, laughing when I disconnected.

I tried Hank again, and this time he answered.

"Howdy. Can you talk?" I was trying to sound offhand and half asleep. I can lie better that way.

"The coast is clear. What happened?"

"Well," I drawled, "your suspect is not a suspect any longer. It's my opinion he's as pure as the driven snow. He spent the morning doing chores without leaving his land. At eleven-thirty, while sweating like a pig, I emptied my water bottles, and me and Marjorie strolled out of the woods when he was glancing our way. I introduced us and politely requested some much-needed cold well water. He wasn't alarmed at seeing us. He took us around the house to the back and thoroughly watered us. We had a nice conversation. He's proud of his house and offered to show it to me. I pretended reluctance at leaving Marjorie unprotected. He owns a huge Rhodesian Ridgeback that was standing nearby, stiff-legged, with his back hairs standing straight as a rooster's comb. He was eyeing Marjorie like she was cold cuts for lunch." I heard Hank chuckle but he didn't speak. I continued my tall tale.

"Stringer then invited us both inside. I drank a Coke in the kitchen, toured every room of his house, and ended up on the front porch from where I spotted his new truck. We circled it while I oohed and aahed. I can't tell you Marjorie's opinion of the truck, and I don't mean to digress, but I really learned more about his vehicle than was necessary. Before Marjorie and I left the woods, I alerted her that we were on a pot sweep. She didn't blink an eye or shift an ear throughout the tour. Case closed. He's clean."

"Thanks, babe, I owe you," he said, lowering his voice. Hank is the only one who can call me babe. He started calling me that during our fling and only uses it now in private. From him, the sexist label is acceptable. All others beware.

"You owe me about two pints of sweat, which I'll collect sometime in the future. How's the biggie perking?" I was referring to the kidnapping.

"A big fat nothing, so far. The principals in charge are spinning their wheels and infighting to beat the band. I stand on the sidelines and cheer them on."

"Do they suspect anyone yet?" I was careful not to sound much interested in his answer.

"They're equal opportunists," he said. "They suspect everyone, but nothing's been said in particular about any individual. They haven't a clue."

"Well, I have to go do some work," I said lazily. "Take care." Maybe the surveillance of Tim was just routine.

"You too."

I headed to the kitchen for a dose of the fizzy stuff. My gut had been clamoring for an Alka-Seltzer ever since I started lying. Hank despises liars. I can lie beautifully, but my body parts make me pay. Rudy and Bobby Lee made the journey with me. I ignored their expectant looks. Their diets were in shambles, and I had to regain control. Not having to open the refrigerator helped.

The phone rang as I entered the office. I assumed it was Bubba—it could be the start of another silence and hang-up routine—but it was Tim.

"Sorry to miss your calls, but I was on a sweep," I apologized.

"No problem," he said cheerfully. "I've decided the assorted agencies following me are just honing their skills. I've even quit looking for them. I'm an upright citizen, and I'm in security. They can think what they like."

"A new attitude. Anything happen to convince you?"

"Nah. I kept getting a crick in my neck from trying to spot them. I'm not breaking any laws, so why bother? What's happening with you?"

"I'm just getting started. I met Cannon last night. He's

cooperating—reluctantly. He's gathering keys so I can search some of their properties. Find out anything yet?"

"Rumors are mushrooming at the plant. Everyone has a different theory about what's going on. A lot of suits are in and out with no explanation. Frank's absence is being covered with illness as the reason. Everyone's concerned. Our bad guys, the three sons, aren't helping any. They're in and out, looking worried and snapping at the employees. They were never popular, but now they're considered enemies by all. Why do you think they haven't made any attempt to collect the money?"

"I have no idea. Maybe they've argued over the plan and can't agree on a new approach. If Frank's still alive, he's more at risk with each day that passes. Still think they're responsible?"

"I know they are." He put a wealth of meaning into the four words. So be it. He knew them and the plant. I'd have to trust his judgment. His suspicions about the sons were all I had.

"Anyone there have any weird tales to tell about anything happening six months ago?"

"I only started asking yesterday. I've talked to about ten people so far. It's hard to remember six months ago with all that's happening in the here and now. Everyone I've asked so far seems to think I'm the one who's weird. I've told them there's a twenty in it if they come up with the right answer. Maybe I'll get some feedback by tomorrow."

"Keep asking," I encouraged him. "We won't know if anything's important until we check out each suggestion. Listen, I have to have someone who knows the make and model of cars. He has to be able to spot the sons' vehicles and recognize each one's mode of transportation when it's described. I'd like to use him a couple or three hours each morning, starting tomorrow. Does anyone come to mind?"

"I know the perfect person, but you can't use him in

the mornings, just afternoons. It's my cousin John's younger stepson, Kenton. He's out of school at three, and he's an expert on cars. He lives, eats, sleeps, and breathes them. He's twelve years old. I'm sure John would agree, if you can assure him there's no possible danger and Kenton would be safe."

"There's no danger," I said absentmindedly. I thought about it. He'd probably be better than an adult, since most of the people he'd ask questions of would be kids themselves. Also, when he was questioning adults, they wouldn't wonder about the motives of a twelve-year-old boy as they would an adult. Who'd suspect a young kid of being devious?

"On thinking it over," I told Tim, "he sounds just like what I need. Do you think you can set it up with John and have the kid available tomorrow afternoon? By the way, is he easy to get along with? How sharp is he?"

"Sharp as a tack," he replied quickly. "But I have to warn you, he's a smart-ass and doesn't interact too well with adults. John's straightened him out a lot, but he still has work to do. Personally, I don't care too much for him. He's as prickly as a cactus."

I sighed. Another lame duck. I was beginning to believe that more than half the population had problems, or was it just me?

"Set it up. I'll give him a try."

"Will do. Anything else?"

"Yeah. Find me a couple of volunteers at Cannon Trucking to help with an in-plant drive for Jarel. He's the black boy in jail accused of shooting the female deputy. It's money for his defense."

"You don't want much, do you? I don't think it'll be a popular cause around here, but I'll try."

"Surely you have a couple of secretaries who like campaigning for lost causes?"

"I'll try," he repeated.

"Good. We'll talk again tomorrow," I said, ending our conversation.

I called Sheri but she wasn't home yet. I'd try later. I'd see Susan and Jasmine at supper. I wouldn't be able to get much done, it was already after five, but I left to check on the animals. I also wanted time to question Wayne on how the trainees were doing before we sat down to eat.

The evening meal was fine, but the prevailing mood seemed a little subdued. Simon Clemments, our fire chief, sat at one end of two tables that were shoved together. With Jonathan and Gainey gone, we only filled the two tables. He was being charming for Rosie's benefit, so we all relaxed and let him be the unofficial master of ceremonies.

Carol had made an appearance just before we sat down to eat. She appeared sullen and withdrawn. I ignored her, but watched to see what she'd do without Gainey dancing in attendance. She looked the field over carefully and settled on Corporal Randall Jordan, who, at thirty-seven, was nearest to her age. I had to smile. By showing pictures of his wife and children, he'd obviously demonstrated that he was both a loving husband and a loving father. Carol was wasting her time. She'd missed these facts, because she'd only had eyes for Gainey. I hid my amusement with my napkin when I saw him, only two or three minutes into their conversation, whip out pictures of his family again. He bored Carol silly with his lengthy explanation of each face in the photo. She suffered in silence with a sickly grin on her face, then left in total defeat just minutes after finishing her meal. Good riddance.

During the meal Susan sat at my left and Jasmine at my right. I had a chance to enlist both of them in raising money for Jarel.

"Do you think your Reverend Euttis B. Johnson of the Pentecostal Holiness Fundamental Gospel Church will help us with the defense fund?" I asked Jasmine.

"I'm surprised you remembered his name—and his church," she said, smiling. "Of course he will and be happy you asked."

"I'll never forget him or his help," I told her, "but if you don't mind, will you do the asking?"

I was tired from my morning workout and suspected the trainees didn't have too much steam left either. A little after nine, they started, one by one, saying their good nights and heading for their rooms. Jasmine left for her college class after the meal. Rosie and her chief had disappeared.

A little before ten, Susan and I straightened the common room and Susan left for home. I was in bed by half past ten.

I awoke in the early morning darkness, sweating and trembling. A weird nightmare still ensnared me with wisps of cobweb bonds and lingering dark shadows. I was crouched on a cold floor feeling trapped and panicky, but the memory stopped there. I shuddered. Turning my pillow, I closed my eyes and willed myself to sleep.

32

Any Old Port in a Storm
November 17, Wednesday, 8 A.M.

Breakfast was over, and I was ready to begin my work on the Case of the Missing Caliph. I refused to dwell on how far behind on dog training I was. Since Wendell had no trainee, with Gainey out of the picture, I'd started him working with the puppies. I was three lessons behind on their training schedule, but he had infinite patience and would soon have them current. Clifton Holcombe, my other trainer with no trainee, could keep on exercising the animals and working with next month's seminar hopefuls. Donnie was to tape the morning workout and Wayne was everywhere, watching, soothing jitters, calming dogs, and generally overseeing the bonding of the dogs with their new handlers. My small kingdom was temporarily perking along without me.

I entered the office and glanced at my watch. Petula, Ramon's receptionist, should be opening the clinic about now. I wanted to remind her to have Ramon here, ready to speak to the trainees at eleven. Earlier, I'd informed Carol to make herself scarce until suppertime. I had to make a quick visit to see Sheri; I hadn't reached her yesterday on the fund-raising. I also wanted to know how she was coping with the plenitude of cash. Busy, busy me. I fondled Bobby Lee's velvety ears while I dialed the clinic's number.

"Petula. Jo Beth. Will you—"

Petula's shocked voice overrode mine. "I think you should come here right away, Miz Jo Beth, right away!" The volume climbed with each syllable.

"I'm on my way," I said, carefully replacing the receiver.

Oh, shit. I got out of there fast.

Petula was leaning against the reception counter, weeping copious tears.

"What's wrong?" I asked, trying to keep my breathless dismay under control.

"The Carshes' chow is sleeping now, but when Jack wakes up, I won't be able to control him. He weighs over a hundred pounds! Honey still has stitches in his paw. Arabella is recovering from bloat surgery. I don't know what to do!"

"Who's Honey?" I asked, mystified at the feminine-sounding name and Petula's use of the masculine pronoun.

"You know Honey," she replied with impatience. "He's Miz Mary's white poodle that bows his head for his prayers and can say Ma-Ma."

I had to regain control of this conversation.

Placing my hands on her shoulders, I gently guided Petula to her chair and made her sit. Pulling up a chair, I lowered myself so I wouldn't appear to be looming over her. I felt like shaking her, but hell, I was as nutty as she was.

"What is going on?" Reasonable and calm.

"I put on the coffee first thing," she explained. "Then I came to my desk and found the notes. He's gone!" she wailed, groping for a tissue.

"Ramon?"

"Yes'm!" She took some papers from the desk and thrust them at me.

There were two envelopes and her unfolded note. I read it. It was short and to the point: *Petula, I've gone. Jo Beth will tell you what to do.* It was signed *Ramon*.

Such a warm and considerate missive. I imagined mine would be more of the same. I closed my eyes briefly and silently recited my calming mantra: *I will not get upset, I can handle this, I will not get upset. Amen.* Tearing into the envelope, I digested its contents, only wasting a nanosecond. *Jo Beth, the books are up-to-date and on my desk. Tell Carol.* It was also signed *Ramon*.

My gut shot a generous amount of red-hot acid into my digestive system. I reached for the phone and called Jasmine. She'd planned on spending an hour or so bringing our daily log on each dog up to speed and then mixing the dogs' lunch formula before leaving for a sweep.

"Drop everything," I said when she answered. "We have a problem. I need you here at the clinic. Ramon has flown the coop."

"Coming."

I turned back to Petula. "Feeling better?"

"Yes'm." At least she'd stopped crying and had her compact out to repair the damage. "How could he just walk off without telling anyone? He's been real moody and depressed with Miz Carol gone. He's been acting strange, but to just get up and go?"

I had to agree with her. I wouldn't have thought Ramon would be so reckless with his career as to quit without notice. That's hard to forgive. I was also pissed at him for leaving me high and dry during my first seminar. It was unacceptable behavior, but where did I voice my displeasure?

"Let's have a cup of coffee," I suggested.

I was pouring three cups when Jasmine arrived. We sat and sipped while Jasmine read the notes. I gave both of them a pad and pen.

"Petula, I'd like you to start calling the pet owners who have animals here. Tell them Ramon was called out of town on an emergency. Tell them we're trying to arrange for another vet to take care of their pets until they're well enough to go home. See if they have any suggestions or preferences. If they scream and holler, let me talk to them. Think you can handle it?"

"I think so," she answered, sounding doubtful. At eighteen, I'd felt I could lick the world. Different strokes for different folks. Maybe she'd gain some confidence with this experience.

"Jasmine, start composing a short announcement for the paper along the same lines. If we call it in by noon, it should be in tomorrow's paper. I'll use Ramon's office to try and get a local vet. Christ, I'm not thinking. Will you call Rosie? Ask her if she'll go over and break the news to Carol and sit with her for a few minutes. I'll take over as soon as I'm finished here."

I entered the hall, opened Ramon's office door, and was two steps into the room before my eyes could telegraph my brain to halt. I stood, rooted to the floor, and stared uncomprehendingly at Ramon lying on the couch. An IV stand was near him, its tube taped to his arm. I stood frozen with shock. He could be asleep, but never for one second did I believe it. I forced myself to turn and take careful slow steps to get out of there. I felt weak, and the exertion of movement made me feel unbearably tired.

I got to the waiting room doorway and clung to the door facing. Jasmine glanced up, saw me, and frowned. She pushed back her chair and started toward me.

"Don't go in there," I croaked out the words, hoping they came out in the right order.

Jasmine grabbed me and managed to get me seated.

"Don't go in there," I repeated clearly. Barely trusting my voice I added, "Call Hank. Tell him Ramon is dead." I lowered my head between my knees and closed my eyes.

Hank arrived with half his force, it seemed. Jasmine, Petula, and I moved to the large couch in the waiting room. At Hank's suggestion, the county doctor checked my pulse and raised my eyelids to look at my pupils. I assured him I was fine. He turned around and told Hank the same. I should be making phone calls, locating a vet, taking care of business, but Hank said to sit, so I sat.

Jasmine produced my cigarettes and fetched Classic Cokes from the vending machine. She said we all needed the sugar. I sipped and smoked.

Now I'd never know which version of Ramon and Carol's disagreement was true. The point seemed unimportant somehow. Ramon had been twenty-eight, two years younger than I. How could he, or anyone else, cease living because of a marriage that faltered? I realized how little we know about what makes anybody tick.

People were tromping back and forth. The front door was propped open and they rolled Ramon out. That couch would have to go. I never wanted to see it again.

"Has Carol been told?"

"Hank sent P. C. He and Rosie will tell her," Jasmine answered.

"Do I still have a job?" Petula sounded shy and uncertain.

"Of course you do," I assured her. "Whoever takes over the practice will need a receptionist. I'll give you a good recommendation." I patted her knee.

"Thanks." She produced a weak smile, even though she still looked like a young horse ready to bolt. Someone had dropped something in Ramon's office a few minutes before, producing a sharp crack. Petula had levitated from the couch, wall-eyed with fear. It took both Jasmine and me to calm her down.

Hank returned and stood in front of us. "Jo Beth, would you like to go lie down at home for a while?"

"Hank, I haven't got time to indulge myself and have the vapors like a proper southern belle," I snapped. "I've got a business to run and a lot of phone calls to make. What I want to know is, when can we get to use the phones?"

"Welcome back," he said with a grin. "P. C. wins the bet. He said you'd be your usual cantankerous self within the hour. I was foolishly worried about you and disagreed with him."

I made a face. "I hope you lost a bundle."

"Just a sawbuck." He glanced at his watch and looked toward the reception area, where Deputy Tom Selph was talking on the phone. "We should be finished within the next twenty minutes or so, and you can start making your calls then."

When everyone finally cleared out, Jasmine and I tackled the phones. We got permission from the owners of Jack, Honey, and Arabella to transfer their pets to Balsa City Clinic; the vet there would take care of them. He'd also try to steal them away from my clinic, but at the present, I didn't have much choice. They had to go somewhere, and he had a good reputation. He arrived within the hour and picked them up.

Petula started calling pet owners who had scheduled appointments. After she made a couple of calls, she perked up and sounded almost professional. I was proud of her.

None of us admitted hunger, but Rosie sent us Donnie Ray with three hot lunches. After inspecting the contents, we nibbled a few bites with feigned reluctance, then polished off the rest. We felt guilty about eating where someone had recently died just a few feet away from where we were working.

Petula didn't want to go alone to the back and clean the cages the three patients had occupied, so Jasmine went with her. I entered Ramon's office. Keeping my eyes averted from the couch, I gathered up the ledgers. I didn't exactly scurry from the room, but I'll admit I didn't waste any time piddling around.

When Tim placed his daily call, Rosie gave him the number at the clinic. I told him I hadn't achieved anything and explained what had happened. I also told him I still wanted to pick up the kid, Kenton, as planned.

I'd started thinking of the kidnapped victim as Frank. He was always in the back of my mind, along with a clock ticking off the hours and days. Common sense and my analytical mind told me he was dead. This was the thirteenth day since he'd disappeared. My hopeful heart insisted he was alive and, wonder of wonders, my gut agreed. I always go with my gut feeling. It's the body part that can cause me physical pain.

I checked the two refrigerators and bagged the perishable items for Miz Jansee. I composed a short message of explanation for the answering machine while Jasmine taped a note on the door above the emergency bell. I couldn't bear the thought of the clinic being totally dark, it seemed so final. I set the light panel on nighttime lighting for forty-eight hours. I'd be back before then. I told Petula to take a couple of days off and I'd call her; she'd be paid for the time she missed. I sent her home a little after two and locked the door.

Jasmine and I walked around the clinic and back to the house that sets back from the road about fifty feet. It had been home to Ramon and Carol for the past three years.

Jasmine bagged the perishables while I went around checking the rooms and turning on night-lights. This house wasn't going to be totally dark tonight, either.

I drove up Tim's street, checking house numbers. When I spotted the correct numbers on the next house, I saw a well-built teenager with dark hair, weighing at least a hundred and fifty pounds. He rose from the curb and stepped back onto the sidewalk. This couldn't be Kenton. It had to be his older brother, Keith, who's fourteen.

I pulled to the curb and stopped in front of him. He stuck his head in the window but quickly withdrew it when he realized he was eye to eye with a very large bloodhound. I leaned over so I could see his face.

"Kenton?" My doubt was plain in my voice. I was unhooking Bobby Lee's safety harness and moving him over to the middle cushion.

"Yeah."

"I'm Jo Beth. Hop in." I gave him a big smile. This man-child could log for a living right now. It must be something in the water. Each new crop of kids was turning out taller and with bigger feet. My mother had worn a size six shoe and swore that her feet were bigger than other women of her age. I wore an eight, and Jasmine and Susan wore nines. Mother had been of average height at five feet two and a half inches. We three were five feet seven and over. This kid probably wore a size twelve shoe, and if he wasn't five feet five inches tall I'd eat my hat.

The kid hadn't moved. "Hop in," I repeated.

"I don't like dogs," he said, looking sullen.

"You're kidding!" I was surprised. "Didn't your Uncle Tim tell you what we'd be doing?"

"He didn't mention you'd be bringing Cujo." His sarcastic retort let me know two facts: one, it was Bobby

Lee's size that bothered him, and two, he wasn't happy about this assignment.

"The dog is gentle. He doesn't bite," I said. "He's lovable. He likes to be petted and touched mainly because it's the only way he has to get to know you. He's blind."

"So what good is he?"

"Well, if you'll get in the van," I said, with a touch of asperity, "I'll explain just how good he is on the way. Time's awastin'."

"I think I'll pass." He folded his arms, looking belligerent.

"Listen, Kenton," I began, trying to hang on to my temper. "You gonna wimp out on me just because the dog's head is bigger than yours and he has larger teeth? I get your message. You're not too hot to trot on this one. I think you should reconsider. Your Uncle Tim and your father want you to help me out. They both owe me a big one, and you're it. I don't think they'd take your refusal to go along too kindly. So get in and quit wasting time."

His eyes were shooting daggers at me, but after a brief hesitation he jerked open the door and plopped down on the seat. I floored the gas pedal before he could change his mind. I didn't know what had convinced him: being called a wimp or having to encounter the wrath of two adult family members. And I couldn't care less. I started the introductions.

"My name is Jo Beth Sidden. You can call me Miz Jo Beth, or Ms. Sidden, whichever you prefer. This is Bobby Lee, a pedigreed champion and an amazing mantrailer." I rested my hand on Bobby Lee's head. "Why don't you feel his ears? He likes to meet people. Give him a couple of pats. He loves it."

"No way," he muttered, staring straight ahead.

I began to see what adults mean by "Children should be seen and not heard."

"Be a scaredy-cat, then," I taunted. "Did some dog frighten you when you were a child? If so, let me know now. If you have deep-rooted fears about canines, you'll be of no use to me. I'll explain to your father. Maybe he can get you some help with your problem."

"I ain't scared of no dog!" He turned and glared at me.

I pulled the van over on the edge of a grassy field and shut off the motor. I tapped Bobby Lee's right shoulder and said, "Shake, Bobby Lee." He laid his huge paw in my waiting hand. I looked at Kenton.

"Prove it," I said in a calm tone. "Feel his paw. He'd like to be your friend. I told you he's a loving dog. Any minute now he might choose to lean against you. He loves to lean on a person. He won't harm you, and I really need to know if you can work with him. This isn't a game we're playing. This is real; a man's life hangs in the balance. Will you try?"

Kenton reached over and gingerly felt Bobby Lee's paw. He tentatively rubbed it with one finger.

"What man?" he asked, sounding a little more civilized. "What d'you mean about his life? Is he lost, or what?"

I had to decide just how much to tell him. He went to school each day. The urge to brag to his contemporaries could be irresistible. And he was twelve years old.

"Can you keep a secret and not brag to your friends about what we're gonna try to do? Cross your heart and hope to die?"

"Do I have to spit in the crick too?" He said it dead-pan, but I saw the glint of humor in his eyes.

"It helps seal the vow," I agreed with a smile. "Pity there isn't a crick in sight. We'll have to settle for crossing and hoping."

He made the age-old gesture and raised his hand with two fingers straight up and the rest folded.

"Scout's honor," he added. I had to trust him if we were going to accomplish anything. I added a little insurance.

"Your dad and your uncle will lose their jobs if this gets out. Mum's the word." It was the best I could do. "Bobby Lee loves to have his ears rubbed."

I started the van, pulled back onto the road, and kept my eyes straight ahead. Making a right turn, I saw he was fingering Bobby Lee's right ear. Maybe we were in business. I drove out to the Highway 301 overpass and pulled close to the low concrete parapet. It was prime time to see a lot of vehicles. We got out and leaned over the four-foot railing. Both lanes had commuters and tourists zipping along just a few feet below. I looked back and pointed to the inside lane. There was a temporary break in traffic.

"Tell me the make and model of the next five cars." We watched as they approached.

"Ninety-four Ford pickup, Dakota Club Cab," he recited in a strong voice full of confidence. "Eighty-one Ford pickup. Ninety-two Dodge Caravan. Eighty-six Ford pickup. Ninety Chevy four-door sedan. Ninety-three Nissan. Eighty-nine Toyota—"

"Enough," I said laughing. "You've convinced me you know cars." I wasn't sure if he was totally accurate, since I couldn't distinguish a Chevy from a Ford at fifty paces, but I didn't think at his age, he had enough guile to fake it.

I pulled the list of the three sons' cars from my jeans. The list I handed him didn't have the license plate numbers. My list with those numbers was in my other pocket.

"Let's load up and go see if we can spot some cars."

At Cannon Trucking Company, I slowed the van and drove slowly through the parking lot. Bobby Lee was now leaning companionably against Kenton's side, his eyes closed, savoring the human contact. As we neared the turn at the back of the building, Kenton turned to me, frowning.

"They ain't here." He sounded disappointed.

After rounding the building, I slowed again when we approached the executives' reserved parking spaces.

"There!" He was excited. "There's the red Ford pickup! Look! There's the silver Trans Am!"

I was sneaking a peek at my list, checking the plate numbers. He'd correctly identified David's pickup, the oldest son, and the Trans Am belonging to Donald, the youngest. The license plate numbers matched the numbers on the list Little Bemis had compiled.

"The black Ford Bronco ain't here," he said.

"Isn't," I corrected. "Isn't here. Good work."

He grimaced. "I get English lessons too?"

"Yep. Let's go check out some warehouses."

I drove to the address of the first warehouse and took out the large ring of keys that Susan had brought me last night from the glove compartment. I presented Frank's sweater to Bobby Lee. He went to work nosing the ground. We made a circuit of the lot, entered, and searched the abandoned building. We didn't find a thing. Kenton was disappointed. He'd watched Bobby Lee's progress with fascination and wanted him to find something. We tried two more locations on the list and came up empty. On the way back to drop Kenton at his Uncle Tim's house, I explained what we were doing.

"It's called the process of elimination, Kenton. We have a long list of properties to check. Each afternoon we'll search some more. I'll pick you up tomorrow at the same time. Okay?"

"I could stay out of school tomorrow. We could search all day long!" He was now an eager recruit.

"No way."

33

Stout Fences Make Good Neighbors
November 18, Thursday, 10 A.M.

After watching the trainees, trainers, and dogs depart for field work, Jasmine and I spent most of the morning helping Carol pack. She'd been brisk, orderly, and fully in control. Ramon's parents wanted his body for burial in his hometown. Carol agreed without turning a hair. When I tactfully suggested we should maybe have a memorial service here, she said that would be fine but not to count on her, she was going to her mother's as soon as she finished packing. She promptly sat down and wrote out her mother's address, asked me to close out their bank account after all the checks had cleared, and mail her the balance. She said she'd stop by the bank and sign a power of attorney. I'd phoned Wade at nine on her behalf and then left the room. I guess he advised her on how to handle everything. I bit my lip and kept my mouth shut.

Her car was loaded to the gunnels with her possessions—only. She had us carefully sort all of Ramon's clothes and refused to take any keepsakes. She even left their wedding picture, his desk accessories, personal papers, the lot. It was sad to see just how little he'd left. He didn't play any sports, fish, or hunt. I knew he loved to do crossword puzzles, but I couldn't remember anything else he did in his spare time. I suddenly realized how little I knew about both of them after living just a few hundred feet away for over three years. Ramon had wanted it that way, and I hadn't tried to cultivate Carol's friendship. Saying I was busy was no excuse. I was beginning to feel guilty.

Wayne and Donnie Ray found a waterproof tarp and finished lashing her trunk and two suitcases onto the roof of her car. The four of us stood hovering over her, trying to say the right words to send her on her way.

She stood in the sunshine looking cool and crisp in bright pink shorts and a white halter. No widow's weeds for our Carol. The others finished their good-byes and stepped back.

"I should have been more of a friend, Carol," I said softly. "I'd like to apologize for that. I wish you well. If you ever need me, just give me a call."

Her mouth formed a small moue. "I've never liked you, didn't you know that? In fact, I've avoided you as much as possible."

"I'm sorry," I said, taken aback. "Did I hurt you in any way?"

"Don't flatter yourself. You never had the capacity to hurt me. You always acted so high and mighty, like you were the queen of the hounds, like I was dirt beneath your feet. You're laughable the way you strut around. Ramon didn't like you either!"

"Is there anything else you'd like to get off your chest?" I gave her a patient smile.

"No. I think you get my drift." She lifted her head a bit and appeared satisfied. I was going to let her have her day in the sun and enjoy her denouncement, but after she was seated in her car, she looked up at me and whispered,

"Bitch." That tore it. I'm fifty-one percent sweetheart and only forty-nine percent bitch.

I gave her a saintly smile. "Go with God, my child," I told her in a soft voice, then turned and walked back to the others.

"Go to hell!" she yelled, as she gunned the engine and left rubber on the driveway.

Donnie Ray was laughing and Wayne was signing, wanting to know what was so funny. Jasmine looked shocked.

"What was that all about?"

"Our little widow was bidding me a fond farewell."

Jasmine frowned. "She's acting irrationally. We shouldn't have let her leave so soon. She could still be in shock."

"Jasmine, she knows exactly what she wants. I just hope she gets it. I wish her the best in life." I then explained how Carol had described me and the way she thought I acted. "Was she right? Give me truth, not platitudes. I need to know."

"Only a teeny, weeny little bit, just on very rare occasions," she said, grinning at me.

"Thanks," I said wryly. "You know, when people ask for the truth, they don't really want to hear it. They expect to be reassured, not deflated."

"I know. I just couldn't resist. I'm trying to make you humble and sweet-natured."

"Fat chance."

"I know that, too."

I went to the office to make some calls. The first was to Sheri. I explained about the defense fund drive for Jarel. She agreed to start organizing the women at the library. She asked about Ramon and I filled her in.

"Are you enjoying clipping coupons?" I asked.

"You bet. Everything is running smoothly."

"I keep trying to make time for a coffee visit, but I keep getting jammed up. Sure you're okay?"

"I'm fine," she declared. "Don't worry about me. Take care of your business. Wade is too busy with Jarel's defense to worry right now. I'll pay the taxes in a week or so."

"Don't cut it too close to the deadline. We might have to improvise if he proves stubborn."

"Jo Beth, I could talk him into shaving his head and wearing boxer shorts. He's putty in my hands."

I laughed. "I'll see you later."

My next call was to David Sherwood, my attorney in Fontain, New York. He and Wade are handling a civil suit for me. I needed a favor.

"Hi, David, how are you?"

"Fine, personally, but your case is stalled again."

"Whoa," I said. "Don't start telling me about it. I've heard enough about that sucker to last me a lifetime."

"Well, you didn't call New York from Georgia to inquire about my health. What can I do for you?"

"A favor. Can you hire someone to run a fast check on a veterinarian who should be currently practicing in Andrel?"

"I have an agency I use. Their rates are reasonable, but they charge more for express checks. Seems everybody's in a hurry for information nowadays."

"I'm willing to pay the extra freight. My dogs are without a vet, and I'm getting antsy."

"Give me his name and what information you need." Straight-to-the-point Sherwood. I sometimes can't help but admire a Yankee. This one surely didn't indulge in frivolous chitchat.

"His name's Harvey Gusman. I need a criminal check,

a fast buzz on his finances, and a faster check on his license. I want to know if he's ever been in trouble with the state board."

"I'm just guessing, but I'd say at least four days."

"Tell them I need it by late tomorrow afternoon. Have them call me direct."

"Anything else?"

"That'll do it."

"Good-bye."

"Nice chatting with you, David," I told the empty line.

I called Hank and asked, "Can you talk?"

"Yep. I gave FIB and GIB the conference room. They don't call me unless they run out of coffee or doughnuts."

"Any new leads?"

"I had to put out an APB on a fired employee from Cannon Trucking who's probably back in Mexico, raising babies instead of Cain. They're reaching for any and everything they can. Also, a new face has appeared. It seems she's a profile expert. Nice legs."

"Is she giving you the come-hither look?" I teased.

"Moi?" He chuckled. "I'm a small-town hick sheriff. She gave me the keys to her rental car. I checked her in, deposited her luggage on the bed, and took her the room key."

"Does she wear silk underwear?"

"Plain white briefs. I was disappointed. But her perfume was nice."

"Letch!" I was thinking about my next question and how to sound casual. "How about the sons? Have they considered them? Are they suspects?"

"Nah, they're clean. Funny you should ask. The grandpa and a security dude were making all kinds of accusations a few days ago. They stirred up such a stink, the FIBS started investigating *them!* Goes to show you what assholes they are. Hey," he said softly. "Don't you do sweeps at Cannon Trucking? How tight are you with the security people out there?"

"I know that the top man in security is near retirement, but I can't remember his name. I deal with the peons," I explained. "I just remembered hearing one of the guards making a joke about the sons awhile back. Must've been almost a year ago. Don't know what made me remember now." I was trying to sound vague and seem as if I could barely recall the incident. "I don't think they're well liked out there, from the way personnel acts."

"You got that right," he agreed. "Most of the workers are trying to figure out what's going on with all those suits swarming around the place, but they're quick to badmouth the boss's sons. The latest rumor circulating is that the plant's under investigation by the Justice Department for some kind of interstate violations. Some are beginning to wonder about the boss, thinking he might've taken a powder instead of being ill. FIB and GIB better work fast. They're going to give away the ball game themselves."

"How's Jarel doing?" I wanted to change the subject.

"He's not happy with solitary confinement, but it's the only place I can keep him safe. I'd like to ship him elsewhere. I sweat every day he's under my roof." He sounded apprehensive.

"I know it's rough," I commiserated. "I gotta run. Take care."

"You too," he answered.

During lunch I listened for Tim's call. When it finally came, I was sorting harnesses in the grooming room.

"What's happening?" he asked. "Find out anything?"

"I know three places where he isn't," and explained about the warehouse search.

"How's Kenton working out?"

"So far so good," I said cautiously. "He does what I

tell him, and he definitely knows cars. I'm not positive, but I think I know why the initials are giving you a hard time."

"Give," he demanded.

"You and Frank Senior were so vocal about the boys, they thought you were trying to divert suspicion from yourselves."

"Christ, I can't believe they're so thick!"

"Believe. Do you have anything for me? Something someone remembered?"

"Yep, here's the latest skinny. About five months ago, one of our local drivers had a fender bender with a Mexican woman who belongs to that bunch of fortune-tellers out on Three-oh-one. Naturally, the old woman sustained more damage—our driver was in an eighteen-wheeler. Since the accident, the driver's been in two more accidents, one small, one large, and neither one was his fault. He's also lost thirteen pounds he can't afford to lose. He's convinced the woman put a spell on him. That she's practicing voodoo, or something.

"A dispatcher is positive that the routing number on a forty-eight-foot trailer has been altered and that the total cars on-line in the computer have been changed to make the count balance.

"One of the drivers thinks his wife's having an affair with one of the other dispatchers. Seems his wife turns up missing when the driver's on haul. He's put two and two together and come up with five. He's been charting the dispatcher and his wife's whereabouts for months. We found a loaded shotgun in his locker last week. He says he likes to duck hunt, but I'm skeptical. I notified the sheriff. That's it, so far."

"Whooee," I replied, "I hope your company insurance covers mental health. Your fender basher needs some help if he believes in voodoo. As for the suspected wife, did you notify the sheriff or the sheriff's department?"

"Sheriff's department. What's the difference?"

"Maybe whether the wife keeps breathing. Call Hank personally. Act like it's a routine follow-up. I bet the good ol' boys haven't done a thing to warn her of the danger or to have a serious talk with the husband."

"I'll call him this afternoon."

"Why is the dispatcher so sure that the numbers have been changed on one of the trailers and the total count altered?"

"He plays the Florida lotto faithfully. He claims he's played the same number on Play Four since they began the game in nineteen ninety-one. Said he hit the number twice within the first twenty-five days. Said he made five grand on a twenty-five-buck investment. He's played the same four numbers ever since, but admits that lately he hasn't had much luck."

"The four numbers are the routing numbers for the trailer?" I made an educated guess.

"Only the last four. The routing number has eight digits."

"Do you believe him?"

"I haven't given it much thought. He says he's saved all the tickets he played on the game. Over four years' worth."

"Did he report it to anyone?"

"I didn't ask." He was embarrassed.

"So you didn't believe him." My voice was flat.

"It isn't that. As I was laying it out for you, I started thinking, Who could've changed the numbers if the guy's telling the truth? I didn't like the name I came up with. I should've checked it out." Tim was disgusted with himself.

"Who?" I knew it had to be one of the three boys.

"Donald, the youngest son. He's in charge of the computer system."

"All right, let's doodle here," I said, thinking out loud.

"Let's assume the dispatcher's correct, and a trailer's missing. We'll also assume the total was altered to cover the loss. Why would the boys need an empty forty-eight-foot trailer?"

We said the words at the same time.

"Damn!"

"Shit!"

The "damn" was mine. "How long has it been missing?" I was pumped. Maybe we had a lead.

"Several months, he wasn't sure. It was something he wouldn't have noticed every day. He said he gradually became aware of not spotting the number on the screen. I'll go back and get the answers we need." His voice was grim.

We must've been thinking the same thoughts, visualizing a man held captive in one of his own freight-hauling trailers. Where had the sons parked it? A forty-eight-foot object is not easy to hide. It could be parked inside an abandoned warehouse we didn't know about, or hauled into the deep woods and hidden among acres of pine trees, or—I swallowed—it could be buried underground.

"Does Cannon Trucking own any earth-moving equipment?" My question was asked in a very low voice. I didn't feel so hot.

"Oh, God." Tim groaned. "I hadn't thought of that. Do you think they buried him?"

"Anything's possible. Don't jump the gun, Tim. We've made some quantum leaps with our logic. I don't think you should go back and ask the dispatcher anything. If, and it's a big if, we're correct with our conclusions, we don't want to let them know we're suspicious."

"This is the fourteenth day he's been missing, Jo Beth."

"I know that. What would you like me to do? Tell me your plan. I'm all ears."

"I just feel so damn helpless. I'm not doing anything!"

"Yes, you are," I soothed. "You found out a trailer's missing. You also had me called in, and you produced Kenton for me. If Frank's still alive, we'll find him. Hang in there."

I heard him sigh. "I'll call tomorrow. I gotta go."

"Right."

I felt for him. It's hard to sit on the sidelines with your hands tied.

Kenton was waiting when I pulled over in front of Tim's house. I moved Bobby Lee over while he stood watching.

"Hi," he said as he climbed in and settled in the seat. He reached over to fondle Bobby Lee's ears and got a handful of dewlap and drool just as Bobby Lee turned to greet him.

"Gross! He slobbers!" He made a face and rubbed his hand on his pants leg.

"There's tissue in the glove compartment. All bloodhounds slobber. A little drool won't hurt you. How did school go today?"

"Boy, the guys were really impressed when I told them about the blind bloodhound and searching the warehouses!"

"Say what?" I was pulling away from the curb, but I braked suddenly when I heard his words. Kenton hadn't fastened his seat belt. He threw his hands up and braced himself against the dash.

"Just kidding!" he yelled when he saw my face. "That's what you were really asking, wasn't it? When you asked me about school? You wanted to know if I'd blabbed about what we were doing, right?"

"I was making polite conversation, you lit—big jerk!"

I was angry more at myself than with him. He'd caught me napping, and I'd reacted. I felt foolish.

"I'm sorry," I said, regaining my composure. "You startled me and caught me by surprise. Are you hurt?"

"Nah."

"Pity," I said, under my breath but loud enough for him to hear. He tried to suppress a grin when he caught my glance. I grinned back.

We traveled a couple of miles in silence. Bobby Lee was leaning companionably against Kenton and enjoying his attention. Kenton looked at me.

"How long have you been using Bobby Lee for searches?"

"Since July."

"He's a good dog, huh? I bet your other dogs ain't as good as this one."

"Bobby Lee's good," I agreed, "but I have a lot of excellent dogs. Don't use ain't," I corrected. "Aren't."

"Yeah, I bet," he said with a quirky grin. He ignored the grammar lesson.

A light bulb glowed above my head. Now I knew why he was looking so smug. Back in April, Kenton and his brother had planted a small bag of marijuana in their stepfather's—John's—rig, hoping he'd be sent to the big house and out of their lives. They resented him for marrying their mother and giving them orders. The dogs had found the weak stash, called shake. After questioning John, I knew it wasn't his and didn't report it. I also knew it wouldn't help John in his effort to win the boys over. It was a cruel prank and could've gotten him fired and caused him to lose his certified driver's license. The boys weren't told and were never punished. It was far enough in the past. I felt it was safe now to indulge myself.

"I have two dogs named Tolstoy and Frost," I began. "I was working with them in your dad's place of employment, Cannon Trucking, back in April. Tolstoy found that pitiful bag of poor-boy you and your brother planted in the sleeping compartment of his rig." I watched Kenton's eyes go wide with shock. "He wouldn't let me report you. He wanted to help you and your brother and be a good dad to you both. Has he been a good dad?"

"Yeah," he admitted. "He didn't say anything about it!" he whispered with awe. "Why didn't he give us a lickin'?"

"I think you can figure it out if you put your mind on it."

As I turned onto Big Alligator Road, I slowed the van.

"Here's the plan. We're gonna stop at each house that faces the road. We're looking for your friend from school. He moved out here about six months ago, and you don't know where he lives. We'll make up a name. We'll only stop at houses that show evidence of having kids. You get out and ask the questions; you'll be better than I. Kids sometimes get tongue-tied around strange adults. What we're trying to find out is if they saw anything, somewhere in the neighborhood of six months ago. Don't be rigid. We're not sure of the exact time. Describe the three cars. Also mention that any of the three cars could've been on this road about two weeks ago. Again, we're not sure of the exact day or time. It could have been morning, noon, or late at night. Oh, also ask about any large pieces of equipment being transported on flat-bed trucks."

"I'm looking for my friend, and I ask all them questions? It'll take me a week!"

"Improvise. Help me think up a name for your friend."

"What's that word? Imp—?"

"It means you're a sharp cookie and will find the right words to say, if you try." I gave him a smile of encouragement.

"What if we pick a name and there's someone with that name living on this road?"

"How about Kilroy Swartzenager?"

Kenton snickered. "You're kidding, right?"

I pulled over, motor idling, and studied my helper's face.

"Are you sure you want to do this? You don't have to, if it makes you feel uncomfortable."

"I'll do it," he said, avoiding my eyes. "I'll just feel like a dork!"

"We'll just jump in and get our feet wet. See what happens. How about Kenny Jones?"

"Suits me," he muttered indifferently.

I put the van in gear and pulled back onto the road. Maybe he was experiencing stage fright. I had to keep reminding myself he was only twelve. His size made me expect more maturity.

Slowing, I pulled into the drive of the first house on the left. It was a large red brick with a plain-looking landscape, two trucks parked in the dirt driveway, and—bingo!—a bicycle, lying carelessly tossed near the front door.

Kenton unbuckled his seat belt and opened his door.

"Stand near the door until you're sure there's no Cujo in residence. I'll honk the horn. Good luck."

Not answering me, he stared at the house. He hadn't stepped far from the van's door when a lanky teenager came out of the house and approached him. I saw the teenager shake his head, and I assumed that Kenton was inquiring about dogs. They met in the middle of the lawn, and I couldn't hear their voices. I settled back to wait and lit a cigarette. Bobby Lee leaned in my direction and I rubbed his neck.

The route I had decided to try this afternoon, Big Alligator Road, is a wide unpaved thoroughfare approximately twelve miles long. Where it intersects with three other similar roads it forms Teeterville Junction, which consists of one small independent grocery store with a gas pump. The rest of the land is planted pines, miles and miles of planted pines. About halfway along this road, Frank Cannon owns blocks of timber totaling 15,272 acres. It was the first parcel of land on the list that Little Bemis had supplied. Frank Senior bought the land back in the late forties, when you could hardly give the stuff away, for twenty dollars an acre. At that time, government subsidies were a joke, and most people didn't want to wait forty years for the land to produce natural tree growth for harvest.

Even Georgia became mechanized after World War II. Agriculture experts and tree farmers grew new strains of slash pine, which matured as a money crop within twenty-five years. Frank Senior had lived long enough to gloat over the wise investments he'd made almost fifty years ago. Now the timber is very valuable, fetching higher prices each year.

Kenton strolled back like a triumphant warrior returning from a successful joust. He had a self-satisfied smirk on his face and was walking tall. I hadn't timed him, but I'd finished my cigarette, so at least ten minutes had passed.

Kenton concentrated on fastening his seat belt, ignoring me. I backed out of the driveway, fast, angrily turned the wheel, sped down the dirt road a short way, pulled over, and slammed on brakes. I turned off the engine.

"Well?" I put a wealth of meaning in my lone utterance.

Kenton turned in his seat sideways and gave me a huge grin. "Boy, was he cool! He knows cars almost as good as me! He's the quarterback for the Rebels. He's in the ninth grade at Balsa City Junior High. Man, is he cool!"

"Kenton." I strained to sound reasonable. "I've never, ever, entertained the thought of strangling a child, but I'm now on the bubble. Gimme some fast-speak."

"Sorry 'bout that." He giggled. "I was joshing you. Can't you take a joke? I got what you wanted on my first try. And, boy, am I glad, 'cause I don't like to talk to no kid I don't know. Ain't that cool or what?"

34

The Devil Dances in Empty Pockets
November 18, Thursday, 5 P.M.

I didn't bother to correct his use of ain't because I saw that he was delighted he'd provoked me. He was hugging his information tightly and hated to spend any nuggets of what he'd learned.

"You're shining me on," I suggested, with obvious disbelief.

"Cross my heart!" he said quickly, flashing his hand across his chest in the ageless gesture.

"Why won't you tell me what you learned?"

"'Cause you're mad at me. I just wanted to surprise you. Maybe tease you a little. Then you got crappy." He was playing with Bobby Lee's ears and looking sullen.

I forced a smile, reached over, and punched him lightly on his shoulder. "Let's start over. I'm Miz Jo Beth and you're Kenton. You're doing me a favor and I'm grateful. We're looking for Kenny Jones. You've just gotten back into the van from asking questions of a young man who came out of the house when we blew the horn. Now, *what did he tell you?*" I yelled.

Kenton glanced up, saw my grin, and returned it.

"The dude saw the Trans Am twice. He said it was silver, and when he got eighteen he was going to get a job and buy one just like it, only his will have about twenty layers of lacquer where you can look down into the surface and see these flecks of glitter. It's his favorite car, so that's why he remembers."

"Great. Does he remember the last time he saw it?"

"He said about two weeks ago. He ain't sure what day it was. He said it could've been Thursday or Friday. Both days he was throwing his football through an old tire his dad hung up so he could hit his receiver better. He said it was late, after football practice, 'round five-thirty. He was getting ready for the game on Saturday. The night-light had just come on, and the car was going slow, like it was trying to miss the potholes. Two men were in the front seat. His mother called him in for supper right after."

My heart was beating against my ribs. The time sounded right. Cannon was supposed to have been taken later on Thursday night, but the sons could've waited until the next day to bring him out here. Friday could be the right day. There are nine different pieces of property owned by Frank and his father in this county. I couldn't quite believe we'd started checking and hit the correct one on the first go-round. My luck just isn't that good.

Common sense quelled my enthusiasm. "When did he see the car the first time?"

"Way back in March or April. He can't remember 'xactly when. He saw it twice. Both times were late at night. He said he was practicing for spring training and blew a muscle. His arm was hurting like crazy, and he couldn't sleep. He was afraid to tell his mom. She didn't like him playing football, 'fraid he'd get hurt. He was lying out on the screened patio, both nights, when he saw the

Trans Am. Said he didn't know what time it was. The noise of the diesel grinding gears made him get up from the swing and watch for it—"

"Diesel?" I interjected.

"Yeah, diesel." He sounded pleased with my reaction. "He wanted to see how many pieces were coming in to log. Said his mom and dad get uptight when trucks are logging nearby; they mess up the road. They won't let his younger brother ride his bicycle out on the road when they're hauling back and forth."

"Pieces to log?" I knew what he meant, I just wanted to check that our quarterback could recognize heavy machinery as well as his favorite cars.

"You know, logging machines, timberjacks, skidders, loaders, pinchers, stuff like that."

"I know them, you've demonstrated you know them, but the question is, could our quarterback recognize them?"

"'Course, you must think all of us is dumb!"

"Are," I corrected automatically. "With using 'all of us.' *Are* is plural. *Is* is singular."

Kenton flushed and gave me a look of contempt.

"Sorry." I tried to look contrite. "It grates on my ears, can't help myself. I use a lot of poor English. I try to learn something new every day. You should try it. It would help in tests and things." He appeared mollified.

"Aw, it's okay," he said, shrugging. "This Trans Am probably isn't the same one we saw today. The dude said those guys in the Trans Am he saw were moving in somewhere down the road. The guy you're looking for don't live down this road, does he?"

"No, but what makes our guy think he does?" It was an idle question. I felt it wasn't possible either, but he hadn't gotten around to explaining the diesel sound. I was still curious.

"The guy mentioned that trucks always change gears

near his house. It takes them that long to build up speed after slowing to turn onto the road."

"What trucks?"

"He said the excavator came first, then the Trans Am, and then the eighteen-wheeler."

I stared at Kenton while my heart flopped in my chest like a gaffed fish. I asked the first question that popped into my mind.

"What made him think they were all together?"

Kenton tried to be patient. "They had to be together. No Trans Am is going to idle along behind a big rig hauling an excavator. On a wide road like this, he would've left him in the dust as soon as they made the turn. It takes those heavy babies a long time to shift through all their gears and get up speed."

"I don't understand the moving in part. What does an excavator have to do with moving?"

I did understand, but I wanted to hear the quarterback's explanation. My daddy had called them draglines. Those big machines look like prehistoric monsters, with large jagged toothlike jaws to bite the dirt and a long cranelike neck to move the dirt to a pile or load it onto a carrier. The kids were calling them excavators now. I was still hazy on why he associated the digging machine with moving to a new place.

Kenton looked at me like I was thickheaded.

"For the septic tank. If you move onto new land, you have to have a hole dug for the septic tank so the toilet will flush. You must live in the city."

"No," I said absentmindedly. "I have septic tanks, but mine were dug with a backhoe. A excavator sounds like overkill, but then I haven't dug any septic tanks recently, so who knows? What was the eighteen-wheeler for, moving the furniture?"

"Well, yeah, but he could also be a truck driver and own his rig," Kenton answered with wry tones.

"True, very true," I agreed. "You mentioned that he saw the Trans Am twice, and both times were late at night. Did he mention when he saw the car the second time?"

"He didn't mention it, I don't think."

"Try to remember, Kenton, it's important."

"I'm pretty sure he didn't say."

"Then we have to go back and ask him. I need to know if the equipment was returning from up the road and—and this is the most important question—if the semi was still pulling the trailer or was it just the tractor. Also, the time span between the two trips. Have you got it?"

"What's with the 'we'? You got a mouse in your pocket?"

"I stand corrected. *You* must go back and ask him."

"Aw, come on. I can't go back. He'll think I'm a dork!"

"Remember the man we're trying to help? This could save a lot of time if he remembers. Please?"

"Uh-uh, no way." He crossed his arms over his chest and looked stubborn.

I cranked up, turned around, went back to the driveway, and turned in. I tooted the horn twice and hopped out.

"Do they have a dog?"

"It died." Kenton's voice was subdued.

The same teenager came out of the house and stood on the stoop and looked at me. I started toward him, and he moved slowly toward me, looking uncertain. I gave him a big smile.

"Sorry to bother you twice, but Kenton forgot to ask you something. It'll only take a minute."

He looked embarrassed. "My mom said I shouldn't have talked so much when I didn't know where the kid lived. She said you might be a bill collector or a repossesser, looking for the car."

"Oh, no," I said, laughing and indicating my van. "I raise bloodhounds. I just need to know when you saw the car and equipment the second time. Were they headed this way and was the trailer still attached to the semi, or was it just the cab?"

His eyes lost focus as he tried to remember. I held my breath. A wisp of a woman stepped out of the house, held the screen door open, and stared at us.

"Dwight!" Her call had the imperative ring of command.

"I gotta go."

"Please," I mouthed softly, as I gave the woman a large friendly wave. "It's important."

"It was the next night about the same time," he mumbled. "It was just the cab—without the trailer—the Trans Am, and the excavator." He turned and headed back.

"Thank you!" I called. I gave his mom another wave and got out of there. I backed out and headed back to town.

"Kenton, I need to find a phone fast. You look on the right side and I'll take the left."

He was slouched down in the seat and avoided my eyes when I turned his way.

"Did you find out what you wanted to know?" He straightened in the seat and appeared to be looking for a phone.

"Yes, yes, yes!" I sang in happiness. "I think we have a good chance now. Boy, were we lucky finding that teenager!"

"There's one!" he exclaimed, pointing toward a convenience store. I pulled up beside the phone, dug for change, and held out a five-dollar bill to Kenton.

"Get us a soda. Make mine a Diet Coke. Get yourself a candy bar, if it won't spoil your dinner or get me in hot water with your mom." He took off for the store, and I stepped into the booth and dialed Hank's number. I glanced at my watch. I hoped he was still at his desk.

"Thank goodness you don't keep banker's hours," I said when he answered. "I know it's very short notice, but how about coming out and eating supper with me and my trainees? Miz Jansee Tatum is the cook, and she really puts out a delicious spread."

"You want something, right?"

"Jeez," I said, sounding hurt. "When did you get so suspicious?"

"When you start fattening me up for the kill," he answered, chuckling. "What time do we eat?"

"Between six-thirty and seven. Don't be late."

"I'll be on time. I've tasted Miz Jansee's cooking."

"See ya."

Kenton came back with the sodas and change. He saw me eyeing his large Butterfinger candy bar.

"Want a bite?"

"Just break me off a small piece. I'm supposed to be on a diet." He handed me a generous portion, and I munched as I drove.

Pulling up in front of Tim's house, I turned in the seat and gave Kenton a grateful smile.

"I won't be needing you any longer, Kenton, but I want to thank you for your help. Maybe later I'll be able to tell you just how valuable the information you helped me uncover was."

Disappointment and dismay washed over his face. "I . . . I wanted to see Bobby Lee find someone. I'm sorry I wouldn't go back and ask that dude some more questions. If you'll give me another chance, I promise I'll do everything you ask."

"Hey, I'm not angry with you. I honestly don't need you any longer. A long time ago I was twelve, and I know how things can bug you. Listen, I'm really busy right now, but in a couple of weeks, when I get caught up, I'll give you a tour of the kennel, and you can watch us practice field exercises. In fact, I'll let you hide from a dog and see if he can find you."

He perked up. "Honest?"

"Cross my heart," I said, making the fast motion with my hand.

He opened the van door and got out.

"Bye," I called and waved.

"Don't forget!" he yelled as I pulled away.

When I reached home, I took a quick tour of the kennel. Now that I was without a vet, I'd worry about the animals until I had a replacement. Bloodhounds are not an easy breed to raise. Maybe all breeds are difficult, but bloodhounds have special problems because of their size. All the dogs looked well, so I hurried in to shower and dress for supper. The trainers had left, and the trainees were drifting back in for their pre-meal drinks. I put on a navy raw silk dress with a daring neckline and added pearls and high heels. I was dressing to please Hank. I was gonna ask for a big favor, and he likes silk and high heels. I'd need all the ammunition available. Hank can be as stubborn as a mule. I wanted him mellow.

Supper was over and I was on my second beer. I had a chance to check with Wayne before Hank arrived, and he assured me that the trainees were finished with their exercises and everyone had done well. He signed that he had no hesitation about sending the four dogs to their new homes tomorrow. Only then did I relax and stop feeling guilty about missing so much of the seminar. If Wayne said they passed muster, they were very good indeed.

Susan wore royal purple, and Jasmine had on a soft wool dress in yellow. Chief Clemments had picked Rosie up right after supper. They were going shopping for drapes. Their wedding was less than three weeks away, and Rosie was nervous about every detail. Shopping soothed her.

When Hank went to the bathroom, I huddled with Susan and Jasmine. "I need to talk to Hank alone. I'm gonna split for a while. Secrets, and all that. Will you two dance, talk, and make merry with the four trainees? I sure would be obliged. I don't want them to feel neglected on their last night here."

Susan smiled. "Since you ask so nicely, Sidden, I'll personally and gladly take over your duties as hostess."

"Jasmine?"

She smiled too and made a shooing motion; Hank was returning. I picked up my beer and white sweater and stopped in front of him.

"Want to go with me on a kennel check?"

"Sure. Let me get a beer."

As soon as we cleared the door, Hank helped me put on my sweater. A cool front was moving down and over from the middle of the country. The temperature had dropped ten degrees in the last four hours. Finally, some fall weather was arriving to break the heat. The wind was crisp and cool, blowing about fifteen miles an hour. The sky was clear, the stars were bright, and the air held a faint hint of winter. It felt wonderful on my face. We strolled along the walk, and I opened a wooden covered box and pulled a flashlight from its bracket.

"Carol went home to her mother?"

"This morning. We weren't friends, exactly, but I'm going to miss both of them." The flashlight beam revealed sleeping dogs that lazily raised their heads and then put them back down. Very few took the trouble to get up and walk to the fence to see who was out here.

We progressed along the cages and turned right into the north wing.

"What happened to Mr. Initials and his handcuffs?" Hank asked.

"Chief Webber? He left. He had just stopped by to tell me his sergeant couldn't make the seminar."

"I saw Cathy in the bank Monday. She mentioned you were driving around town with a strange man beside you."

After checking the last of the pens, I snapped off the light.

"Why don't you just say what's on your mind, Hank, and quit pussy-footing around the subject?"

"I just wondered if you miss me."

"I miss what we had for maybe two weeks," I said carefully, "until we started ripping out each other's vital organs. You can't tell me you miss our verbal brawls."

"I even miss them sometimes late at night when I'm sleeping alone." His voice had deepened.

"Surely you jest!" I forced a laugh. "Let's go sit on the porch. I need to ask a favor."

"I should have known."

I ignored his comment and chattered brightly about nothing until we were seated on the back porch. There was enough light to see his face.

"Hank, I want to tell you something. Then we can figure out just how you can present it to FIB and GIB. I know approximately where Frank Cannon is being held. It would take forever, on foot with the dogs, to find him. He doesn't have much time left. Can you get the initials to search for him in the air and keep me out of it? I also can't tell you how I know where to look."

"You're serious? You're not pulling my leg?"

"Nope, I know within a few thousand acres where he is."

"Jo Beth, get real. You can pull this crap with me— I've fallen for some of your schemes more than once—but you can't con the FBI or the GBI. They'll chew you up and spit you out. I sadly regret giving you confidential information. I've been worrying about that fact ever since you called me up and started asking questions. Back out of this now, and don't tell me another word. Are you trying to make me an accessory before—or after—the fact?"

"Hank, he's been buried underground for two weeks. We're his only hope," I pleaded. "Listen, I think about him every minute. No one's looking for him. The suits are playing around with past employment records. Say a reliable informant called it in. Would that work?"

"Nada. They'd want the informant and a signed statement in triplicate, but that isn't the point." He reached over and clasped my hands in his. "He's dead, Jo Beth. It's been two weeks. Something went wrong. He's out in the swamp somewhere in water, and the alligators will clean up all evidence. I don't know what you've heard or surmised or whatever, but you don't have a hope in hell of finding him alive. You're playing a dangerous game. Get out of this while you still can, or *if* you can. You hear me?"

I pulled loose from his grasp and stood. Smoothing my skirt, and running a hand through my hair, I gave him a polite, pleasant smile.

"Thanks for coming to supper. I enjoyed your company, but I can't abide your moralistic drivel and incorrect assumptions. I'd like to wish you good night before I lose my temper."

I stuck out my hand. Hank took it, held it briefly, shook it, and fled. He knew I wasn't whistling Dixie. I went back to my guests alone.

I was completely buried in dirt. My mouth was packed with crumbly sour-smelling soil, and I was choking. When I tried to blow it free, my inhalations clogged my throat again. Horror and panic pushed me into a frenzied attempt to break free. I couldn't move my arms! Oh, God, Oh, God! I was weakening, and my legs wouldn't respond to my pathetic commands. I couldn't breathe. My lungs were bursting from holding my breath. I made a final desperate lunge and sat up in bed.

Sobbing, I took in great gasping breaths until dizziness made me realize I was hyperventilating. I threw back the covers, turned on the lamp, and stared wide-eyed at my bed. I couldn't shake the nightmare of being entombed. I rose, shaking, and clutched my shoulders, chilled to the bone. I was drenched in sweat. I saw the sweat-dampened tangle of sheets.

I made coffee, took a shower, and changed the bed linen. Wrapped in a flannel muumuu and a fleece housecoat, I drank coffee and smoked. Bobby Lee sat and leaned heavily against my leg. His large warm torso banished the last dregs of fear. Disturbed from his night's rest, Rudy was sitting in front of his dish, angrily demanding a snack to compensate for his loss. I ignored him.

I settled back and started to plan. I'd get the damn helicopter myself. Cannon had money and was willing to spend it to find his son. If I failed, and if the thousand in expenses didn't cover it, I'd at least know I'd put my money where my mouth was.

Relenting, I fed Bobby Lee and Rudy a token snack and went back to bed. Less than an hour later, I awoke again in the grip of the powerful nightmare, which was just as debilitating and scary as the first time. I gave up all thoughts of sleep and spent the rest of the night washing and drying two loads of clothes and waiting impatiently for the dawn's early light.

35

Better Than Snuff and Not Half as Dusty
November 19, Friday, 10 A.M.

After breakfast, I spent a miserable and frustrating two hours on the phone trying to locate a helicopter. Either the machine was under repairs or out doing someone else's business or they didn't have a pilot available for today. They all suggested reserving a day the following week. They also suggested, tactfully, that a deposit equaling the day's charter had to be physically in their hands before the bird would spread its wings.

I called Jasmine into my office, told her only the pertinent facts so she could continue searching, and said I was going to my bedroom to make other calls. I told her to give up on Waycross and try Jacksonville.

She nodded acceptance of my instructions and gave me a pleasant smile.

"Let's see if I have the correct information. I'm to rent a chopper in order to search fifteen thousand acres for an object that was buried underground at least six months ago. The object's dimensions are about ten feet high by ten feet wide, forty-eight feet long. The ground will be camouflaged.

When spotted, they aren't to land but take careful coordinates and phone you immediately. Is that correct?"

"Perfect."

"Are you out of your gourd?" She was smiling. "Waycross is already calling the funny farm, requesting the butterfly net patrol. I trust you didn't give them your name?"

"Sounds kooky, huh?"

"The kookiest," she agreed.

"I didn't stop to think. My mind is ten jumps ahead on this caper, and I didn't get any sleep last night."

"I have a suggestion."

I propped my elbows on the desk and rubbed my weary eyes. "Shoot."

"Tell me what you're attempting to do. I'll be thinking about it until this afternoon at three when we wave farewell to our boys in blue." She glanced at her watch. "You're not needed until lunchtime. Go lie down. Take a nap. I'll unplug the phone and call you when it's time to eat. After we get rid of the troops, you and I together will solve your problem. You know our motto, 'Two women on hand are worth more than four men in the bush.'"

I laughed and told her everything.

After Jasmine shook me awake, I washed my face and joined the happy dinner guests. This was graduation day. I really felt guilty for not spending every minute with them. Tim called during lunch, and I told him nothing had happened. I didn't want him joining the search and bringing the initials with him. He wasn't too happy, but I told him that when the seminar ended today, I could devote more time to the search.

Hank called also. "Are we still friends?" he questioned.

"As ever was, big guy," I vowed. "I have a message for Tall Chief Who Doubts." Hank's proud of Indian blood he inherited from a grandmother, several times removed.

He chuckled. "What's the message?"

"I'm gonna make you eat your words from last night," I jeered, as I gently cradled the receiver. He didn't call back.

We posed for pictures and said cheese too many times. Donnie Ray was everywhere, fussing, rearranging groups, and being obnoxious to boot.

I said good-bye individually to Shakespeare, Margaret Mitchell, Hemingway, and Scarlett O'Hara. I knew I might never see these wonderful animals again, and I dripped tears with each final hug. I whispered into each ear that I loved them and that, if they ever felt the need, they were to return home immediately. I shook hands with the men and made them check to see if they had my telephone number. I said good-bye to Corporal Randall Jordan, Sergeant Curtis French, Deputy Sergeant Ralph Vaughn, and Sergeant Julian Tyre.

"If the dogs are ever unhappy, ill, lost, or stolen, call me immediately. Anytime day or night. No matter how late or early. Understood?"

"What about us?" They called out in chorus.

"You can find a good psychiatrist, internist, or psychic or pay the ransom. Just don't call me!"

They all hooted with laughter.

Wayne loaded two dogs into the van for the trip to the airport, and drove off with Donnie Ray and the dogs' new masters. The other two graduates loaded their newly acquired mantrailers into their cars. Jasmine, Rosie, and I waved until they were out of sight.

Rosie looked tearful. "It's so quiet! Lord, I'm gonna miss you all." It was now fifteen days until her nuptials. She was sniffing back her tears one minute and reading us the riot act the next.

"Would you look in on the dogs, Rosie? Jasmine and I have to load up for a field trip practice."

"You're leaving now?" She was surprised.

"Yes. You don't mind, do you?"

"Me? Why should I mind? Don't matter to me one way or the other!" she snapped. "Don't I always watch the dogs?"

She strode off still fussing, with all sails unfurled.

"I'm loading Bobby Lee, with Ulysses for backup. Don't forget to fill your water bottles."

"I've already filled the bottles and loaded them," Jasmine said. "There're also six Diet Cokes iced in your cooler and a bag of deer jerky. I'm taking Gulliver. I'm also loaded for bear."

We were both excited.

"Before we leave, take your rifle out of the rack and hide it under the straw in the middle dog cage on the left. I'll use the same cage location in my van. That way, we'll know where they are in both vans."

"Explain," she said.

"We're in the middle of hunting season, and we're going into a hunting club's territory. They'll probably board us and want to search for hunting guns, even with our go-free card from Cannon. You have the copy I printed for you?"

"Right here," she said, patting the pocket of her jeans. "They'd really go that far?"

"They act nuts all year, but during hunting season they're scary. If you spot them blocking the road, roll up your windows, leaving a two-inch crack in order to pass the permission letter to them, and lock your doors. If they turn ugly, grab your radio and thirty-eight and wedge yourself between your seat and the doorway bulkhead. I'll ride to the rescue. I'll do the same, if I get into trouble. There can't be a hunting accident with both of us present."

"Gotcha."

"Wear your hunting jacket and matching orange cap, even if you get out to pee. Game wardens come out of the woodwork during hunting season. The warden would give you a ticket if you weren't wearing the vest, even if you had no gun. They try to save lives. There're lots of itchy trigger fingers out there. Some would shoot an elephant if it walked into range."

"Got it!" Jasmine gave me a snappy salute. We grinned at each other.

I reached under my seat for the soft leather bag holding the mass of keys Cannon had sent me. I picked out the correct ring from the attached tag and saw it held three keys. I slipped one off and handed it to Jasmine. We loaded the dogs and pulled out with Jasmine's van behind mine.

The day was perfect and the air smelled wonderful. Our cool front was finally here, and I rejoiced with all the others. Summer had overstayed its welcome. Bobby Lee had his head out the window, the wind rippling his elongated ears.

When we turned off Big Alligator Road, I pulled up to the locked cable and shut off the motor. I hopped out and went back to Jasmine's window.

"You turn left on all roads leading left. When you reach a crossroad, always turn right. Keep turning right and you should come back into this road we're on. I'll do the same on the right. These roads don't have names. Use your map and our special numbers to remember where you are. It's easy to get lost. When you unlock a gate, be sure and lock it after you pull through. An unlocked gate will have hunters chasing you. I'll do a radio check every fifteen minutes. If I don't call on time, come looking. Who do you want to be today?"

"How about Protector?" Jasmine suggested.

"Okay, I'll be Avenger." We enjoy picking out code names for the radio. We get silly sometimes.

I unlocked the cable. Both sides have locks. One side has the timber company's lock, and the other has the hunting club's lock. Naturally, with a fifty-fifty chance of being right, I chose the wrong side. I drove through and then Jasmine. I watched her in the side mirror as she ran back, pulled up the cable, and locked it.

A road leading to the right appeared in less than a quarter of a mile. I gave Jasmine a wave as I turned onto the narrow three-path road. I watched the overgrown ruts carefully. Some potholes are spring busters. On both sides of the road the timber had been clear-cut for the first mile. After that, half-grown timber was on my left and trees old enough to log were on my right. I passed several sloughs where the big machines had scooped out shallow basins in order to get enough dirt to build up and repair this road. Overflow from ditches could cover the road and wash away the sandy soil. Then the backhoes would be off-loaded to scoop dirt, and the road grader would level and pack it down. It's a constant battle to keep the roads passable out here near the swamp. They could dig here and get sandy soil; fifty yards down the road they'd get black gooey muck with tannic sediment.

At four-fifteen, I keyed my mike.

"Avenger to Protector. Over."

"Protector. Over."

"Check. Out."

"Out."

We keep our transmissions very brief.

"Was that you calling me, Bud?" boomed out of my CB.

Oh-oh, we had some hunters nearby. It pays to listen in.

"Bud, you there? I was taking a piss and didn't catch

what you said. Boy, this beer runs through you, don't it? I'm on Narrow Road. It's slipperier than a limp dick! You been on it today? Bud, you gotcha ears on?"

I rolled my eyes in the silence. Such a gentleman.

"Slick, you calling me? I was taking a dump. You got any extra beer? I've only got twenty-two cans left! Hee, hee, hee. Come on?" Bud's voice was not as loud as Slick's. He wasn't as close.

I just wished these guys would finish their conversation and get off the airwaves. Their CB transmission would override my hand radio. I couldn't send Jasmine a message if they continued their verbal garbage, and she wouldn't be able to reach me. They jawed back and forth for another five minutes before they signed off. I breathed a sigh of relief.

I reached an intersecting road and turned left. This road was in better condition, and I could travel a tad faster. I wasn't expecting Frank to be on the edge of the road waiting for me. I knew that aimlessly driving the roads wouldn't produce where they'd buried him. This was a scouting expedition to see, personally, where the roads led. To grid-search this area of more than fifteen thousand acres, using two working teams and making the trails a hundred feet apart, working eight hours a day, would take approximately twelve years. With a hundred-yard path, you could still miss him. Walk within twenty-five yards and not see a thing.

I had really been kidding myself. This was an impossible mission. Finding out the who and when and where had bolstered my enthusiasm, but driving mile after mile through this timber, I realized my where was just too big. If they buried the trailer months ago, they had to have a way to get in and out of it because Frank was taken only two weeks ago. If the digging, in order to place him inside, was done two weeks ago, it might show from the air, or if I could walk within fifteen feet of the spot. If they had smoothed the dirt, tamped it down, and scattered pine needles and leaves over the raw earth, I could walk over the spot where he was buried and not see it.

That's where a bloodhound is a miracle with its scent ability. If they're given a person's uncontaminated scent article, they can tell you if that person is under ninety feet of water, tons of concrete rubble, or tons of dirt. Their ability is uncanny.

I came to my second crossroads and again turned left. This road should lead me back to the road where I started the search. It was four-thirty and time to call Jasmine.

"Avenger to Protector. Over."

"Protector. Over."

"Check. Out."

"Out."

I listened, but Slick and Bud remained silent.

I passed a decent-sized slough filled with water and covered with lily pads. A large water bird was standing in its shallow depths, balanced on long pipe-cleaner legs, motionless, fishing for his supper. I scanned the edge of the shallow pond, looking for its mate. The water bird was alone. It made me feel sad. I'd read somewhere that they mate for life. If their mate dies, they never mate again. I caught a glimpse of movement and spotted another water bird, a little shorter, near some tall reeds. I'd missed it on my first scan. I grinned. I felt better. The sun was down behind the trees in the west, and the air was growing cooler.

My route fed into the road I'd started on. I turned right and drove past Jasmine's first road and continued on to the second road on the left. I pulled over to the edge and turned off the motor. I got out and walked over to the edge and studied the ground. There were plenty of tracks, but Jasmine hadn't traveled here. I'd sit here and wait for her to come out. I'm not good at reading tracks, but Wayne had made it easy for us. He had cut a small *V* in the fat part of the tread on Jasmine's back left tire. Mine was on the right side. You could spot it quickly if you knew what to look for.

I walked back across the road and heard the sound of a motor approaching. I got into the van and locked the doors but left the windows down. A red truck with oversized tires and lifts stopped quickly when it pulled around and in front of me. I watched as a man climbed down from the cab and walked toward me.

"Howdy." He had a wide grin. He was short and appeared to be in his late forties.

"Howdy."

"You alone?"

"Nope."

"He on a stand or in the bushes?"

"Neither. I'm working, not hunting. Partner's in another van down the road."

"What kind of dog is that?" He had just spotted Bobby Lee. I bit down on my lip to refrain from a sarcastic retort. The bright easily read letters on the van said BLOODHOUNDS. What did he think I'd haul around, shelties? He either didn't notice or couldn't read. A lot of adults around here can't read.

"He's a catch dog."

"Hogs? You hunt hogs?" His eyes widened as he spoke.

"Forced to. Big dogs eat a lot of meat."

His eyes narrowed. "Thought you said you were working, not hunting. What you bring catch dogs out here for? What kind of work you do out here? Your partner a member of this here hunting club?"

"Mister, are you writing a book? I have permission to be on this land, by the owner. Written permission. You asking for it?"

"Yep, sure nuff. We catch a lot of poachers out here!"

I unhooked my seat belt, reached over, opened the dash, and handed him a folded sheet of paper. It was a recipe Rosie had written by hand for me to pass on to Sheri. It was for an eggplant and squash casserole.

He squinted and studied the paper, then handed it back.

"Need some light?"

"Nah, it's okay. Had to check. No hard feelings?"

"Nope."

"Want a beer?" He put both hands on the door panel and moved a step closer. His wide grin was back. I couldn't resist.

"Mister, step back," I commanded sharply. "This catch dog's mean as a snake! Guy stuck his hand in the van 'bout a month ago, and this here dog took off two of his fingers! Caused me all kinds of trouble with my insurance company."

He stepped back at my command and was staring at Bobby Lee, who at the moment, had moved over and was peering over my right shoulder, looking at the man, or appearing to. He had really moved over to get closer to his voice. He likes strangers' voices; they usually pet him. He could barely reach my shoulder. I guess there wasn't enough light for the man to see Bobby Lee's restraining harness.

"Why do you carry him in the front seat and not in a cage?"

"Some fools come on to me when I'm working. All I have to do is open the door. Beats carrying a gun."

"Well, I gotta go. See ya around." He was illiterate but not dumb. He got the message.

I lit a cigarette, popped the top of a Diet Coke, and smiled. Time to call Jasmine, but she beat me to it.

"Protector to Avenger. Over."

"Avenger. Over."

"Sector four. Last leg of first turnoff. No emergency. I repeat, no emergency. Need to see. Over."

"Coming. Out."

"Out."

When I heard her voice, I placed my Coke in the holder, put out the cigarette, and grabbed the map and flashlight. I took a second to find the real sector four on the topical map of the county. It was quite a way over from my position. Good. If anyone was curious and checked the sector, they'd be going to a distant location.

Jasmine was on the road where I had sat waiting. I cranked up, turned onto it, and fought the urge to go faster. She'd said there was no emergency, just a need to see. Speculation would be useless. I had no idea what she wanted me to see. I turned on the high beams. It was dusk now, and the lights were more of a hindrance than a help. It wasn't completely dark yet, but I didn't want to run into her if she didn't have her lights on. It isn't easy to see the light green paint of the vans in the waning light. At least she could see my lights and turn hers on if I was close.

In less than a mile, I saw two small lights to the right and realized she had her parking lights on. When I got close enough, she hopped out of the van, ran between our bumpers, and was by my side before I turned off the ignition.

"Turn off your lights! It spoils your night vision!" Her voice vibrated with excitement.

"What is it?" I turned off the lights and got out of the van, clutching my flashlight. She grabbed my hand, pulled me to her door, reached in, and turned off her parking lights.

"Now, stand here facing the clear-cut and let your eyes adjust."

"What? What? Don't keep me in suspense!"

"You have to see it to appreciate it. Now, look about seventy-five yards over there."

I followed her pointing arm and gazed off into the almost darkness.

"I don't see a thing!" I complained.

"You're looking for a dark rectangle with a slightly lighter area adjoining it to the right."

"My God," I whispered softly when the implication of what I was staring at registered in my brain.

"Sherlock, did Watson find the dog that didn't bark?" The whites of her eyes were flashing at me. I could see them clearly.

"Watson," I said with growing excitement, "I believe you have!"

36

Let Sleeping Dogs Lie
Somewhere, Sometime

He lay in the sleeping bag and took stock of his health. He knew that whatever the illness had been, he had survived it. He felt much weaker but his head was clear. He'd crawled out of the bag earlier, drunk a bellyful of water, and passed some. Just the thought of food nauseated him. He chuckled. The irony of his earlier fears amused him. Fear of running out of food and water, being ill, alone with no medicine.

He had plenty of water. The third jug was still full and another held over a quart. More groceries than he would ever desire were waiting within reach. And medicine? Who needed medicine? Here he was, proof that you don't need a doctor or an emergency room to recover. He had also feared death. All that needless worry, for naught.

Death was going to be pleasant. He was warm, dry, and comfortable. He wouldn't die under bright lights, probing hands, stabbing needles, intrusive scalpels, and the harsh reality of pain. No highway crash, with some terrible moments of knowing that his body was beyond repair and that his flesh was going to be consumed by hungry flames.

No struggling to breathe with lake water filling his lungs, nose, and mouth when a painful cramp or bursting heart muscles failed to function.

He was lucky. He'd been given the gift of a painless death, with time to savor the knowledge and contemplate his few regrets. Regret for his father: the father who would grieve and be saddled with all the sad details, paperwork, rituals, and maybe not ever knowing what had happened to his only son. Regrets of not being able to sit in a courtroom, publicly point the accusing finger at his conniving wife and rotten sons, and listen to their lying denials of guilt.

He would sleep and wake, sleep and wake, and soon sleep for eternity. He heard a tiny voice calling his name, a surrealistic, repetitive refrain. Hallucinating didn't bother him. It comforted him to know that the end was near. He napped. A weird asymmetry of light coming from the ceiling made him open his eyes and quickly close them. Random beams bored into his clinched eyelids. He ignored them and went back to sleep.

37

Looks Like Death Warmed Over
November 19, Friday, 5:15 P.M.

"They dug a pond," I said with wonder. "They didn't bury the trailer, they just covered it with dirt!"

"My same reasoning!" Jasmine was impatient and excited. "So let's go dig him out!"

"Whoa, there. Let's not count our chickens before they hatch. How much growth was on top of the dirt pile? Did you notice while there was still enough light? I can't see squat from here."

"As a matter of fact, I did notice." She sounded smug. "There're pine saplings 'bout a foot high. Dog fennel 'bout ten feet high. Plenty of wild grass and some wild berry bushes. Couldn't tell what kind."

"Sounds about right for six months' growth in summer. I bet you didn't check this clear-cut. It looks fairly level, but the weeds are too high to judge in the dark. Wonder how hard the dirt is farther in. Think we can get the vans in there?"

"After I called you, I ran out a ways into the field. They've already taken out the fat-lighter stumps, burned all the dead woodpiles, leveled, and planted. The weeds aren't as high as they seem in the dark. I think we can pull the vans off the road. Ground's hard enough. I jumped up and down in several places."

"Just pulling them off the road won't cut it." I was turning to view the land opposite where we were parked. "All this land is clear-cut for at least a quarter mile on both sides. Night hunters passing by would shine their Q-Beams on both sides. They'd spotlight us for sure."

"I thought you said there were hardly any poachers on the hunting club's land."

"Correct, but these wouldn't be poachers," I said wryly. "They'd be members of the club."

"You mean the club members fire-hunt?" She sounded shocked.

"Each hunting club has a few members who'll break the club rules and the law. You have to understand their viewpoint, Jasmine. They're working men. They invest a lot of money they can't afford because they love hunting. They burn a tank of gas every day they hunt. They buy hounds and feed them all year just to use in hunting season. Their licenses and club fees are over a grand a year. They feel they deserve their limit of two deer. If they can't bag them legally in daylight, they try at night with a light. I don't condone it, but I can understand why they do it."

"So what do we do?"

"Well, let's turn on our parking lights and let Bobby Lee tell us if we are barking up the wrong tree. If we aren't, then we'll try to drive across this clear-cut and hide the vans behind the pile of dirt. If Frank's under that shit, we're gonna have one hell of a time digging him out with shovels, regardless of how talented and beautiful we are."

Jasmine giggled and turned on her parking lights. I turned mine on too, stuffed my flashlight into one pocket of my jeans, and crammed the bag of jerky treats in the other. I put on a lightweight denim jacket, placed the bag containing Frank's sweater against my chest, and zipped the jacket closed over it. I needed my hands free to work with Bobby Lee. I reached behind the back seat and pulled out my small hunter's walking light. I tucked the six-volt battery into my jacket pocket, ran the thin wires up to my head, and placed the headband with the lamp on my forehead. Jasmine was watching me. She was already wearing her jacket, and when she saw my headlamp she ran back to put hers on.

"Put on your snake leggings," I called. "Snakes feed at night."

"Ugh!" she exclaimed.

I walked to Bobby Lee's side of the truck, unhooked his seat belt, and attached his short lead. After drawing on my gloves, I patted his shoulders.

"A-hunting we will go, a-hunting we will go," I sang softly into his ear. He was quivering, raring to go. He jumped gracefully to the ground and started prancing with excitement.

We both turned on our headlamps, and I walked to the shallow ditch on the side of the road. It was dry enough to walk in. Our footprints would be less obvious here than pacing down the road. We walked in the ditch until we were almost level with the dark rectangle of the pond, about seventy yards away. We had our lights adjusted to shine where we walked. I pulled up some dog fennel and placed it on the road for a marker. The plant paid me back for crushing it by giving off an astringent odor. It smells like dog piss, hence the name. I told Jasmine we should try and keep our wheels about a third of the way up on each side of the mounds. I didn't believe we could straddle a planting mound. The bottoms of the vans might drag, and I didn't want busted oil pans.

About halfway along the route into the clear-cut, Jasmine spoke. "What do we do if a fire hunter should appear?"

"Drop flat on your tummy and put your face in the dirt. Pray they don't come. If they scan the fields with the Q-Beams and don't spot us, they might use the vans for target practice. We have two dogs in there."

"Oh, no!" she said. "I wish I hadn't asked!"

"The odds are with us. There are a lot more roads around here than fire hunters to ride them."

This fact didn't make me feel any better, but maybe it would ease her mind. I'd feel a lot safer with the vans out of sight. We walked parallel with the pond, then turned and headed toward where we'd hide the vans. Bobby Lee stopped on a dime. I didn't notice and took another stride. I felt the lead go taut, and I was jerked to a stop. When a large dog doesn't want to budge, you don't move him with a tug of the lead, you need a truck with four-wheel drive. Bobby Lee held his nose high, and his bay burst forth, filling the crisp air with his wonderful cry of success.

"Hot damn!" I yelled, pumping my clenched fist into the air before dropping to my knees to restrain him. I called, "Retreat! Retreat!" I repeated the command over and over as I clung to his neck.

Confused, Jasmine hovered over my left shoulder, screaming to be heard. "What? What's wrong? Talk to me!"

Bobby Lee was lowering his cries and choking back his urge to bay, per my command. He sat and whined and accepted my praise and pats.

"Jasmine, say hello to a champion! My God, my God," I crooned. "I've got me a winner! Bobby Lee has just found Frank!"

"But he couldn't have," she said. "You haven't presented a scent article. How could he know?"

"Jasmine, this talented hunk of canine has the

intelligence to match his gifted nose, and he knows how to apply it. He's got scent *memory!* He retained the memory of Frank's scent from the warehouse searches, where he *didn't* find him. Tonight, when he sniffed the air, he knew it was Frank's scent because he remembered it. I've got a champ!"

"Are you sure?" She was doubtful. Very few animals have this ability. I'd read about it, but I'd never had a dog who was this talented.

"I'd bet the bank," I said, with great conviction. "We have to move fast. Let's get the vans and try to move them in. We have to dig for Frank. Double-time. Ho!"

My adrenaline level was high as we raced toward the vans. It was reckless to move so fast over uneven ground with headlamps as our only source of light. We didn't break a leg, trip over an armadillo, or even fall. I backed up my van, weaving like a drunken sailor. Backing any vehicle, much less a large van, is very difficult for me. I back in fits and starts, trying to hold the wheel correctly, but the minute my vehicle's in reverse with gas applied, gremlins take over. They turn the wheel to the right when I should be going left. They do it to make me look inefficient and silly. It's really not my fault.

Jasmine was driving toward me, slowly, and I noticed she was going opposite of where I'd traveled. She was closing the curves to make it appear that someone else had created an aimless pattern on the road. Smart girl—or was she just teasing me about the one flaw I couldn't correct?

I turned cautiously at the dog-fennel marker, eased into the ditch, and went up the dirt bank. We rocked and rolled along slowly, trying to miss holes and keep from going up too far on the planted hills. I wanted to save the van's springs. We were destroying some recently planted pine saplings, but I also knew I could destroy every damn one of them if I brought Frank home to his father.

We finally made the journey and parked behind the dirt pile. Jasmine hurried to check if her van would be visible from the road.

I moved to Bobby Lee's side and whispered in his ear.

"Where's your man? Where's your man? Shush. Shush. Where's your man?"

This was a routine I'd have to repeat every five minutes. It's the command for a silent search, a very difficult command for a bloodhound. They run mute, but they want to bay as they near their quarry. I didn't want a hunter driving the road looking for stray dogs to hear his cry. They'd think their animal was caught in a trap or injured and come to investigate.

I hooked him to his lead, and Jasmine indicated that she was ready. She had two water canteens strapped onto her left shoulder and was balancing two round-point shovels with her right hand, the handles tucked under her arm. I signaled that I wasn't ready and reached into the van for the radio.

"I'll try to reach Rosie. We may be here all night. She'll worry." I tried three times without success. I thought the clear dry air would help the transmission, but no such luck. I could be in a dead zone where timber, or low ground, or something else prevented the signals from reaching their target. Hank had added two more towers to his county area to aid in radio transmissions, and I knew one was in the northeastern quadrant not too far from us. Maybe the radio was having a bad signal day. Anything was possible. I replaced the radio.

I looked for Jasmine and saw her standing by her open van door holding her mike. I strolled back to see if she was having any luck and arrived in time to overhear part of her conversation.

". . . didn't want you to worry. Over and out." She replaced the radio and grinned at me. "Your gremlins are busy tonight. Mine worked just fine. Got her on the first try."

"Uh-huh," I replied and acted like a lady. I didn't cuss or spit.

I returned to Bobby Lee, repeated the silent command into his ear, and we were off. Straining against the leash, he led us right up the dirt bank. He was scrambling for toeholds and shifting a lot of loose dirt backward on top of me. I was doing some scrambling of my own, trying to balance on the slope and keep up with him.

Glancing back to check Jasmine's progress, I noticed she had moved to the left of me, so my dislodged dirt wasn't landing on her. It looked like a good move. I pulled back on Bobby Lee's lead and scurried up to his side. Now his dirt wasn't falling on me either.

We reached the top, a fairly narrow plateau about fifteen feet wide and more than seventy feet long. I visualized a parting of the dirt and me sliding downward and being covered with tons of it. I shivered. I was remembering my nightmare. I pointed my light at the ground below. We had to be at least twenty feet above ground level. Bobby Lee kept straining to go forward. I eased the pressure on the leash and let him advance. He lunged forward, hurried around a clump of dog fennel, and stopped at a vine-covered stump. I stood patiently waiting for him to find the perfect spot to pee. Suddenly, I noticed his tail was wagging with abandon, something he doesn't usually do when he's getting ready to lift his leg. I moved forward, adjusted my headlight, and leaned over and down so I could get a better look. I was reaching for my flashlight in my pocket, when Jasmine grabbed my shoulder and hissed at me. I heard the noise of an engine too.

"Get flat," I told her. I wrapped my gloved fingers around Bobby Lee's harness, turned his large head toward me, and gave him the silent signal to rest. I was putting pressure on his nose, and pushing downward. He obediently lowered his body to the ground as I stretched out beside him.

We saw the radiance of a Q-Beam slowly advancing down the road toward us. The light was scanning the field opposite us. When it switched to our side of the field, the lower part of the beam raked across the roof of the truck cab. We could see the outline of the man with the light. He was standing in the bed of the pickup, directly behind the cab.

"Just keep your head down," I said in a normal tone. I knew the idling engine would cover my voice. "If he shines this way, turn your head away from the light."

"Why? You think my pale skin will show up in the light?"

"Funeeee," I drawled. "I thought everyone knew a cat's eyes glow in the dark and reflect bright lights."

"Meow, meow," she mimicked. Bobby Lee turned his head toward her voice. We both giggled. The light's beam came closer and brushed across the top of the pile. We both lowered our heads and turned them toward Bobby Lee. I placed a hand over his eyes. He lay quite still, my hand caressing his ears. The light moved to the other side of the clear-cut.

"Why was he shining up here anyway?" Jasmine complained.

"Because deer love to play on sand piles. When my kennel was being built, I got there early one morning and there were three deer on top of the sand the men used to mix the concrete. They were trying to push each other off. They looked just like kids playing king of the hill."

Once the truck had moved out of sight, we got up and brushed sand from our clothing. Bobby Lee strained to get back to his stump. I let him. Squatting, I used my flashlight and saw that the vine-covered stump was three-inch plastic plumbing pipe. It had been painted dark green. Dark green plastic grape vines were wired onto its circumference all the way to the dirt. Even in daylight, it wouldn't be obvious from ten feet away. Bobbie Lee held his nose over the pipe and whined softly, breaking his silent command. I was so happy, I didn't say a word.

My heart was singing with excitement. I turned my head Jasmine's way.

"Do you hear any motor noise?"

She walked about twelve feet away from Bobbie Lee's soft whining and listened.

"Nothing."

"Okay, I'm going to start calling Frank. I'll pause after each call while you listen."

"Frank!" I yelled and waited.

"Nothing," reported Jasmine.

"Frank Cannon, can you hear me?"

"Nothing."

"Frank! Answer me!"

"Nothing."

After twenty calls I quit trying. I wrapped Bobby Lee's lead around the post, walked over and sat down on a clear spot of sand, and lit a cigarette. I asked Jasmine for a water canteen. The liquid eased my throat. It felt strained from all my yelling.

Jasmine took a few swallows from her canteen. "It was his airhole. He should've been able to breathe."

"Yep. Either he's never been down there, or they moved him, or he's unconscious—or dead. Scratch the option that he's never been down there; Bobby Lee smelled him. Breathing in the odor coming from the pipe, *I* smelled him. The air's very ripe and very bad. Which means," I said wearily, "it's weeks of accumulated body and human waste odor, or he's decomposing down there."

"Stop it," Jasmine replied with anger. "Quit thinking negative thoughts!"

"Well, I'll sit here and smoke while you go sniff at the pipe and voice an opinion."

I was being facetious to cover my disappointment. Damn! I wanted so badly for him to be alive. In my nightmares, I'd lived just a tad of what he'd faced in that hole in the ground. I wanted to set him free.

I sat and voiced my thoughts. "The sons dug the pond in late March so the summer rains would fill the pond and nourish some growth on the dirt pile. They kidnapped him sometime Thursday evening, two weeks ago. They had five days before anyone knew he was missing. Sometime during those five days, when they weren't under constant scrutiny, they brought him out here and placed him inside the trailer. How'd they manage that chore?"

"They left one trailer door uncovered?" suggested Jasmine.

"Not feasible. It'd be too risky to bring back the big machinery so close to the time he disappeared. And don't say the boys covered the trailer door with dirt using three shovels. It would be a lot of work and take too long. I have the feeling they wouldn't want to work that hard."

She shook her head. "You tell me."

"They put in an airhole. They wanted to keep him alive, at least long enough to collect the ransom. They had to have a way to reach him quickly if they had to prove he was still alive in order to collect the money. They put the airhole on top. Why not add a trapdoor? The top would have less dirt than the sloping sides."

"By Jove, Sherlock, I think you're right!" Jasmine exclaimed. "Where do we start digging?"

"It's only been a couple of weeks since they covered him up. Nothing would have time to grow on the trapdoor. I suggest we look for a square where there is no growth."

"Great! Let's find it!" She jumped up, turned on her headlight, and started pacing the dirt in a straight line down the middle. I got up slower, still reasoning. Even if the dirt wasn't as deep on the top, it would still require moving at least five cubic feet. That's a lot of dirt. I couldn't see a hole with shaped sides, edges squared, at least three feet deep. I think it would've made it easier for them to have placed the trapdoor nearer the edge so they could slide some of the dirt over the side. That seemed more logical than digging straight down. Being a covert operation, I felt they'd want the hole away from the road and on the back end. I'm not a dirt removal expert, but I remembered the trouble Sheri and I encountered trying to dig straight down in a small area.

I stood and paced the narrow width of the large pile of dirt. I stopped about two feet from the sloping edge. I didn't want to hit a soft spot and slide over the edge. I made the width to be eighteen feet, not counting the edge I couldn't walk on.

I walked to the approximate center, then paced out nine feet, and still had my two feet of safe footing. I turned and studied the long length, then started hoofing it down to the back end away from the road. Jasmine was in the center searching the area near the pipe. When I turned my head to shine the light on the pipe, I saw Bobby Lee lying curled in a ball. He was sound asleep. He can also sleep standing or leaning against my leg, when we're at Jacksonville's dog trials for certifications and have to wait and wait.

I removed the flashlight from my pocket when I was twenty feet from the back edge. I trained the beam ahead of me and did a slow sweep of the area. I stopped walking and took a deep breath of satisfaction. My guesses had been right on the money. The light revealed just where they'd dug. It had rained at least twice, and the loose dirt from their digging had settled several inches below the undisturbed edges. Water seeks its own level, and with more flowing here in the sunken area, we now had a perfect blueprint on where to start digging.

"Bring the shovels!" I called to Jasmine.

Dew had settled on the growth of weeds. I shed my jacket and spread it on the ground. I emptied my pockets of jerky, wallet, and the note giving permission to trespass, placed them on the jacket, and flipped over the edges to protect the items from dampness. I rolled up my sleeves and was drawing on my gloves when Jasmine arrived with the shovels and canteens.

I explained the reasoning that had allowed me to come straight to the correct spot. She was lavish with her praise, which I tend to take with a grain of salt. After all, I do sign her paycheck. However, I still enjoy hearing it.

I walked as close to the back edge as I dared and sat down. I drew up both legs close to my body, turned my feet sideways, and pushed both of them out, trying to dig my heels in as deep as possible.

"What are you doing?"

I laughed. "I'm pretending I'm a baby bulldozer pushing dirt off the edge." I was heartened by the amount of earth that slid down the slope. I dug my heels in and shoved again.

"Lord have mercy," Jasmine remarked as she sat down about six feet over at the other indentation line and duplicated my movements.

Our labors quickly grew tiring. We rested by standing and shoveling more dirt near the edge. Finally, I stopped and smoked a cigarette. Jasmine had to prove that, by being five years younger, she was in better shape. She worked through my first smoke break but stopped and sat beside me when I took my second one.

By ten o'clock we were exhausted and still hadn't reached the roof of the trailer. I began to doubt my calculations. Maybe this area had formed a natural watershed and wasn't the correct spot to dip a shovel. What stopped me from checking the entire roof was: I really didn't want to know for sure that we'd busted our butts in the wrong place. I was afraid Jasmine would turn homicidal if she found out I'd erred in my hasty guessing.

Jasmine slid-walked down the slope to collect the cooler that held Diet Cokes. I was almost too tired to move. My thighs throbbed from bulldozing, my shoulders ached from lifting the shovel, and my back was killing me. I was sitting on the elevated edge we'd produced with the removal of so much dirt. I stared at my feet and saw a darker batch of dirt six inches from my foot. I kicked at it listlessly, and it moved over. I was staring at a patch of tarpaulin. I dropped to my knees, found the edge, grasped it, and pulled it up. Dirt slid off, revealing a larger area of material. When Jasmine returned, she found me energetically tugging the tarpaulin, my weariness forgotten.

"It's about time," she grumbled, as she stepped down to help me. "I suppose this was placed here to keep dirt and water off the door?"

"If it wasn't," I said, grunting, "I'll lie on this spot and sob like a baby." We were nearing the edge. "Stop," I ordered. "Let's sit down and push it over with our feet."

"My push is too tired."

I snickered weakly. We sat and pushed until the tarp slid off the side for a foot or so. "Enough."

I glanced at the horizon. A pumpkin-colored disk had appeared. We'd have more light shortly; the moon was full tonight.

I held the flashlight inches from the edges of the crudely cut square trapdoor. No wonder they'd covered the opening with a tarp. Sand and water would've poured inside the trailer. The outline was roughly three feet square. I slid my gloved finger into a jagged notch and pulled.

When the trapdoor cleared a few inches, Jasmine helped and we were able to throw it back to rest against the higher dirt. The odor emanating from the opening was comparable to rotten eggs. Jasmine gagged. We squatted and turned both beams into the fetid dark hole.

A man—Frank—was lying in a sleeping bag some ten feet below us and eight feet back from the opening. He was either asleep, unconscious, or dead. I could see no movement. I moved the light around, seeing discarded cans, three five-gallon jugs, and two cartons, but the light wouldn't reveal the contents. Probably food.

"Come on," I said, and walked some distance away from the hole. Jasmine followed. I lit a cigarette. I couldn't think or breathe properly while staring down at that pitiful tableau.

I dragged on my cig and turned to Jasmine.

"We got us a big problem. We can get down there, but how do we get out?"

"My suggestion is to call Hank on the radio. Let him figure it out. You've found him; you'll get the reward."

"I'll figure it out," I snapped. The reward was the last thing on my mind. It was my giant ego. I'd keep proving I could handle my load as long as I was able. I was too competitive for my own good.

I walked to Jasmine and placed my hands on her shoulders.

"Sorry I was sharp with you. We're both tired. Let's move my van."

"Where?" she asked, sounding bewildered.

"We're gonna use the van to pull him out of the hole. Let's go figure it out."

We slid down the pile of dirt, our feet sinking into the soft sand.

38

Sitting on Dead Ready
September 19, Friday, 11 P.M.

Jasmine and I walked to my van. I traced the path the tires would travel and saw no formidable obstacles. I turned the van and backed it close to the edge of the dirt pile.

"We're gonna use the van to haul Frank out of there," I explained as I moved to the van's storage locker. I picked up a leather belt and threaded it through the belt loops of my jeans and slipped on the sheath holding my hunting knife. I also took a seventy-five-foot rope, a hand pump, and an inflatable mattress.

"Inflate the pad while I tie the rope to the axle."

"I hope I get to drive the van," Jasmine said nervously, as she took the objects from my hands.

"You got it," I told her.

I smiled as I crawled under the back of the van. She didn't want to enter the trailer. I wasn't exactly looking forward to it myself. I scooted backward and drew the rope taut.

"Would you bring Bobby Lee down and water the dogs?"

"Sure."

I picked up the end of the rope, sliced off a fifteen-foot length, and laid it on the hood of the van. I lit a cigarette and waited for her to return. The moon was rising fast. Cool dim light was washing over the fields. I snapped off the flashlight, climbed into Jasmine's van, turned it around, and backed within twenty feet of my van. I wanted to leave enough room for her to pull forward. Part of the van might be seen by a passing truck, but I doubted if any poachers would be out with a full moon shining. Deer don't move around to feed when the moon is full.

After Jasmine returned and we watered the dogs, I indicated the short piece of rope in my hand.

"Hop in the van. Can you see this piece of rope without a light?"

"Yes. What's it for?"

"See where I'm placing the end?" I laid it on the ground six feet away from her window and stretched it out to its full length. I walked back to her side.

"We'll measure how far to pull us up when I get Frank tied to the hauling rope. With your motor running, you won't be able to hear me. I don't want you banging our heads against the ceiling of the trailer. We have to get this right the first time."

"You're making me nervous," she said.

I laughed. "Piece of cake. Just remember, a slow steady pull."

I picked up the length of rope and handed it to her, letting it uncoil as we struggled up the slope. I stopped and rolled down my sleeves and put on my jacket. The sweat from my exertions was drying, but I felt chilled from the wind. I gave my wallet and the jerky bag to Jasmine.

"When I get Frank under the door, I want you to pull hard on the rope and keep it taut, so when I tie him to the rope we don't leave any slack."

"Gotcha."

I tossed the rope into the hole and stuck my flashlight deep into my jeans pocket. I could smell the polluted air from here. I took a deep breath and backed into the hole. Holding tightly to the rope, I swung free and quickly slid down inside the trailer. It was only a short distance to the floor, but I was still swinging from the drop, and I carefully eased downward until I felt the floor beneath me. Jasmine was shining her light on me, and I didn't look up. I clicked on my light and slowly walked over and knelt by Frank.

I pulled off my glove and touched his face. God, the air was unbelievable. I was taking tiny inhalations and keeping my mouth shut. I could almost taste the smell, it was so thick.

Frank opened his eyes and squinted at me. "The light hurts," he mumbled.

I moved it away from his face. "He's alive, Jasmine!" I yelled to her.

"Wonderful!" she called.

"Are you hurt?" I was leaning close in order to hear him, and his breath almost made me gag. I shut my mouth, warning my gut to behave.

"Who are you?"

His voice was weak, but I could easily understand him. He didn't sound delirious or feel hot to the touch.

"Are you hurt?" I repeated.

"I'm weak. I've been sick. Who are you?"

"Had a cold?" I'd just noticed this place was cold as a morgue.

"Something. I'm over it. You haven't answered me. Who in the hell are you?"

He sounded petulant and I chuckled. The boss in him, used to being answered quickly, was rising to the surface. I began to think he just might survive this horror and retain his sanity.

"I'm Jo Beth Sidden. My bloodhound, Bobby Lee, found you. Your father hired me to search for you."

I was leaning close so I could watch his reaction to my news. In the dim light, with the flashlight shining away from him, I saw his eyes water and tears appear.

"Thank your dog for me. Now get me out of here." He closed his eyes.

I patted his shoulder. "Hold on. We're on our way."

I placed the light on the floor. Walking backward, I pulled Frank near the rope.

"Pull as hard as you can on the rope, Jasmine, pull it tight!"

I grabbed the rope and wound it around Frank under his armpits as tight as I could get it. I heard a short grunt but ignored it. I had to have a taut rope.

"You can turn loose," I called to Jasmine. "Leave your light shining down till I can cut the rope. Hold your measuring rope about a foot below the ceiling, against the hauling rope, and let the balance fall." I couldn't look up; her light would blind me. I ran over and picked up my flashlight and put it back in my pocket.

The second rope arrived. I tightened it, running my hand down and holding it tight against the hauling rope. Where it touched Frank's head, I cut it with my knife.

"Leave your light shining away from the hole." When she had placed it, I called to her.

"We're ready here. Haul away, and hurry back to help me."

I had wound the excess rope around my waist. I put on my glove and grasped the rope and crouched beside Frank. When the rope began to move slowly upward, I took a firm grip. I dangled along beside Frank as we were lifted into the air. When our heads were two feet from the opening, I was ready for Jasmine to stop. I took a deep breath. We stopped moving, with our heads less than six inches from the opening. I closed my eyes briefly. That was too close for comfort. I reached with my left hand and grabbed the rope that was above the hole. I got a firm grip and placed my right hand palm down on the roof and lunged upward. I hooked my right elbow and scrambled out of the hole. Jasmine arrived, breathless from running up the slope.

I raised my head and took a deep breath.

"Take a couple of deep breaths," I told her. I needed a couple myself. My muscles, sore from shoveling and pushing dirt off the ledge, wanted to rebel. It had taken all my effort to force them to work. We'll sleep till noon tomorrow, I promised them when I made the final lunge. My muscles groaned but cooperated. They knew as well as I did that Jonathan was returning tomorrow, and we wouldn't be sleeping till noon.

"Ready?" I asked.

"Ready," she replied.

We braced ourselves against the opening, lifted him out and over the edge of dirt, and stretched him out.

I knelt beside him.

"Frank, we'll get you to a hospital very soon. It won't be much longer."

"No," he said with alarm. "No hospital. Don't tell anyone I'm free. Promise me. Swear you won't tell!" His volume was rising with each word.

"That's not possible," I said, trying to soothe him. "All the law-enforcement agencies are looking for you. Your kidnapping isn't common knowledge, but the FBI, the GBI, and the county sheriff's department are all searching for you. Because Tim Fergerson was actively trying to find you, he came under suspicion. He recommended me to your father, who hired me. When you turn up, everyone will start asking questions. If I didn't answer them, I'd be an accessory after the fact in a federal offense—kidnapping. It isn't possible. I'm sorry. I realize you want to protect your sons. I think it would be a foolish thing to do, but I can understand your wanting to do it."

Frank gave a weak laugh. "I don't care a whit about their miserable hides. Did the agencies guess? Are they suspects?"

"No," I answered with amusement. "They're busy checking out your former employees from five years ago."

"I see you aren't fond of our protectors either," he said, giving me a wintry smile. "How'd you like to pull the wool over their eyes? Who knows you're here?"

"No one," I admitted.

I didn't like the way this conversation was heading.

"We can keep this under wraps. My father and I will remain silent. I give you my word. How about her?" He cut his eyes to Jasmine and back to mine.

"That's the rub. She's here, and I won't put her in jeopardy."

"How much does she pay you, young lady?" He smiled up at her.

"Enough." Her answer was curt and harsh. "I'll do what she tells me to. You don't have enough money to buy me . . . now."

Uh-oh. Her "now" had been said so softly, I knew I was the only one who'd heard it. I would've missed it too, but I'd been looking directly at her face. Her glittering eyes reflected the moonlight.

"You just lie here and rest," I told him. "My associate and I will be right back." Jasmine and I walked several yards away, and I lit a cigarette.

"Former customer?" I kept my voice matter-of-fact. I didn't want to embarrass her.

She sighed. "I don't hold it against him. I was for sale, and he bought some of me. In a different life," she said, qualifying her statement. "Don't hold back and do anything different because of me. You want to help him. I can tell by your voice. I promised you when you hired me that if I ever became a problem, I'd leave. If you don't help him, I'll leave."

"No," I said quietly. "I'll wring your neck if you even look like you're getting ready to leave. Think we can get away with it?"

"Piece of cake." We grinned at each other.

"Go move Bobby Lee and Ulysses to your van and pick up the measuring rope. Then come back and help me drag our Frank down the embankment."

Lord, she took off running. She was in better shape than I was. I had to quit smoking and go back on my diet. As soon as Jonathan left, I promised.

I picked up my cigarette butts and scuffed dirt on some of the heavier prints. I didn't try to cover all of them. Rain was expected tomorrow after our brief cool spell moved off and into the Atlantic. I walked back and stood over Frank.

"I'll give it a try. My associate and I will keep quiet."

I didn't use Jasmine's name. I didn't think he'd recognized her, and I didn't want to jog his memory.

"Thank Jasmine for me later," he said politely.

Well, scratch that theory.

I walked to the trapdoor, slammed it shut, and started kicking dirt over the top. When I had a thin layer, I stopped to rest. Frank had turned his head to watch me.

"The shovel would be more efficient," he said.

"Frank, while you were snoozing down below, my muscles and Jasmine's got you uncovered. They now refuse to even think about a shovel, and I agree. Take a nap."

He was sensible and didn't offer any more suggestions. I glanced at the indention where we'd dug. I had blurred the outline by kicking the sand in around the perimeter. It wasn't obvious that a hole had been dug here, but it was much lower than the sand around it. It suited the hell out of me. I grabbed the rope, still attached to Frank, and started dragging him downhill head first. It wouldn't hurt him for the short journey. I would've retied him and he would've gone down feet first, if he hadn't mentioned the shovel.

Jasmine ran to help me. "I can handle Frank," I told her. "Grab the tarp and use the back of the garden rake on our prints on the slope. Just fill in the deepest ones. The dirt slide looks natural."

I pulled Frank to the edge of the back door on my van and opened it.

"Think you can step into the van with me helping you?"

"I think so."

I cut the ropes, unzipped the bag, leaned down, and, with both arms extended, pulled him to his feet. "Hold on to the door a second."

He seemed steady enough to release him. I pitched the smelly bag in the back on top of the inflated mattress, smoothed it out, and went back and helped Frank step up and in. After he lay down, I zipped the bag.

"Are you okay?" I thought I could hear his teeth chattering.

"I'm cold," he admitted.

I crawled over him to the locker, pulled out a blanket, and tucked it around him.

"Thanks," he managed through his dancing teeth. "Where are we?"

"On your dad's fifteen thousand acres off Big Alligator Road."

"How did you find me?"

"Frank, since Jasmine and I are both accessories now, I don't think I'll discuss anyone else who helped me. I followed a clue that Tim supplied. I found you; that's all that matters. You owe Tim Fergerson a great deal. I hope you don't get him into trouble. He and your father were your only allies."

"Will you tell me what day it is?"

I took out my flashlight and looked at my watch. "It's just after midnight, or early morning of the twentieth of November. It's Saturday. If they brought you out here late on Thursday night, November the fourth, you were down there about fifteen days."

"Thanks for getting me out." His voice broke. "Is my dad paying you enough?"

"A ridiculously high reward, which I'll promptly accept. I have many canine mouths to feed. However, I won't accept any more from you, and neither will Jasmine. I'm dividing my reward with her. It's plenty for both of us, so say no more."

Jasmine stuck her head in the back door. "Ready?"

"Ready. I'll follow you to our driveway." I walked back to her. "Keep an eye peeled for Bubba. He roams at night."

"Check."

"Wait," Frank called out weakly. "Will Ms. Jasmine allow me to thank her?"

I looked at Jasmine. She stepped into the van, turned sideways, eased past me, and knelt by Frank's side.

"Thank you for rescuing me. Will you allow me to shake your hand?"

"Sure." She took his hand and said, "I wish you well."

"The same to you," he whispered.

She stepped past Frank, pushed up my seat, and left the van. I closed the back door, walked around to my door, and climbed in. We drove slowly over the bumpy road, but when we reached the main road, Jasmine picked up speed. In fifteen minutes we arrived at the kennel's driveway. I looked around for Bubba and touched the butt of the .32 concealed in a compartment near my leg. It was just for reassurance. I didn't plan to ever use it.

Jasmine walked back and listened in on my car phone call. I dialed Mr. Cannon's number. Henry answered after five rings.

"Cannon residence." He sounded sleepy. I must've woken him up.

"Henry? Jo Beth Sidden. I know it's so-o-o-o late to call, but I'm worried about our precious puppy!" I was trilling and sounding like a silly twit. "I just woke up from a horrible dream. Is our little darling ill? I just *have* to know!"

"I don't know," Henry stammered. I'd caught him unaware.

"You don't know?" I screeched. "Oh, my poor baby, Mama's coming. You get that silly gate open, Henry! You wake up that boss of yours and say I'm coming. I want to tell him face to face that he doesn't deserve my puppy. I'm coming right now!" I placed the phone in its cradle.

"Beautiful," said Jasmine, laughing.

"See you later," I told her.

I pulled out and raised my voice above the engine noise so Frank could hear me.

"I seriously doubt that your father's house is under twenty-four-hour surveillance, but we take precautions just in case. Tim discovered your father's phone was bugged during his interrogation when he became a suspect. That sounds reasonable. The kidnappers could call him, knowing he has money and you're his only son. Be careful when we reach the house. Don't utter a word until we get near some cover noise like radio, TV, or a noisy shower. Even then, whisper.

"If we are going to resurrect you successfully, you and your father will have to think up a very clever story that excludes me and mine. My participation's over when I deliver you to your father's door. Tell your father to have his lawyers draw up a contract, predated from July first of this year to run until July first of next year. This will be for my services and my bloodhounds. The check should read *Advance payment in full of the contract* et cetera. He can call me a consultant."

When I reached the correct street, I strained to see the ornate gate and was relieved to see it was open. I drove up to the house, pulled under the portico, and stopped the van directly by the side door. It was thrown open. Henry stood there looking nervous, with Cannon directly behind him.

"I'll be back in a couple of minutes," I whispered back to Frank.

I threw open my door, pushed the driver's seat forward to make a path for Frank, and started screaming before I reached the door.

"Where's my puppy? I want my puppy!" I grabbed Henry's shoulder and whispered in his ear. "Yell back at me. Make some noise." Pushing Henry aside, I yelled again. *"Give me my dog! Now!"*

"You can't do this," Henry said, sounding more quarrelsome than angry.

I leaned close to Cannon's ear. "Frank's outside in the van. He's alive. Just weak. Don't talk until both of you are in the bathroom with the water running."

"You can't do this," Henry said, gaining volume. He wasn't very inventive, just repeating himself like a broken record.

"Frank?" It was the only word Cannon uttered. He sat in his wheelchair, his mouth agape, giving me a blank stare.

"I'll search and find him myself!" I boomed toward the ceiling. "Get hold of yourself, you old fart!" I spit out my disgust in his ear. I wanted to shock him back to normality, back to his take-charge haughty ways.

I saw Cannon's mouth snap closed. His eyes cleared, anger flicked away, and great uninhibited joy spread across his features. He made shooing motions for me to hurry and get his son. I resisted the impulse to give him a finger and saluted instead.

From the joy displayed on his employer's features, Henry finally caught on. He actually jumped up in the air while he shouted, "Come back here! Come back here!"

I peeled Frank out of his sleeping bag, guided him through the front of the van, and across to the door. He was using both hands to hold up his trousers. He wasn't wearing a belt, and he must've lost fifteen pounds during his ordeal of imprisonment and illness, a fact I hadn't noticed earlier when he entered the van.

I let Henry take over when I had Frank inside. I left, yelling that I was taking my dog, and threatening legal action. I was looking forward to a hot soak in the tub while I drank a dozen cold brews. Food never entered the picture.

39

Be Still My Heart
November 20, Saturday, 8 A.M.

Sitting on the back porch in fleece pajamas, ratty robe, and padded socks, and with untamed hair, I was feeling comfortably slobbish. Sleeping late is a rare treat, but I felt no guilt. I'd seen Wayne and Donnie Ray entering the kennel several minutes ago, so I knew the animals were under Wayne's watchful eye. I'd missed the New York agency's report on the vet yesterday, but I'd briefly glanced at Rosie's notepad on my journey out here and knew it would be here soon.

Savoring the morning's last dregs of coolness, I could feel the warm front creeping in on cat feet, insinuating warm humid air to mingle with the crisp, cool air of yesterday. Within the hour, my attire would be too warm for comfort, but right now it was perfect. I sipped my second cup of coffee and lit my third cigarette. Two days of accumulated mail was stacked on the chaise beside me. Rosie's notepad was on top.

I'd riffled through the stack of envelopes, scanning the return addresses, looking to see if my favorite fantasy was about to unfold. But not one letter was postmarked Singapore, so it wouldn't unfold this morning. The awaited envelope would have crisp chop marks, to signal its oriental origin. Inside, on expensive ivory-colored bond, a famous old law firm would inform me that a long-lost unknown relative had gone peacefully to his maker, leaving me a large, completely outfitted junk, with crew, and a mysterious scrap of parchment: a treasure map that I alone had the expertise to translate successfully and the uncanny ability to find. Ah, well, if not today, possibly Monday.

I planned my morning. After my agency report on Harvey in New York arrived, I'd take a hot soak in the tub. Muscles I wasn't aware of possessing had been creaking and groaning since I awoke. Next, my favorite breakfast, a bacon and banana sandwich on white untoasted bread, maybe two. No supper last night.

I was sitting left of center on my wide canvas-covered chaise. Rudy took up a relatively small area. He was curled in a ball and catnapping. At my right, Bobby Lee was stretching out and inching my way using his large shoulder muscles. He placed his head in my lap. He was lying on top of the mail and the notepad, but, since I was in no hurry to peruse its contents, I set the empty coffee cup on a low table and fondled his ears.

I didn't expect Jonathan until after lunch. If he'd left Tampa at eight o'clock this morning and traveled state roads, it would be a five-hour trip. On the faster Interstate 75, he'd have to leave it at Valdosta and travel sideways another seventy-five miles on back roads to reach here, which would take almost the same amount of time. His choice of roads would tell me more about him. If he took the back roads, he could enjoy a more leisurely pace, travel down the main streets of small Florida towns, fifteen to twenty miles apart, and see some pastoral and uncrowded countryside. If he took the Interstate, he'd roar up the highway, doing at least seventy-five miles an hour just to keep pace with traffic. He'd read hundreds of very large billboards advertising factory outlet malls, hotels, motels, cheap gas, and places to eat. When he had to jog over on the comparatively snail-paced back roads for the last push, he'd feel resentment at the loss of time gained by speeding. It would be interesting to find out which route he chose.

I heard the *bing-bong* of the first gate alarm and saw Wayne walk out of the grooming room where he could see who was approaching. I relaxed. It was probably Bertie. Wayne gave me the okay sign, and I caught a glimpse of her vivid yellow compact through the hedge to my right as she pulled into the courtyard. She stopped close to the back steps and hopped out. She's short and pear-shaped and has an enormous rump. She's always cheerful, cusses like a sailor, and owns numerous cats and dogs, periodically rescuing more from the pound. We've been friends forever.

"Come sit!" I called, as she started toward me waving an envelope.

"Jesus Christ, you look like a Sunday-morning whore who worked Beal Street's Saturday-night rough trade! Here it is practically noon, and you're still in your jammies! Tied one on last night, did we? Got any more of that swill?" Her glance raked the coffee table, spied my cup, and settled on Bobby Lee.

"Shi-i-it! Who's the monster?"

"You remember Bobby Lee. He's still a puppy."

"Is that the small bundle of wrinkles I met in April at the SPCA picnic?" she asked with pretended awe. "Let me know when he turns one. I'll buy him a goddamn horse collar!"

"I'll make a pot of coffee. Won't take but a minute. I haven't seen you in ages."

"Don't get up. I can't spare a minute. My clients go crazy on Saturday, trying to catch up on last week or trying to get a jump on next week. Either way, they keep me jumping like a cat on a car hood hot enough to fry eggs!"

Bertie worked out of her home, delivering messages for lawyers, medical files for doctors, summonses for small claims court and civil cases, telegrams, alterations from department stores, and prescriptions from the local pharmacies. She eked out a living for herself, her widowed mother, and her many pets.

I laughed, took her envelope, and fished out the five-dollar bill I'd crumpled in my robe pocket.

"*This* client is loaded, and I'm on a fat expense account. I'll give you five as a tip and charge them ten."

"Fucking deal," she said, grinning. "Stick it to the suckers!" She ran down the steps and sped away with a clang of gears.

So I lied. I was the client and knew it was the only way she'd accept a tip from me. A tiny extra to help feed her brood. Rudy and Bobby Lee sat sleepily watching me as I gathered the mail and started inside.

"Aren't you guys hungry? Yum, yum!" I heard toenails scrabbling on the floor as I slammed the screened door.

I was dressed in an emerald-green polished cotton sundress and staring at the matching headband nestled atop my carefully coiffured mop of hair. I personally thought it looked silly, but Susan's estimate was mentally ringing in my ears.

"Wear it, Sidden! It makes you look soft and feminine. Two attributes you sorely need!" Remembering her earnest delivery, now several weeks in the past, I didn't remove it. My full war paint looked great. Usually, I don't take the time to apply it correctly.

The phone rang. Glancing at my watch, I saw it was five minutes to one. I hoped it wasn't Jonathan reporting car failure or a sudden change of plans. It was Hank. He sounded pissed.

"Sidden, don't leave. I'm on my way over."

"Anything wrong?" I asked.

"Everything's just peachy," he replied in disgust. "Twenty minutes." Before I had a chance to answer, he hung up.

I frowned. It couldn't be . . . nah, it was too early yet. He probably didn't even know Frank was safely back at his father's place, much less think I had anything to do with his return. But something was bugging him. I just wished he'd hurry and get his visit over with before Jonathan arrived.

I was pouring a glass of iced tea when the first gate alarm bonged. I walked to the window and saw Jonathan proceeding up the drive. Oh, no, Hank would arrive after Jonathan! I set the glass down and went to greet him.

"Jonathan, how nice to see you! How was your trip?"

He walked toward me and gave me a hug and kissed me on the cheek. He held me at arm's length and admired my efforts.

"You look beautiful!" he said, smiling. "I like this second greeting much better than the first one I received."

"Darn it, left my gun in my jeans when I changed clothes. How was the road coming up?"

"Great. Going down I got tired of maintaining eighty just to keep from getting rear-ended. I'm a compulsive reader and didn't skip a billboard. I found out more about Georgia and Florida's tourist offerings than I care to know. Coming back I came up the middle of the state. First on SR Fifty-one, then Four-forty-one north, enjoying the scenery a lot better."

"Wise choice," I agreed.

"Did anyone fail your training course?"

"Everyone passed with flying colors. I tell you true, I

think this past week was the second longest I can ever remember. I'm just glad it's over."

"When was the first one?" He gave me a quizzical raised brow.

"The first week in traction after Bubba's attack."

"Sorry, I shouldn't have asked."

"Nonsense. No apology needed. I gave you the lead-in, and I'm not sensitive about it now. Enough. What would you like to do first?"

"Gentleman that I am, I won't touch that line with a ten-foot pole. What would you suggest?"

I felt my face redden. I rarely blush. I did the first thing that popped into my mind. I gave him a solid punch on his right biceps.

"That's for stepping on the line."

"Ouch!" He rubbed the spot, giving me a rueful grimace.

I smiled sweetly. "Have you eaten?"

"Only an early breakfast. Let me take you to lunch."

"Rosie has made her famous three-cheese lasagna casserole and a beautiful salad to celebrate your return. I myself slaved over a store-bought loaf of French bread, smearing it with store-bought garlic spread, and wrapping it in foil. Let's go eat."

I stuck out my elbow. Jonathan ignored it and clasped my waist. I put my arm around his waist, and we were entwined as we walked toward the porch. I loved his touch. Solid and warm, his big hand softly embracing my waistline.

The harsh noise of the first gate alarm caused me to shy like a startled horse. It broke Jonathan's grip.

"Damn!" exploded from my lips.

"Expecting company?"

"Unfortunately, yes. The local sheriff is a friend of mine. He called a few minutes ago sounding upset. Said he

was on his way over. He didn't give me a chance to tell him
I had company coming."

"Maybe he won't stay long."

"I hope he's already had lunch," I said, sounding
grumpy.

"You said he was a friend?" Jonathan looked into my eyes.

He was asking, and I didn't want to pussyfoot around.
I took a deep breath.

"He was a very dear friend ... a few months ago ...
for a very short time. Now he's just a friend."

"Well, in that case, I also hope he's had lunch."

I took my eyes off the driveway entrance and met his. He
smiled, the flesh around his eyes crinkling from the effort.

"I won't even ask if he's hungry," I said, feeling a
lump in my throat.

Hank left his car, strode to the porch, and focused his
attention on Jonathan. He didn't glance my way until he
was standing at the base of the steps.

"Hank, I'd like you to meet Police Chief Jonathan
Webber, from Eppley, Georgia. Jonathan, Hank Cribbs,
sheriff of Dunston County."

They shook hands awkwardly, Hank taking one step
up and Jonathan taking an equal step down. They mumbled
greetings in low voices, then stepped back and looked my
way.

"May I speak privately with you, Jo Beth, if Jonathan
doesn't mind?" Hank was flicking glances at me, then
Jonathan.

"Not at all," Jonathan replied with ease. "I'll just go
inside."

"Pop the casserole and bread into the oven," I called to
Jonathan's retreating back. "I'll be in shortly."

"Righto," Jonathan called back over his shoulder.

"I thought you said he'd left," Hank said, as soon as
Jonathan was out of hearing.

"I did, and he had. He's just returned. What is it you wanted to see me about, Hank? Jonathan and I are running late on lunch, and I'm starved." I tried to speak in pleasant tones.

His face was grim. "David Franklin Cannon the First called a press conference at his home at ten this morning. He invited Fred from the local paper, Henderson from the Waycross paper, me, and the suits. He was flanked by two lawyers. He said his son had returned this morning from an unnamed sanitarium, somewhere in an undisclosed location in the Midwest. Stated his son wanted to put to rest the rumors that he'd been kidnapped and wanted to apologize for the misunderstanding—personally. We all trooped into the guest bedroom, and Frank Junior was lying in bed looking like death warmed over. You can sure tell he's been sick. He's dropped a lot of weight. With just the right amount of humility and embarrassment, he explained away the abandoned car and not letting any of his family know where he was. Said he became ill on the way to his father's house, and a friend picked him up and drove him to the clinic. Another friend was given a message over his answering machine to pick up the car. But this second friend's son came home, listened to the messages, erased them, and forgot to tell the father to pick up the car. He planned to call the family and explain, but he became too ill. Only now was he strong enough to return. He had no idea, quote, that everyone was looking for him, unquote.

"Did I mention that Doc Phillips was standing by his bedside? The minute Frank Junior finished his tale of explanation and the suits and reporters started throwing questions at him, Doc Phillips threw us all out. Said his patient was still weak and unable to be questioned. Try again next week. Translated: That means never. The three sons and the wife were also present but didn't open their mouths to say boo. The four of them had expressions that reminded me of frozen cod or terminal shock. Also, four additional men were present but not introduced. I recognized two of them. They are high-priced bodyguards from an agency in Jacksonville. How do you like the news so far?"

"I'm glad he's back with his family," I said, testing the waters. "What do you think?"

"Well, the suits bought it. They gnashed their teeth, fumed and fussed over wasted government time, et cetera, but they bought it. The newsmen didn't. They went away with knowing looks, thinking the family had paid the ransom, Frank was released, and they want to keep it hushed up so the scavengers out there won't think he's an easy mark. They just pretended to believe the whole scheme."

Hank waited. I knew he wanted me to ask again, so I obliged him.

"You didn't give me your opinion. What do you think?"

"After the press conference was over, the suits invited me to share a conference with them. This was unusual, so I tagged along. They let me hear a short portion of the taped log from Frank Senior's house. Happens they thought it was worth a laugh. They believe you're a flippity flibbertigibbet who doesn't have sense enough to get out of the rain. I know different. They were proving that nothing unusual was on the tape. You see, the suits hoard all the facts when they think there's a chance they can make a headline arrest. When the case fizzles, like this one, they point at the locals. That's me. They're blaming my department for calling them in, in the first place. I don't like that one damn bit. Now for the bottom line: Where was he and how did you find him? I know you brought him home, from the asinine conversation last night. It was cover for you to get him into the house. I should've become suspicious when you started asking particulars about the kidnapping on the phone. Give."

I debated trying to con him into believing he was wrong, but I decided to be straight. I didn't want to keep Jonathan waiting.

"Sorry, Hank, my lips are sealed. I am not the only one in this. I can't explain without involving others. Maybe later I can fill you in. If I can, I will. Promise."

"Friends don't do this to each other. I told you about the case. I broke security for you because I trusted you. Don't you trust me?"

"Hank, we bent a few rules. I can't squeal on the others. Sorry."

"Yeah, I'm sorry too. The next time you need my help, think twice before you call." He turned, took a couple of steps, and turned back. "Enjoy your lunch."

I watched him depart and sighed. He'd forgive me.

I went inside and straight back to the kitchen and Jonathan. He had the iced tea poured and was sitting at the table, his napkin tucked under his chin, a knife in one hand, and a fork in the other. He had a large grin spread over his face.

"When do we eat?"

I passed him without comment, opened the oven door, removed the casserole and the bread, and turned off the oven.

"It's not ready yet!" he protested.

"It may not be, but I am," I said, as I removed the napkin from his shirt. He rose to meet me. I put my hands on his shoulders and my lips on his. Much later, we ate lunch.

Epilogue

Rosie's wedding was simple, beautiful, and went off without a hitch. The vows were said in the rose garden adjacent to the house, and the reception was held in the grooming room. Firemen and dog handlers mingled and sipped champagne—which was quickly replaced with moonshine—and a good time was had by all. I'd secured five gallons for the occasion from a friend in the flatwoods. It sat on the serving table in a white plastic jug adorned with a band of white ribbon and a blue crescent-shaped paper moon. If a fire had occurred on Rosie's wedding night, I would've feared for the structure and the water dousers, but fate was kind. I didn't worry about the following morning. The one property of moonshine that's most appreciated is: no hangover when one awakes.

Bubba's still using his predictable pattern of harassment: phone calls, then hanging up without saying a word. He's now calling twice a day, the last one coming after midnight. I'm careful and alert and still angry that I have to practice tight security and can never completely relax in my own home. I've mellowed just a tad. I now whisper *Que sera sera,* or whatever, when the dark shadows move on sleepless nights. Sometimes it works.

Hank hasn't forgiven me yet. However, he sent me a

Christmas card. He waved when I passed him on Main Street a few days ago. I perceive these acts as tiny chinks in his unforgiving armor. I'm certain we'll be friends in the future, maybe.

Susan, Jasmine, and I still spend Friday nights viewing old movies and consuming lots of beer and popcorn, but now it's every other Friday night. Jonathan and I commute, taking turns to see who has to drive the long stretch up and down Interstate 75. This long-distance romance really suits both of us because we both work long hours. When it's my turn to drive, I leave early Friday, which gives us Friday night, Saturday, and Sunday morning. Then, after breakfast, I start back. Jonathan does the same. It's long enough for two nights of romance, but not long enough for major disagreements. So far, it's working, but it's early days, fragile with newness and with absolutely no commitment promised or assumed.

Harvey Gusman, formerly of Andrel, New York, is the new veterinarian for my small animal clinic and Bloodhounds, Inc. The quick investigation of him I'd ordered didn't turn up any problems. I called and sent him a round-trip plane ticket, which he used to fly down here and look me and the place over. I was thankful the weather cooperated. It was mildly crisp with a rare low humidity. He said the plane had left New York during a blizzard. I think the weather sold him on flying back to New York, closing his office, and moving back, all within two weeks. I'm afraid when the spring humidity skyrockets, he may think I cheated a little when I extolled the local weather. I'm counting on my beloved Georgia to grab him by the throat with her beauty, southern manners, and lovable natives and never let him go, as it has so many other transplants.

I split Frank Senior's fifty-grand check with Jasmine. When I mentioned later that I'd given John, Kenton

Fraley's stepfather, five grand to start a college fund for Kenton, she immediately donated five grand out of her share. On a crisp Saturday more than three weeks ago, Kenton had a ball, hiding from Caesar during a field exercise. He comes often now.

With my balance of the rescue check, I purchased a black economy Ford Tercel for my long commutes to Eppley. I chose black because sometime in the future my nosy attitude may afford me an opportunity to actually tail a suspect. I always thought Magnum looked silly tailing a subject in broad daylight, driving a bright-red seventy-grand-plus Ferrari.

Jarel's trial will start this month. Wade says he is sitting on dead ready and loaded for bear. He's become quite proficient with our local colloquialisms. He's free from worry about meeting next year's taxes now. He and Sheri have decided to postpone their wedding until after Jarel's trial. They want time for a leisurely honeymoon.

Sheri's managing to save a whopping two grand a month out of their two salaries—and by dipping frequently into the treasure loot. Wade brags to anyone who will listen about her uncanny ability to squeeze a buck till it whimpers. Sheri demurely accepts the praise and gives me a wink, if I'm present.

I'm sitting on my porch chaise, wrapped in a blanket, watching the sun slowly lighten the early morning darkness on this first day of the new year. My coffee's hot, and I just lit my first cigarette, breaking my New Year's resolution to quit cold turkey.

I'm trying to think of a way to get out of starting a college class on the third, two days hence. Jasmine won the bet fair and square, but I'm not above cheating if it will free me from the odious chore.

Wayne appears at the base of the porch steps, tossing the rolled-up newspaper so adroitly that I manage to hold on to it without fumbling. We sign good morning to each other, and he trots off for breakfast. I unroll the slim paper, take a sip of coffee, and choke: THREE LOCAL BROTHERS VANISH!

My eyes wouldn't focus on the tiny print below, but I didn't need confirmation of their identities. I stared unseeing into space. What had the two old farts been thinking? I knew in a heartbeat that both Franks, Senior and Junior, were responsible. My thoughts flew to Jasmine. I was thankful she didn't take the paper. She said most of the news in it was bad and depressed her. Wait till she saw this hot item!

I kept taking deep breaths trying to calm my fears. Jasmine did listen to the radio in the mornings. Maybe she'd sleep late today since it was a holiday. She could arrive any second, wild-eyed in shock and fear. I believe I could survive in jail, if I was convicted. It would be unpleasant and hard to take, but I was sure I could take it. Jasmine couldn't. The old Jasmine, in another life, had spent a lot of time in jail between the ages of twelve and nineteen. She had pulled herself up and, with Hank's help, made a new life. She'd spent almost six years in virtual seclusion in two small rooms behind her tiny restaurant with only her newly found religious faith to sustain her. I found her and hired her and encouraged her to venture out into the world again. I had also gotten her involved with this mess. Oh, God. Oh, God. Oh, God. Hank. He'd be here shortly and wouldn't walk away without answers this time.

Did the bastards think we'd just let three men rot in that hole without doing anything to save them? Obviously yes, or they wouldn't have done the deed. I had not a moment's doubt that the brothers were, at this minute, down inside that trailer where they'd placed their father.

*   *   *

It's three hours later and I'm still sitting here on the porch, only now Jasmine is sitting beside me. We've been fitfully suggesting to each other ways of rescuing the three bad boys without getting caught. I'm still in my nightclothes, wrapped in a blanket. Wayne doesn't miss this fact as he steps up on the porch, giving me a closer look. He hands me yesterday's mail. With New Year's Eve preparations yesterday, it was forgotten. I listlessly flip through the contents, while he and Jasmine sign some comments I'm not following. A regular-sized envelope catches my eye. My name in square print. No return address, either on the front or on the back. I rip open the envelope to find a four-word message on a folded note, also block printed: THEY ARE NOT THERE.

Now what?

Has a Killer Been Set Free, or Are the Authorities Barking Up the Wrong Tree?

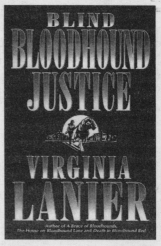

Join Southern sleuth Jo Beth Siddon and her trusty bloodhounds in their dogged pursuit of the truth in *Blind Bloodhound Justice*, the fourth book in Virginia Lanier's award-winning mystery series. This time, Jo Beth delves into the decades-old murder of a nanny and child, spurred on by the early parole of the man convicted of the heinous crime, a man who for thirty years has steadfastly maintained his innocence. With the sheriff worried and the locals in an ugly mood, Jo Beth and her dogs may be the only means to discover the truth...and keep a killer at bay.

HarperCollins*Publishers*
www.harpercollins.com